Praise for Starr Ambrose
and her fresh, sexy romantic suspense novels

THIEVES LIKE US

"A sparkling, sexy, and sassy romance! Guaranteed to make you grin!"

—Karen Hawkins, *New York Times* bestselling author

"Lighthearted romance. . . . Ambrose deftly balances Janet and Rocky's steamy relationship with the suspense plot."

—*Publishers Weekly*

"Ambrose has the great ability to create snappy, spunky characters that are easy to relate to and root for. . . . Her latest novel is yet another demonstration of her ability to blend lighthearted romance with a suspense theme. . . . A good read."

—*Romantic Times*

"This fast-paced romantic suspense will keep you spellbound with its adventurous escapades."

—Fresh Fiction

"Ambrose delights with spirited characters and a clever story line."

—Single Titles

OUR LITTLE SECRET

LIE TO ME

"An excellent debut novel. . . . With this stellar (pun intended) beginning, Starr Ambrose is a name to watch for in the romantic suspense genre."

—Romance Reviews Today

"A truly wonderful read!"

—Wild on Books

"An entertaining read from start to finish. . . . Starr Ambrose has written a great story full of romance, twists, and one very hot accountant."

—Fallen Angel Reviews

"This book really grabs you and doesn't let go. I was hooked from the first page."

—Book Binge

These titles are also available as eBooks

Also by Starr Ambrose

Lie to Me

Our Little Secret

Thieves Like Us

Available from Pocket Books

Silver
SPARKS

STARR AMBROSE

Pocket Books
New York   London   Toronto   Sydney   New Delhi

Pocket Books
A Division of Simon & Schuster, Inc.
1230 Avenue of the Americas, New York, NY 10020

This book is a work of fiction. Names, characters, places, and incidents either are products of the author's imagination or are used fictitiously. Any resemblance to actual events or locales or persons, living or dead, is entirely coincidental.

First Pocket Books paperback edition December 2011

POCKET and colophon are registered trademarks of Simon & Schuster, Inc.

For information about special discounts for bulk purchases, please contact Simon & Schuster Special Sales at 1-866-506-1949 or business@simonandschuster.com.

The Simon & Schuster Speakers Bureau can bring authors to your live event. For more information or to book an event contact the Simon & Schuster Speakers Bureau at 1-866-248-3049 or visit our website at www.simonspeakers.com.

Cover design by Anna Dorfman, photo ©Westend61 GmbH/Alamy

Manufactured in the United States of America

10 9 8 7 6 5 4 3 2 1

ISBN 978-1-4516-2363-5
ISBN 978-1-4516-2365-9 (ebook)

To Ariana
for infinite patience and
the best fact-checking skills anywhere

Acknowledgments

Pulling the first plot ideas from my head is a lot like pulling teeth—painful tugs, with much kicking and screaming from the patient. Diane Lutz, Patti Shenberger, and Cheryl Anne Smith always let me whine through those early days, and never flinch when I needed to brainstorm. I owe a special thank-you on this book to Philine Tucker, who forced me to describe each character's deepest fears and desires, then wrote it all down for me and made me believe I actually had an organized story line. Cal and Maggie came to life partly because of her.

Thanks also to Andy Cohoe and Kyria Joyner, who spent many years living in the Rockies and helped fill in the gaping holes in my experience. Any mistakes are my own.

Silver
SPARKS

Chapter One

Rafael De Luca had his hand on Maggie's ass. Again.

If they'd been at Del Tanner's bar in Barringer's Pass, she would have planted a vicious elbow jab in his wonderfully ripped midsection and told him to get lost.

But they weren't in the valley. They were in The Aerie, the posh nightclub at the Alpine Sky resort on Two Bears Mountain, where people came to play and be seen, especially if they were rich or famous.

Rafael De Luca was both. Anything she did to him would be seen by hordes of his fellow vacationing Hollywood glitterati. Plus, management frowned on pissing off the guests, especially the famous ones. Since management included her sister Zoe, Maggie spared Rafael's pretty rib cage and settled for grinding her three-inch heel on his toes as she turned to leave.

His hand jerked away. "Ow! Shit, baby, watch where you step."

"I did." She leaned close so the reporter lurking in

the press of bodies at the bar wouldn't hear. "Time to go play with someone else."

Rafael's lip curled in a cynical smile. "After buying you drinks for the past hour? I don't think so, baby." He slipped his arm around her waist and pulled her close.

She stiffened, but reminded herself that she should have seen this coming. She should have blown him off five minutes after he hit on her, when he'd scanned the room then sauntered over with his smoky-hot gaze and confident opening line: "I always like to meet the most beautiful woman in the room first." He'd flashed his TV smile. "I'm Rafe. And you are . . . ?"

Despite the lame line, Rafael and his reality show costars had been fun to joke around with for an hour. But she preferred men with more depth, and an hour of Rafe and the cast of *Trust Fund Brats* was enough, especially after the unwanted ass-grab.

Her toe-crunching move should have worked, but all those drinks he'd been buying had gone down *his* throat, not hers. His extremities were probably half numb by now. Unfortunately, it didn't affect the strength of his grip as he held her against him.

For Zoe's sake, Maggie gathered some restraint and didn't slug the drunken jerk. But she put her fists on his chest, holding him at a slight distance. "Get your hands off me before I hurt you," she hissed.

To her surprise, he released her. Laughing, he growled like a tiger. "*Rowr!* Feisty Maggie."

She took a step back while she could. "Look, Rafe, it's been fun, but I'm going to go mingle."

"Perfect. Mingling's what I had in mind, too." He snagged a lock of her strawberry-blond hair where it brushed her shoulder, rubbing it with his fingers. "I hear redheads are hot."

"That's hot-tempered, genius." She hated to prove the cliché, but he was pushing her limits. She turned to the man next to her. He had biceps like twin picnic hams and had hovered around Rafael De Luca all evening as if he might be a bodyguard. "You want to help me out here?"

The guy sipped his drink—not his first one—and gave her a dispassionate glance. "Nope."

Rafe smirked. "Baby," he crooned, "be sensible. I'm about to change your life. See that reporter over there from *The Hollywood Scene*? If I give the signal, your picture will be all over the country by tomorrow and that little store of yours will be flooded with more customers than you can handle. My name is magic." He released her hair and let his hand slip to the bare skin at the opening of her blouse.

Her flesh crawled and she brushed his hand away. "My store's doing just fine already. And if you don't move right now, I'll give your paparazzi friend an even better picture to splash across the tabloids."

He stroked her arm thoughtfully, and she checked to make sure he wasn't leaving a trail of slime. "You really have to learn to recognize an opportunity when it's handed to you. Especially when it comes in such a *big* package." He winked. "I'd think one of the Larkin girls would know all about that."

Maggie froze. Slowly, she lifted her gaze.

A hard edge touched his smile. "Oh, yeah. People talk, babe. But don't worry, I can spice up those rumors for you, make you more popular than ever." His hand slid up her side and found her breast. "I know exactly what you want."

Rafe's cool gaze cut into her like a knife, slicing right through the frayed bonds of her temper. She could almost hear them snap.

Cal set his beer down with a thunk. Pretty Boy De Luca had just put his hand on her again. Damn it, this was not going to end well.

The redhead had drawn Cal's attention even before Rafael De Luca had hit on her. She was the type who always drew looks, with a smile that flashed as bright as her hair and the kind of laugh that made others smile when they hadn't even heard the joke. She was a distraction he didn't need. But fortunately De Luca zeroed in on her, making it easy for him to watch both of them.

Cal had to give the woman credit. Her engaging smile had grown stiff within minutes of talking to De Luca. If that other woman from the *Trust Fund Brats* crew hadn't claimed Red's attention, she probably would have slipped away. But instead she got stuck next to De Luca long enough for the man to feel possessive.

Even from across the room, Cal could see the woman didn't like it. She didn't look like the type to bow to fame or fortune, either. De Luca didn't have much experience with that, so he wouldn't see it. But Cal did, and in another thirty seconds the whole bar would see it, including the reporters that swarmed after De Luca like flies around manure.

The last thing Cal wanted was to draw attention to himself, but he couldn't stand by and watch another woman be victimized. Red had no idea what she was getting into.

Abandoning his beer, he shoved through the crowd of mostly women who were loitering three deep around the bar. Damn reality stars drew them like magnets.

"Hey, watch it!" A drink sloshed and someone swore. Cal mumbled an apology but didn't pause. A man grabbed his arm with an angry, "Hey, buddy!" but Cal shook it off, cursing under his breath because he wasn't going to make it in time. Twenty feet away, Red's eyes narrowed with icy determination. Maybe De Luca was too smashed to recognize it, though even a ten-year-old could have seen it coming.

Cal watched it happen in slow motion. She raised her left hand to De Luca's shoulder. The gesture looked friendly, even to Cal, who knew better, and De Luca actually smiled. He never noticed her right hand drop, taking aim. De Luca's lips curved in smug confidence.

Red drove her palm upward, smashing into De Luca's nose with an audible crunch. His scream was instantaneous. Reeling back, he covered his nose with both hands as blood seeped through his fingers.

Shocked silence hung in the air for a fraction of a second, then pandemonium erupted. People turned, reporters shoved, and a couple of women screamed. A dozen cameras flashed, held high and pointed toward the center of the action, while De Luca yelled obscenities, blood dripping onto his sparkling white shirt.

Red hadn't moved. Cal noted the satisfaction in her eyes as he pushed through the onlookers and finally reached her side. He also noted the angrily contorted face of De Luca's bodyguard as the man threw his drink aside and lunged at the woman.

Introductions would have to wait. Grabbing her

arm, he spun her aside, putting himself in the guard's path. The man plowed into him like a linebacker. Cal barely had time to turn his shoulder into the blow, and the impact staggered him. Luckily, it also knocked the wind out of the guard. Muscle Man doubled over, gasping for breath.

Behind Cal, Red's furious yell pierced the bedlam. "Hey, what the hell do you think you're—oh, shit!" Her objection broke off as she spotted the now more furious behemoth glaring like a bull ready to charge.

"Get out of here! Now," Cal ordered without taking his eyes off the guard. She'd seen the danger and was smart enough to run.

He braced himself, ready to deflect De Luca's lackey long enough for Red to get away. Instead, she pushed around Cal, shoving him aside as she planted her feet, jabbing her finger at De Luca's bodyguard.

"Don't you dare touch me, you incompetent Neanderthal! If you had half a brain you'd take that mentally stunted, oversexed drunk you work for and lock him up in his room until he learns to act civilized!"

Cal felt as stunned as the guard looked. Red was either oblivious to the danger, or too enraged to notice. Taking a step forward, she balled her fists. "News flash, buddy: women aren't playthings put on earth to stroke your feeble male ego!"

Cal squinted as two cameras flashed in sync, flaring like a nova. Among the raised cell phones, several professional-grade digital cameras clicked furiously, recording frame after frame of Red's tirade and De Luca's bloody ranting from the sidelines. They'd also probably captured clear photos of Cal. Shit! Grabbing Red's hand, he hissed, "Lady, are you nuts?"

She shook him off, apparently just hitting her stride. "Do you even understand what sexual harassment is?" She continued her lecture. "Because it's obviously your job to keep the little pervert in line, and his behavior was beyond inappropriate. No one gets to treat me like that and—"

"Red!" Cal yelled loudly enough to cut through her fury.

"What!" She whirled on him. "Someone has to tell these superficial morons—"

She couldn't see the crazed look on the guard's face, but Cal did. He also heard Muscles snarl, "Bitch," as he reached into his coat pocket.

Adrenaline shot through Cal. He'd hoped to get out of this without more violence, but that option had just evaporated. Bloody noses and barroom tackles were one thing; guns implied a whole new set of rules.

"Gun! Move! Now!" Grabbing Red's arm, he yanked hard. She staggered as he released her, but he couldn't watch to see if she stayed on her feet. The bodyguard extended his arm, black metal visible in his hand.

It was Cal's only chance. In that one moment while the guard stood, body wide open and unprotected, Cal jumped forward, throwing a kick directly at the thug's diaphragm.

His foot hit flesh, hard. The guard went wide-eyed, grunted, and crumpled. In one continuous move, Cal spun, his gaze finding Red's. "Go!" he ordered. Because she clearly couldn't be trusted to do the sensible thing, he grabbed her hand and charged forward. They dodged through the confusion into the resort's elegant lobby and out the main doors into the cool Rocky Mountain night.

Red clutched his hand and ran with him, finally in complete agreement with his agenda. She slowed and would have stopped under the front portico, but he tugged her to the right without skipping a beat. They followed the driveway until it split toward the parking lot. He hopped the low flower-bed border, landing on thick, well-manicured grass. She hesitated before making a cautious jump, and he realized she'd been running in high heels. Slowing to a trot to accommodate her strides, he rounded the corner of the hotel and drew her into the shadows against the brick wall.

Voices faded. Panting, they listened to a few running footsteps and shouted questions as people dashed outside, looking for them. Paparazzi if they were lucky. De Luca's hired guns if they weren't. When Cal was sure they were alone, he finally released her hand. She leaned against the wall, eyes closed, catching her breath.

After several seconds, her breathing evened and her eyes opened. She finger-combed her hair, shaking it away from her face. He tried not to notice its silkiness. It was the kind of hair that tempted a man to run his hands through it to cradle her head when he kissed her.

"Are you okay?" he asked.

She nodded, taking a deep breath and blowing it out. "Yeah. Thanks. Hey, did you see? That palm to the nose really works!"

"It does, and you're welcome." That was the end of the niceties. He gritted his teeth. "You want to tell me just what the fuck you were doing back there?"

The change was instantaneous. Fire shot into her eyes as she came off the wall faster than he expected. "I was defending myself!" Her voice was low and controlled but seething with fury. "I thought that was obvious. Isn't that why you jumped into the middle of things, because I was in the right?" She stuck her hands on her hips. "And who the hell are *you*, anyway?"

"I'm the guy who saved your ass."

They faced off a long moment until Cal finally muttered, "Oh, hell. Come on, let's get out of here before they find us." He took a few steps toward the parking lot before he realized she wasn't following him. "What's the problem now?"

"What makes you think I would go anywhere with you?"

He might have smiled at her tough attitude if he'd been in a better mood. Unfortunately for them both, he was feeling pretty tense and irritable. "How about because you sure as hell can't go back in there without causing a bloodbath? And because I'm going to explain to you how you just ruined both our lives. Is that okay with you?"

She stared him down. "No. Give me your phone."

"What?"

"Mine's in my purse, in my sister's office. She's the assistant manager here. I can guarantee she'll want an explanation for that little scene, and you're going to help me convince her that I was provoked and doing nothing wrong in defending myself."

That might be hard to do, considering she'd thrown the first punch, but she was holding out her hand, fingers wiggling impatiently, and damned if he wasn't curious to see how this played out. Besides, he couldn't leave her alone until she understood just how much danger she was in.

He pulled his phone out of his pocket, and she snatched it away. Dialing rapidly, she tapped her foot while she waited. Finally, she straightened. "Hi, Zoe, it's me."

She winced, and he bit back a smile. Apparently he wasn't the only one who found her aggravating. "I'll explain, just let me in the door by the kitchen. I don't want anyone to see us." When her eyes flicked up to his, he knew her sister had asked who was with her. "The guy who kicked Mr. Universe in the gut."

Smiling sweetly, she snapped the phone shut and handed it back. "Follow me."

She marched off without a backward glance. He narrowed his eyes at the swing of her hips under her short black skirt, and weighed his options. His cover was blown. Red had just jumped into more danger than she knew and—taking a wild guess—she was bound to make it worse.

Shit. Shoving the phone in his pocket, he marched after her.

Her name was Maggie. He gathered that much during the enraged tirade from the highly polished, younger version of her that was her sister Zoe. To be fair, it was probably the official hotel management duds that made Zoe look so prim and proper—navy-blue skirt and blazer, white blouse, and strawberry-blond hair identical to her sister's but pulled into a neat bun. Maggie's loose, stylish bob went a long way toward erasing any hint of prim and proper.

So did her attitude.

"I tried not to start something, I swear," she claimed, brushing by her sister to head down the hall.

Cal trailed them to what was apparently Zoe's office. Maggie paced before the desk, hands alternately combing hair off her neck and gesturing as she talked. "I told him to get lost several times, but the little perv wouldn't take no for an answer."

Since Zoe didn't ask who the perv was, he figured she'd already heard some version of the incident.

"He kept *touching* me." Maggie glared, looking like she'd like to smack De Luca again. "And even then I controlled myself, Zoe. I didn't want to cause you any trouble."

"But you did." Zoe stood with arms crossed, unmoved by her sister's anger.

"Yes, and you know why?" Maggie put her hands on her hips, pretty pink lips pressed into a tight line. "He said he could give me what I wanted, and he knew I'd like it—because I'm one of the Larkin girls."

Zoe's arms dropped. "Oh." A pained look crossed her face. Cal definitely had to look into the significance of their last name.

With all the energy sucked out of her anger, Zoe's gaze finally shifted toward Cal. "Who are you?"

"Cal Drummond. I hauled your sister's ass out of there before it got really ugly."

Maggie planted her hands on her hips. "I was handling it."

"Bullshit," he scoffed. "You were asking to get killed. Rafael De Luca is a dangerous man."

Her eyes narrowed, a look he was getting used to. "Thanks a lot. I brought you along to back me up, not throw me under the bus."

"It happened just like she said," he confirmed to

Zoe, then turned a hard look on Maggie. "And it was incredibly stupid."

"Hey! I stood up for myself. I was brave, damn it." She was seething.

Brave . . . and reckless. The words hit him like an icy splash of water. He'd been attracted to that mix once before and knew how deadly it could be; how devastating. It was something he never wanted to go through again. "There's a fine line between brave and stupid, lady, and you plowed right over it."

Zoe looked ready to side with him. "Couldn't you have been a little more diplomatic? I've got half my staff out there trying to soothe some very powerful, very pissed-off customers. I'll probably have to comp their meals and rooms for several days just to keep them from suing the resort."

"I wouldn't go that far," Cal said.

She arched a condescending eyebrow. "Oh, really? Why not?"

"Because you shouldn't let the De Lucas put you on the defensive. And when I say the De Lucas, I mean their lawyers, because that's who you'll be hearing from. You could have easily called the cops on their precious boy and his hired ape, but you didn't. Be sure to point that out. Forget the sexual harassment part—"

"Sure, that's not important," Maggie muttered.

Cal ignored her. "It's too hard to prove and you'll only get conflicting stories. But the big guy they employ pulled a gun in a crowded room. Maybe he only planned to scare your sister with it, although I wouldn't bet on it. He had two drinks while I was there—seriously unprofessional for a bodyguard. He'll probably get fired for letting something happen in the first place, but if I were you I'd point out what you *didn't* do. You didn't call the cops and make an official report, you didn't have their gun-wielding bodyguard Breathalyzed, and you didn't have Rafe held on charges of harassment. Maybe none of it would stick, but it wouldn't matter because it would already be headlines, and not the kind they want. You know it, and they know it. Rafe caused the mess and *you* minimized the damage."

Zoe stared at him for several seconds, then gave a curt nod. "Thanks, I can use that."

Maggie peered at him. "Who *are* you?"

"I'm a cop."

"Where?"

"Oklahoma City. I'm with the state police, but I'm on leave."

"And you just happen to be in an exclusive resort in the Colorado Rockies, watching me?"

He uttered a short laugh. "You? I was watching De Luca." And okay, Maggie, too, which still irritated him enough to make him deny it. "I've been following him for three weeks."

Zoe tilted her head, puzzling it out. "Not because you're a fan, I imagine."

"Hardly," Cal scoffed. "Flexing and posing for the camera is only one of the things Rafael De Luca does. The other is less pretty." He flicked a glance at Maggie. "He's a killer."

He watched their mouths open and their eyes go wide before Maggie blurted, "*Rafe De Luca*? Star of tabloids and reality TV, famous for being rich and obnoxious?" She looked at him like he'd lost his mind.

"The man can't even go into Starbucks without causing a media alert. How could he possibly get away with murder?"

He noted that she hadn't doubted he'd do it, just that he'd get away with it. At least she had no trouble reading the man's character. "If I'm right, he's gotten away with it several times. He has a violent temper, a lust for power, and a family that will go to any lengths to protect the reputation of their only son."

"You're kidding." Zoe sank into her chair, staring at him in disbelief.

"I wish I were."

Maggie seemed less shocked than skeptical. He didn't know if that was due to his claim, or the fact that it came from him. "You can prove it?"

"Not yet." It was a sore spot, since he wasn't sure how he ever would, short of finding the bodies on Rafe's property. He figured the odds of that were greatest right here, where the De Luca family had a huge estate and where two of the young women in question had last been seen.

"But you're building a case? I can't believe the Oklahoma police would let you trail him to Colorado. Are you working in conjunction with the FBI?"

She was sharper than he'd thought. "No," he admitted. "I took a leave of absence, like I said. I'm doing this on my own."

Maggie took several seconds to absorb the information, rubbing a finger over her lower lip as she thought, which he found distracting all over again. "Why?"

He dragged his focus away from her mouth. Her eyes had softened, and he knew she'd already guessed it was personal. "His last victim was my half sister Julie." The corners of her mouth tightened, but she said nothing. "She lived in L.A. Her body was dumped in the hills. She'd been bound and her throat was cut."

"Oh, my God," Zoe breathed.

"I'm sorry," Maggie murmured.

"Me, too." He heard the gruffness in his voice, and hardened his expression to match it. Anything to keep the vise grip of guilt from immobilizing him now that he'd finally started making progress. When it came down to it, he'd barely known Julie, but guilt could be just as crippling as grief.

Scowling, he said, "Once I started looking into it, I saw a pattern of missing women leading back to Rafe. I don't want to see it happen again. I took a personal leave after Julie's funeral last month, and I'm not going back until I stop the son of a bitch for good."

Maggie nodded once, as if approving his plan. "But he's not going to do that to me." The aggression was gone, but the naive, stubborn confidence was still there. "It would be a stupid move—there were too many witnesses. He'd be the first suspect."

Cal heaved a sigh, his exasperation with her returning. "You don't get it. You made him look bad in public, and the De Lucas *never* look bad. He's going to fix it one way or another." He stepped closer, making sure Maggie's golden-brown eyes couldn't look away from him. He needed her to understand. To *fear*. "Don't underestimate what just happened. Rafe is probably already huddling with the family lawyers, trying to figure out the best way to put a positive spin on your little incident."

"You act like it's headline news."

"It is! Didn't you see the cameras flashing? That place was full of paparazzi."

"But they don't know who I am."

"By tomorrow morning they will." A flicker of discomfort touched her eyes, and he went after it, ruthlessly driving home his point. "You're going to be tabloid headlines, Maggie. They'll have your name, and they'll be digging hard to find mine. The incident will be blown out of proportion and so will the theories they come up with for why it happened. Have you ever read those papers? You're in the shark tank, lady, and they smell blood."

Worry lines creased her forehead. "I don't have to talk to them."

"That's your best move, but it won't be enough."

She blinked, staring, and he saw real apprehension finally settle in. She licked her lips nervously. "Then how can I stop it?"

"You can't. Rafe de Luca's coming after you, and there's nothing you can do but try to survive it."

Chapter Two

Maggie couldn't believe this guy. He was actually glad he'd scared her. How mean could you get?

But she suspected he was right about the press coverage. She remembered the camera flashes, making his scenario of headlines and wild speculation all too believable. Rafe wouldn't take this well. She just didn't know what he'd do about it.

"I'm going home," she announced. "If reporters are going to be calling all day tomorrow, at least I can get a good night's sleep first."

Zoe opened a drawer and took out Maggie's purse. Handing it over, she said, "Call me tomorrow."

"I will."

Cal pulled out his phone. "I'll follow you home. Give me your number."

She managed not to laugh. "I don't think so—to both of those statements."

He gave her a disgusted look. "I'm not hitting on you. I'm following you to make sure no eager reporters are tailing you. And if they do, I have to be able to call you so you can keep going and not lead them to your house. They'll find it eventually, but you might as well make them work for it."

He made it sound like swarms of reporters would be after her, when everyone in their small, nosy town knew there were only three or four at most hanging around the cast of *Trust Fund Brats*. Probably just another attempt to scare her. "I think I'd know if someone were following me."

"Well, I don't, so why don't you humor me?"

She met his stubborn stare with one of her own.

"Makes sense to me," Zoe said, turning traitor without hesitation.

Too bad. Maggie didn't give out her number to just anyone, and she certainly didn't let strangers follow her home. Maybe other women fell for his let-me-protect-you routine, but for all she knew Cal Drummond was worse than Rafe De Luca. Rugged good looks and flat abs weren't enough to make her abandon common sense.

Heck, she didn't even know if he was who he claimed to be.

Thrusting out her hand, she said, "Show me some identification."

He said nothing, but his mouth twitched up on one side as he reached into his pocket and handed over his whole wallet.

It fell open to credit cards and photos. The picture on top showed a pretty dark-haired woman in a formal gown. Low-cut, with plenty of cleavage. A girlfriend? The sister? She didn't look anything like him.

Quickly flipping the photos over, she checked the

driver's license. The same guy, but with shorter hair. She glanced up; the longer style worked better. Something worked, anyway, because if she overlooked the clenched jaw and hard stare, he wasn't bad-looking. In fact, if he weren't being such an annoying ass, she might . . .

"Here." She thrust it back.

Tucking it away without comment, he held up his phone, thumb poised over the numbers, waiting. Zoe waited, too.

Maggie gritted her teeth and rattled off her phone number. Stalking toward the door, she added, "Feel free to lose it after tonight."

She heard the muttered "Gladly" as she walked out with Cal on her heels.

She knew he was behind her on the winding drive down the mountain only because of the constant distance he kept between their cars, two headlights she couldn't shake. When she pulled into her drive he slowed, idling down the street until she closed the front door behind her. When she looked again from the living room window, he was gone.

She didn't sleep well, and blamed it on Cal. He'd been so sure she'd be a tabloid sensation by morning that she couldn't relax, and kept waking every hour until she gave up and decided to open the store early. Saturday shoppers weren't early risers, but she could always find paperwork to keep her busy.

Traffic was light at seven in the morning. Few downtown stores opened before nine, including hers. The town of Barringer's Pass fit snugly into a narrow valley between three towering peaks, with the picturesque downtown crowded alongside a rushing snow-fed stream. The stream was high with May's snowmelt, swirling around boulders and flashing in the morning sun. On the east bank, old brick buildings lined the main road through the pass, most dating back more than a hundred years, to the town's first settlers. Maggie cruised by slowly, scanning the brick sidewalks and the pedestrian bridge over the stream that led to the public parking lot. Only a few people were out, drawn by the coffee shop on the corner. The other storefronts were dark.

Perfect. She could duck inside before any of Cal's rumored reporters showed up, if they ever did, and spend a quiet two hours on inventory before she had to open the doors. Then, if a reporter showed, she'd be ready to give them a few minutes for a polite but brief "no comment."

She drove around to the small employee lot, parking behind the back door of Fortune's Folly. She'd named the store after the abandoned silver mine on Tappit's Peak that had drawn settlers to this area. The mine had fizzled back in the 1930s, but Maggie's store had struck gold. Her eclectic home and office decor found plenty of customers among the wealthy residents and visitors to Barringer's Pass.

Locking her car, she headed for the back door and was halfway there when a car door slammed, and she turned to look. A man in a suit moved briskly on an intercept course, waving when he caught her eye. He didn't look like a reporter. The suit was too expensive, and the portfolio under his arm surely wasn't standard issue for paparazzi. She waited.

"Good morning, Miss Larkin." He held out his

hand, offering a business card. "Parker Jameson, with Finch, Hartley, Bass and Epstein."

She glanced at the card, then at the three-piece suit, and finally met Parker Jameson's smile with a more cynical expression. Cal Drummond had been right. "Let me guess—you represent Rafe De Luca?"

"My firm represents the De Luca family, yes. May we go inside and talk?"

She was tempted to say no, but the forty-degree breeze rippled her thin blouse and slipped beneath her skirt. It might be late May, but winter didn't surrender easily at this elevation. She unlocked the back door, letting Parker Jameson follow her inside, but not into the shop itself. As clean and wholesome as Jameson looked, he worked for the De Lucas; she suspected that something slimy lurked beneath the surface. The back room was good enough. Tossing her purse on the packaging table, she turned to face him. "What do you want?"

Jameson zipped open his portfolio as he went into his pitch. "We are, of course, aware of the unfortunate incident at the Alpine Sky resort last night. The De Luca family would like to offer you reassurances that they believe no action need be taken against you."

"Against *me*?"

"That's correct." He stepped around her and laid a thin stack of papers on the fake wood grain of the worktable. "These papers have already been signed and witnessed, affirming that neither Rafael De Luca nor the De Luca family will bring charges against you or in any way hold you at fault for the unfortunate misunderstanding between you and Mr. De Luca."

She stared at the papers, then at him. "You're kidding."

"Not at all. All you have to do is sign your name, and the matter is resolved." He pulled a silver ballpoint from the portfolio and held it out to her.

Since he was going with the lawyerly façade that all parties involved were reasonable, intelligent people, she kept a civil tone. "There's a slight problem, Mr. Jameson. It seems Rafe and I have differing explanations for what happened."

His smile held a touch of condescension. "There are always two sides to any dispute, Miss Larkin. But in this case, the facts don't matter."

She raised an eyebrow. "That's a unique approach to the law."

"The particulars need not be discussed. In fact, the agreement states that both you and Rafael will refrain from commenting on the details of the incident. A brief statement will be released to the press by the De Luca family explaining that it was simply a disagreement between two passionate people that has since been resolved. A lovers' quarrel, so to speak."

"A *what*? You can't seriously expect me to tell people that I'm actually dating that scum-sucking piece of garbage!"

He didn't even blink. "Miss Larkin, we expect you to say nothing whatsoever. People will think what they will, and you and Rafael need only carry on the charade for a few days before a mutual decision to end your relationship. This will, of course, be announced to the press, at which time the media will undoubtedly lose interest in you."

So much for remaining civil. "Yeah, they'll lose interest, but you will already have trashed my name. There is no relationship! I'm not going to pretend there is, so just forget it." She picked up the papers and slapped them against his chest, forcing him to grab them.

"Miss Larkin, you may want to rethink that decision."

"I doubt it."

"If you don't want to go along with what I assure you is your best option, then the De Lucas will be forced to handle this on their own."

"Fine, whatever." She moved toward the door, a broad hint that he should follow.

He didn't. "Since they will be forced to assume you are opposed to protecting their best interests, they will not be able to protect yours."

His tone was as businesslike as before, but the words sounded threatening. She tipped her head, watching him through narrowed eyes. "What does that mean?"

He shrugged. "I believe it means if you are not with them, you are against them. I really can't say what the actual details might involve."

But it wouldn't be anything good. The De Lucas maintained a home in the area, one of several all over the world. Thanks to their ownership of a major movie studio and record label, they were rich and famous on an international scale. Rafe's playboy lifestyle had only added to the media's fascination with the family. Opposing them wouldn't be smart.

That didn't negate the fact that going along with their version of events would be disgusting, dishonest, and just plain wrong. She wouldn't be able to live with herself. "Thanks but no thanks," she told him.

Parker Jameson tucked the papers back in his portfolio and zipped it shut. "You have twenty-four hours to think about it, Miss Larkin. I'll contact you later." He smiled, not attempting to hide his disrespect. "Unless, of course, you call me before then. If you're as smart as I hear, you will." He walked past her, opened the door, then glanced back. "Have a pleasant day. I believe there are some people here to see you."

She caught the door before it closed and looked outside. Two men stood by her car, camera straps slung over their shoulders, and hands cupped around their eyes as they peered in the windows. Crap—only tabloid reporters could be that bold. Still, that didn't mean she had to put up with fingerprints all over the glass, or scratches if one of those cameras banged against the side of the car.

"Hey, guys!" They looked up. "Hands off the car, okay?"

They straightened immediately. "Maggie! Could we get a quote from you about your fight with Rafe De Luca?" They both jogged toward her. "Is it true your fight was because he was upset about your police record?"

"What?" She scowled, mouth hanging open in astonishment. One of them chose that instant to raise his camera and take her picture. She snapped her mouth closed. "Who have you been talking to? I don't have a police record."

They kept coming, throwing out questions as they did. "How long have you and Rafe been seeing each other?" That was from the shorter one who'd taken her picture.

"Weren't you the secret woman he was with in Hawaii last month?" asked the taller one as he, too, reached for his camera.

"No! We aren't . . ." She realized she was falling into their trap, and shut her mouth, glaring. Another priceless Kodak moment was captured with a flash. "No comment!" She slammed the door.

Leaning against it, she took several deep breaths. Fists pounding on the outside vibrated against her back, and she jumped away. The reporters continued to shout questions, and she moved to the front of the store so she couldn't hear.

She hadn't handled that well, but they'd taken her by surprise with that crap about a police record. She needed to keep her cool and politely deflect questions with noncommittal answers. Next time she would be ready.

Maggie concentrated on calming her anger and her galloping heart. After a few seconds the pounding and shouting stopped, leaving the store in blissful silence.

Light streamed through the two big front windows, but with the overhead lights off, the area near the back wall was dim. Soothing. She took a deep breath and let it out slowly, feeling calm seep back in. Fortune's Folly in the early morning was her favorite retreat from the world, and she let it work its magic on her now.

She was alone here, if you didn't count the hundreds of corpses. "How's it going, George?" Maggie ran her hand over the rippled black body where it hung on the wall, encased in its tomb of limestone. "Sorry about that lawyer. We haven't all evolved to the same level." The giant trilobite was silent, but she imagined tiny black eyes blinking kindly behind the protuberances on George's fossilized head. George would understand—he was that kind of guy. In the four months he'd hung on her wall, they'd had many one-sided conversations, and he'd never once failed to agree with her.

"How's your lady friend? Has she noticed you yet?" The sandy-colored stone slab held the bodies of five more trilobites, all giant specimens about a foot long. One lay nearly within reach of George's outstretched antenna, as if he'd spent the past five hundred million years trying to get her attention. Maggie gave him a warning tap on the head. "Just keep those feelers off her ass, buddy. Girls don't like that."

Pulling a long dusting rod from beneath the checkout counter, Maggie began brushing invisible cobwebs off the displayed fossils—more chunks of ancient ocean mud, teeming with the bodies of pre-historic fish, crustaceans, and ammonites. They were popular items among her customers with twenty or thirty thousand dollars to blow on an interesting con-versation piece.

She worked her way toward the front of the store, humming to herself as she smoothed silk wall hang-ings. She'd nearly forgotten about rude reporters when a tap on the front door made her look up. Through the glass, four men waved and signaled for her to come to the door. Two were from the parking lot, but the other two were new. Were there really that many tabloids? Her first instinct was to ignore them, but she realized they wouldn't go away. They'd just wait until she opened for business and bother her while she had paying customers in the store. It might be better to get it over with now.

The four straightened alertly as she reached for her ring of keys and unlocked the two heavy front doors. They pulled them open before she had the keys back in her pocket. She stepped back as all four pushed inside, holding up both palms while blocking their path. "Hold it right here, fellas. I know you have questions. I'm willing to answer if it'll get you out of the way before I'm open for business. Agreed?"

A chorus of agreements assaulted her, followed by a jumble of loud questions, with each one trying to talk over the other.

"One at a time!" In the brief pause, she pointed to one at random, a man in his mid-thirties, balding, with a thin ponytail. "You first."

He held up a miniature tape recorder as three more arms shot out, all holding recording devices. At least she'd be accurately quoted. Shifting his camera strap aside, he moved the recorder under her nose and asked, "How long have you been seeing Rafe De Luca, and what's the status of your relationship?"

She pushed his hand back to a polite distance, giving him a free lesson in manners. "I'm not seeing Rafe. There is no relationship." She cut off his follow-up question, pointing at the next man. "You."

"Why did you hit Rafe? Was that the first instance of abuse in your relationship, or have there been more?"

She frowned. "I told you, there's no relationship. I never met him before last night. And I hit him because he made inappropriate suggestions and wouldn't keep his hands off me." This was going better than she'd hoped. There was obviously a serious gap in the facts, and they were listening eagerly to every word, allowing her to clear up the story. No matter what spin the De Lucas tried to put on it, at least her version would be out there to counter it. She pointed again, this time to the short guy from the parking lot. "Your turn."

"Was Cara Rockford the reason for your breakup with Rafe?"

"Who?" Maggie shook her head. "I told you, there was no breakup. I don't even know Rafe. We just met last night."

The man nodded, as if she had just confirmed what he'd said. She hoped he replayed that tape before writing his story. Before she could move on, he insisted, "But what about Cara?"

"Never heard of her." Speaking over his next question, she pointed to the tall man behind him. "You."

"What's your response to Blaster's threats against you?"

She wrinkled her brow. "I have no idea what you're talking about."

"The Blaster—Rafe's bodyguard. That's the name he used in pro wrestling. He was fired after you assaulted Rafe, and he swore to get even. What do you have to say about it?"

Four pairs of eyes fastened on her as she shook her head. "I had nothing to do with his getting fired. I imagine it was because he pulled a gun, and had been drinking on the job." Thank you, Cal. It might be a good thing he'd stepped into that mess after all, or she wouldn't be this prepared. "It's not my fault if the man can't keep Rafe from forcing himself on women."

They all grinned, and a couple nodded in agreement.

"You certainly handled yourself well, Maggie," the first one said.

"Thank you." It was about time someone showed some appreciation for how she'd dealt with two bullies.

"Maggie, can you tell us who the mystery man is?" Someone spoke out of turn, and before she could reply, another one took off on the new topic.

"Is he an old boyfriend?"

"Did he force you to leave against your will?"

"What's his name, Maggie?"

Her orderly system was breaking down in the face of their renewed excitement.

There was no way she was going to give them Cal's name. And the way they used hers all the time was beginning to bother her, like they actually thought she might mistake them for friends. "I never saw that man before, and I haven't seen him since."

One man chuckled. "Aw, come on, Maggie, everyone saw you run out of there with him. Who is he?"

She shrugged helplessly. "Sorry, I don't know him, and he didn't stick around, so I can't tell you anything about him." There, that ought to satisfy Cal. He might be overbearing and arrogant, but she owed him something for helping her out of a jam. Maybe now the press would forget about him, and he could go back to shadowing Rafe. Cal's theory about murdered girls might be far-fetched, but he could probably find several lesser offenses to charge Rafe with. She wished him luck.

"Maggie!"

Cool air swirled into the store as a new reporter opened the door and pushed his way inside. He stood on tiptoe, stretching a tiny recorder over the heads in front of him. "Can I get a quote on your relationship with Rafe De Luca?"

Responding to the new competition, the other four abandoned their brief fling with order. Questions tumbled over each other, getting louder with each second. She held up both hands, waving them like semaphores above her head.

"Stop! No more questions." A flash made her blink back spots. Another one followed, stretching her patience to the limit. "Out!" Rather than wait for them to obey, she shoved past them and held the door wide until they all followed her onto the sidewalk. Like a pack of preschoolers, they continued badgering her with questions about Rafe, his TV show, his costars, and her dating history.

Sticking two fingers in her mouth, Maggie blew a shrill whistle. The babble faded. "We're done!" she ordered.

"Just a photo!" someone insisted. She turned to find the ponytailed reporter giving her an encouraging grin. "Come on, a nice shot of you in front of your store. It'll be good for business."

Damn, he might be right. And a posed shot had to be better than any pictures they'd taken so far. Obediently, she stood beneath the dark green awning with the white letters reading, "Fortune's Folly." Cameras clicked.

"Okay, that's it," she said.

"One more! How about—"

Obviously, they'd never be satisfied. She turned away, leaving them on the sidewalk. Before closing the front door, she reminded them, "I answered your questions. I expect you to leave me alone during business hours."

She locked the doors again, then lurked near the checkout counter to see what happened. Within seconds, they dispersed.

Maggie smiled. For her first encounter with the press, she thought she'd handled it pretty well. They were pushy, but she'd kept them at bay. Cal had made it sound like she'd be mobbed by unruly hordes that would rip her to shreds. If he showed up, he'd have to eat his words.

It was nearly three o'clock the next day when Cal walked through the front door. The paparazzi had been shooed away by the police, so they weren't there to spot their mystery man. They'd missed her, too, when she'd stayed at Zoe's last night instead of going home. Another day or two of this and maybe they'd get tired of stalking someone they couldn't find.

The day had started out cold, but heated up to seventy degrees with a high blue sky. Both doors were propped open, letting the warm breeze play against the wind chimes just inside the door. Cal didn't appear to appreciate the tinkling sound as he passed by. In fact, he didn't seem to appreciate any part of the beautiful spring day as he zeroed in on her behind the display cases in the center of the store. It was too bad, because he really had an interesting face and she was betting it would look even better with a big, strong grin. Looked like she'd just have to imagine it, because he seemed incapable of smiling around her.

Maggie replaced a ring in the glass case and straightened as he strode up to her, his boots echoing on the worn wood floor. Despite his tight expression, she put on her friendly greet-the-customer face. "Hi, sourpuss. Is it just me who ticks you off, or don't you ever smile?"

"It's definitely you."

Not even the slightest hint of humor softened the hard line of his jaw. Still, his bad day didn't have to ruin her good one. "What did I do this time?" she asked, not because she cared, but just because he looked like he might explode if he didn't vent.

"You've been busy, haven't you?" He slapped a stack of papers on the glass countertop.

The banner on the top one read *National Tattler*. Tabloids. Mildly curious, she turned it to face her. "Did they mention me?"

He didn't answer. He didn't have to. Her photo filled most of the front page. One arm was extended toward the camera, and she appeared to be lecturing someone. From the pose and the grainy quality, she assumed it had been taken with a camera phone the other night at the Alpine Sky, probably as she faced down the Blaster. Anger wasn't her most flattering expression. Against the dark background, large yellow headlines next to the photo proclaimed, "Rafe De Luca and Girlfriend Caught in Rowdy Bar Brawl."

Maggie wrinkled her nose and shoved the paper toward him. "Don't worry, I cleared that up yesterday morning."

He gave her a tight smile. "I know." Removing the *Tattler*, he shoved the pile back at her.

The Hollywood Scene lay on top. She blinked twice at the large color photo of her, mouth open in a startled expression, before recognizing the moment from the parking lot behind the store. They hadn't wasted any time. Banner headlines declared, "Rafe's Bar Bimbo Denies Criminal Past."

"What!" Sudden weakness hit her knees so hard she leaned against the glass cabinet for support. Grabbing the paper, she held it in shaking hands. "I told that idiot I didn't have a police record!"

"Obviously," Cal drawled. "Which is exactly what he reported—you denied having a criminal past."

She swallowed, but still only managed a whisper. "That bastard."

Wordlessly, Cal took the paper from her hands and handed her the last one. Lurid red headlines on a white background proclaimed, "Rafe De Luca in Love Triangle with Local Hottie!" Next to it, a picture of Maggie smiling in front of the store cut off half the name, displaying just the word "Folly" above her head. Below, in a smaller font, "Mystery Man Flees the Scene," and "Rafe Can't Keep His Hands Off Me! Maggie Claims."

"Oh, my God," Maggie groaned. "It's not over, is it?"

Cal lifted one eyebrow, studying her with disgust. "Lady, it's only just begun."

Chapter Three

Maggie paced the work area between the packaging table and her desk. She had to move; if she stood still, her brain froze up, displaying that startled image of her face with the words *Bar Bimbo* next to it. That picture was on front pages at newsstands and grocery store checkout lines all over the country. Her grandmother would see it. So would her sisters.

She growled her frustration. "Those slimy bastards. They knew better, and they twisted the facts to suit their story."

"That's what they do." Cal stood with arms folded, watching her pace. He didn't even try to look upset on her behalf.

"Well, it's despicable." She wished the whole pack of them would show up just so she could have the pleasure of kicking their butts onto the street. What really ticked her off was that she'd given them the fodder they needed to write their misleading stories. "Damn it, I should have known better," she muttered.

To his credit, Cal didn't agree. He didn't have to. She could see it on his face, that resigned look of contempt that said he'd known she would blow it. That part really irritated her. She should have been the one who knew what to expect. She dealt with celebrities all the time, both in her store and as part of the nightlife at the big ski resorts. Most didn't attract reporters the way Rafe De Luca did, but they were never truly anonymous, and never truly alone. She knew that. So how come this cop from Oklahoma had anticipated the overblown media reaction and known how to handle it?

She faced him, hands on hips. "How'd you know the tabloids would be all over this?"

"Are you kidding? Haven't you ever watched *Trust Fund Brats*?"

"No."

He snorted. "You must be the only one. The show has all these twenty- and thirty-something rich kids who have grown up never knowing what anything costs because everything was always given to them. Then they give them a limited budget and a task, like feeding a family of four for a week, or fixing a leaky faucet, and watch them try to cope. America loves to see the rich people screw up the stuff we all deal with every day."

She wasn't sure she'd call an hour of Rafe De Luca making a fool of himself entertainment, but she took his word for it. "So he's popular."

Cal gave her a condescending smile. "It's not that simple. De Luca's good-looking, and outrageous in his excesses. Women fall all over themselves to be with him. He's the guy we all love to hate. Perfect

headline material. I've followed him around long
enough to know he's a paparazzi favorite. No matter
where he is, cameras are never more than a few yards
away."

She'd had a demonstration of that two nights ago.
Pacing again, she told him, "Their lawyer was here
yesterday. You were right—they want to put a pretty
spin on the whole thing and say Rafe and I had a lovers' quarrel."

"Perfect. Go along with it, and in a couple days
you're old news. It's over."

She shot him a hard look. "That's not gonna happen."

He rolled his eyes upward. "Somehow I'm not surprised."

"What I need to know is, what's their next move?
You seem to understand how Rafe's narrow little mind
works, so maybe you can tell me what I should do to
head him off."

He faked a startled expression. "Are you saying you
might actually follow my advice?"

Maggie gave him an evil squint. "Don't you dare
make fun—" She broke off as her sales assistant,
Holly, poked her head through the doorway and made
a loud "pssst" sound. "What is it?"

Holly nodded her head meaningfully toward the
front of the store. "There's, uh, someone here asking
to see you."

"Can you handle it? I'm kind of busy."

"I think you better come." Her eyes went wide and
she mouthed the rest as if it were top-secret information. "It's Rafe De Luca."

Maggie's mind froze up again. She looked at Cal.
His casual pose disappeared as he crossed the room

to her side. She smiled gamely. "I guess I'll go find out what Rafe's next move is."

"Not alone."

"I thought you didn't want to draw attention to yourself. Besides, he's not going to hurt me." She clenched her jaw. "And I promise not to hurt him."

She started forward, but he clamped a hand around her arm. "Damn it, Maggie, you're the most stubborn woman I've ever met. I said you're not going out there alone."

She opened her mouth to snap out a nasty retort, then noticed the tight creases at the corners of his eyes and the drawn line of his brows. He was worried. She had a feeling that Cal Drummond didn't worry without a darn good reason.

She gave him a cautious nod. "Okay, we go together."

His grip didn't relax. "And I won't tell you what to say, because I might as well be talking to the walls, but please . . ." He closed his eyes as if offering up a prayer that had little hope of being answered. "Think before you talk." Before she could object, he moved his hand to her back and guided her past Holly, sauntering into the front of the store like he owned the place.

Rafe stood by the rock and mineral display, hands clasped behind his back, idly scanning the museum-quality crystals. He might have been fascinated by the huge amethyst geode with its sparkly purple interior, but Maggie thought it more likely that he'd chosen that spot because it was near the large front window. On the other side, faces and cameras pressed against the glass. She wondered why they hadn't followed him inside, until she looked at the front door. Two large men blocked it. From their long hair, tattoos, and bulging muscles, she guessed they were more pro wrestling dropouts.

Rafe didn't turn, even though he had to know she was there—her footsteps were loud in the sudden silence. She realized with chagrin that the three women shoppers who stopped their excited whispering when she entered the room had probably recognized her from the tabloid photos. She glanced over her shoulder. They huddled together, staring, awaiting the next installment in the drama.

Rafe waited to turn until they were right behind him. Maggie enjoyed a tingle of anticipation, hoping to see a gigantic swollen nose, swaddled in gauze and taped in place. Maybe his eyes would be glazed by massive doses of painkillers, purple bruises blooming below them. She was almost smiling as he turned.

She looked at near perfection—wavy black hair, artificially tanned skin perfectly complementing his tailored pale yellow shirt. And a perfectly straight nose that was only slightly wider than usual. Her smile crashed.

Rafe flashed his teeth in a predatory smile and reached for her hand. "Hello, Maggie."

She stuck her hand behind her back. "Why isn't your nose broken? I thought I broke it."

The smile became strained but stayed in place—playing for the audience. As she waited, he glanced over her shoulder, winked, and nodded. Giggles carried across the room. The press would undoubtedly get three excited accounts of his incredible charm when he dropped by the store to see her. Chances were she wouldn't come off as well.

He finally graced her with his phony smile, speaking through gritted teeth. "I don't think you want to talk about your unfortunate lapse in judgment, Maggie. You should just be grateful that I'm willing to make this look good for both of us." Raising his voice, he announced loudly enough for the women to overhear, "Those bug fossils are pretty cool. I might be interested in buying one."

"They're not bugs; they're trilobites."

"Whatever. How much is the big one?"

George. As if she'd let Rafe touch him. "Thirty thousand. Unfortunately, I just sold it this morning." She tried not to get sick over the lost income; he probably would have paid it without blinking.

His mouth twitched as he forced it into a polite smile. "Too bad," he said, then lowered his voice to a quiet rumble. "We need to talk." His gaze settled on Cal as if he'd discovered a clod of mud on his shoe. "Alone."

"No." She and Cal said it together.

Rafe looked Cal up and down, from his ordinary brown hair to his cowboy boots. From across the room it might have looked like he smiled, but up close it was more of a condescending sneer. "This must be the boyfriend."

"That's right," Cal said. Maggie frowned and opened her mouth to protest, but he spoke over her. "And I'm not about to leave her alone with you." Like Rafe, Cal kept his voice so low that she doubted the three ladies could hear.

Rafe took several seconds to assess Cal, head

cocked. "That's not going to work, cowboy. How will the press think she's making up with me if you're standing right there?"

"That's your problem," Cal told him.

Rafe seemed to find it amusing. "Afraid I'll steal her from you?"

Cal gave a disinterested snort. "A spoiled piece of TV trash like you? Don't make me laugh."

Rafe's smile disappeared.

She had to give Cal credit for backing her up even when he thought she was doing the wrong thing. But pushing him into losing his temper in front of all those cameras seemed unnecessary. And it almost worked. From the ripple along Rafe's jaw he had to be grinding his teeth hard enough to crack their pearly white crowns. When he finally spoke he muttered through a fierce smile, "Your opinion doesn't count for shit, asshole. Here's how it goes. You make your little cunt girlfriend do what I need, my family's lawyers kill the story, and I won't have to look at your ugly faces again."

Cal laughed, a sharp-edged insult. "*Make* Maggie do something?"

Maggie didn't see what was so funny. She balled her hands into fists, wishing she could hit Rafe again. "I'm not staging a kiss-and-make-up scene for your benefit."

Rafe shook his head sadly over her ignorance. "Have it your way. I was willing to make it easy, but I don't mind watching the press drag your name through the mud for a few days before you decide you've had enough."

She sighed loudly, determined to set him straight.

"You really don't know how to take no for an answer, do you? This isn't Hollywood, and I don't have to suck up to you or your daddy. Nothing you do can make me change my mind."

From the way he tensed, she knew she'd crossed some invisible line. He leaned closer so their audience couldn't see the hard look in his eyes, or hear his harsh whisper. "Listen, bitch. You're the one who doesn't understand. No woman is going to make me look like a fool. Try it and my lawyers will crush you." The hatred in his voice sent shivers skidding down her back.

"Your *lawyers*," Cal scoffed.

Turning to Cal, he stepped closer, something Maggie would have thought twice about, considering the icy look in Cal's eyes. "And I'll be more than happy to have them crush you along with her."

She expected a rude response from Cal, but a slow smile tugged at his mouth. For a brief second her heart stuttered; she'd underestimated the effect of his smile, but didn't have time to consider it. Leaning in until he was nearly nose to nose with Rafe, Cal said, "You think I'm afraid of someone who let a girl give him a bloody nose?"

Rafe's head jerked as if he'd taken a jab to the chin. He drew a deep breath, his slitted eyes boring into Cal as he let air hiss out through his teeth. For a moment his eyes shifted toward the door and she wondered if he was thinking of calling one of his hired brutes over to twist Cal's arm off and beat him senseless with it. If so, he thought better of it. His gaze touched on the women across the room, and he flashed a tight smile their way, a practiced move that spoke of a lifetime in the public eye. She knew how it would look to the three women: distracted and annoyed by the callous shop owner and her rude friend, Rafe still took a second to appreciate his fans. What a prince.

She'd give a hundred dollars to kick him right now.

Maggie darted a nervous glance at Cal. He looked as calm as usual, but she realized it was deceptive—something was fiercely alert inside him as he watched Rafe. He almost looked disappointed when Rafe took a step back and gave him an assessing look.

"What's your name?" Rafe asked.

"Cowboy."

A muscle jumped beside Rafe's eye. "We're not done here."

Cal's smile gave her chills. "I'm counting on it."

Maggie's heart pounded at the implied violence, even though Rafe's expression went bland again. He studied her as he nodded toward the window behind him. "You see those vultures outside? They'll do anything for an exclusive with me. Last chance—either you go along with my story, or I tell them a completely different one guaranteed to make the headlines. Once I sic them on you, they won't stop picking at you until your bones are clean."

Mutely, she shook her head.

"Fine." He startled her with a wink and a smile, back in full publicity mode. "You let me know when you've had enough, pretty Maggie. But I'm afraid the terms will be tougher next time we talk. I'll be in touch."

He gave them a friendly nod and walked away. She wanted to rip his throat out.

Cal must have felt her impending explosion, because he clasped her hand in his and led her firmly back through the door that said EMPLOYEES ONLY. Fine—she had a few things to say to him, too.

Cal knew she was ready to boil over. He didn't like being the target of her fury, but it was better than letting her spout off at Rafe De Luca in front of half a dozen photographers. She should have already learned that lesson—any reasonable person would have—but reasonable didn't apply to Maggie Larkin.

She lit into him as soon as he closed the door. "You purposely provoked him!"

She was pissed as hell, but he couldn't stop his smile. "Yeah. Wasn't it fun?"

"No!" She threw up her hands in exasperation. It seemed like her hands were always moving when she talked. "I want him to go away! Now he's going to try even harder to ruin me."

"Maggie."

He waited until she huffed impatiently, stuck her hands on her hips, and snapped, "What."

"He was going to ruin you anyway. You're the one who decided not to give him what he wants—to look good in the press. To be the suave Romeo they always make him out to be. So, yes, he'll try to punish you for that. He's vindictive. It's part of his killer mentality. And it's why you should go along with him."

She didn't look the least bit appeased. "Why do I keep forgetting that you aren't here to help me? You have your own agenda. So what's your plan—provoke Rafe into killing me to prove he's a murderer? Thanks a lot."

It was just sarcasm, but the thought of Rafe harming her sobered him fast. "Hell, no! That's what I'm trying to prevent. I don't believe in taking unnecessary risks." Apparently he was just attracted to women who did. Once was enough on that crazy carnival ride, but it seemed he hadn't learned his lesson. Secretly, he admired Maggie's refusal to take shit from anyone, making him all the more irritated with himself.

"Then what's the point?" she demanded. "Because it felt a lot like some macho strutting contest with me in the middle."

"The point is to find his trigger." He moved away from the door, forcing her to follow. He could only imagine what would happen if someone overheard his theory about Rafe De Luca murdering women. Those three women shoppers might be straining to overhear the conversation in the back room if they weren't already on the sidewalk, selling their version of what they'd seen to the press.

Maggie refused to sit at her desk—did the woman ever relax?—so they stood as he explained. "I need to know what makes him kill. Rafe's not like a serial killer who plans and stalks and prepares for each kill. Most of the time he's just your average, everyday asshole, with too much money and power for his own good. But every once in a while something sets him off. He doesn't plan to kill, at least I don't think he has yet. He does it impulsively, in an outburst of temper."

She thought it over, pursing her lips as she did, which he found highly distracting. He tried to focus instead on her eyes. They usually snapped with enough anger to make him forget about demented fantasies like kissing her. She'd probably bite him if he tried it, anyway. "You mean he's like the guy who kills his ex-wife because she leaves him for someone else? If he can't have her, no one can?"

"Not exactly. The kind of guy you're describing tends to zero in on one woman exclusively, maybe for years at a time. Rafe picks up and disposes of lovers on a regular basis, and doesn't care who they go to next. But he does care about controlling them while they're with him. I suspect he has an image of himself that's nearly godlike. He can't tolerate a woman who defies him."

She finally looked cautious. "Like me."

"Like you."

"Are you saying if I don't go along with his lovers' quarrel scenario he'll try to *kill* me?" Her voice went up at the end; at least she took it seriously enough to be horrified.

"I think you're safe for now because everything has been so public. But nothing's certain, and I need to know what triggers his uncontrolled bursts of temper."

"You *think* I'm safe?"

"What do you want, a guarantee? I can't give you that." She raised her eyebrows. He hadn't meant to spit it out so forcefully, but her determination to control the situation was exasperating; it was the reason she was in this mess. He could imagine Julie doing the same thing, and she'd ended up dead. "The man's dangerous and unpredictable, Maggie. If you're afraid of him—and you should be—then for God's sake, give him what he wants. How many times do I have to say it? Pose for the press, pretend to like him for a couple days, then break up."

She glared at him, more angry than he'd expected. "Never. I refuse to be associated with that lecherous moron, even as a pretense. I already take enough flack for being one of the Larkin girls; I don't need to add further proof by dating some Hollywood man-whore."

Ah, there was that reference to the Larkin girls again. "What does that mean, being one of the Larkin girls?"

She gave him a bitter smile. "That's right, you aren't from around here. I guess I should be glad our reputation hasn't spread all the way to Oklahoma." When he just waited, she blew out a breath in a resigned manner. "Let's just say it's nothing I'm proud of. I'd prefer to keep it in the past."

"Well, obviously you haven't been able to, so I want to know." At her stubborn look, he added, "Or should I just ask around?"

He was pushing hard against a sore spot, and was relieved when all she did was turn away until she got her resentment under control. Every muscle in her body was taut, and he half expected her to whirl around and spit out a string of nasty words but, in a minor miracle, reason won out. She shook back her hair and found her determined expression. He was beginning to suspect she met a lot of life with that look on her face.

"My upbringing was sort of . . . unconventional," she said. Starting at the beginning. That was okay with him; he hadn't expected it to be a simple story. "My mom's an original hippie. No psychedelic drugs, but she did have flowers in her hair, communal living, free love lifestyle, the whole thing. Especially the free love part."

He nodded, making sure not to look judgmental. He knew he was getting as few facts as she could get away with telling, and he didn't want her to censor the story too much. When she seemed to be waiting for a response, he said helpfully, "Like Woodstock."

Her smile was bitter. "Yeah, like that, only about a decade later. And more organized—she and her friends started a commune on Two Bears Mountain. My two sisters and I lived there until my grandma took us in. Hippie kids." She said it as if it were in quotes, and he knew it was the name other people had given them.

He imagined three girls growing up in the small town of Barringer's Pass, where everyone would have known about their mother's unorthodox lifestyle. "So people just assumed, like mother, like daughters? That the Larkin girls slept around?"

She gave a rueful smile. "Mostly because we did. Well, Zoe and I did. Not Sophie—she's been smart enough to escape that trap. She's eight years younger than me, six years younger than Zoe. When Zoe and I turned into wild teenagers, acting out and generally living up to expectations, my grandma stuck Sophie in a private school in another town and kept her sheltered from those rumors. Poor kid was practically wrapped in cotton because of us," Maggie said, shaking her head. "But it worked. No one ever looked down on her, and she never had to prove she was as good as everyone else. Or refuse to prove it, and just live up to it. That was my brilliant choice. Not the brightest move, but I was pretty headstrong when I was a teenager, and kind of made my own rules."

He choked back a laugh. "What a surprise."

She allowed a tiny smile. "Maybe I still do. But I don't sleep with every guy I go out with. Anymore," she added with an embarrassed look. "Unfortunately, what you do at sixteen or seventeen isn't forgotten just because you're thirty-two and you've become a responsible member of the community."

His age. He would have thought she was in her mid-twenties. Maybe that fiery spirit made her seem younger. "So to everyone else, you're still one of those wild Larkin girls?"

"Yeah, except the term they use isn't that polite."

"How did Rafe find out?"

"I don't know. I like hanging out at the resorts because I meet people who aren't from here. They don't judge me by my name, and don't hit on me because they think I'm easy. Up there, the past never happened. It's like getting a fresh start."

He knew all about that need from his own childhood. "You fit in."

She gave him a surprised look, but didn't question him. "That's right. But when he threw the past in my face the other night, I kind of lost it."

"It's your trigger."

She sighed. "I guess it is."

Cal didn't want to upset her further, but she might as well be prepared. "You should know that those reporters are going to be asking around about you. They'll use your past in their stories, if they haven't already."

She winced. "I know. I should probably warn Zoe."

"You think she'll be okay with them starting up those rumors again?"

"Of course not, but she won't run and hide from it. She's a fighter." She set her jaw and thrust it forward. "We both are."

"And what about Sophie?"

Maggie narrowed her eyes. "What about her? This has nothing to do with Sophie. She's not even here, she's in grad school at CU—Boulder, just finishing up her semester. The tabloids don't know she exists."

"Right. And how long do you think that will last?"

He hated to be the cause of the sudden, stunned look of fear in her eyes. She licked her lips nervously and said, "You think they'll find out?"

He'd have given anything to reassure her, but it wouldn't be the truth and would only hurt her more in the long run, so he pinned her with a hard look. "Maggie, I think they'll find out the name of the first boy you slept with and ask him how good you were. I think they'll find out what other celebrities you've been seen with this past year. I think they'll track down your first-grade teacher. Hell, they'll find out the name of your dog and do an interview with his veterinarian." He took a deep breath and blew it out in a disgusted sigh. "Yeah, I think they'll find Sophie."

She finally dropped into the chair at her desk. "Shit."

He gave her enough time to imagine the repercussions, then pushed again. "Does that mean you want to back off and do it Rafe's way?"

"No, I . . ." She shook her head, her hair partially shielding her confused expression. "I don't know."

"Then prepare for things to get worse."

She looked up. "Worse how?"

"Exaggerations, even outright lies, about your past. Suggestions that you're mentally unstable. Maybe more hints about run-ins with the law. The De Lucas will see that it gets to the press."

She rallied at that. "But that's ridiculous! My run-in

with the law amounts to one speeding ticket when I was nineteen. They can't make anything of that."

"You'd be surprised. All they need to say is, 'confidential sources report' or 'a friend of the family revealed,' and add anything they want."

As the magnitude of it registered, she paled. He watched her closely, determined to convince her to go along with Rafe's cover story and avoid the virtual bloodshed sure to come.

"I need to think about it."

Not good enough. "There's another consideration, Maggie. Your store."

She frowned, and he saw the concern behind it. "What about it?"

"The De Lucas have a home here in Barringer's Pass. They probably have friends—or people who are afraid to cross them, which is just as good as far as they're concerned. All they have to do is let it be known you're on their blacklist, and people will stop shopping here. How much of your business is local?"

She pressed her mouth into a tight line. "Maybe half."

"And how many of your customers from out of town are from the Hollywood crowd or the music industry?"

She bit her lower lip. "I don't know." Her voice had lost its steely quality. "I guess I'll find out, won't I?"

"I'm afraid so."

She muttered a few swear words under her breath, then looked up with renewed fire in her eyes. "Can I get back at him? Hit him first and distract the reporters? If they focus on him, they might leave Sophie alone."

Damn—he was torn between cheering her fighting spirit and warning her to back off. How could he encourage someone not to stand up to an injustice, not to defend the innocent?

By remembering that some people preferred to live in the midst of chaos, and were more than happy to drag you into it with them. He'd seen it up close. His fault. It didn't have to happen again.

Frustrated, he said, "I don't recommend it, but I'm not sure that makes any difference to you. You know, this wasn't supposed to be my fight. I'm just trying to keep De Luca from killing you while I figure out how to prove he killed Julie."

Any camaraderie she might have felt toward him disappeared in a flash. She shot to her feet. "Well, excuse me for dragging you into it and involving you in my personal issues. Oh wait, that was your idea, wasn't it, *boyfriend*?"

He couldn't argue, which made it all the more irritating. Everything about Maggie Larkin was irritating. How had he gotten this mixed up in the problems of a stranger? Maybe he needed to let her handle things on her own. She'd been right about one thing—Rafe probably wouldn't hurt her, at least not physically. Maggie was under too much scrutiny now. And anything else De Luca did to her, like shredding her reputation, was not Cal's concern. Julie was. It was time to remember that.

"You're right, I chose to get involved," he told her. He walked to the back door, then turned with one hand on the knob. "But I don't have to stay involved. You want my advice? Here it is: Stay out of dark alleys and don't accept rides from strangers. And if Rafe threatens to kill you, call the cops. See you around."

He left without waiting to hear her response. From what he already knew of Maggie, he'd lay bets it was colorful. And loud.

Cal caught himself wondering about Maggie at least ten times the next day as he tracked down resort employees who might have seen the two missing girls. He wondered what Rafe would do to her. What the press would do to her. Each time, he furiously blocked the thought and turned his focus to Julie. Julie, who at twenty had been too naive to see the shallow side of Rafe De Luca that Maggie had pegged within minutes. And too stubborn to call her big brother for help when things had turned ugly and dangerous.

But blaming Julie for not calling him was a cop-out. She would have been too proud to admit she'd misjudged the handsome, famous man who'd swept her off her feet. Too embarrassed to ask the brother she barely knew for help getting away from him. Still, their mother had figured it out. Cal might have intervened in time to save Julie if his mother had known how to reach him.

But she hadn't. He'd intentionally cut himself off from her, left without giving her so much as a phone number. But if Sherrie June Drummond Ellis Howard knew one thing it was men, and she'd recognized the evil in Rafe De Luca. She'd known her daughter was in over her head. And she would have turned to Cal for help if she could.

Because she couldn't, Julie had died.

He had to live with that guilt. Assuming his two half sisters could depend on whatever man happened to currently be in their mother's life had been stupid.

He'd failed Julie as badly as their mother had. All he could do for her now was prove that Rafe De Luca was the monster who had killed her and dumped her body like a piece of garbage.

That would be a lot easier if Rafe didn't find out who he was. Claiming to be Maggie's boyfriend might actually help—there was no reason for Rafe to connect Maggie's local friend Cal Drummond to Julie Ellis, a brief fling in California.

A bigger danger might be the reporters. Being in their sights would restrict his ability to monitor Rafe, and it wouldn't take long for them to figure out that he wasn't local. He had to be extra careful, which included not letting them follow him straight to his cabin.

Cal cruised slowly by the slightly shabby main building of the Lost Canyon Lodge and the cabins that trailed deep into the trees on either side of it. His gaze lingered on a blue car parked by the main lodge with a man behind the wheel. The guy might be waiting while his wife paid the bill or bought a souvenir T-shirt in the tiny gift shop. Or he might be a reporter, staking out the place in hopes of finding the mystery man who'd helped Maggie escape from The Aerie bar.

He wasn't willing to risk it. Turning around at a gas station, he drove back to the small family restaurant across the street. He could watch the driver of the blue car and anyone else who might be loitering near the cabins for the next half hour to make sure they weren't looking for him. He wasn't in a hurry; Rafe probably wouldn't be prowling for women until later tonight.

He walked in and scoped the place out. All the tables along the windows seated four or more—they'd never let a lone diner monopolize one. A perky young girl led him to a table for two in the center. He chose the chair that faced the windows and the lodge across the street. The blue car and driver were still there. Cal ordered a piece of pie and a coffee, scarfed down the pie, then sat sipping the coffee as he watched the blue car.

"Hey, you want this?"

He looked up to find the lone diner at the table next to him offering a folded newspaper.

"I'm done with it, and you looked like you needed something to do."

"No thanks."

"Suit yourself." The guy dropped it on his table. "Can't say I blame you. It's nothing but speculation about that scuffle between Rafe De Luca and some local chick."

"I already heard about it." Cal took another sip of coffee and returned to watching the lodge across the street. The blue car hadn't moved.

"It's nothing but trash journalism."

Cal agreed but didn't answer. Better to let the subject die.

"'Course, you gotta wonder, anytime a woman hits a man," the guy said. Apparently some people couldn't take a hint. "Mostly, women don't like to make a scene. Unless they've been drinking. No telling then. Maybe this Maggie chick was drunk."

He should ignore him. Or grunt agreement, reinforcing the idea that he didn't want to talk. But the idea of another nasty rumor about Maggie floating around town ate at his conscience like acid on metal. "She wasn't drunk," he muttered.

"Really? Seems unlikely—"

"I got it firsthand from someone who was there," Cal said, cutting him off abruptly.

"Oh."

Yeah, oh. Now shut up and find something more important to think about. People needed to get a life and stop wasting time reading celebrity gossip. Or hanging around cheap tourist cabins waiting to see if he showed up. Damn reporters were going to have him looking over his shoulder until this thing died down, which didn't look to be anytime soon.

"Of course, there's that whole other piece of the puzzle, the guy who stepped in and decked the bodyguard," the man reasoned aloud. "Could be he started the whole thing. Jealousy can make a guy do strange things."

Cal pushed his coffee away, even though it probably wasn't the reason for the sour feeling in his stomach. He turned sideways to face the guy. Long hair brushed the man's eyebrows in front and covered his collar in back. Cal figured a haircut was about two months overdue. A shave wouldn't hurt, either. Combined with the guy's worn denim shirt and jeans, he could have been a man in need of a job. Except for the glasses. The square black frames imparted a serious, slightly professorial air to a face that was not much older than his own. Or maybe it was the steady gaze behind the glasses. The guy looked too smart to care about some no-talent rich asshole's bar fight.

Cal gave him his stern cop face, the one he saved for argumentative drunks. "Sounds like you've read all about it. I thought you said it was trash journalism."

He shrugged. "Entertainment for the masses."

"More like crack cocaine," Cal told him. "Feeds an empty craving while taking the focus off real life. I told you, I'm not interested."

"You don't think it matters if a woman slugs a man in a bar, then ducks out like she has something to hide?"

"I think it's between the man and woman, and the cops. And just because a woman doesn't want to get shot by a raging, drunk bodyguard, doesn't mean she has something to hide."

The guy cocked his head, thinking it over, nodding sagely. "You could be right."

"I am." Cal turned back to the window.

"I guess you would know." He let a pause hang in the air for a few seconds. "Since you were involved."

Cal turned back. The guy's frank gaze looked pretty damn sharp now as he waited for a reaction. Cal scowled. If he was fishing for a quote, he wasn't going to get one.

The guy held out his hand. "Rick Grady. You got a name, other than Mystery Man?"

Cal ignored the hand. The name sounded familiar, probably from one of the bylines in those trashy tabloids, and he had no desire to shake hands with one of those hacks. "Congratulations, you found me. I have nothing to say to you or the other slugs who live under your rock."

He shrugged. "That won't stop anyone from writing about you."

The reporter's lack of concern only aggravated the frustration that had been building since last night. "And you have the scoop on that, don't you? You can tell the world that I like apple pie and take my coffee black. Or do you just make shit up like all the other vultures?"

Rick Grady leaned back in his chair, unmoved. In fact, Cal thought he looked slightly amused. "Your diet is fascinating stuff, but I'm not interested in writing about you."

"And yet you sit here making wild speculations and pumping me for comments on the big incident. That doesn't sound like a lack of interest to me." The problem was, Cal hadn't been the only subject of those speculations. The thought of Rick Grady spreading more lies about Maggie jabbed at his gut like a hot poker, spreading heat through his whole body. He leaned closer, dropping his voice. "If you even think of writing one of your sick, twisted lies about Maggie Larkin, I'll find you and break your fingers one by one."

"Jesus, buddy, back off." But instead of looking scared and retreating, Grady leaned forward. "Pushed your buttons, huh? I suggest you learn to control that reaction, or you'll be their next big headline instead of a mildly interesting sidebar."

Cal curled his fist around his chair instead of smashing it into Grady's face, and forced himself to take several deep breaths. Rick Grady might have sold his soul to whatever tabloid he worked for, but he was right. Despite his best instincts, Maggie Larkin had gotten under Cal's skin. She was impulsive, bossy, and a giant pain in the ass, and defending her was distracting him from his main objective. He should be thinking of Julie.

But he couldn't stand by and watch Rafe De Luca and the tabloids rip Maggie to shreds. If he had to take them on one by one, he would. He stood, looming over the reporter and forcing him back in his chair. "Listen, asshole, if you write one word that isn't true—"

Grady held up both hands. "I'm not writing anything. I'm not interested in the lady."

Cal frowned. The guy looked sincere, but you could never tell with his species. They'd rat out their own mothers for a good story. "Then what the hell are you doing?"

"Looking to burn Rafe De Luca's sorry ass. Without collateral damage—that means I don't care about you and your girlfriend."

"Right. You just happened to be eating here while keeping an eye on the Lost Canyon Lodge, where I just happen to be staying."

"I eat here because I like the prices. And I'm watching the blue car over there, same as you. That's Rob Ventner with *The Hollywood Scene*. If he's still there when we're done talking, I'll get rid of him for you."

Cal eased back, more puzzled now than angry. Grady pointed at the chair across from him. "Have a seat. I think we might be able to help each other out."

Chapter Four

Cal didn't see how a reporter could help him, but Grady obviously wasn't the typical tabloid stringer. Not unless he was lying about not being interested in him or Maggie, and Cal didn't think he was. He pulled out the chair across the table and sat. "Who do you work for, and what makes you think you can help me?" he asked.

"I don't work for anyone. I freelance. Mostly I do articles for online news sites." His superior look revealed what he thought of the tabloid reporters. "But about a year ago I happened to be in the right place at the right time, and I took a picture of Rafe De Luca arguing with a woman—a girl, really, about sixteen— outside a club in Acapulco. No one else was there, I was the only one who caught it. I sold it to a tabloid for fifty thousand dollars."

"Holy shit." No wonder those photographers were on De Luca like leeches.

"No kidding. That was way more than I made on my articles that year. And I only took the picture because two seconds before that I saw Rafe hit her. He looked like he was going to do it again, and if I couldn't scare him off I wanted to at least document it."

"Son of a bitch," Cal muttered. He gave Rick a hard look, noting the decently muscled build and flat stomach. The guy was no wimpy pencil pusher. "Why the hell didn't you do more than take a picture? He was abusing a girl. You look like you could handle yourself in a fight."

"I was in a parking lot, separated from them by a chain-link fence. But I yelled, and he saw the flash from the camera. That was enough to stop him. Caught him with his arm raised and a look of desperate fear on the girl's face."

Cal raised his eyebrows. "I remember that picture. It caused a brief stir, but he explained it, and the girl backed him up. Something about practicing a scene for a TV show."

"At two a.m. behind a Mexican nightclub?" Grady gave a derisive snort. "He bought her off."

Cal grunted, not surprised. But the story was nothing without proof. "You know that for sure?"

"Sure as I could get. I tracked the girl's family to a little run-down apartment across town, but I couldn't talk to them. They'd moved away. Left town the day before in their brand-new pickup truck, the neighbors said."

Cal believed it. But that didn't mean he trusted Rick Grady. Gesturing at the camera and zoom lens on the chair between them, he said, "So you moonlight now as a tabloid photographer to pay the bills?" For that kind of money he could hardly blame him, but he still found it distasteful.

"Not exactly." Rick fiddled with his water glass, his expression grim. "I'm hoping to catch him in another act of abuse. I heard in Mexico he likes his girls underage, and he's not gentle."

Cal bit back a string of curses only because he was conscious of the two young kids dining with their parents a few tables away. He wasn't surprised at Rafe's behavior, but it still infuriated him to hear it. Worse, horrible possibilities started playing in his head, making him wonder if Julie had gone through the same sort of abuse. Or maybe she'd been a willing participant until things got rougher, or more degrading. Images he didn't want flashed to life in his mind, nightmare scenarios of what Rafe might have done to Julie before the final, outrageous assault on her young body.

"I thought you should know what you're dealing with," Rick said, "since your girlfriend crossed him and he looks mad enough to kill her."

Cal gave him a sharp look. "She's not my girlfriend."

Rick looked confused. "Sorry, I just assumed, since you rescued her like that . . . or did they exaggerate?"

He ran a hand through his hair and heaved a sigh. "No. It was a train wreck—I saw it coming and I couldn't stop it, and couldn't look away. Couldn't leave her to handle Rafe on her own either, especially after she made it worse by charging back in to shake her fist at that hulking idiot bodyguard of De Luca's. Crazy woman."

Rick chuckled. "I thought it was great. Dangerous as hell, but great."

The problem was, somewhere deep inside, so did Cal. He admired Maggie for not backing down, for not letting Rafe use her. But it didn't outweigh his fear for her, and for the rage she aggravated further every time she defied Rafe. He'd seen what that bold approach to life could do. It didn't always turn out well.

"How do you figure you can help me?" he asked.

The determined look on Rick's face was the same one he'd seen on Maggie's. "I'm going to nail the bastard. He's obviously unstable if he's pushed too far, and it's bound to happen again. I intend to be there when it does."

"So you can get a picture and another big check?"

"No." Rick looked annoyed. "So I can expose him for what he is. Sure, I'll take the money. But the guy's got women throwing themselves at him, and they have no idea how dangerous he is. I know his type and I can guarantee that someday he'll take it too far."

Finally, someone else who realized the truth. He gave Rick a hard look, and decided to trust him. "He already has."

Rick grew still and Cal could sense the man's journalistic instincts going on high alert. "What do you mean? Did he do something to Maggie?"

Cal noted the barely leashed tension—Rick wanted to bring Rafe down as badly as Cal did. He still wasn't sure if it was a passion for justice or simply lust for a juicy story, but maybe it didn't matter. He also recalled where he'd heard Rick's name before. They might be able to help each other in more ways than one. "Let me ask you something first. Have you ever done any investigative pieces, the deep-background type of exposé?"

"I did one on a police chief involved in a bribery scandal. Why?"

Cal allowed a smile of satisfaction. The article had been sensational, but gutsy and true, and he'd noted the reporter's name. "Because you're right about De Luca. And if you're looking for another big scoop, I have a personal connection to a story that might interest you."

Maggie had assured Zoe that the media attention didn't bother her. She'd lied. Her sister bought it for only one day. By Monday evening she insisted on coming over.

Zoe stepped inside the house, took Maggie by the shoulders, and searched her eyes. "Are you okay?"

Maggie smiled, washed by a warm wave of affection for her sister. She hadn't realized how badly she'd needed to hear someone ask that. Nodding, she pulled Zoe into a quick hug. "I am now. Thanks for asking, it's been brutal. And Zoe, I'm so sorry if they've dragged you into it, too."

"They haven't. At least, nothing more than reciting some old news to prove you come from a degenerate family. They can't hurt me with what this town already knows and has discussed to death. I've been squeaky clean for years, which translates to boring. But the way they're ripping into you . . . I saw the stories. Brutal is the right word. It's like they *want* to hurt you."

"They do. From what Rafe implied, his family can control some of the stories. He threatened to make my life miserable." She led Zoe to the living room and dropped onto the couch, glad to finally be off her feet. "A couple friends said they tried to tell reporters that I wasn't anything like what those articles said, but they weren't interested in printing it." She gave her sister a grateful look. "It's nice to know I have some support. But you shouldn't have bought those horrid papers. I resent every dime they'll make from shredding my private life to ribbons."

"I didn't buy a paper," Zoe said, sitting beside her. "I read it online."

A weak feeling hit her stomach. "I'm on the Internet?"

Zoe looked apologetic. "Just the entertainment sites." She winced as she added, "With links."

"Great. The gossip section, which is probably what pops up as soon as you turn your computer on."

"Well, no, you were after the president's trip to Europe and that airplane accident. . . ." Her voice trailed off at her sister's annoyed look.

Maggie sighed. There was no point in being the only one who hadn't read it. "What did they say? Was I vilified for being a bar bimbo, or was it about my supposed criminal past? Or maybe they speculated about the mystery man in my love triangle with Rafe?"

"Uh, no, actually the one I read was about your loose morals and how you go through men like candy. They got a few quotes from some guys you dated, or so they claimed." She frowned. "I didn't recognize the names."

Maggie's muscles coiled inward as if she'd taken a punch in the stomach. "You're kidding. Someone I dated told the press I had loose morals?" Not that she'd always been as discriminating as she should have been in choosing her dates, but it still felt like a betrayal to know that one of them had talked to the tabloids about her. Grabbing her laptop off the coffee table, she shoved it toward Zoe and demanded, "Show me. Find the article. I want to see who said that."

Zoe obediently tapped keys and pulled up the article, then turned the computer toward Maggie. Large headlines read, "Rafe's Accuser Has Questionable Past."

"Accuser," Maggie muttered. "I'd love to give that witless wonder some real accusations to deal with." Then she began reading.

It was worse than Zoe had said. "Will Brenton? I never even went out with Will Brenton! And he has the nerve to say I'm an easy lay!" She burned Zoe with a blazing stare. "Did you read this whole thing? This is outrageous! Mitch Rutkowski says I probably slept with half the senior class—what a crock!" Even as promiscuous as she'd been then, the claim was outrageous. "How can they get away with saying this crap? Maybe I should sue them."

"I don't think you have a case if that's what people told them, and you know it probably is. People in this town will believe anything bad about the Larkin girls."

"You're right," Maggie grumbled. "And besides, the tabloids are just following where the De Luca family points. Rafe said his family would go after me, and this is what he meant."

Zoe's jaw tightened. "Big deal, we've taken hits before. So we fight back. Go after Rafe."

Rather than fire her up, the words pricked Maggie like pins, leaving her deflated. "I can't."

"What?" Anger mixed with incredulity as Zoe's mouth dropped open. "Why not? You know I'll support you. I'll do whatever I can."

"I appreciate it, but that's not it. It's Sophie. Cal said if I keep this fight going, the tabloids will find her and drag her into it."

"What can they possibly say about her?"

Maggie raised her eyebrows in weary defeat. "Anything they want, apparently. If they hurt her, they hurt me, and that's what Rafe wants. Just saying she's related to me would be bad enough. Having her name dragged through the tabloids won't help her get a teaching position at a university. Plus, she's never dealt with this crap. She never had to develop that hard shell, and I like her that way."

"Damn. I'll bet that's why she wanted to meet us here."

Maggie frowned. "When? Next weekend when she comes home?"

"No, tonight, any time now. She left school early and said she'd meet me here so we could talk about it. You think she's worried about how this might impact her?"

"Oh, God. Probably. She should be." She pressed her lips together and gave Zoe a pleading look. "I can't let them drag her into this, Zoe. I'd rather let everyone think I had some brief fling with Rafael De Luca than turn the tabloids loose to ravage Sophie. At least one of the Larkin girls can walk through this town without causing whispered comments, and I'd like to keep it that way. Can you understand?"

"Sure." Zoe reached out to take Maggie's hand in her own. "I agree; we need to keep this from touching Sophie. And we can always put the true story out later, that you just lied about having an affair with Rafe in order to stop all the lies."

"No, I can't. I'll have to sign something that says I can't talk about it."

Zoe made a disgusted face. "Well, I don't, and I'll be glad to tell everyone exactly what sort of arrogant asses the De Lucas are."

At the crunch of tires on gravel, they both looked toward the front window. Zoe flipped back the curtain and confirmed, "It's Sophie."

They met her at the door, each of them drawing their slender, chestnut-haired sister into a firm hug. "You cut your hair," Maggie said, fingering the locks that barely reached past Sophie's jawline. "I love it. It's even shorter than mine."

"Thanks. Listen—"

"God, those are cute shoes. Where'd you get them?"

"Boulder. I have to—"

"Adorable," Zoe agreed.

"It's so good to see you," Maggie gushed, hugging Sophie again. "Will David be coming soon? I'm dying to meet him."

"Maggie!"

Maggie paused, blinking at her youngest sister. "What?"

"I didn't come to discuss my shoes or my boyfriend. Well, not exactly," she corrected, letting the vague statement hang there. "I want to hear about this stuff with Rafe De Luca. I know whatever I heard can't be true, and I want the whole story from you."

Maggie shrugged it off as she guided Sophie toward a seat in the living room. "I'll tell you everything, but don't worry about it, it's all going to be over soon anyway. The De Lucas are going to spin it as an affair and a lovers' quarrel, and they'll make sure all the nasty stories stop."

"What!" Sophie popped back off the couch. "You had an affair with that little prick?"

Maggie scowled while Zoe laughed and pulled Sophie down again. "I'm not that crazy," Maggie said. "But that lie is better than the lies they're spreading now, so I decided to play by their rules. It'll be better for everyone in the long run."

"Better for whom?" Sophie demanded, dark brown eyes snapping with anger. She scooted to the edge of the cushion, leaning intently toward Maggie. "How can it be better to just ignore all those things they're saying, and let everyone who knows us assume they're true?"

A sick feeling began in Maggie's stomach. Everyone who knows *us,* she'd said, not everyone who knows *you.* "Did someone on the faculty connect you to the stories about me?"

Sophie wrinkled her nose. "I think one of the tabloids called my advisor. They called my landlord, too. But I don't care about that," she said, waving it aside. "I was more upset that some reporter called David and asked him about our family, and hinted about how hot I must be in bed."

"No!" Maggie stared in shock at her sister. "They called your boyfriend? They already know who he is?"

"Oh, yeah. But more important, do *you* know who he is? David is the son of a minister." She raised her eyebrows significantly. "A nice, conservative minister. His parents get hives at the very thought of sex scandals. They conspicuously avoid talking about their son's living arrangements, just in case he might be fornicating with me on a regular basis, as he is, and he's quite happy to keep them in the dark. But he loves them dearly and he's a bit jittery about their finding out that my sister is a Hollywood Jezebel."

"Oh, my God," Maggie groaned. "I'm so sorry, Sophie!"

"Don't be sorry," Sophie ordered. "If David's afraid to defend me to his parents, I'd rather know that now. But you need to stick up for yourself! Tell the truth!"

Maggie scrunched her eyebrows. "I don't think you want me to do that, sweetie. Rafe is a snake, and his family is a writhing nest of vipers. If you think it's ugly now, Cal assures me it will get worse if I don't go along with Rafe's story of a lovers' quarrel, and he's been right about everything else so far."

"Who's Cal?"

Maggie hesitated, censoring the first words that came to mind, such as *smart, stubborn, bossy, arrogant,* and *sexy as sin.* She gave an involuntary jerk. Where had that last one come from?

"He's Mystery Man in the stories," Zoe summarized for her. "A cop from Oklahoma who helped Maggie out when Rafe got aggressive. He says Rafe killed his half sister."

Sophie blinked, trying to absorb the information. Her gaze darted back to Maggie. "You can't let them make up more crap and pretend that it's true," she said, her eyes pleading. "You have to fight them, Maggie."

Maggie's stomach twisted at the pain in Sophie's eyes. This was exactly what she'd tried to avoid, but the story had raced ahead of her like wildfire through tinder. Faster than she'd thought possible. She scowled over the logistics of reporters tracking down her sister, finding out where she lived, who her academic advisor was, and who she was dating. It wasn't even about Maggie, who was supposedly the star of the scandal. The information had to have been fed to the tabloids, and there was only one obvious source—the De Lucas.

Hot fury roiled inside her until she felt the heat of it rising off her skin. She'd been ready to play it their way, but the De Lucas had crossed the line. She'd destroy Rafe for this.

"That son of a bitch won't get away with this," she growled at her sisters. "I promise I'll make him pay, Sophie. If he thinks I'm going to crawl in a corner and lick my wounds, he's in for a surprise."

"Good," Sophie said grimly.

Zoe nodded. "We're both with you, Maggie. What do you want to do, and how can we help?"

"You don't need to do anything. I'll talk to those tabloid reporters. They're digging around for stories, so I'll give them one."

"About what?" Sophie asked. "Something positive, like your volunteer work at the Children's Clinic?" She looked doubtful, as if realizing she might not be able to count on Maggie to get this done. Sophie had a lot to learn.

"Hardly. They don't want to know good stuff, they want a story with teeth. Scandal. Innuendo. Backstabbing. It's what they thrive on, the stuff that sells papers." She sat back, tapping her thumbnail on her teeth as she thought. "If I'm going to fight back, I'll have to come up with something equally scandalous about Rafe."

Zoe raised her eyebrows. "Like what?"

"I don't know yet." She flashed a wicked grin. "But you can bet it'll be good. Are those reporters still hanging out at the Alpine Sky at night?"

"As long as Rafe's partying there, they are. But he doesn't always stay at the Alpine Sky. The production company provides a suite for him, but I hear sometimes he stays at his family's estate if he wants privacy."

From what she'd seen, that wouldn't be very often. Rafe enjoyed the limelight too much to hide out at Mom and Dad's, no matter how big their place was. And if he wanted to put a negative spin on her part in the incident in the bar, he'd have to be out where the press could find him. "Could you give me a call if the reporters show up later tonight?"

Zoe nodded, but didn't look enthusiastic. "Don't you think you should talk to Cal about it first? He seemed to know a lot about Rafe."

"No." Definitely not. Cal would advise caution and restraint, and nothing ever got done that way. "This isn't about Cal, it's about me, and our family's reputation."

"It's just that he seemed pretty smart."

"You mean he sounded like he wouldn't do something reckless and impulsive."

Zoe nodded, unabashed. "That, too."

Maggie stood, a hint that she was done talking. "I'm not impulsive, I'm decisive. Cal would probably think about it for a week, then do the same thing."

Zoe shrugged as she and Sophie got up to leave. "I hope you're right."

"I am. Call me later."

"I will." Zoe followed Sophie to the door, then

turned with a wry smile. "Something tells me you're going to hear from Cal tomorrow."

She was probably right. The man was a big buttinski. Well, too bad. He'd just have to accept that she had her own score to settle with Rafael De Luca, and it had nothing to do with him.

The Backstreet Bar on the edge of Barringer's Pass was smaller and darker than The Aerie, and the clientele more rowdy, even on a Monday night. Rafe was obviously in the mood for rowdy. He was in the thick of the noisy group that sporadically burst into roars of approval as one more person downed a shot.

Cal didn't have to duck reporters at the bar—the reporters were with Rafe, cheering and drinking along with the others. He nursed his beer at the bar, keeping his alcohol consumption low. When Rafe moved on he needed to be able to follow, and only one of them had a chauffeured car waiting outside.

Another cheer from Rafe's group drowned out the background rock music. When it died into hysterical giggles, the old man next to Cal sent the group a disgusted glance. "Damn celebrities. They should stick to the resorts and let the real residents have a beer in peace."

Cal gave an amused grunt. "I'm with you." Although, as long as he was trailing Rafe, he preferred these small local dives to the generic glitz of the resort nightclubs. Where else could you still find Bruce Springsteen on the jukebox and Invaders from Mars on a pinball machine?

"Never seen you here before," the man said.

"Never been before." The guy looked a little more

distant, and maybe a little offended. Cal felt obligated to add, "But it's a nice place."

"Nicer without the likes of him. I been comin' here for near forty years, and that one right there and his friends, they been ruinin' it the last few years."

"But you still come here."

A smile played at the corners of his mouth. "Owner's a friend of mine. He cuts me a deal on my tab."

They went back to drinking beer and staring at the glow of the Coors Light sign behind the bar. Across the room Rafe had gone from tossing back shots to making out with the young woman on his lap. Cal kept half of his attention on Rafe, while the other half went over what the old guy had told him. He'd lived around here a long time. In forty years of sitting at this bar, he'd probably heard every rumor or bit of gossip in town. And he didn't seem averse to voicing his opinions.

"So you must know about everything that goes on in this town," Cal said.

"Reckon I do."

"I haven't been here long, myself. Maybe you can give me some information."

"'Bout what?"

"About where to find some available women. It's tough competition here, what with all the Hollywood types throwing money around. I can't compete with that."

The man nodded. "Ain't that the truth. There's not many women what can't be won over by flashin' a wad of cash."

The guy obviously didn't associate with the right class of women, but that might be just as well for what

Cal wanted to know. Maggie's comment about the Larkin girls had grabbed his curiosity and wouldn't let go. He wasn't from a small town, but he couldn't imagine her having a reputation so persistently bad that mentioning it still raised her hackles. Only one way to find out.

"I hear I missed some good times in this town. Something about a couple of sisters. Lark? Larking?"

"The Larkin girls." The response was too fast and sure for Cal's comfort. "They was too young for me." He flicked his gaze over Cal. "You woulda liked 'em if you was lookin' for a good time. They was lookin', too. Way I hear it, they always found one." He chuckled. "They musta gave as good as they got."

It was pretty much what Maggie had implied, but it bothered him to hear some old guy recite it like it was town history. He had to work at keeping a neutral expression. "They aren't around anymore?"

"Oh, sure. Just toned it down a whole lot. 'Course, that might not be true, from what I heard. One of 'em just got in a tangle with some big movie star up at the Alpine Sky. Got in a fight over her sleepin' around while she was supposed to be sleepin' with him. It's all over the papers, so I guess it's true. A leopard don't change its spots, do it?"

Cal bit down hard for several seconds until he could talk without coming unglued. "I heard about that. But the way I heard it, he was coming on to her and she was trying to get him to leave her alone."

"Huh. You gonna hear it all different ways, but the way I figure, once a slut, always a slut."

Cal stared at him, imagining choking him until his pasty white face turned purple. The visual helped him keep his hands to himself until he was sure he could speak calmly. No matter how despicable, he couldn't afford to ignore a good source of information.

"Heard there was some trouble with abductions of young women around here."

The guy screwed up his face. "Where'd you hear that? Ain't much crime around here, and sure as hell none of those psycho killers, if that's what you're talkin' about."

"Maybe I misunderstood. I thought some girls disappeared about a year ago. They never found their bodies."

The man nodded several times as his memory kicked in. "I bet I know what you're talkin' about. It was just one girl who disappeared; my sister knew the family. One of them kids what's out of control and the parents can't do nothin' about it, you know? Fuckin' idiots. Way I heard it, this girl ran off with some guy is all. They investigated, but naturally they didn't find nothin'. Little shit's probably turning tricks somewheres, too ashamed to call home. Happens all the time."

Not in Cal's world, but then, he lived in the real one. "I thought there was another disappearance, too."

"Not that I heard of." The guy squinted at Cal over his beer. "Who you been talkin' to, boy?"

"The wrong people, I guess."

"I guess."

"Well, thanks for the information. I'll see you around." He slapped some money on the bar and walked out the door. He'd learned all he needed to know. Barringer's Pass clung to its favorite scandals and swept others out of sight. The difference lay in how titillating the scandal was.

Maggie's had been plenty titillating. He'd rather spend the rest of the night huddled in his cold car than sit next to a guy who trashed her so easily and so thoroughly.

So that was what she was up against. No wonder she'd reacted the way she had. He figured Rafe was lucky he still had all his teeth. If Cal had known Maggie's story a few days ago, he would have stepped in sooner. Rafe would have been sipping his dinner through a straw for the next few months.

He still didn't like the idea of her tangling with De Luca. It was reckless—his least favorite attribute in a woman.

But damn, he was glad she'd taken the little bastard out.

Maggie had braced herself for an immediate reaction to her most recent evening's efforts at The Aerie. It actually took two days before the next papers hit the stands. And about two minutes after that for Cal to react.

Her doorbell rang at seven in the morning. Maggie muttered curses as she looked for her robe, belting it over her tank top and panties as she shuffled to the front door. Braced for a furious lecture, she flung the door open, prepared to yell back.

Cal was half sitting, butt propped on the porch rail, arms folded. Smiling. It hit her with a punch low in her stomach, taking the breath from her lungs. Covering quickly, she squinted in confusion. Cal never looked at her this way. Maybe the rising sun was glaring off his scowl, making it look like a smile.

He shook his head when he saw her. The smile

definitely grew wider. Her heart beat faster. "Good morning. Remind me never to get into a throw-down fight with you."

Besides being breathtaking, his good humor made her suspicious. "Why?"

"You're too good at it." He reached for a folded paper on the rail, holding it up so she could see the bold headlines: RAFE WANTED A THREE-WAY, MAGGIE CLAIMS. Smaller print below it read, "Third Person Was a Man!"

She blinked in surprise. "Wow. I'm a one-name star, like Cher."

"Congratulations." He opened to the article, cleared his throat dramatically, and read aloud. "Maggie Larkin, the woman at the center of a torrid public brawl with actor and entertainment heir Rafe De Luca, is finally telling her side of the story. In a private interview with the *National Tattler*—"

She snorted. "Real private—talking at The Aerie bar."

"—she claimed Rafe invited her to his suite, making clear he wanted to have sex, then asked another man to accompany them." Cal looked up expectantly.

"Absolutely true." She couldn't hold back her smile. "He told his bodyguard to come with us and make sure we weren't disturbed. That was before I turned him down, of course."

"Of course." He picked up another paper. "I thought this one was particularly inventive on your part," he said, displaying the headlines for her appreciation: "Sex Shocker: Romeo Rafe Is Impotent!"

She bit her lip to keep from smiling. "I didn't say that." She reconsidered. "Not exactly."

"Let me refresh your memory." Cal opened to the article. "'I saw him pop a couple pills shortly before he hit on me,' Maggie claimed. When asked what they looked like, she said they were small and might have been blue." He lifted one eyebrow, waiting for confirmation.

"He *did* pop a couple pills."

"I know, he was doing it all night. They were Tic Tacs. White, not blue."

She shrugged. "If you say so. I couldn't recall."

His mouth twitched. "Right." He picked up the last paper and flipped to an article inside. "This one is my favorite. 'Rafe De Luca Consults with Alien Ambassador.' See the picture?" He held the paper up so she could see the grainy photo of Rafe with his arm around the shoulder of what looked like a small gray alien.

"Cool. I don't remember him from the bar."

"Apparently he and Rafe were trying to recruit you for their breeding program, and you objected. Not very sporting of you."

She tried to keep a straight face, but couldn't. Laughing, she held her hand out. "I want to keep that one."

"You can have them all," he said, handing them over. "Start a scrapbook. I hope you live long enough to finish it."

Maggie lost her smile. "You're a real downer, Drummond, you know that?"

"Yeah." He stood. "Invite me in, Maggie."

Ignoring the way her nerve endings started tingling, she looked down at herself. "In case you haven't noticed, I'm not dressed for company."

"That's okay, it's not a social visit. You've just drawn a line in the sand, and Rafe's not going to stay on his side. If you're going to survive, I think we'd better consult on strategy." Without waiting for an answer, he brushed past her into the house, taking a long look at the robe where it came together over her chest, then an equally long look into her eyes that made her heart trip as she held the robe together at the front. . . . "Maybe you better get dressed first. I'll wait."

Chapter Five

He waited quite a while, killing time on her couch until she'd gotten dressed, fixed her hair, and made herself a cup of tea. Carrying the steaming mug into the living room, she settled in an adjacent chair.

He wasn't sure her skirt and blouse were any better than the robe. They certainly weren't less distracting. At least the long robe had covered those shapely legs, which were now crossed at the knee and angled toward him as her bare foot bounced an impatient rhythm. Some part of her always seemed to be moving. If she was ever completely still he'd have to check her pulse.

Maggie cradled the mug and sipped gingerly before speaking. "So what's your strategy, other than making me practice saying 'No comment' to anything a reporter asks me?"

"I really wish you'd tried that," he said sincerely. "But it's nice to know you learn from your mistakes."

She gave him a dark look. "And it's even better when you point them out to me."

He laughed out loud, and her mouth nearly slipped into a smile. That small victory warmed him. He was surprised to find how much he wanted to make her laugh, to create that sparkling, musical sound he'd heard when he first noticed her at The Aerie.

Unfortunately, what they had to discuss was not the least bit amusing. He lost the smile. "To start with, I don't want you to be alone, Maggie. Ever. Rafe is going to start playing dirty, and I'm not sure how far he'll go."

"*Start* playing dirty?" She gestured at the tabloids on the coffee table. "You don't consider the other day's pack of lies dirty? And that's only half of it—Sophie said reporters have already contacted her grad advisor and her landlord, among others."

He raised an eyebrow. "That was fast."

"That was crossing the line. I know the De Lucas put them on that trail, and it's already enough to hurt her. Image counts if you want to get hired to teach at a major university, you know. Trashing my name is one thing, but messing with my sister is a whole new ball game."

He waited for her anger to subside, but it didn't look like that would happen anytime soon. He couldn't blame her—this shouldn't have anything to do with her family. But escalating the fight was a dangerous tactic. "I hope you know what you're getting into."

"I'm only giving him back what he gave me."

"But he can do much worse than imply that you sleep with half the men you meet."

She glowered at her cup of tea for several seconds before flicking a glance at him. "I don't, you know."

"You already told me."

She raised her chin. "I just want to make sure you believe it."

"I do."

"Thanks." She relaxed a little. "At least someone does."

Tight lines lingered beside her mouth. He hadn't realized how battered she must have been by her past, and by those years of slander about the Larkin girls. Even though her back had lost its stiffness, her eyes remained shadowed by memories. It was that look that touched him, that made him recognize a similar pain in himself. Reaching out, he laid his hand on her knee.

"I understand," he began. That was all he got out. He lost the rest of his thoughts as his hand met her warm skin and her eyes lifted to his. It was like being hit with a double whammy, the intensity of her gaze, and the sizzling awareness of her body as it radiated up from his fingers and shot through his chest. He'd touched her before, but never when she looked so vulnerable and . . . desirable.

Her leg stopped its impatient bouncing. For a few seconds everything stopped, as if his fingers on her knee had completed some connection between them. She stared, and he swore he heard an electric buzzing in his ears.

He drew his hand back. The buzzing faded. A tiny pucker creased her brow.

Cal struggled to find his train of thought. And his voice. It would be easier if she weren't watching him so closely. He cleared his throat and tried again. "I understand about regretting your past, Maggie. About living with the results of bad choices you made and can't take back. I've been there."

Her soft chuckle was full of disbelief. "You have a promiscuous past to live down? You'd be the first guy I ever heard of with that problem."

"There are other bad choices. Worse ones."

She studied him for a long moment. "Like what?"

"I walked away from my sisters when they needed me most." He made himself say the rest; he needed to admit it as much as she needed to hear it. "I wasn't there for Julie, and she died because of it."

Sudden sympathy touched her eyes. But, with the same full-on, honest approach she used in her own life, she didn't let him gloss over the details. "Why do you think you should have been there? What could you have done?"

He leaned back. It was easier to talk when he wasn't so close to her bare legs, thinking about touching more than her knee.

"I wasn't there because I don't get along with my mother." He blew out a heavy breath, the same exasperation he felt every time he was forced to talk about her. "Sherrie June Drummond. She also has a couple more last names from subsequent marriages. She goes through men faster than I can keep track. Fast enough that I never knew from one day to the next if the guy who'd driven me to Little League the day before would be the same guy eating supper with us that night.

"When I was eleven she married a guy named John Ellis. By the time I was thirteen, Ellis was gone and

Julie had been born. My mother needed to work, but she couldn't afford a sitter, so she decided I should stay home from school to watch the baby."

Maggie blinked. "Every day?"

"She said keeping her job was more important than me going to school."

She shook her head in disgust. "She can't do that. The school must have told social services."

"They didn't know. She told the school I went to live with my father."

Her mouth fell open, but it took several seconds before she found words. "So you took care of your baby sister and missed school for—what? A few months? A year?"

"Unfortunately for my mother, I wasn't that complacent about giving up my future. I knew I needed school if I didn't want to be stuck in her world forever." He hesitated, braced for criticism. "I called the cops and turned her in."

Maggie brightened. "Good for you!"

He could have kissed her for that. No shock or pity for the boy who'd chosen to tear his family apart. He should have known that fighting spirit would color every aspect of her life.

"Social services put me in foster care. Julie, too. My mom ended up getting Julie back about nine months later, after she hooked up with some new guy and convinced the county that she could provide a stable home. She never tried to get me back."

"You wouldn't have gone, anyway," she guessed, staunchly taking his side.

Cal smiled. "You're right. And I got lucky—my foster families were pretty nice."

"Ahh," she breathed, realization lighting her face like a sunbeam. His chest tightened in response. He rubbed his breastbone, wondering how her smile could make his muscles spasm. "You were a foster kid," she said. "That's why you understood when I said I liked going to The Aerie because no one knew my background, and I fit in."

He nodded, surprised that she'd remembered. Maybe because she was interested in him. Or maybe she was just observant.

"I was better off that way," he told her, "but you're right, I didn't always fit in. That's part of why I joined the army right out of high school—it gave me a place to belong. Police academy after that. My mother and sisters were in L.A. I tried to reconnect once, but it didn't work. Visited the girls once more, but never really got to know them. I gave them my phone number." His smile was bitter. "A lot of good that did when I lived in Oklahoma, right? I didn't know how to connect with them and it made me feel less guilty."

"You have a right to a life of your own, Cal."

"That's what I told myself, right up until Julie disappeared. But I had an obligation to look out for my sisters when I knew no one else was doing it. When my mother finally figured out Julie was in over her head and took a moment from her life to be concerned, she didn't know how to contact me."

"Didn't your other sister know?"

"That would be Amber Howard. She believed Julie when she told her everything was fine. She's not quite seventeen, for Christ's sake. She thinks she can handle anything, so naturally she thought her twenty-year-old sister could, too."

He must have looked as disgusted with himself as he felt. A weary smile tugged at Maggie's mouth and she shook her head. "You're being too hard on yourself. No one blames you for your sister's death."

"They should. I think Amber does." He'd heard the strain and accusation in her voice when she'd surprised him with a phone call last night, asking where he'd disappeared to after the funeral. "I'm not looking for sympathy, Maggie. I'm saying I made some questionable choices, the same as you. All either of us can do is learn from them and be the best people we can be today." He winced. "Hell, I sound like a self-help book."

She looked more amused than annoyed. "Maybe you should write one."

He sat up straighter, energized by her words. "That reminds me, I met someone who might want to do just that, a sort of true-crime exposé on Rafe. I talked with one of the reporters following him around yesterday, Rick Grady. He actually sounds like a respectable journalist. He happened to catch Rafe in an abusive situation last year, and he's worried Rafe's the type who will eventually take it further. He's determined to catch him at it again and stop him, so I told him about Julie."

She put her mug down. "What did he say?"

"Totally believed me. He's the only person I've met who has seen Rafe for what he really is. It looks like I might have an ally in connecting Rafe to those disappearances. We're going to meet again today."

She smiled. "I like it. Let's turn the tables and put a little pressure on Rafe."

Perhaps he shouldn't have sounded so excited; he already knew Maggie wasn't big on taking a cautious approach. "Eventually. Right now I don't want him to get suspicious that anyone is looking into his connections to the missing women."

She leaned forward, pressing her point, and he struggled to keep his eyes on hers and not the cleavage he glimpsed beneath her V-neck blouse. "But it would take some of the heat off me if he had something else to worry about."

"You can accomplish that yourself," he reminded her. "Stop antagonizing him."

Maggie's stubborn look came back. Her golden-brown eyes turned stormy and her lips pursed, as if she were contemplating how best to rip his head off. "You mean I should stop fighting back? Is that the strategy you wanted to consult on? I don't think so." She stood, snatching the mug off the coffee table. "I'm not going to let Rafe destroy me and my family without lifting a finger in defense. I can't believe you'd ask me to do that." She stalked to the kitchen.

Cal followed on her heels. "I didn't ask you to not defend yourself—you're going off half-cocked again."

She turned, her eyes cool and dangerous. "Just what did you mean, then?"

He chose his words carefully to avoid making it sound like he was trying to control her. Even if he was. "We have to make this a team effort. You don't go planting stories in the tabloids without at least talking to me first. And for God's sake, learn to be objective."

"About what?" she scoffed. "Blaming him? We both

know he's the one who sicced the tabloids on me."

"I'm talking about how you react to it. I'd like to smash him in the nose and embarrass him in the press, too, but it won't help me prove he's a murderer, and that's more important. Besides, De Luca's dangerous. Rick's experience confirms my suspicions that Rafe is not the kind of man you want to rile up, especially not for something as trivial as your own pride."

He knew it was the wrong thing to say as soon as the words left his mouth. She slammed the mug on the counter and whirled to face him, eyes snapping golden darts of fire. "*Trivial?* My pride is trivial?"

"Compared to your life."

"You think I shouldn't have enough self-respect to care what lies Rafe spreads about me and my sisters?" She jabbed a finger into his chest. "What would you say if he were attacking Julie's reputation? How would you like that?"

He scowled, but she didn't give him a chance to answer.

"Not so nice, huh? But I'm supposed to let him trash my reputation and ruin my sister's life while I stand by quietly, playing the helpless victim? Didn't you just tell me you should have done more for *your* sisters? I thought you were on my side!"

Cal shook his head, annoyed with himself as much as with her. "I *am* on your side, damn it! I'm trying to keep you from pushing Rafe into a violent reaction when no one's there to help you." It was the thing he feared most, but it didn't seem to faze her.

"Bullshit. All you care about is your own agenda." She poked his chest again. "*Your* quest for revenge."

Another poke. "*Your* search for evidence that might be compromised by my trivial concerns. But don't worry, it's only my personal and financial life he's trying to ruin. While *you*—"

He grabbed her wrist before she could land another sharp stab against his chest. "Cut it out," he ordered. "You know that's not true."

"Don't tell me what's not true!" Instead of calming down, her fury only increased. "You've been telling me what's true and what I should do since the first second I met you. Don't make Rafe too mad. Don't get his family upset. Be objective! Like that's supposed to protect me!"

"It is, damn it!"

He still held her wrist. Instead of trying to pull away, she leaned closer as she lectured him, her fingers closed into a fist. He had a strong suspicion that if he let go, her fist would come straight up to meet his nose.

"Well, maybe I don't want your protection. Not if it means letting Rafe drag my family's name through the mud. I told you, I've been there before, and I'm not letting anyone do that to me again, and they're especially not doing it to my sister."

Her anger did nothing to lessen the impact of her closeness. Her fresh scent, her soft skin beneath his fingers, the passion in her eyes—even if the passion was telling him to go to hell. "It's not worth dying for, Maggie."

"I'm not going to die. I'm not a naive twenty-year-old girl, Cal. In case you haven't noticed, I'm a grown woman."

He'd been having a hard time *not* noticing.

"I can take care of myself. I appreciate the information on Rafe, but if you're not going to help me fight him, then stand aside." With her free hand, she pushed his chest, as if that might move him.

"Damn it, Maggie . . ."

"Damn it yourself!" She yelled her frustration. "I don't even know why you're pretending to help me when all you want to do is stop me!"

"I just want you to use some common sense!" He yelled back. "I know what I'm talking about. I've seen this happen before, Maggie, and it ended badly."

She gave him a confused look. "You've seen a Hollywood celebrity go after someone in the press?"

"No. Hell," he muttered. He hadn't wanted to bring it up, but maybe knowing the bare facts would convince her to be more cautious. "A cop I worked with was in a similar situation, except instead of a celebrity, it was a powerful drug dealer."

Her mouth pulled with disgust. "That's hardly the same thing."

"You'd be surprised. The big drug dealers engender a lot of loyalty in their communities. It's mostly based on fear, but it still gives them a lot of power. The cop—her name was Diane—was determined to stop this guy. And she was as fearless and reckless as you."

Inches from his chest, Maggie still felt coiled to strike. Her eyes watched his closely. "Was she your partner?"

"No, she . . ." She'd been so much more. And been just as careless with his heart as she'd been with her life. A hard lesson learned. "We were friends. The point is, she thought so little of the guy, she didn't believe he could hurt her. She broke with procedure, tried to do things her own way, without backup. He killed her."

She gave it a few seconds thought, the muscles of her arm tense beneath his grip. "It's not the same," she said, her eyes flashing in warning. "And I'm not Diane."

He bit back the string of swear words that hovered on the tip of his tongue. He knew she wasn't Diane. She didn't look anything like her, didn't even remind him of her. Except in this one thing. "You're just as impulsive as she was. Just as reckless. And damn it, Maggie, you could end up just as dead!"

"Thanks for your objective assessment." With a twist, she yanked her arm away. "I can't run everything by you first, Cal." The words sounded bitter, final. "Why do you even care what I do?"

He knew why. The answer ricocheted through his mind, as hot and wild as her temper, but he couldn't make himself say the words.

He could only show her. With a sudden jerk, he pulled her against him and crushed his lips to hers. Her body went stiff but he didn't pause, delving into her heat with a sweep of his tongue.

He'd acted on impulse, silencing her tirade, but as soon as he felt the softness of her lips against his own, he knew it was what he'd wanted to do all along. His mouth moved on hers, tasting, devouring. Showing her what he felt. After the first startled moment he feared she'd explode in anger, but the fist she'd raised to his chest unclenched and her lips softened, moving with him, accepting. Her rigid body relaxed against him, and her hands crept around his neck, pulling his body against hers.

It was more than he'd hoped for. He grasped a handful of luxurious hair and took what he wanted.

He hadn't expected her to be passive—she wasn't passive about anything, as far as he could tell. But the silken stroke of her tongue on his nearly sent him over the edge. Heat, flavored with the faint taste of mint from her tea, spun through him, waking an even larger need. Lust flared, a sudden awareness of her breasts pressed against him, her thighs brushing his leg . . .

He pushed her away, hands on her shoulders, breathing heavily. Wide eyes blinked back at him and she weaved slightly before regaining her balance.

"That's why," he said, his voice harsh, gravel on sandpaper.

Her tongue made a slow pass over her lips and he had to force himself not to kiss her again. Her silence made him nervous. "Nothing to say?"

She folded her arms tightly against her body, as if protecting herself.

Maybe it was better if he left before she decided to kill him. "I'll see you later."

He was almost at the door when she said, "Cal." He turned.

"That wasn't objective."

He considered it. "No. Not one bit. And don't expect it to change."

She stared at the door for nearly a full minute after he left. It didn't help. Her brain still couldn't reconcile the resentment she knew she should feel toward Cal with the naked desire that his kiss had ignited. Part of her wanted him to stay the hell out of her life. The other part—a much larger part—wanted to take him to bed for a week of exhaustive mutual exploration. And wouldn't that be a good way to prove that she didn't hop into bed with every guy she met?

Damn it. She didn't need this sort of distraction.

She wasn't going to figure it out now. She had a store to open, and probably a dozen photographers and reporters to deal with. She had to be ready.

Thirty minutes later she was out the door.

The day was bright, already unseasonably warm for May, and she paused to admire the view. Across the road, the mountainside fell away sharply toward the nestled shops and houses of Barringer's Pass. The shallow terraced lots on her road allowed her to look over neighboring rooftops right into the downtown area, and beyond to the rising slope and ski runs of Tappit's Peak on the other side of the valley. Sunshine bathed the town, improving her spirits. Smiling, she turned away to lock the dead bolt on the front door.

Something moved in the corner of her vision. Barely more than a shadow. She raised her head, turning toward a soft rustle in the forsythia bush by the steps.

The world went black.

Maggie gasped at the feel of cloth over her face. Before she could raise her hands, an arm came around her neck from behind, jerking her head hard against a firm chest and pinning her.

The keys dropped from her hand, clattering onto the wooden porch.

Male. Strong. Rough.

The impressions swirled in a dizzy kaleidoscope as

she clawed at the arm pressed against her throat. Hard forearm. Nylon jacket sleeves. Leather gloves over the hand that dug into her shoulder.

She opened her mouth to scream, but his other hand clamped across it, pulling her even tighter against him. A muffled cry escaped her, the most she could do. It sounded weak and frightened.

Helplessness infuriated her, and she fought with the only thing left to her—her feet. Kicking backward, she connected with a shin as she thrashed her weight around. He countered immediately, ramming her against the porch rail. She sucked in a sharp breath as her lower abdomen met the wooden rail with bruising strength. He pressed against her to hold her there while spreading his feet enough to keep his legs away from her feeble kicks.

Fear soaked her, momentarily sapping her strength. The pressure against her windpipe didn't help. She drew deep, panicked breaths down her aching throat, exhaling through flared nostrils and heating the suffocating darkness around her face. Each breath became more difficult as his grip tightened.

Beside her right ear, his face pressed against the cloth, millimeters from her clammy skin.

"Like this," he whispered. The words were soft, feathery against the dark cloth. In one swift movement his hand left her mouth and slid below her chin. Before she could even try to scream, her jaw was forced shut by the pressure of his forearm below it, cracking her teeth together and arching her neck outward. He held her there as his free hand marked a slow, thin line on her neck below his arm. A weak scream stuck in her throat as the gloved finger drew slowly, almost lovingly, across her neck. "It would be so easy," he breathed.

The next second the gloved fingers clamped around her trachea. Her heart thundered in terror as the last of her air was cut off. Breath rasped in her throat without making it to her lungs, and dizziness closed in. As she felt herself fading, he pushed her sideways. She fell onto the porch, one hand clutching her throat, gulping raw, harsh breaths into her lungs.

Fresh air fanned her face as the hood was ripped away. Maggie opened her eyes. Sunlight stabbed her expanded pupils, blinding her for the first few seconds. She sat still, gasping, and squinted against the brightness until her vision returned. The familiar peaceful view wavered into focus in front of her eyes. Off to her right and out of sight behind a stand of aspen trees and scrub brush, a car squealed its tires as it took off down the road. He was gone.

Her purse lay five feet away, contents spilling onto the porch. She crawled toward it and pulled out her phone.

Cal told himself there was no need to hurry, the police were already with Maggie, but he cursed under his breath at the tourists who ambled across intersections or held up traffic while searching for parking places. The last skiers of the season were using the morning to shop while the sun melted the crusty top off the ski runs. Right now, he hated every one of them.

He cut off the main road and sped up just as his phone rang. Bluetooth on his ear, he snapped out, "Hello."

"Cal, they're taking me to the police station."

Maggie's voice made heat rush through him, relief and tension in one confusing mix. She sounded composed but strained, as if it hurt her to talk. He gripped the wheel tighter. "Why?"

"Pictures."

She was using as few words as possible, but he understood. They wanted to photograph the marks on her neck. Just imagining the red blotches on her fair skin made him want to hit someone. No, not someone—Rafe. "The station just off the interstate?"

"Yes."

"I'll meet you there."

Whipping into the first driveway, he turned around and headed back through the congested downtown of Barringer's Pass, cursing the lack of alternate routes through the narrow valley. The ten-minute drive seemed like forever to his frazzled nerves, proof that Maggie had become more important than he wanted to admit.

He never should have kissed her. Before, he'd been able to pretend she was no more than an irritant, that his concern for her was professional and platonic. He'd almost believed it. He wasn't sure exactly what he felt now, but it sure as hell wasn't platonic.

The thought caused a weird twisting in his gut. He forced it away, assuring himself that *not platonic* didn't mean *love*. Desire, sure—Maggie was undeniably hot. But what he felt for her was responsibility. The woman obviously needed someone to watch out for her.

He finally cleared the downtown and gunned it to the station. He used his police shield to get past the

front desk without prolonged explanations, and found
Maggie standing near the wall in a large office, holding
her hair up for the man who was snapping pictures of
her neck. Cal strode past desks, ignoring looks from a
couple of officers.

Maggie spotted him. "Cal. I was telling Sergeant
Todd that—"

She broke off as he took her by the shoulders and
pushed her hair aside to get a better look. Angry red
blotches dotted her neck where fingers had dug in to
close off her airway. A vision of Maggie gasping for
breath burned through his mind. His gut clenched into
a hard knot of pain and he swallowed back bile.

"It doesn't feel as bad as—"

The rest was muffled as he pulled her against his
chest, tucking her head under his chin as he squeezed
his eyes shut against the image of the fingerprints on
her neck. Surprisingly, she stilled, allowing him to take
a couple of deep breaths as the red haze cleared from
his mind. When he finally set her back, she watched
him as if unsure what he might do next.

"I'm okay," she tried.

He clenched his teeth, biting back the rebuttal that
she was certainly not okay, not with those red marks
on her neck. "Was it Rafe?"

Sergeant Todd stared at him. "Rafe De Luca?"

"I didn't see his face." She pressed her shapely lips
into a tight line, obviously annoyed with the admission. "I couldn't tell."

"One of his bodyguards, maybe?"

She shook her head. "He seemed less, I don't
know . . ." She searched for a word. "Less bulky?
Strong, but more lean."

"Rafe isn't that muscular."

"I know." She coughed lightly and massaged her throat, and Cal figured in another minute steam would be coming out of his ears if he couldn't find the guy and slug him.

"You can't be sure it was him?"

She huffed out an irritated breath and shook her head.

Todd studied Maggie. "You're the owner of Fortune's Folly? The one who got into it at The Aerie with De Luca?"

"Yeah," Maggie grumbled.

"Did you tell that to the officer who took your report at the house?"

She nodded again, then bit her lip and looked at Cal. "There's something else. He ran his finger across my neck and . . ." She took a deep breath, steadying her voice. "He told me how easy it would be to cut my throat." Her hand went to her neck as she said it, fingers splayed protectively.

"Son of a bitch," Cal growled. "It is him."

The sergeant's gaze shifted between them, settling on Cal. "Does that mean something to you, other than the obvious?"

Maggie kept her eyes on him, letting him decide whether to tell.

He had no evidence, nothing but a string of coincidences. But this latest one involved Maggie, and he wasn't willing to take a chance with her safety. "A month ago, my sister was killed by having her throat cut after a sexual assault. She was dating Rafe De Luca at the time."

Todd's face got the shuttered, emotionless look

Cal recognized from having used it so often himself. "Doesn't prove anything."

Cal stared him down. "Forget he's a celebrity. Just think about the facts. One girl he's dating ends up dead with her throat cut. He has a public fight with Maggie, then goes after her in the press. Next thing you know, she's attacked by someone who chokes her and threatens to cut her throat. And that's not even considering a couple girls he's gone out with here who have disappeared."

"Who?" Todd snapped out. "When?"

"Rachel Anders and Tara Kolinowski."

He nodded. "I know those cases. The detective thought Rachel was a runaway, but the case is open. Tara had a history of hooking up for short-term flings. A drug rep from Dallas was a person of interest."

"Rafe was in town both times—I have witnesses."

"He was in town. That's it?" Todd held his gaze for a long time before finally speaking. "How come I never heard of your sister's case?"

"It was in L.A. Julie lived there and started dating Rafe after they met at a party. He has a house out there." Reluctantly, he added what he knew Todd would ask next. "De Luca had an alibi—his bodyguard and a friend. They both said he was with them, for what it's worth."

Todd scowled as he thought about it, obviously unhappy with this new wrinkle. Cal knew he'd just handed the sergeant a messy situation that he wouldn't have been happy to have dumped in his lap, either. He waited it out until Todd muttered something under his breath and gestured to a chair beside one of the desks. "Sit. Both of you. I want the whole story."

Cal drew up a chair from another desk and sat beside Maggie. He kept his voice unemotional as he recited the basics of Julie's death and the police investigation. Todd wrote it all down, then wiggled a finger between the two of them and asked, "How do you two know each other? You live in L.A., or here?"

"Neither. I'm from Oklahoma." He laid his shield on the desk so Todd could copy down the badge number, and added a business card with his phone number. "I'm on leave, but my captain can tell you anything you want to know about me."

Todd took the card and handed the shield back, giving Cal a long, assessing look. "As long as I don't hear that you're some whacked-out cop with a grudge against De Luca, we'll be looking into this. If they tell me you're a nut job . . ."

"You'll be looking into me. I know." It was more than he'd hoped for. "I'll help in any way I can."

He shook hands with Todd and walked Maggie out, one hand at her back. He needed to touch her, to reassure himself that she was okay. They paused outside, tolerating the cool breeze in order to soak in the bright, cleansing sunlight. The snowcapped peaks around them sparkled against the blue sky, as majestic as anything Cal had ever seen. It would be easy to pretend that the ugliness of the attack had never happened, except for the red blotches he saw on Maggie's neck when she stretched her face toward the sun.

She closed her eyes and inhaled, letting her breath out slowly. It seemed to work like a yoga exercise for her, erasing the lines of tension from her forehead. It didn't help him at all.

"That's what I meant by escalating the argument," he told her.

Maggie nodded.

"You have to stop fighting him in the press."

Her brows snapped together, creases instantly returning to her brow. "Excuse me?" He couldn't believe she really intended to argue the point, but she turned on him, hands on hips. "Whether or not Rafe did this"—she pulled her collar out to expose her neck— "we know it's because of him."

"Absolutely."

"Then do you expect me to show Rafe that threats work? That violence against women is the way to get what he wants?"

"I don't care what Rafe wants! I'm more interested in what I want—to keep you safe."

"Oh, what *you* want." She lifted one delicately arched eyebrow. "You think that just because I let you kiss me, you can tell me what to do?"

Throwing their kiss into the argument didn't help his disposition. "I don't think you ever let anyone tell you what to do. I just had this crazy hope that you might use common sense." He lifted an eyebrow at her, unwilling to let her skim the facts. "And you didn't just let me kiss you. You kissed me back."

"So I like the way you kiss," she said, the admission so casual he nearly lost the thread of their argument. "It's not an invitation to run my life." She huffed out a breath, signaling that the topic was closed. "Now could you please give me a ride to my store? Holly can drive me home later."

He rubbed the center of his forehead, the sore spot that was beginning to feel like it had her name on it. Forcibly shutting down the part of his brain that wanted to dwell on how much she liked his kiss, he concentrated on her ridiculous request to go to Fortune's Folly. She obviously had no idea what she was going to find when she got there. He could tell her, but she didn't seem to be in the mood to take advice from him.

He shrugged. "My pleasure."

Chapter
Six

Maggie sat quietly in his pickup truck for the three-mile trip back to town. He pulled into the small lot behind the store, letting the truck idle in park. "I'll just wait here."

She gave him a quizzical glance. "I'm not just dropping in, you know. I'll be here all day."

He smiled. "See you in ten minutes."

She gave him a suspicious look, but got out without another word. He watched her disappear through the back door, then looked at the clock on the dash. And waited.

Nine minutes later Maggie hurried out the back door and slid into the passenger seat. "Go!"

He threw the truck into drive without a word. Several photographers rounded the corner of the store at a run, snapping pictures of them as Cal zipped past, bounced over the sharp dip where the lot met the street, then slid into traffic. Two photographers jogged beside them for half a block, cameras pointed at the truck's windows, but fell back as Cal lucked onto a green light and sped up.

Maggie slunk low in the seat. "How'd they find out so fast?"

"Police scanners."

"They were all over the store," she complained, wrinkling her nose. "Like an invasion of cockroaches. Holly said they'd stopped asking her questions, but as soon as I came in they swarmed around me. They wouldn't leave, and if I'd called the cops it would have caused an even bigger scene." She sighed. "Holly finally slapped a handful of phone messages at me, and begged me to leave. Even then, they tried to catch me."

"Vermin," he agreed.

She was quiet for a minute, then darted a sidelong glance his way. "So how long was I in there?"

He smiled, savoring his minor victory. "Nine minutes."

"Crap."

She sulked until they reached her street, then gripped Cal's arm as they approached the house. "Oh, my God, don't stop!"

He'd already seen it. "Don't worry," he said grimly.

She scooted down low in the seat as they drove past, peeking at the string of crime scene tape around her porch and the three white vans out front topped with satellite dishes. Where had they come from? There wasn't a TV station within a hundred miles. On the sparse grass of her front yard, photographers roamed or sat on the rock outcroppings, smoking. By one of the vans, a man with a microphone conferred with a man holding a large video camera.

"Holy shit," she breathed. "This thing is out of control!"

"I should have anticipated this," Cal grumbled.

"How could you?" She wrenched her body sideways, watching the spectacle until the neighbors' trees blocked her view. "How will I ever get into my house again? Maybe I should call the police."

"Don't bother. They can't make the TV people leave, they're parked on public property. And the paparazzi will just scuttle off the grass until the cops leave, then come creeping around to look in your windows again."

She made a frustrated sound, then gave it some thought. "I have a rifle."

"Jesus, Maggie!" The truck jerked as he shot her a startled look. When she smiled, he turned away to scowl out the front window. "Shit, don't scare me like that."

"You thought I might really shoot someone?"

"It doesn't strike me as impossible."

She laughed. "I'm flattered."

"Of course you are. Jesus."

Rattling him made her strangely happy. Cal always seemed so controlled and organized, so damned *right* about everything, that it made her want to do something to knock him on his delectable ass. She snuck a look toward the part of him in question, then let her gaze roam down the well-muscled thighs, then back up to the wonderfully broad shoulders and the firm jaw that was currently locked tightly enough to make muscles jump in his neck. A contented hum rose in her throat. If he ever let go of that control, it could be mighty interesting.

As if sensing her gaze, he looked at her. She snapped back to reality. "Where are we going?"

"Lost Canyon Lodge. That's where I'm staying. Shouldn't be any press there. One guy had it staked out, but he gave up and left when he couldn't find me."

Considering her most recent thoughts, going back to his place didn't sound like a smart move. Looking indulged her fantasies; touching was out of the question with such a control freak. He'd probably tell her where to put her hands and how loudly she could moan. He didn't exactly seem like he was thinking about making a move on her, but he'd already taken her by surprise once. She hadn't seen that devastating kiss coming.

"Why are we going there?" If he made some casual excuse about hiding from the media, she'd question his motives for sure, because they didn't have to do that in a crappy one-room efficiency cabin that was little more than a glorified bedroom.

"That's where I'm meeting Grady."

"Oh." He was thinking business. She was the one with her mind in the gutter.

She didn't say anything else for the ten minutes it took to get to the Lost Canyon. Cal drove by the main lodge and followed a curving gravel drive through the trees, passing several scattered cabins and parking in front of the last one. Tall pines crowded around it, blocking even the neighboring cabin from view. She followed him up the steps to a rustic front porch with four inexpensive deck chairs, feeling out of place in her skirt and heels. Quiet enveloped them, save for the distant hush of traffic on the highway and the faint buzz of a bee. He unlocked the door while she noted management's stab at beautification, a lone clay pot holding three stunted daffodils.

He pushed the door open and stood aside. "After you."

She stepped over the threshold onto worn linoleum and looked around. The cabin was small, maybe twice the size of a motel room. To her left, a small kitchen table and counter were cluttered with groceries. She counted four boxes of macaroni and cheese, cereal, a small bag of potatoes, and another of apples. Bachelor fare. To her right, a couch, chair, and TV anchored a small square of carpet. The bed directly across from her was neatly made. She guessed that the door next to it led to a bathroom.

"Classy."

He smiled. "I knew you were a snob."

"You have to admit, it doesn't look anything like the Alpine Sky."

"I can follow De Luca around, but I can't live like him. I don't have a trust fund or a pretend job that pays me a million dollars a week. The place is clean; that's good enough."

She laid her bag on the kitchen table, checking for crumbs first. "When's this Grady guy coming?"

"About fifteen minutes." Cal stuck his hands in his pockets and looked around, as if just noticing his limited entertainment options. His gaze settled on the kitchen counter. "Want an apple?"

"No thanks."

He scanned the room again. "Watch TV?"

She stood and opened one of two kitchen cupboards, taking down a glass. "I think I'll water your flowers."

She filled the glass at the sink as he watched, bemused. "What flowers?"

They were sitting on the deck when they heard the crunch of tires on gravel. She kept her eyes on the heavily treed drive as an ancient Honda appeared around the last bend and parked next to Cal's truck. A man with shaggy dark hair got out, slammed the door, and shaded his eyes as he walked toward them. Maggie thought he looked studious with his dark-framed glasses, and handsome in an absent-minded-professor sort of way. His eyes lit with curiosity when he saw her, and darted questioningly between her and Cal as he walked up the steps to the porch.

He went right to Maggie and stuck his hand out. "Rick Grady. I recognize you from the papers."

She gave him a halfhearted smile as she shook his hand. "Not my best moment."

"I thought it was brilliant!" Rick beamed in admiration. "Exactly what De Luca needed. I only wish I'd seen it myself."

She gave Cal a triumphant look. "*He* thinks I was brilliant."

Cal scowled. "I never said he was smart." He cocked his head at the door to the cabin. "Come inside. We don't want to risk someone spotting us. So far, the media haven't found me and I'd like to keep it that way."

Rick nodded, suddenly serious. "Right."

"Intrigue," she murmured happily, following them inside.

They sat at the small kitchen table and Rick

recounted his experience with the damning photo of Rafe for Maggie's benefit. He seemed to revel a bit at being the unsung hero of the story, and Maggie couldn't blame him.

"Thank God you were there to catch him in the act!" Fury raged through her at the thought of Rafe charming some young girl with his wealth and star power, then slapping her around, maybe even forcing himself on her. "You did a service for women everywhere by selling that photograph."

"And for himself," Cal pointed out. "He made a lot of money."

"Cynic," Maggie accused, then told Rick, "He's good at finding the negative side of anything."

Rick looked resentful. "I lost money over it, too. The De Lucas can buy loyalty, and some publications avoided me after that."

"You didn't say that before." Cal finally looked interested. "Do they still refuse to deal with you?"

He brushed it off. "I have no idea, because it doesn't matter. I have other outlets to write for. The point is, the incident opened my eyes. Rafe De Luca likes young girls and is sexually abusive. His family hates that I know it. Up until now, they've had enough money and power to cover it up." He curled his lips over the words *money* and *power* as if finding them personally offensive. "We have to let people know what sort of man Rafe De Luca really is before he hurts more young women."

"Exactly!" Maggie agreed. Finally, someone else who believed in being proactive. Why couldn't Cal be this directed?

"We will," Cal said. "But only if we can connect

him to the disappearance of those two missing girls from this area."

"We can try. We *will* try. But I've been thinking about this ever since we talked." Rick leaned forward, intent on selling his point. "Maybe we don't have to watch him as closely now, because Maggie planted the idea that he takes advantage of women, and the press will be watching for it. So we're free to figure out how to connect him to the missing women."

"But what if we can't find any evidence?" Maggie asked. "We can't just give up and let Rafe kill again."

Cal frowned. "Who's giving up?"

"I say we mount a two-pronged attack," Rick continued. "We try to find evidence that links Rafe to the missing girls, sure. But we could also try to catch Rafe in an unguarded moment, like I did before, but something so bad it will mark him forever. Use the power of the press against him."

Destroying Rafe had appeal, and Maggie had a new respect for the power of the press, but Cal looked annoyed. Before he could reject the idea outright, she offered her support. "It could work," she told him.

"It could also get someone killed. You're talking about putting Rafe in a situation where he'll respond with violence."

"A *controlled* situation," Rick emphasized. "Scripted by us. A setup."

She couldn't read Cal's expression as he took a long look at Rick. "You plan to lure him into it?"

"Why not? We know what he wants," Rick said.

She looked from Rick's confident expression to Cal's closed one, not following. "What does Rafe want? A girl?"

"You." Cal turned to her. "Rick's talking about using you to tempt Rafe into violence."

"Oh," she said slowly, trying not to reject the idea out of hand just because the thought of Rafe touching her made her skin crawl. "But you guys would be right there to make sure he can't hurt me. Right?"

"Of course—"

"No, we wouldn't," Cal said, squashing Rick's reassurance before it left his mouth. "If Rafe did those kinds of things with other people around, he would have been caught by now. He wouldn't respond violently unless he felt no one was around. And we aren't in Mexico," he added sharply, forestalling Rick's objection. "We're on his home field. If he wants to get kinky, or thinks a woman might resist, do you think he'll try something at The Aerie? Or maybe in the Alpine Sky lobby, while you lurk behind a potted plant with your zoom lens? He'll take her to the family estate, where no one can follow him."

He was right. Maggie sat back in her chair, dejected. "Damn."

Rick didn't give up that easily. "It doesn't have to work that way. Think outside the box," he urged, the cliché drawing another annoyed look from Cal. "Maggie could entice him to a place where he thinks they're alone, like her store. At night." He warmed to the idea as he talked. "But we would already be there, hiding and watching."

Rick gave her an encouraging look, waiting for her approval. Maggie didn't want Rafe to touch George the trilobite, much less her, but for the chance to humiliate and destroy him, she might be persuaded. "Maybe," she equivocated.

"No." Cal's forceful answer made it clear he didn't care if she approved. He looked between them, like they'd both lost their minds, then focused his irritation on Rick. "In your little scenario, exactly when do you plan to step in—when Rafe slugs her for the first time? Is that when you snap a picture? If he just breaks a rib, or cracks her cheekbone, that won't show on camera, you know. Will you let him keep going until she's black-and-blue and dripping blood?"

Maggie flinched, feeling bruised already.

Rick frowned and started to reply, but Cal talked over him. "What if he shoves her across the store and you don't have a good angle because the display case is in the way? Do you sit quietly and hope Maggie can drag her battered body back into the shot? Exactly how much are you willing to put her through to get that million-dollar photograph?"

Rick's gaze darted to Maggie, as if to explain, but Cal wasn't done. Arms on the table, he leaned toward Rick. "And here's one more thought—what if he comes after you, too? When he killed my sister, he slit her throat. Is your camera going to be enough defense against a raving lunatic with a knife?"

Rick frowned and held up a hand. "Okay, okay, I get it. You're right, my plan has a few bugs."

"Your plan is shit."

For a few seconds Rick pressed his mouth into a stubborn line, then gave a reluctant nod. Maggie blew out a sigh of relief, surprised to find she'd been holding her breath. Cal's description had seemed all too real. His anger was real, too, and palpable. She wondered if it was because Rick had proposed a poorly constructed plan, or because it involved putting her at risk.

"So what's *your* plan?" she asked him.

"Good old-fashioned detective work." He gave them each a look as if assessing their capabilities. "The two missing girls I want to investigate are Rachel Anders and Tara Kolinowski. Rachel was eighteen and from Barringer's Pass. She disappeared almost a year ago. Tara was twenty-three, from the Denver area, but was vacationing here when she disappeared eighteen months ago. I've already determined that Rafe was here during those times. He overlaps Tara's visit by only two days, but that's enough. We need to find witnesses who can put the girls with Rafe on the day they vanished."

Maggie had to admit that Cal's bossy attitude lent itself to leadership. He just needed a dry erase board to make it feel like a police briefing. Thankfully, Rick listened as attentively as a rookie cop, taking notes in a spiral notebook. "How do we know he even met them?" he asked.

"It's a weak link right now. I've talked to people who can place both Rafe and Tara at the Glacier Pass resort on the last night she was seen. She was staying there, and partying with a large group of people in their lounge. If she left with Rafe, someone must have seen them, but I haven't found anyone who can swear to it yet. Rachel, the local girl, will be harder to pin down. She didn't hang out at the resorts, since they were too expensive for her. But she was well known at the bars and restaurants in town."

"So how do we pin her disappearance on Rafe?" Rick asked.

Maggie hid a smile at his wording, which made it sound as if Rick was willing to blame Rafe whether or not it was his fault. No question, he was on their side.

"I think it's likely she met him that night. Maggie can help confirm this," he said, glancing at her. "A lot of celebrities have vacation homes or permanent residences in the mountains around Barringer's Pass, so it's not uncommon to see them around town. Right?"

She nodded.

"And even though most of them hang out at the high-end resorts and restaurants, a few of them are known for slumming at the cheaper bars and clubs."

"Some do, especially a few rock stars and comedians I can think of. I don't know about Rafe."

"From what I've been told, and what I've seen, he does. Rachel told her friends she intended to meet Rafe De Luca the next time he showed up in town." The corners of his mouth tightened a bit. "She made a bet with her best friend that she could get him in bed. Apparently the two of them had a contest to see who got him first."

Maggie winced and muttered a few select words under her breath about teenagers and bad judgment. Only sheer dumb luck had kept her from a similar fate.

Under the table, Cal squeezed her hand. She looked up, surprised to see understanding and reassurance in his steady gaze, the kind of empathy she got only from her sisters. Something warm and fluttery bloomed inside her.

She never felt fluttery. Flustered, she pulled her hand away and pressed it to her breastbone, trying to rub out the strange sensation.

Cal went on. "I have a list of Glacier Pass employees, both current and former, who might remember

Tara. I've eliminated six so far. Technically, Rachel still lived at home, but her parents said she often stayed with friends. They don't seem to have a clue about her social life. I think her friends are the way to go there."

"Wouldn't the police have already talked to these people?" Maggie asked.

"Probably, especially the employees at Glacier Pass. But they weren't asking about Rafe De Luca, and some might not volunteer that they saw him there even if they did—I've found that most of the townspeople try not to piss off the De Lucas. Except for you, of course," he added dryly.

"I happen to think it's one of my best qualities."

Cal clearly disagreed, but Rick gave her an enthusiastic nod. "You've got guts. Good for you."

Guts, but no brains. She knew Cal was thinking it. Whatever attraction he felt for her didn't extend to the decisions she made.

Cal consulted a small notebook. "I suggest we divide up my list of names and cut the work in half."

"There are three of us," she pointed out.

"You're with me. You don't go anywhere alone." When she bristled, he added, "Unless you can't wait to go another round with your latest admirer."

Rick looked between their resentful glares. "What are you talking about?"

"The guy who jumped out of her bushes this morning, nearly choked her to death, and threatened to slit her throat."

Rick straightened, his eyes gleaming behind his glasses. "Rafe?"

"I don't know," she muttered, still disgruntled that she couldn't pin it on him.

"Rafe, or someone doing his dirty work," Cal said. "And he's still out there, which is why she shouldn't go anyplace alone." He gave her a hard stare.

"Fine," she grumbled. "Then you two work out a schedule of who talks to whom. You don't need me." She grabbed her purse and took it to the couch, not caring if she looked like a pouting thirteen-year-old. It might be Rafe's fault that she couldn't walk around in public without drawing a crowd of reporters and couldn't walk around alone for fear of being assaulted by some De Luca goon, but it was more convenient to be pissed at Cal.

Rummaging in her purse, she pulled out the five pink while-you-were-out slips that Holly had thrust at her as she left Fortune's Folly. She read the large, looping script on the top one: *Mrs. McNabb changed her mind about the velociraptor.*

Damn. But it wasn't too surprising. Mrs. McNabb had dithered for forty-five minutes over which fossilized dinosaur claw her son might like for his birthday. Personally, Maggie wouldn't have paid nearly three thousand dollars for *anything* for an eleven-year-old's birthday, but she wasn't married to a wildly successful real estate speculator, so she didn't have to worry about those decisions.

She flipped to the next pink slip: *Alyssa Burke canceled on the rugs.*

For a moment, Maggie felt the blood rush from her head. The Burkes were adding a recording studio to their mountain retreat, and Alyssa had selected three of Maggie's best Persian rugs to provide the proper ambiance. The order had been Maggie's largest in months, and totaled over $45,000.

Even in her light-headed state, she made the connection—Aaron Burke was a music producer for one of the De Luca labels. Maggie didn't know if they were friends with the De Lucas, but it wouldn't matter, not when their income depended on the De Lucas' goodwill.

Frantically, she flipped through the last three message slips. Each one was a canceled order, totaling another $12,000 in business.

Stunned, she stared at the message slips. Almost $60,000 in sales had disappeared in a matter of a couple of hours this morning. Who knew how much since then? The panicked thought jolted her, and had her digging into her purse for her phone.

One bar. It disappeared as she watched. Crap, she was tucked too closely against the mountainside. "Be right back," she threw over her shoulder as she walked outside. The sky was overcast with a bite to the air, but it felt good against her fevered skin. She kept an eye on her phone as she stalked past the cars onto the gravel drive. Two bars—good enough. She dialed the store.

"Fortune's Folly, may I help you?" Holly sounded tired.

"It's me. Are you busy?"

The sarcastic laugh was sharp in her ear. "Hardly. It's dead here, except for the phone calls and returns. Even the reporters are gone. There's no point in you coming back today."

"Damn." Returns, too. She kicked at some stones, which didn't work well with pointed toes. They moved a couple of inches. "How many more cancellations?"

"A few." Holly hesitated, then changed it to, "A lot. But no more big ones. Most of them are small."

"How small?"

"A few hundred dollars." Another hesitation, this time longer. "Including returns, they total about fifteen thousand dollars."

"Shit."

"It's the De Lucas, isn't it?"

"Probably." Definitely. She sighed. "Thanks for holding down the fort, Holly. I promise I'll be there as soon as I can."

"Don't hurry. I hate to say it, but you could probably just close up early."

She could just imagine the De Lucas gloating over that. "No way. I'll see you soon." She snapped the phone shut with renewed vigor and marched back up to the cabin.

Cal was looking at her expectantly even before she slammed the door, which startled Rick into looking up, too. "What's wrong?" Cal asked.

She wasn't surprised it showed; she probably had steam coming out of her ears. "The De Lucas," she said, tossing her purse on a chair. "They must have put out the word, because I'm getting lots of returns and canceled orders, like you said." She winced. "Including one big order that I really needed."

Cal's face was grim. "I'm sorry."

She nodded. It was better than "I told you so," which he had every right to say. "I have to get back to the store."

"I'll take you."

"Just take me to my house and I'll get my car—"

"I said I'll take you."

She rolled her eyes. Fine. If he wanted to spend all his time chauffeuring her around, let him.

"What are you going to do about the De Lucas?" Rick asked.

Cal shot him a dirty look, but it didn't matter, her mind was already working on the problem. The trouble was, she didn't have any ideas.

Rick couldn't leave it alone. "I didn't think they had that many friends around here."

"They don't," she said. "But they have money, and power. A lot of people here can't afford to piss them off."

Rick snorted his disdain. "Personally, I'd love to piss them off. Whatever ruins their day makes mine better."

Maggie hummed a noncommittal reply. She didn't need vengeance; she'd settle for being left alone. It was becoming clear that Rick invested too much energy into hating the De Lucas. Not that he was the only one—pushing people around tended to make them annoyed, and the De Lucas had done it enough to earn a reputation for being ruthless. Power bought loyalty, but it also earned enmity.

She twirled a strand of hair absently, wondering how many people felt as strongly as Rick did . . . and how she could use that to her advantage.

She stared unseeing at the speckled linoleum for several seconds before the silence made her look up. Cal and Rick were watching her, and Cal didn't look at all pleased to see her formulating ideas. She freed her finger from the corkscrew of hair and flashed a smile. "So what did you guys decide to do first?"

Cal's eyebrow twitched. He wasn't buying the innocent act.

She wouldn't have cared except for that glimmer of worry in his eyes. The death of a fellow officer still haunted him. Maggie wasn't convinced that she was like his friend Diane, but she couldn't deny she'd acted recklessly. And knowing that it revived Cal's fears was enough to curb her plans.

"We'll talk later," she told him. "Right now I just need to get to my store while I still have one."

From the way he relaxed, she knew he understood—she'd tell him what she planned to do about the De Lucas later, before she did it.

It didn't mean she had to listen when he said no.

She spent the rest of the workday making returns and fielding calls for canceled orders. At the end of the day she was down another $8,000, which she considered good after the meltdown that morning. When Cal came to pick her up at 7:30, she was glad to lock the door behind her.

It was still light as they approached her house, and she could see that the line of news vans out front had grown.

"Good Lord, how many news outlets are there?"

"Hundreds. Do you want me to keep going? You could stay with me tonight." When she shot him a look, he smiled and shrugged. "Or with your sister or grandmother. But I'd be better company."

"I'm staying in my own house. They can't drive me away."

But they could give her several unpleasant minutes. They swarmed around Cal's truck when he pulled in, yelling questions before she even had her door open.

"Who attacked you, Maggie?" she heard as she stepped out, nearly knocking the reporter over when she opened the passenger door. She moved quickly, ducking into the protective shelter of Cal's arm as he pushed past the gathered reporters and cameramen to escort her to the door.

"Did he threaten other members of your family?"

"Did you see the knife?"

"How many stitches did you get? Show us where he cut you!"

They followed her up the driveway but stayed off her front walk. She opened her door and turned to Cal. "Thanks. I'm sorry you have to go back through them."

"I don't think they'll follow me; they're stuck on covering you."

"Slug a TV star and you too can have your own news following."

"I'll stick with dodging yours."

She shut the door, then watched out the window as Cal strode back to his truck, making the reporters stumble out of his way. That was the way to do it, she decided—get pushy. She'd probably get a chance to try it in the morning.

She surfed the entertainment networks that night and saw replays of her huddled rush to the house, along with embellished descriptions of her assault and speculation about whether it related to some previous relationship. They made it sound like she had a string of bar fights and pissed-off men in her past. She sensed the De Lucas' hand in that.

Rafe had apparently lain low all Sunday, as there was no recent footage of him. From the tone of the reports, you'd think he'd spent the whole day in church.

Maggie didn't sleep well at all.

Cal dropped her at work the next morning and kept himself from calling her until noon. "Hi, how's your morning going?"

"It's dead. No calls and no customers. I'm debating having Holly bring a deck of cards when she comes in at one."

"How about you let her play solitaire and hang out with me? I'm going to visit Rachel Anders's parents."

He wanted to take it back as soon as he'd said it. Chatting with the parents of a missing and probably dead girl didn't sound as enticing as he'd like. But despite his lame offer, her tone perked up.

"Okay. I can leave as soon as Holly gets here."

"I'll take you to lunch first."

He was smiling when he hung up. Sure, she'd agreed to go because she was helping with his investigation. But there was more there, a mutual interest he knew he wasn't imagining. It crackled between them even over the phone. He'd have to be careful. He was far more attracted to Maggie Larkin than he wanted to be.

You don't do reckless, he reminded himself.

He had sworn he'd never give his heart to a woman who would be as careless with it as Diane had been, putting his love second to her need for the thrill of danger. But it wasn't love that made his pulse race and his groin ache when he looked at Maggie. It was pure lust.

That wasn't necessarily a bad quality in a relationship.

He could handle lust. And with Maggie, he could enjoy the hell out of it. He should probably be worried about that.

He arrived a few minutes early. She came out before he could park, as if she'd been watching for him. The morning's dull sky had changed to a deep gray overcast, but it didn't dim the radiance she seemed to carry with her.

"Pick a restaurant," he told her. "Something touristy. I might as well see all the attractions while I'm here."

She chose a place that overlooked the rushing stream downtown and they ate while watching water tumble and swirl over rocks as it cut its way down the mountain. He drank it in, loving the wild, restless feel of the high country. It suited Maggie's personality; she belonged here.

By the time they left the restaurant, the cloudy sky was spitting snowflakes. Cal zipped his lightweight jacket, silently thankful that Maggie had a coat so he didn't have to give her his. Being a gentleman didn't make him immune to the cold. "What's with the snow?" he asked, hurrying into the truck. "It's nearly June, for Christ's sake."

"Snow happens, especially around here. Ignore it." She buckled her seat belt and turned to him. "Where do the Anderses live?"

"Beats me. Here's their address—you navigate."

She glanced at the paper. "Shouldn't we call first?"

"So they can refuse to talk to us? I'd rather show up at their front door and rely on my charming personality to get us in. Which way am I going?"

"Through town, then left on Elkhorn." She paused

for only a second. "I can help get us in. I have a charming personality, too."

"Nah, you have an abrasive one."

The corner of her mouth twitched up. "Bullshit. Just with you."

"And you're argumentative."

"That's true."

He smiled, not sure why, since everything he'd said was true. Abrasive wasn't an exaggeration. They disagreed constantly, and he'd been mad at her fully half the time he'd known her. But the other half . . .

That had been consumed by thoughts of kissing her smart mouth until all she could do was moan with desire. Then he'd undress that tempting body, find some even better spots to kiss, then slide inside her and take them both to paradise.

And she might just let him. As contrary as she was, they'd seemed to be in complete agreement when he kissed her. There was a definite spark between them. Hell, more like a wildfire.

He stole a glance sideways, enjoying the way her skirt rode up her thigh. If he could get her to twist to her right and look behind them, he bet it would ride up all the way to—

"That's it, the A-frame on the right."

Well, damn, now he had to hope the cold air took care of the bulge in his pants before they got to the front door.

From Maggie's experience at The Aerie, Cal didn't exactly have a smooth way of introducing himself. Fortunately, he used a more professional method on Mrs. Anders.

The woman who answered the doorbell was fifty-something with poorly dyed, short brown hair, wearing a sweater and jeans. She opened the door all of six inches, blocking the cold air. "Yes?"

"Mrs. Anders? I'm Cal Drummond and this is Maggie Larkin." The door opened wider as the woman took a look at Maggie. "I'm a police officer in Oklahoma." He held up his ID.

"Oklahoma?"

"Yes, ma'am. I'm on leave, so I'm not here in an official capacity. I'm looking into some missing persons cases, and I wondered if I could talk to you about your daughter Rachel."

Mrs. Anders's gaze went flat and her lips pursed tightly, etching creases into her cheeks and chin that immediately aged her another ten years. "My daughter ain't missing. She ran away from home."

"You've heard from her?"

The creases deepened. "No, and I don't expect to. Sorry I can't help you. . . ."

Cal put a hand in the door as it started to close. "You still can, ma'am. Perhaps I can confirm that your daughter isn't missing. I just need to check with the people she hung out with. If you can give me some names, it would be extremely helpful."

While she pondered it, Cal stomped his feet and hugged his arms close to his body, waiting patiently while he apparently froze to death in front of her.

Maggie saw the woman's mouth go through more displeased motions while she thought it over. The door swung open. "I don't know much, but you best step inside so I can close the door."

"Thank you."

"And stay on the tile, your feet are wet."

They stood close together on the small tiled floor of the entryway.

"I ain't got much time. I work banquets at the Eagle's Wing resort, and we got a big dinner there tonight. What do you need to know? I don't know most of the kids Rachel hung around with."

Cal pulled out a notepad and pen. "Whatever names you know."

"Well, mostly she mentioned Amy and Sara."

"Do you know their last names?"

"No idea. I think they worked with Rachel at The Peak. That's a restaurant."

He nodded, writing. "Anyone else?"

Mrs. Anders shrugged. "She was always seeing some guy or another, but I don't know any names. She never brought them here. But I wouldn't be surprised if she ran off with one of them."

"Why do you say that?"

"Because she called men her ticket out." Mrs. Anders folded her arms and raised her chin in a defensive posture. "I don't know if you've seen a picture of my daughter, but Rachel's a pretty girl. She was always going out with men she met at The Peak. It's a fancy place, you know? She said she was going to find her a man with money who would take her out of this town. I figure she finally did."

Cal nodded, taking notes. "Do you know the names of any more of Rachel's friends or coworkers?"

Mrs. Anders flattened her mouth into a tight line and shook her head. "No. We didn't talk much."

"Thank you for talking to me, ma'am."

She watched him put the notebook inside his jacket,

eyes darting nervously as she bit her lower lip. "Will you tell me if you find out anything?"

"Of course." He handed her a card. "And I hope you'll call me if you hear from Rachel."

She took it and gave a quick nod.

Maggie turned and reached for the door, but Mrs. Anders's voice stopped her. "Ain't you the one's been in the papers and on the news? The one that got into that fight with Rafe De Luca?"

She turned, feeling slightly uncomfortable at being recognized from media coverage. "Yes."

"Did you really hit him like they said?"

She started to offer an explanation, a defense for her actions, then thought better of it. From the hard expression on Mrs. Anders's face, she'd already made up her mind about the type of woman who gets into fights at bars. "I'm afraid I did."

Rachel's mother looked at her like she'd just tracked wet footprints all over her clean carpet. "You ever think about anyone besides yourself when you're partying with those Hollywood folks?"

"Sorry?"

"Lots of people in this town depend on those tourist dollars to make a living. I do. My husband does, too—he does maintenance at the airport over by Juniper, where all the rich folks keep their private jets. What do you think happens to our jobs if those people decide to stop coming here?"

"I, um, I don't think giving Rafe a bloody nose will make them stop coming here."

"Well, think again, missy. Those De Lucas have big parties and bring in lots of business acquaintances. Who do you think got that *Trust Fund Brats* show to film here? The De Lucas, that's who. And how much business is this town going to lose if they all decide to up and leave?"

"I really don't—"

"More than you can replace, that's for sure. You need to think before you take some lame-brained feminist stand and hit one of the biggest sources of money in this town, lady."

Maggie's mouth hung open and her brain spun. Cal gave her a sharp nudge in the ribs. "Yes, ma'am," she murmured.

He thanked Mrs. Anders again and practically pushed Maggie out the door into a landscape of blowing snow. Maggie threw her hood up and shot him a resentful look. "I'm not the B-Pass Chamber of Commerce. Since when am I responsible for the flow of tourist dollars into this town?"

"The lady was pissed. She needed an apology. I'm sure the citizens of Barringer's Pass thank you. That is, the ones who are still speaking to you." And she'd handled it well, no reckless accusations or comebacks. He turned up the short collar on his jacket and hunched into it. "Come on, let's get out of this stuff."

They trotted for the truck, slamming the doors quickly on swirls of snow. "Damn, I need to buy a winter coat!" Cal exclaimed, brushing snow from his jacket.

"No, you don't. Tough it out, I promise it'll be gone in a day."

He didn't look like he believed her. Maggie waited while he started the truck and fiddled with the heater until it was blowing hot air on them.

She turned her brooding stare away from the

Anderses' house. "Cal, if Rachel took off with some guy, she would have called one of her girlfriends and told them where she was. Even if it didn't work out with the guy. She might have made something up if she had to, made it sound like she'd found the better life she was searching for. But either way, she would have said something to her friends. I don't think Rachel ran away."

He didn't look at her. "I know."

Maggie looked back at the house through the wind-whipped curtain of snow. "It's going to be hard on her mother if they ever find Rachel's body."

His jaw set grimly. "It always is."

Chapter
Seven

She had him stop on the way back to Fortune's Folly so she could see if any new tabloids had hit the stands. They hadn't, and she breathed a sigh of relief at not having to deal with more vicious lies and hate. It didn't last.

She stood by the jewelry display counter in Fortune's Folly between Holly and Cal, looking out through the front window. Two bright yellow splatters partially obstructed their view of the snowy street beyond. "What happened?"

"Paintballs," Holly said. "There's one that landed on the bricks, too. It was a drive-by shooting."

Maggie felt sick. "Just our store?"

Holly nodded miserably. "The police said you're lucky the glass didn't break. I'm sorry, Maggie. I would have called you, but there wasn't anything you could do."

She nodded. "Thanks for handling it. I'll see about getting it cleaned off tomorrow, once the storm is over." She gave her assistant a hug. "And thanks again for watching the store today. I don't know what I would have done without you."

"Same as always—you would have been here, doing everything yourself. You needed a break."

Maggie didn't bother explaining that she was even deeper into it than before, helping Cal look for a connection between Rafe and two missing women. She sent Holly home with a reminder to drive carefully.

The back door shut behind Holly, leaving an empty silence behind. Maggie surveyed the store. It was as devoid of customers as if it were closed, even though she would be open for nearly four more hours. With only a few shoppers braving the blowing, drifting sidewalks outside, she decided to blame it on the weather.

Her gaze settled on Cal. He stood near the marine fossils, absorbed in studying Maggie's favorite group of trilobites.

"His name is George."

Cal turned, amused. "The one getting fresh with the other trilobite?"

She joined him by the display, oddly pleased that he imagined the same relationship she did between the long-dead creatures. "She's a hot chick, as trilobites go."

"Clearly."

"So naturally he's hitting on her."

"A romance frozen in time." He cocked his head at the slab of sandstone. "Of course, you do know they were both lying dead on the mucky ocean floor at the time."

"Some guys never give up," she said, unswerving in her fantasy. "George is one of them."

"Good old George." They contemplated the trilobites for a moment. "You know, I think George had the right idea."

Maggie was suddenly aware that his gaze was on her, not the trilobites. She looked up into Cal's shadowed gray eyes. Prickles of excitement slid over her scalp. His expression was nothing like the passive, blank stare on George's fossilized face. It was a look of frank interest. And intent.

He gave her time to step away and pretend the moment hadn't happened. She tried to convince herself to do it. But when he slipped one arm around her waist, she stepped into his embrace as if it were the most natural thing in the world. He ran his hand beneath her hair, urging her closer, and she lifted her face to his.

Maggie expected the same barely restrained hunger she'd felt in their first kiss. She quivered with anticipation, ready to respond in kind. Cal could be a control freak at times, but damn, the man could kiss. But instead of taking her mouth with the expected ravenous need, his lips met hers gently, almost cautiously. A caring but safe kiss.

She repressed a twinge of disappointment. Safe was probably smart. And it was still a very nice kiss.

Cal must have decided it was safe to do a little more, because he continued caressing and tasting, the tender kiss apparently having no end. Her pent-up energy eased into blissful enjoyment. She found herself savoring every slide of his lips, every touch of his tongue.

She heard him groan and the kiss deepened further. She melted into him. Within seconds she was lost, aware only of Cal's hands where they cradled her back and head, and his mouth, gentle yet insistent, loving hers.

She felt caught in slow motion, liquid heat seeping through her body until she found it easier to simply mold herself to him. His hand on her back encouraged it, pressing her closer as his other hand explored her hair, her cheek, and the curve of her neck. It was a lover's touch, languid and sensual. The effect was as powerful as a lightning bolt.

Desire hit her so hard and fast she nearly shook with it. What had happened to *safe*? Part of her knew it was crazy to want a man who opposed her at every turn, and wanted to control her every action. Another part of her thought nothing mattered but what he was doing to her body, most especially the part that had been jolted out of dormancy and throbbed eagerly between her thighs.

There was no doubt he felt the same way. The evidence pressed hard and hot against her abdomen. They were way beyond safe.

Cal pulled away suddenly, eyes unfocused, breathing heavily. She blinked, staring at his shoulder and concentrating on clearing the fog from her mind.

He cleared his throat. "Maggie." It was almost a groan.

She drew a deep breath. "We probably shouldn't do that," she whispered.

"Right."

She took a step back. He didn't let go of her. A muscle jumped in his jaw and she saw him dart an uncertain look toward the door to the back room.

Oh, God. She hoped he had enough willpower to cancel that thought, because she knew she didn't.

As they stood there, a loud ring broke the silence. Startled, Maggie stepped back, and this time he let go of her. They both looked at his pants pocket.

"Probably Rick," Cal said. "He can leave a message." He fastened his gaze on her, his gray eyes narrowing decisively.

Her heart kicked into overdrive. Without taking his eyes off hers, he pulled his phone out and set it on the fossil case, where it continued to ring. Then he pulled her back into his arms.

Damn. It would have been easier to end this if he weren't touching her. But now he was sliding his hands up and down her arms, his dark gaze heating her blood and making it impossible to think.

"Just tell me no, Maggie." He growled it in her ear, his breath sending goose bumps skittering down her body.

She should say it. His phone had gone silent, but her pulse thundered in her ears as she tried to remember why she didn't like Cal. Was it simply because he didn't like her? Because right now he looked like he liked her a lot. . . . .

His phone began ringing again.

"Shit! What's so damn important?" He glanced down at the phone, then did a double take. Grabbing it, he stared at the display. "It's Amber."

She recognized the name of Cal's youngest sister. As she watched, his face went from puzzled to annoyed and back to puzzled again. "She hardly ever calls me."

His mind was not going to be able to let it go. "Answer it," she said.

He gave her an apologetic glance while keeping a tight hold on her hand. "Ten seconds," he promised.

"I'll tell her I'll call back later." With the other hand he grabbed the phone. "Hi, Amber."

She could wait ten seconds. In fact, it might be a good idea to lock the front door and put up a closed sign. Just in case. She slipped her hand from his and started toward the door.

"You're *where*?"

Cal's startled voice pulled her up short, and she turned toward him.

His brows puckered as his gaze locked on hers. Still speaking into the phone, he said, "How in the hell did you get . . ."

He was obviously getting a complicated explanation. She watched his expression go from stunned to angry to confused. She wondered if Amber always put him through an emotional workout. He finally settled on exasperated. "I'll be there soon. And don't go anywhere!"

She knew she didn't need to lock the door even before he took her hands in his. "My sister is at the Days Inn."

"The Barringer's Pass Days Inn?" She barely kept her voice from squeaking. "I thought she lived in L.A."

"She does. But it seems my featherbrained mother took off with some new guy. She put Amber on a train to stay with me for two weeks."

Maggie frowned. "There aren't any trains to Barringer's Pass."

"I know." Cal looked pained. "When she got to Denver she talked her way into the sympathies of a group of senior citizens on a bus tour to Salt Lake City. Naturally, they fell for her poor-me routine. They let her hitch a ride into the mountains and dropped her off at the Days Inn." He pulled his keys out of his pocket. "I have to go pick her up and try not to strangle her." He added the last part so low she barely heard it. His gaze lingered on hers. "I'm sorry, Maggie."

She nodded. What else could she do, say forget your sister, we're in the middle of something here? As much as she wanted to, she couldn't let a sixteen-year-old girl cool her heels in a snowstorm while she . . . She wasn't going to think about what they might have done in the back room.

"You should still lock up while I'm gone."

"No, I'm open for business."

He didn't look happy, but he didn't bother arguing. "If Rafe or one of his Neanderthals walks in, you call the police. Promise."

She nodded. He waited, not satisfied, and she sighed. "I promise. Here, take the key to the back door."

"Back in twenty." He grimaced. "With Amber."

Maggie already disliked the kid.

Cal knew he had a lot to learn about being part of a family, especially one as dysfunctional as his. When Julie had been killed, he'd resolved to establish a relationship with his one remaining sister. At first it had looked simple—find one sister's killer and get to know the stranger who was his other sister. That seemed like enough for someone who'd lived without family ties most of his life. No one told him it might mean putting his love life on hold to take in a temporarily homeless teenager.

He wouldn't bail on her, but this family thing was getting more complicated than he'd expected.

He needed four-wheel drive for the slick road up the ridge where the motel overlooked the highway. He pulled up to the front door, stopping in the pool of yellow light spilling from the bright lobby. No one was waiting near the door. Leaving the truck running, he went inside.

She was easy to spot. Near the registration desk a girl with long mostly dark hair laughed flirtatiously with a young man in a dark green blazer. Three weeks ago, at Julie's funeral, Amber's dark hair had been streaked with strands of shocking pink. Now the streaks were bright blue. The young man stood with one elbow propped on the tall counter in a pose of casual ownership as he grinned at whatever the girl had been saying.

"Amber."

She turned. "Oh, hey, Cal," she said, as if they'd last seen each other yesterday and not for the first time in three years at Julie's funeral. Something winked on her left nostril and he realized she'd gotten her nose pierced. She turned back to the young man, who clearly belonged on the business side of the desk. Cal raked him with one long glance. He looked too young to be in charge of anything, but too old to be flirting with a sixteen-year-old girl. "That's my ride," she told him, jerking a thumb at Cal.

She picked up a backpack and slipped it over her shoulders, the straps pulling at her top until it strained across her breasts. She adjusted it with a little shimmy. The desk clerk followed the move appreciatively, then grabbed a Styrofoam container off the desk. "Don't forget this."

"Thanks." She beamed at him. "See you around, Ryan."

"Remember, Fridays at the Black Diamond."

She walked across the lobby in a loose, rhythmic stride that made Cal wonder how a five-foot-three girl could make her legs look so long. "Ready," she told him.

He frowned at her thin scoop-neck sweater that looked like it covered nothing more than an equally thin tank top. "Don't you have a coat?"

She gave him a look that asked if he'd gotten stupid since she'd last seen him. "It was eighty-five when I left home."

He ground his teeth. "Here, put this on." He started removing his jacket.

"No thanks." She gave him another look that seriously questioned his intelligence, or at least his fashion sense. "You have heat in that truck, don't you?"

He didn't argue. He tossed the bulging backpack on the backseat, went around to his side, and waited while she buckled herself in. A rich, meaty aroma filled the truck. He glanced at the Styrofoam container. "What's in there?"

"Beef stroganoff. Ryan had the kitchen fix me something to eat. He's really sweet."

He doubted Ryan would have done the same for him. "I could have taken you somewhere," he grumbled, irritated that he felt he had to compete with Ryan. They both knew somewhere was probably McDonald's. The stroganoff smelled better.

Cal drove carefully through what already looked like three inches of snow. He'd listened to the radio on the way over; the forecast was for six to eight inches. The weatherman had been joyous. Cal imagined you had to be a skier to understand.

Amber gazed in horror at the snowy landscape and cranked the heat up higher.

"So what's the deal with Mom?" he asked.

"She got married again and went to Hawaii for her honeymoon." She sounded as resentful as he felt.

Three weeks after her daughter's funeral. He wasn't even surprised. "At least this one must have some money, if he can afford that."

She sneered. "He's old. Probably has buckets full of it."

He didn't bother telling her that money didn't automatically come with age. But if his mother had married an old man, Amber was right—the guy had money. Enough for his mother to stick her daughter on the first train to Denver.

"I can't believe you found a bus driving into the mountains in this weather." The thought of a bus full of senior citizens slipping off a sheer rocky cliff brought on an involuntary shudder.

"Well, of course not. They got through the pass before the snow started."

He took his eyes off the road long enough to give her a sharp glance. "When did you get here?"

She shrugged. "I don't know, around ten or eleven this morning."

"This morning! Why didn't you call me right away?"

"What's the hurry? I was hanging with Ryan and Carrie. That's the girl who worked the desk earlier. They're pretty cool. Carrie's in college."

That was another thing. "Shouldn't you be in school?"

"I'm only missing three days, then we're out for the summer." She scrunched her brow with concern. "Dude, are you always this stressed? Just chill."

It was possible he'd never chill again. He started to rub the ache that was beginning in his temple, then thought better about taking his hands off the wheel.

"I didn't ask to be here, you know. You want me to take off, just say so."

Jesus. Take off where? "I want you to stay." Sort of.

Amber peered through the snowy twilight at downtown Barringer's Pass. Hundred-year-old brick buildings blended seamlessly with newer architecture built to match the old style. "Cute town," she said grudgingly. "Do they have a mall?"

"No."

"No?" Apparently it was difficult to comprehend. "Where are we going?"

"To a store called Fortune's Folly. A friend of mine owns it."

He thought she might object, but she looked interested. "A store, huh? Like a boutique? Do they have clothes?"

He snorted a laugh. "I didn't see any."

Ahead, some poor schmuck in a Mustang spun and slid as he tried to negotiate the slight hill. Cal idled at a safe distance, watching for a minute, then sighed. The guy was never going to make it without a push. Turning up his collar, he opened the door. "Be right back," he told Amber.

She was already digging into the stroganoff and didn't look up.

Maggie turned as the front door opened. Finally, a customer! The man stomped and brushed snow from his long wool coat, then looked up.

Her face fell. "Mr. Jameson."

The De Lucas' lawyer smiled as if they were old friends. "Miss Larkin." He looked pointedly at the yellow blotches on her window and motioned with his head. "It appears someone is unhappy with you."

"Kids." She shrugged. "What can you do?"

He nodded, not looking especially sympathetic. "It's fortunate nothing was broken."

"Yes, isn't it?" She watched nervously as he began wandering around the store. "Can I help you with something?"

"Nice place." With hands in pockets and head cocked, he studied the slabs of fossilized sea creatures on the back wall. "You sell many of those?"

She suspected he knew the answer to that. "Not lately."

He made a disappointed sound. "Pity."

"Retail is like that. Sales will bounce back."

"One can only hope." He made a point of scanning each quiet corner of the shop. "I don't see any customers. I guess that means you've had some time on your hands. I wonder if you've had a chance to rethink the De Lucas' generous offer?"

"Yes, I have." She took a few seconds to enjoy his confident look. "I've decided it's even more repulsive than I initially thought." Before he could react, she added, "But don't you think the offer has become irrelevant?"

His eyebrows drew together. "Why is that?"

"Because after all the mud that's been slung in the press, who is going to believe that Rafe and I simply had a lovers' quarrel? It looks more like a nasty, prolonged breakup at this point, one that's lasting longer than the so-called relationship. Which, I remind you, never existed."

He nodded once. "I see your point. Perhaps all that is necessary is that you and your boyfriend call an end to your open hostilities against the De Lucas and allow us to handle the explanations."

"My boyfriend's not involved," she corrected. "And that would mean not defending myself against accusations already made. I can't do that."

After a moment of confusion, his face cleared. "Ah, I see the problem. It's your provincial attitude about the press." His condescending smile made her itch to hit something. Like him.

"Let me explain," he said, oblivious to her anger. "The public forgets, Miss Larkin. In the world of tabloid journalism, you are but a flash in the pan. Here today, gone tomorrow. Rafael, on the other hand, was famous before he came here and will be famous after he leaves. And in his world, reputation equals money. Therefore it is my job to refute irresponsible, negative stories like yours. This public dispute with the De Lucas is merely your fifteen minutes of fame. Should it disappear today, I guarantee your name will be forgotten tomorrow."

She stared. He really thought that solved everything. It was too bad he wouldn't understand her anger, because he was about to get a big dose of it.

She folded her arms so she wouldn't punch him in the nose. "Now let *me* explain something to *you*, Mr. Jameson. Here in my provincial little town, the things said in the press will *not* be forgotten tomorrow. Or next month, or next year. So, naturally, I feel a need to defend myself against false accusations. A minor detail in the De Lucas' lives, but a major one in mine. Unless Rafe or the De Luca family cares to retract statements made about me—"

"They didn't make those statements. The press did."

She smiled without a drop of sincerity. "Of course. Unless they care to make a statement defending me, and to tell the press to back the hell off, I will continue to do whatever I can to protect my reputation."

"Your solution seems unlikely."

"Then so does yours."

He shook his head. "I confess I'm disappointed, Miss Larkin."

Since he really meant *fuck you*, his formal language irritated her like nails on a blackboard. "Life is full of disappointments, Mr. Jameson."

She was hoping to at least make a dent in his professional calm, but he nodded serenely. "Yes, life has disappointments." To her surprise, he savored it like a precious nugget of wisdom. "I understand your morning was also rather disappointing. Or perhaps frightening is a better word?"

Anger flashed, bright and hot, helping her ignore the twinge of fear beneath it. "Perhaps harassment would be a better word. Where was your client this morning?"

"I'm sure his whereabouts can be accounted for by several witnesses."

"I'm sure." She'd had about enough of this. Starting toward the door, she said, "If there's nothing else, I think you should leave."

"How's your sister?"

She froze. "Excuse me?"

"The youngest one. Sophia, isn't it?" He didn't even raise his head as he fingered a box of ancient bivalves. "I heard she was home from school."

She gave him a long, cold look. "I don't think it's any concern of yours."

He picked up a sharply pointed tooth, larger than the palm of his hand, from an extinct megalodon shark. He turned it idly as he spoke. "I heard she applied for a research assistant position. Sounds like a smart move—if she can get it, of course."

Beside her eye, a tiny muscle began to twitch. "Mr. Jameson, you need to leave. Now."

He ran his thumb over the serrated edge of the tooth. "This is a nice piece."

"They're especially popular with lawyers."

Cool amusement touched his mouth for a second, then was gone. He made his way toward the door as she concentrated on not bursting out of her skin with impatience. "Good-bye, Miss Larkin. Perhaps I'll see you again soon."

Her only response was a stony stare, which didn't seem to bother him in the least, and did little to ease the prickle of fear he'd raised between her shoulder blades. With a slight nod, he walked out.

Maggie squeezed her eyes shut and took several deep breaths. Then she called Sophie.

Her sister seemed preoccupied, so she got right to the point. "Sophie, did you apply for a research assistant position?"

Sophie hesitated. "Who told you that?"

"The De Lucas' lawyer. Is it true?"

This time she heard a heavy sigh. "I didn't get it."

Clammy sweat suddenly dotted her forehead and upper lip. "Because of me? They can't deny you a position because of something your sister did!"

"They didn't. Not exactly." She heard the reluctance in Sophie's voice. "Maggie, my grad advisor called and asked what I'd done to piss off the De

Lucas. Apparently they made a big donation to fund his proposed research project, with one stipulation."

The sick feeling in her stomach congealed into a rock. "That he couldn't hire you."

"Right." Her voice turned bitter. "And he didn't have any choice, because the asshole chairman of the department had already accepted the money."

"Shit," Maggie swore viciously. Sophie, untouched by scandal, had aspired to far more than either she or Zoe. The two of them had wasted several years living down to expectations, but Sophie had followed an ambitious career plan since high school. They were enormously proud of her accomplishments. Now the De Lucas were ripping away any further opportunities.

"I'm so sorry, Sophie."

"Don't be." Her sister's voice was surprisingly harsh. "I want you to destroy that bastard, Maggie. And I want to help."

She'd do everything possible to keep Sophie away from anyone connected to the De Luca family. "Thanks, I'll let you know if I need you."

She hung up, sure of one thing: the only way to keep Sophie out of it was to keep the De Lucas focused on something else. She'd had an idea about how to do that earlier, while thinking about how much Rick Grady hated the De Lucas. Others in Barringer's Pass felt the same way. But some of the residents obviously felt as Mrs. Anders did, that the De Lucas provided employment for many people around here. Those people would hate her for rocking that boat.

Her idea depended on a good number of people actively and publicly disliking the De Lucas. Or a small number of the right people. It was a huge gamble, but it might work if done right.

The reluctant thought occurred that she still needed Cal's approval. She might do it regardless, but she'd come to respect his knowledge and experience.

As if aware that she might be considering another independent plan, he walked in through the back room, trailed by a short girl with neon-blue and brown hair. Amber turned in a circle as she walked forward, trying to take in everything at once, giving Maggie a chance to look her over.

Not a girl, she corrected, assessing the mature figure and makeup. A sixteen-year-old who could easily pass for twenty-one, and probably did on occasion. Her knit top didn't quite make it down to her low-slung jeans, and the glimpse of tanned skin in between revealed a pierced navel with a stone that flashed purple in the bright lights. On the back of her neck a tattoo peeked above her scoop-neck sweater, and another farther down disappeared into her jeans. Maggie could only wonder how many she couldn't see.

Not what she'd pictured as Cal's little sister. She bit her cheek to repress the grin that threatened to break out.

"Amber, this is Maggie," Cal said.

The girl turned, settling her curious gaze on Maggie. "Hi," she offered. Her smile was guarded as her eyes traveled over every inch of Maggie from hair to shoes. She gestured at the wall. "People actually buy this dinosaur stuff?"

"They actually do."

"Huh." Amber wandered around the large central display counter, lingering over the gemstone rings. "Nice jewelry."

"Thanks." Maggie smiled at Cal, who watched the girl with a slightly puzzled look, as if wondering if he'd possibly picked up a space alien disguised as his sister. She stepped closer to him and spoke in a low voice. "How long since you last saw each other?"

"Except for the funeral, three years."

From age thirteen to sixteen. Her smile got bigger. "Girls change a lot during those years."

"No kidding."

Amber finished her circuit of the store. "I like the rugs," she told Maggie, then made a disappointed sound with her tongue. "No clothes, huh?"

"Sorry."

Amber nodded, accepting her misfortune stoically. "At least the jewelry's cool. Can I try some rings on?"

Cal frowned. "I don't think—"

"Sure." She cut him off and went behind the counter to unlock the case. "Come around here and show me which ones you want to try."

Amber didn't need encouragement. She dropped the backpack behind the counter and huddled over the display case with Maggie, trying on rings set with everything from common quartz to diamonds. Maggie understood her fascination, having done the same thing herself when she first opened Fortune's Folly. Lifting out a whole tray, she let Amber try each one, admiring the results along with her as Cal watched, bemused.

Amber stretched her hand out in front of her, wiggling her fingers under the strong overhead lights. Colored fire flashed from four different rings. "Wicked sparkle," she approved. "Got anything like this in black?"

"I have onyx, but you won't get the sparkle." She passed her another ring.

Amber took one off and slid the new one on, holding her hand out. "Mad fresh!"

Smiling, Maggie glanced at Cal to see what he thought of his sister's assessment.

He was no longer watching them. Gray eyes focused on the front window, intent on something outside. As she watched, his expression changed to concern, then alarm. A shiver slid down her spine—Cal didn't worry without reason. She turned to see what he was looking at, but barely had time for a glance. He was suddenly in motion, rushing toward them, yelling, "Get down!"

Amber looked up, confused. Maggie had a brief glimpse of headlights before Cal threw himself on top of them, dragging them down to the floor behind the display counter. Even as she ducked, her mind worked to make sense of what she'd seen. Two headlights. Headlights were normal; all the cars had their lights on in the gloom of the early-evening snowstorm. But the lights that had pinned her in their bright glare had been pointing right at her. That wasn't possible. Before she could figure it out, the world exploded with a ground-shaking crash.

A deafening roar filled her ears. Shattered glass rang as it flew into the display case and clattered against stone fossils. A blast of cold air swirled in, chilling her even as she huddled beneath the shelter of Cal's body. He pulled them close and held on until the world stopped shaking and glass stopped raining down. The roaring went on and on, filling her ears, as if a beast had broken down the walls and stood inside the store, bellowing its anger.

Cal lifted his head. Maggie wiggled out from under him, standing cautiously.

Cold air and snowflakes hit her face. The front window was gone.

The store lay open to the snowy sidewalk and the cars that had stopped in the street. She could barely see them. The view was blocked by a huge black truck with a snow blade that sat half in and half out of her store. Its diesel engine roared as if the accelerator was stuck, while steam hissed from beneath the hood. The eight-foot blade hovered over shards of pottery, dripping slush. One front wheel spun, held aloft by the low brick wall that had caught the undercarriage of the truck just in front of the rear axle. Behind it, the double wheels of the dually pickup blocked the sidewalk.

Maggie felt dizzy. How many things could go wrong in one day? She wanted to believe it was a freak accident, but knew better. Small hairs rose along the back of her neck.

As she watched, Cal picked his way past bricks and glass to yank open the driver's door. He reached inside past the white mass of the inflated air bag, and suddenly the store went quiet as the engine fell dead. Maggie became aware of people yelling in the street. A man stepped right through the missing front window to help Cal as he pulled the dazed driver from the cab of the truck.

Beside her, Amber stood. Glass crunched beneath her feet. "Shit," she breathed.

Maggie didn't have any better words for it, so she just nodded.

They both stared for several seconds as people ran out of stores and gathered to gape on the sidewalk outside Fortune's Folly. A couple more used the front door to come inside.

"Want me to gather up the jewelry?"

Maggie looked down. The display case was cracked, and the one next to it was broken wide open. She snapped out of her daze and threw Amber a surprised, grateful look. "I'd really appreciate that." So would her insurance company, no doubt. "Just grab one of those cardboard boxes under the counter. I'll help in a minute—I want to see how the driver is."

He looked fine, actually, sitting on her glass-covered floor talking to Cal. What she really wanted to know was how it had happened.

Cal squatted in front of him, questioning him about injuries.

The man shook his head. "No, no, I'm fine. Just stunned by that air bag. Damn thing packs a punch." He rubbed gingerly at his bearded cheek where reddened skin showed through beneath the short hairs. A split on his lower lip was already puffing up from what appeared to be a sudden impact with his own incisors, and blood trickled from his nose.

He looked up at Maggie, taking in her skirt and heels. "You the owner?"

She nodded, hugging herself against the cold air.

"I'm really sorry about this. I guess I hit a patch of ice, 'cause the damn truck wouldn't stop. Skidded right across the other lane and over the sidewalk. I'm just glad no one was walking by at the time."

"So am I," she assured him.

He looked around, as if noticing the damage for the first time. His eyes widened with shock at the magnitude of what he'd done. "I got insurance," he told her.

"You must have been going pretty fast," Cal said.

"Twenty-five, that's the speed limit," the guy said, looking Cal directly in the eye. "But I hit that ice and, man, the son of a bitch just flew. Couldn't stop it. You know how it is with those icy patches."

"Yeah, I do." Cal stood. Someone else knelt in front of the man, asking if he was sure he was okay, and the driver began repeating his story. In the distance, Maggie heard sirens approaching.

Cal grabbed her elbow and pulled her aside. He took a long look at her, forehead creased with concern. "How are you? Are you okay?"

She nodded. Words seemed too difficult to form.

"Amber?"

Another nod. "She's fine."

He glanced at Amber, on her knees behind the counter, picking up handfuls of jewelry, then back at Maggie. The lines on his forehead didn't ease. She wondered if he was even aware that he rubbed her arm and back as they stood there, as if reassuring himself that she was all in one piece. It reassured *her*, anyway, and she didn't want him to stop.

"He's lying," he finally said in a low voice.

"What?" The ominous prickling touched her neck hairs again.

"The driver. He never tried to stop. I watched him turn off Tannery onto Division and accelerate. He never straightened out, just headed at an angle across the other lane and straight for the front of the store. He had to have floored it."

She stared at the driver, who was repeating his story to the owner of Carly's Café, then back at Cal. "You're sure he did it on purpose?"

He nodded.

She didn't question it, since it only confirmed what she'd felt in her gut. But it didn't make sense. "I don't even know that guy."

"I wouldn't expect you to." Cal's eyes held hers. "How long do you figure before you can open the store again?"

The question seemed like an abrupt segue, but she tried to answer. She looked at the truck sitting in her display window and the shattered glass and merchandise all over the front of the store. Insurance claim, cleanup, repairs, ordering new merchandise . . . She swallowed her dismay. "Best scenario, several weeks."

"Know anyone who might be happy about that?" He nodded as she reached the obvious conclusion. "Exactly. What do you want to bet I find a connection between that driver and the De Lucas?"

Chapter
Eight

He didn't want to leave her alone. Who knew what could happen? As cautious as he'd been, he hadn't anticipated a truck plowing into her store. What if she'd been near the front window instead of behind the display case? Sweat beaded his forehead just thinking about it.

He looked around Maggie's small living room again, as if a De Luca bodyguard might be crouched behind the wingback chair, just waiting for him to leave.

"You checked the whole house. I'll be fine, Cal."

Amber sat on the small couch, watching the two of them, waiting to see how he'd handle it. She'd been watching them all evening, as if she was trying to figure out their relationship. Well, good luck, kid. So was he.

"I still don't like the idea of leaving you here alone," he told Maggie.

"I'm hardly alone. We must have had at least ten

vehicles following us up here. They're probably setting up TV cameras in my front yard as we speak, hoping I'll put on my boots and parka and step outside for a late-night interview."

Ten was an exaggeration, since they'd lost a few vans on the hilly streets that led to her house. They'd make it eventually, though.

He scowled. "Reporters aren't going to protect you, Maggie. They'd be overjoyed to film an attack on you, but they aren't here to stop one."

They'd been over it before, so she just sighed. "Exactly what is it you think might happen?"

"I don't know." He ran a hand through his hair in frustration. "That's what worries me. What will they try next? This has gone way beyond what I'd expect in response to a tabloid story."

She flopped into a chair. "Well, I agree with you there. I had the same thought when I talked to that lawyer, Jameson. How can they be this upset over one little scuffle in a bar? In fact, I'll bet you anything the show's ratings go up because of all the publicity. I even had to let him know that you had nothing to do with it, because he specifically mentioned you, too." She laid her head back wearily and closed her eyes.

An icy feeling crept over him, freezing him in place. "He mentioned me?"

She dismissed it with a tired wave. "You know, as my supposed boyfriend. As in, 'you and your boyfriend' have to stop harassing the De Lucas."

"Oh, shit," Cal groaned.

She cracked her eyelids. "What?"

"They know. They must have found out I'm a cop," he explained.

She sat up, looking confused. "How do you figure?"

"The tabloids just tagged me as your boyfriend, which makes me pretty inconsequential. The De Lucas don't care what your boyfriend does. They *do* care about some cop sniffing around. Now all their extreme measures make sense. This isn't about your fight with Rafe, Maggie. Not anymore. It's about you and me asking questions about Rachel Anders and Tara Kolinowski. They don't like it, and they just told us to stop."

Her mouth dropped open. "Oh, crap."

Amber sat up straighter. "Who are those girls? What have you two been doing?"

Her sharp look of interest sent another surge of ice water washing through him. Shit, shit, shit! He'd drawn the attention of the De Lucas just when his little sister happened to blow into town. His only surviving little sister. No matter what, he had to keep them unaware of her presence in Barringer's Pass.

"Rachel and Tara are two women who disappeared from this area. The local police never looked at Rafe as a suspect, but my guess is that one or both met the same fate as Julie."

She jumped to her feet. "Can you prove it? Can we nail his ass?"

"Not yet." He looked at Maggie. "But I'd say we're on the right track if the De Lucas want us to back off."

"Good!" Amber looked ready to spring into action. "Let's do more of whatever it is you've been doing. How can I help?"

"You can't." He could tell she didn't like his tone, and he couldn't care less. "You aren't involved, Amber, and you're not going to get involved."

She glared. "I sure as hell am involved. Julie was my sister. If that putrid little fucker killed her, I have the right to personally kick his balls up his ass."

He didn't react to her language. Some things transcended the rules of propriety, and he figured having your sister murdered was one of them. "I understand how you feel, Amber, and I don't blame you. But the De Lucas are dangerous."

"I don't care!"

God, couldn't he have one woman in his life who was meek and obedient for a change?

He put his hands on Amber's shoulders, getting in her face. "Amber, listen to me. This is serious. You saw what happened to Maggie's store tonight. Do you realize how it might have turned out if any one of us had been closer to the window?" He gave her a moment to think about mangled limbs and bleeding bodies. Her mouth set in a stubborn line as she stared back, unconvinced.

He tried again. "That wasn't even the first event. Someone jumped Maggie yesterday morning right outside that front door, and nearly choked her to death. He even mimicked cutting her throat."

The throat-cutting did it. Amber's eyes darted to Maggie, then back to his. She swallowed. "But if I helped . . ."

"Amber, they'll use you against me. They'll target you in order to get me to back off. Trust me on this. I want to get him, too, but I don't want anyone hurt in the process."

Amber looked pained, the first crack he'd seen in her tough armor. "She was my sister," she repeated in a tight voice that was little more than a whisper.

"And you're *my* sister," he told her. "I can't lose you, too, and I don't want to have to worry about them going after you. Let me handle this."

He saw tears pool in her eyes. Saw her fight them back, determined to stay strong. That got to him, and he pulled her into a hug, wrapping his arms around her. For a second she stiffened, then she buried her face in his shirt and sniffled once as he stroked the bright blue streaks in her hair.

He'd give anything if he could make her world easier. He couldn't give her back her sister, or give her a mother who put her child before her husband of the moment. But he could at least give her a brother who cared, and put the bastard who'd killed her sister in prison where he belonged.

He looked up and saw Maggie watching them with an expression he couldn't read. She had to understand, though—she was also trying to shield a sister from the De Lucas. He envied the close relationship she had with Zoe and Sophie, and wondered wistfully if it was too late to find that with his own sister.

He set Amber back with a last stroke down her hair. Blue? He might get to know his sister better, but he feared he'd never understand her.

Maggie spoke up. "You'd better get out of here with Amber before the rest of the news crews get here and start asking who she is. They didn't see her come in, but now they're parked outside. They'll see her when you leave."

He couldn't argue with her if she was going to be careful and sensible. "I wish you'd come with us. You don't need to stay here."

"It's my house, and unless the De Lucas drive a

truck through the front window, I'm staying." She walked to the closet and pulled out a parka with a fur-trimmed hood. "Here, Amber. Put this on. They won't be able to recognize you."

Leaving her with no one to see if the De Lucas' thugs came creeping around her bushes again. "You have dead bolts—use them," Cal told her sternly. "And promise me you won't open the door or go outside for any reason until I come get you tomorrow morning."

"You don't have to—"

"Promise, Maggie. I mean it. Not even if Publishers Clearing House is standing on the porch with balloons and a huge check."

"I'm taking the check."

She wasn't taking it seriously enough, but it was the best he was going to get. Muttering to himself about being cursed with stubborn women, he grabbed Amber's backpack and opened the front door.

Then looked back at Maggie.

Oh, hell. Let Amber wonder. In three quick strides, he went back and pulled Maggie against him, kissing her with all the passion he could manage with his sister watching. He'd probably get peppered with questions all the way to his cabin, but it was worth it just to see the warm flush that heated Maggie's cheeks.

"'Night," he said quietly.

"Um, yeah."

He smiled. Damn, he loved catching Maggie off-guard. She could use a bit more of that in her life.

He figured he was the perfect man for the job.

Maggie discovered that nothing dislodged report-ers when they smelled a story. When temperatures dropped, they simply left their trucks running all night and kept the heaters on. They were still in front of her house in the morning when Cal showed up, ramming his truck through the melting snow in her driveway. She opened the door, stepping onto the porch to enjoy the return of warm weather, then flinched at the barrage of questions the reporters yelled from the street.

"Cal, how do you know Maggie? Is it true she left you for Rafe? Are you two engaged? There's Maggie! Maggie, what did you think of Rafe's comment—"

The second Cal was over the threshold she slammed the door, reveling in the silence. "Where's Amber?"

"I left her at my place." They were alone together, exactly as they were before Amber showed up. She already knew there would be no such thing as mild flirting if she got close to Cal.

She started for the kitchen but he grabbed her hand, bringing her up short. "Listen, Maggie, something came up. I don't want to leave you alone, but Tara Kolinowski's parents agreed to meet with me this afternoon if I can get to Denver."

"I can't go to Denver. I have a million things to take care of at the store."

"I know."

She smiled at the worried creases on his forehead. "Cal, I'll be fine. Contractors and insurance people will be in and out of Fortune's Folly all day. Plus, you can leave Amber with me and you won't have to worry about either one of us."

He gave her a rueful smile. "Good, because she refused to go to Denver with me. Said she was just there yesterday. And I think she's already had enough of trees and rocks, which is all the Lost Canyon Lodge has to offer." He frowned. "She resents me for not being in their lives, and I can't blame her. I think she's decided to be opposed to anything I want to do to keep her safe."

"Teenagers. Aren't they great?"

He snorted. "More like obstinate. I swear it's easier to deal with gang members and street thugs than with Amber."

"You mean when you have a badge and a gun to back you up?" At his look of interest, she wagged her finger at him. "Unh-uh. If I can't shoot paparazzi, you can't shoot Amber. Just learn to deal with the frustration."

"Funny you should mention that." The gleam that lit his eyes wasn't even close to funny. "I've recently thought of a good way to deal with my frustrations."

She'd forgotten he was holding her hand until he tugged her closer. Her forehead nearly bumped into his chin and she had to tilt her head back to look into his eyes. Up close they were smoky gray, with a lazy sexuality that knocked the breath out of her. It was hard to get it back when his fingers brushed beneath her hair, sending shivers all the way down her back.

While she concentrated on remembering how to breathe, he brushed his lips against her ear, then her cheek, then took her mouth in a long, deep kiss that left her heart racing and her pulse hammering in her ears. "I think my frustrations are beginning to go away," he murmured.

She inhaled deeply, smelling a hint of shaving lotion. "I think you're creating whole new ones," she told him, unable to resist burying her nose against his neck to enjoy the scent.

"Don't worry, I know how to relieve them."

She was sure he'd be very good at relieving them. Then afterward he'd remember how much she irritated him, and she'd remember that she no longer jumped into bed with guys she barely knew, and they'd both regret the whole thing. "You don't like me," she reminded him. "I make you crazy."

"I like you just fine. In fact, I like you a lot. It's your reckless ideas that make me crazy."

"Then you might not like what I have to tell you."

He stopped the nibbling that was sending delicious tingles down her neck, sighed, and laid his forehead against hers. "You've done something else?"

"Don't be so pessimistic. This time I waited to run it by you."

He raised his head. "Really? I'm honored."

She dove into her explanation. "I'm sure Rafe and his family think they've finally shut me up for good. They made sure I lost business, then wrecked my store on top of it."

He gave her a wary look. "What, that's not enough for you?"

"It's more than enough. It's overkill, which might work in my favor. The De Lucas are arrogant. A lot of people in this town don't like them for that."

"And they love the Larkins?"

"No," she admitted. "But people do sympathize with the underdog. And in this case, that's me."

"So you want sympathy?"

"No, I want to save Fortune's Folly! Rafe and his family made sure I lost a ton of business from canceled orders, and with the store closed for repairs I'm going to lose even more. But maybe if people know what they did, I could entice others to place orders with me simply to show the De Lucas that they can't willfully destroy the people and businesses they don't like."

"A retail showdown?"

"Why not? Because who knows what other business will be next? Will we all have to tiptoe around, making sure not to piss off the De Lucas? Or do we stand up to them by showing them they can't get away with it?"

"By buying something from Fortune's Folly."

She nodded, then nervously chewed her thumbnail. "What do you think?"

He was silent for several seconds as he thought about it. "I think it won't work."

Instantly, her brows slammed down as her temper shot up. "I knew it! You're opposed to anything I want to do."

"No, I'm not."

"Yes, you are! And if it would help you prove that Rafe is a killer, I'd let them trash my reputation, I really would. But I'm not going to roll over and play dead while the De Lucas trash my sister's professional reputation before she barely even has one. So unless you have a better idea, I intend to play the pity card, because it can't hurt and it might help."

With a satisfied huff, she crossed her arms and stared him down.

Cal pinned her with a direct look. "I didn't say it's a bad plan. In fact, I think you're onto something."

She squinted suspiciously. "You do?"

"Yes. But I think it won't work if you run to the press with a sob story about how the De Lucas are victimizing you. It'll just make you look whiny and petty."

"I don't intend to whine. I intend to give them cold, hard facts. Present my case objectively."

"Because so far the press has shown a real fondness for objective reporting?"

Damn it, he was right. She bit her lip, unwilling to back down so easily. Besides, it was her only idea. "You said it wasn't a bad idea."

"It isn't. I just don't think you should be the one to implement it. People don't respond to self-pity. But you're right about their responding to the underdog. So what do you think about having Rick pick this up as a heart-wringing story about the little guy getting trampled by the evil De Lucas? He's an objective source—well, as far as anyone knows, anyway. And once he starts the story I think he might be willing to urge others to play it up."

She stared for a few seconds, surprised. Then grinned. "I like it! That could work! Very insightful," she admitted. "For a cop." Couldn't let him get too cocky.

"And notice how I asked what you thought about it instead of saying 'This is what we're going to do'? It's called teamwork, Larkin."

The admonition didn't ruin her happiness. "True, I'm not used to consulting anyone. But I graciously admit that your idea is better than mine. I'll call Rick right now, then I'll pick up Amber."

"Okay. I'll get in touch when I get back this evening." Without warning, he pulled her close and kissed her until her head spun. "Maggie," he murmured next to her ear, wrecking even more havoc with her equilibrium. "I have other good ideas. And I'm *very* big on teamwork."

She was still staring as he walked out the door.

A dozen possible responses leapt to her mind,

smart-ass comments about showing him some real teamwork, or confident declarations that she'd be the judge of whether his ideas were good. Or the safe response—*I thought we weren't going to do this.* Or the one she yearned to say—*Can that trip to Denver wait another hour?*

But he was already gone, so he'd have to just wonder how she felt about it. She wasn't sure herself, but she was leaning toward exploring that teamwork idea, and it made her nervous.

Men never made Maggie nervous. The fact that Cal Drummond did shook her clear down to her toes.

She couldn't think about him, not if she was going to get anything done today. She started by calling Rick about the article, getting the expected enthusiastic response. Feeling herself again, she drove to the Lost Canyon Lodge to pick Amber up on her way to Fortune's Folly.

Amber didn't waste time dithering over what to say. As soon as she settled in the car, she asked, "Are you sleeping with my brother?"

Maggie ignored the sudden flutter of nerves and shot her a get-real look. "Do you really expect me to answer that?"

Amber smirked as she lowered the visor mirror and started applying makeup. "None of my business, right? That's what Cal said. I think that means yes."

"Think what you want. Just don't talk about it to those people in the cars following us. We're going to pretend you're my part-time employee, but if they somehow corner you when you're not in the store, your answer to any question they ask you will be, 'No comment.' Don't volunteer anything, ever."

She rolled her eyes. "I already heard it from Cal. And I'm not stupid, you know. Hollywood's crawling with paparazzi. I see them all the time, and I know how they work."

Maggie didn't point out that seeing them was hardly the same as being their quarry. Amber had the confidence that went with being sixteen years old and knowing all the answers. Hopefully, she had some street smarts to go with it.

At least she was interested enough in retail sales to be useful. Maggie put her to work inventorying the jewelry while she dealt with her insurance agent, various repair people, and more questions from the police. The morning went by so fast she didn't even notice it was past noon until Rick Grady banged on the locked front door, holding up a large take-out bag from the Silver Nugget across the street.

She let him in, inhaling the aroma of the Nugget's specialty burgers and fries. Her stomach growled in anticipation as she peeked in the bag. "That's so thoughtful, Rick! But you don't have to buy us lunch. I'll pay you back."

"Pay Cal, he's the one who called in the order." He turned full circle, taking in the destruction. "Damn, that truck wiped out the whole front of the store. What'd he do, back up and ram it again and again?"

"He had a snow blade on the front." Turning, she called out, "Amber! We have lunch!"

Rick backed up, shoving his glasses up his nose as he eyed the boarded front window and wrecked shelves like an artist contemplating his model. "You mind if I take some pictures? They'd really help sell that article you and Cal want me to write. Which is a brilliant idea, by the way. I'll have people so sympathetic toward you . . ." He broke off as Amber sauntered out of the back room. "Hello."

She gave him a glance. "Hi." Her gaze settled on the bag in Maggie's hand. "What do we have? I'm starved."

She handed it over. "Amber, this is Rick Grady. He's a reporter who's helping us go after Rafe."

"Cal told me." Apparently Cal had filled her in on everything, and nothing could compete with food. She pulled out two Styrofoam containers and two large drinks, setting them on the glass top of the surviving display case. Five seconds later she closed her eyes blissfully over a large mouthful of the Miner's Special Deluxe Bacon Cheeseburger.

The heck with the table in the back room. Maggie unwrapped her burger and took a bite, standing across from Amber. Rick leaned on one end of the case, watching Amber eat. "I heard about your sister, Amber. I'm sorry."

Amber's eyes flickered and she stopped chewing for a second, darting a glance at Rick. "Thanks." Maggie winced in sympathy; the stiff response obviously hid a world of pain.

"What was Julie like? I'll bet she was pretty, like you."

Maggie gave him a cautionary frown, but he wasn't looking at her. Amber answered softly, "Julie was prettier than me."

"Did she have any special talents? Like singing, or drawing . . ."

Maggie lowered her hamburger and opened her mouth to drop a strong hint to change the subject, but before she could say anything, Amber smiled at

Rick. "Julie was real good with hair. That's an art, you know. She had her beautician's license and was going to get a job at Universal Studios."

"No kidding? Good for her!"

Amber nodded. "She had a contact there. You have to, if you want to get in anywhere." Munching on fries, she began telling Rick about Julie's career plans, her personality, and the guy she'd dated who later costarred in a big action film and now dated only "name" actresses. She was animated and obviously happy remembering her sister. Maggie mentally kicked herself for not encouraging her to talk about Julie earlier. Cal still beat himself up with guilt when Julie's name came up, but Amber had been close to her sister. She needed to keep the memory alive. She told Rick anything he asked about, and more.

Rick was another surprise. He hadn't seemed the sensitive type, but Maggie had to admit that talking about Julie was excellent therapy for Amber. She laughed as she related an incident to Rick, and even offered him some fries. Rick helped himself, flashing a perfect smile in thanks, looking downright charming.

Maggie narrowed her eyes. Wait a minute—how old was Rick anyway? She guessed about forty, which was too old to be bonding with a sixteen-year-old girl, especially one whose tough façade barely covered the recent loss of her sister and a mother who regularly threw her aside in favor of her boyfriend du jour. True, he didn't sneak glances at Amber's generous breasts or ask uncomfortable, personal questions, but there was no doubt he'd established a trust between them. It could be harmless, but . . .

Cal would want her to be protective. Nervously

Maggie crinkled used napkins and prepared to cut Rick short as soon as she could interrupt Amber.

"Julie could handle people, you know? They never took advantage of her." Amber paused, her pride in her sister slowly collapsing into pain. She stared at the french fry she held, unseeing. "That's why I didn't worry about her going out with Rafe, even when she said he was bossy. You know, a real alpha male. She liked that type. She could always . . ." Amber swallowed hard. "She thought she could handle him," she finished in a weak voice.

Rick shook his head. "He's more than domineering, Amber. It's not Julie's fault she couldn't handle that, or your fault you didn't know it. Rafe's not normal. He's sick."

"He's evil," Amber pronounced. Her brown eyes speared Rick as her face turned cold and hard. "He deserves to die. But I want to torture him first, and make him cry and beg. Then slash his throat, the same as he did to Julie."

Well, so much for their pleasant lunch.

"Hey, Rick," Maggie said, "aren't you supposed to be watching Rafe, keeping track of where he is?"

Rick didn't look perturbed. "I know exactly where he is—at a house about a mile from here, with the whole production company and the other pampered Brats. They're filming Rafe taking over child care duties for the day. Poor kids. It's a closed set; I can't get on the property. So, as long as Rafe is babysitting the kids, I don't have to babysit him."

Wonderful. Now she had to babysit Rick to keep him from digging around in Amber's mind—as if she didn't have enough to do.

Her annoyance must have showed. Rick took one look at her and straightened. "But I do have an article to write, so I should be going." He slung his camera over his shoulder, but didn't move. "Um, Maggie, I wondered if I could talk to you about that article."

"Sure. What's the problem?" The way his eyes kept glancing nervously away, it looked like there was one.

"I guess you and Cal talked about having me sell it to one of the tabloids."

"Of course. They're the ones who are chasing after me trying to create emotional issues, and we thought you could play it up."

"Oh yeah, I can. But the thing is, the tabloids don't want to deal with me since the De Lucas pressured them about that picture of Rafe hitting that girl." At her disappointed look, he rushed to add, "But don't worry. I think we can do even better. Those papers aren't the only ones following you around. You're hot news and you've got TV stations all across the spectrum chasing after you. I've been talking with some of the guys from their crews, just networking, you know? And I think I might be able to convince one of them to do a piece on you as the victim of the De Lucas' power play. That's good exposure, Maggie. I might even get it on *Entertainment Tonight*. Or *Good Morning America*. What do you say?"

She bit her lip and thought it over. She hadn't realized Rick's break with the tabloids was so severe, but he might be right about the TV shows being able to spin it into exactly what they wanted. The visuals of her store would certainly encourage speculation, if they could get a camera crew in before the contractors started repairs.

She nodded. "Okay, do it. But we have to make it look like I'm letting them in reluctantly. As a favor, because I know you, not because I want them to do a story about me. Remember, we have no proof the De Lucas are behind this. I'm just the victim of a random attack and a freak accident. *They* have to be the ones to raise suspicions about who might be behind it."

He held up a hand. "I got it, I got it. I'll call you guys when it's set up. Is it okay if we arrange to do it today?"

"You're that sure they'll go for it?'

He grinned. "Oh, yeah. This has scandal written all over it, and they've been desperate for the next episode in the Rafe and Maggie saga."

She'd been convinced it was a good idea until Rick ran with it. Now she wondered if she was stepping into quicksand and about to get sucked in over her head. She didn't know what could go wrong, but she had a bad feeling that if something did, it would be on a big scale. A *Good Morning America* scale.

Chapter Nine

Cal shifted on the edge of the blue-flowered armchair, facing Tara Kolinowski's parents on a similarly flowered sofa. More flowers crawled up the drapes and bordered the rug, splashy blue roses unlike anything he'd ever seen in nature. He suppressed the urge to sneeze.

Mrs. Kolinowski folded her hands in her lap. "I'm glad someone is looking into Tara's case again. It's so frustrating to try to get answers from a police department a hundred miles away. It seems like they forgot all about Tara."

"Well, ma'am, like I said, this isn't an official investigation, and I'm not with the Barringer's Pass police. But I will be sharing any information I discover with them."

Mr. Kolinowski leaned forward a little, legs apart as if prepared to make a quick exit if necessary. Maybe he was uncomfortable with the strange flowers, too. "Just what do you think you can discover that the other detective didn't find?" he asked.

"I don't know. But it can't hurt to have a fresh pair of eyes look at the case."

He nodded his satisfaction, and his wife said, "What can we tell you?"

"Let's start with the names of the girls who went on the trip with Tara. I understand she worked with one of them, and the other was a friend she'd known for years?"

Mrs. Kolinowski jumped to her feet and crossed to a small rolltop desk in the corner. "I have their names and phone numbers right here," she offered, coming back with an address book.

He copied the information and set the book on the coffee table. Mrs. Kolinowski bounced up again, put it away, then returned to the sofa, waiting for his next request.

This was great—Tara's parents couldn't be more cooperative. "Had Tara been to the Glacier Pass resort before?"

They looked at each other, double-checking, before shaking their heads. "I don't think so," her mother said. "Tara's a good skier, and she likes to try lots of different places."

"She usually goes to one really nice resort every year," her husband added. "That's all she can afford. She always has a roommate to split the cost."

A twinge of sadness hit him—after eighteen months, Tara's parents still spoke of her in the present tense. They were the only ones he'd encountered so far who did.

"She doesn't have any friends in that area, anyone she might have visited?"

Tara's father looked to his wife, as if she'd be more

likely to have that answer. "No," she said, shaking her head firmly.

He hadn't expected she would, but it was a good way to lead into the subject he'd really come to talk about.

"Then our best bet is to talk to the people who saw Tara most recently before she went missing. I think some people connected to the case definitely deserve another look."

Mrs. Kolinowski bit her lip and nodded encouragement.

"For instance, the local people who ski at Glacier Pass. They often meet resort guests on the slopes, then hang around to socialize with them in the evenings." It was a polite way to refer to the men who hoped to pick up vacationing hot chicks looking for some bedtime recreation. From what he'd heard, Tara had been one of those chicks. "They might remember seeing Tara with someone they recognize."

"Detective Sanders had a long list of people who were there the night Tara disappeared, including all the employees," Mrs. Kolinowski said. "He told us he talked with all of them."

Cal nodded, not wanting to imply that the Barringer's Pass detective hadn't done a good job. From what Cal could tell when he'd spoken with him, he had. But local cops were subject to local pressure. If the chief had told Sanders to treat the resident VIPs with kid gloves, he would have, especially without any other reason to suspect them. The scenic real estate and renowned ski slopes around Barringer's Pass drew a lot of prominent people to the area, people who couldn't afford to have their names attached to the investigation of a missing girl. People who paid exorbitant taxes that helped keep the local police department well staffed and driving late-model SUVs. There had been no cruisers more than two years old in the station parking lot. Depending on the ethics of the local police chief, that could buy a lot of deferential treatment.

He had to approach this carefully. "It's possible some witnesses didn't like the idea of being involved with an investigation. People with images to protect. But that doesn't mean they don't know anything, and you might want to press the police to take a second look at anyone like that. Sometimes things that seem insignificant can provide vital clues."

Mrs. Kolinowski twisted her rings. Mr. Kolinowski appeared suddenly distracted by a clump of blue roses on the rug.

Cal pushed harder. "Some of the waitstaff at the hotel remembered Tara being with a group of people that included a couple of movie actors earlier that week. One of them said Tara seemed intent on meeting as many stars as she could." What he'd actually said was that Tara was a slut for celebrities, but he couldn't say that to her parents. Could hardly even think it, sitting in their flowery living room. "She'd been seen having drinks with two *CSI* actors and a rapper earlier in the week."

"She collects autographs," Mr. Kolinowski said stiffly.

Is that what the kids called it these days? "Yes, sir," Cal agreed. "And she's a pretty girl, and I'm told she likes to meet new people, so I imagine she often had conversations with the celebrities she met."

Her mother smiled a bit too tightly. "Tara's always been popular."

"Did she talk with you while she was there, maybe mention any of the celebrities she'd met?"

"She e-mailed me every day. That's what she does. She told me about meeting the *CSI* actors and that singer." She went back to tugging on her wedding ring, sliding it back and forth on her finger. Never taking it completely off, but never leaving it alone.

"Did she happen to mention meeting Rafael De Luca?"

"No." She shook her head emphatically.

"You recognize the name?"

"Of course, we've heard of him," Mrs. Kolinowski answered for both of them.

Cal had the distinct feeling Rafe's name had come up before, and not because they were fans of *Trust Fun Brats*. But their faces remained carefully blank. "A couple of the waiters thought they saw her with him the night before she disappeared," he prodded.

Mrs. Kolinowski shrugged. "I wouldn't know."

He found that hard to believe, especially if Tara had mentioned the actors and the rapper, whose names weren't nearly as recognizable as Rafe De Luca's. For young women interested in celebrity "autographs," Rafe was a major coup. Certainly exciting enough to write home about, even if she left out the intimate details. "Would you possibly have those last e-mails from Tara?"

"Sorry, we didn't save them," Mr. Kolinowski said. "It was over eighteen months ago, you know." His wife got the ring all the way off this time, before slipping it back over her knuckle.

Cal couldn't imagine the parents of a missing girl deleting e-mails they'd received from her, especially her final communications with her family. He studied their faces, but they avoided his gaze.

Time to be blunt. "Apparently she talked about him quite a bit the night before. She almost certainly spent time with him Thursday."

No reaction.

"One of the employees thought she would have willingly left with Rafe Friday night if he'd shown up again."

Mr. Kolinowski frowned. "Conjecture."

Mrs. Kolinowski made a fist, holding her rings in place, and didn't look up.

Cal studied their tight-lipped expressions. "Perhaps I should speak to Rafe De Luca about it."

"I don't see the point," Mr. Kolinowski rushed to say. "He wasn't there."

"The point is, he might have been. He was there the night before, and police say he was definitely in town that night. He might have even seen Tara leave."

Tara's father scowled his impatience. "Seems to me you've got plenty of other people who saw her Friday night. There's no need to bother with people who *might* have been there. That's the kind of thing that slows an investigation down."

Cal's neck prickled with sudden suspicion. "Is it?" he asked quietly.

He nodded sharply. "Celebrity names come up and folks get distracted from the real focus—Tara." His voice quivered, and he took a moment to swallow back the emotion. "Look, we don't care where

Rafe De Luca was Friday night, we care where our daughter was. Where she *is*. If you can help us with that, we'd be grateful. If not, I don't see the point in dragging other names into it and muddying the water."

Cal's hopes sank. The De Lucas had gotten to them.

The Kolinowskis were spouting the De Luca spin— we're famous, Rafe's name will just distract everyone from looking for Tara, and after all, it's your daughter who's the important one here.

The De Lucas knew what they were doing. They'd obviously applied enough ego stroking and feigned concern for Tara to keep Rafe's name out of it. If the media detected even the tiniest connection between Rafe and the search for a missing girl, it would be headlines. He could end up tried and convicted in the tabloids. The De Lucas would have done whatever they could to stop that.

He stood. "Thank you for talking with me."

Mrs. Kolinowski raised a pleading gaze to him. "You'll call if you find out anything? Anything at all?"

"Of course." Although they'd just reduced his chances significantly. The only progress he'd made was having his worst suspicion confirmed—Tara Kolinowski had almost certainly spent her last night on earth with Rafe De Luca. Now it was only a matter of finding her body.

Cal almost turned off the main street a block before Fortune's Folly in order to enter the employee lot without passing the storefront. He was glad he didn't, or he might have missed the sight of Rick Grady being interviewed by a beautiful woman on the sidewalk in front of the boarded-up window of the store. Cal stared as he crept by, traffic going even slower than usual as people gawked at the TV camera and crowds. Probably trying to spot whatever celebrity the press had cornered this time.

Cal wedged his truck into a corner of the employee lot next to a minivan sporting a satellite dish and the legend *Entertainment Tonight*. Maggie and Rick had been busy.

The back door was locked and no one responded to his knock. He pulled out his phone and called Maggie's cell.

"Hi. I'm at the back door. Can you let me in?"

"Oh, that was you! Be right there."

Seconds later she opened it, then shut it quickly behind him, throwing the dead bolt. She grinned, using her wrist to brush a few untidy hairs off her face, careful not to touch her face with fingers that appeared to be covered with dust and dirt. "I should have known it was you. No one else bothers to knock, they just walk right in if I don't keep it locked."

"The pitfalls of celebrity, huh? Where's Amber?"

"Out front, peeking through the window at the *ET* reporter. Did you want to talk to—"

He pulled her against his chest and kissed her. She switched gears seamlessly, wrapping her arms around his neck and kissing him back with enthusiasm. It only inflamed the growing need for her that he already had a hard time controlling. He was starting to wonder why he fought it.

He'd been wrong. Maggie wasn't like Diane. She might have the same incredible passion for life and determination to succeed. She might be impulsive. But she listened to people she trusted, and lately that seemed to include him. She'd consulted him, weighed his advice, something Diane would never have done. Maggie might have reckless impulses, but she allowed him to temper them.

As far as talking himself into a relationship went, it was good reasoning. Plus, he was wearing down Maggie's resistance. She seemed more interested every time he kissed her.

She pulled away now with a satisfied sigh. "You really are very good at that."

"I can do more. What do you say we ditch the kid sister for a few hours?"

"Leave Amber on her own?"

"She's sixteen, Maggie."

"That's exactly what I told the cameraman who invited her to meet him at Del Tanner's bar tonight. She accepted, by the way."

"Shit." He'd been responsible at sixteen. What was with kids these days?

Maggie chuckled as he followed her into the shop area. "Were you like that at sixteen?" he asked her.

"Worse, I'm afraid. But you have your work cut out for you."

As if to prove her point, he saw Amber stand on tiptoe as she let Rick in the front door, looking past him at someone outside. She waved and called, "'Bye, Josh, see you later!"

Like hell she would.

"Cal!" Rick interrupted Cal's scowl as he strode across the room, more energized than Cal had ever seen him. "Great idea you and Maggie had. They went for it big-time. What do you want to bet you have at least three more stations here tomorrow morning, clamoring for interviews?"

"I didn't know you were going to turn it into a publicity event." He wasn't entirely comfortable with the idea, either. He'd prefer that the Rafe-and-Maggie press party died out. Instead, it seemed they'd just cranked up the excitement.

"Had to. This story has all the angles—powerful bad guy, titillating rumors, hardworking independent businesswoman. Pretty, too, which always helps. And a truck driver who—get this, Cal—just happens to work for the landscaping company the De Lucas use at their fancy estate up the mountain. Big surprise, huh? I dug up that bit of information this afternoon. I just love when it all comes together like that."

So did Cal, but he liked to make sure it stayed under control. Rick's enthusiasm made him nervous. "You didn't actually accuse the De Lucas of being involved, did you?"

"Of course not. I didn't have to. It was one of the odd 'coincidences' Tiff cited. That's Tiffany Martin, the cohost of the show. Cohost, do you believe it? She flew in just for this. I tell ya, this is going to blow up big."

Even Maggie looked a little apprehensive, so Cal said, "As long as it doesn't make Maggie look bad."

"No way. We're good, don't even worry." A chime sounded from his pocket. "Excuse me, gotta get this."

Rick pulled out his phone and started texting, looking every inch the busy professional.

Cal looked around the store. Broken items had been swept up, windows boarded, and shelves emptied of merchandise. In fact, the whole front of the store, including the jewelry display cases, was empty. "Where is everything?"

"We packed it up," Amber told him. Dark smudges covered her hands, too.

Maggie surveyed the store with satisfaction. "Got most of it done, too. There's going to be a lot of workers in here creating a lot of dust. I'm not letting that get all over my merchandise, especially the Oriental rugs. And frankly, I don't want anyone tempted to slip something in their pocket. My insurance company is upset enough already."

He looked at the fossilized slabs of stone hanging on the back wall. She'd told him how much the clusters of ancient sea creatures and the dinosaur footprints were worth. "What about George and his friends?"

"I thought I'd hang tarps from the ceiling, cutting off the back of the shop from all the mess we'll have up here. Besides, no one can slip a three-foot slab of stone in his pocket and stroll out the front door." She tilted her head and scanned the back section in question. "What do you think?"

"I think you've done an amazing amount of work, getting this all under control in one day."

"Amber was a big help."

His sister shrugged. "I've got nothing else to do. And some of Maggie's things are majorly fine."

He felt an unexpected twinge of pride in his sister. Okay, so the kid wasn't entirely a pain. "If you can scrub that dirt off, I'll take you ladies out for dinner."

Amber was suddenly in motion. "God, food! Take me now! And make it someplace nice, because we deserve it." She was already in the back room when she called over the sound of running water, "What do you want to do after that? This town looks like it has some decent nightlife."

Cal's gaze flicked toward Maggie. Not the kind of nightlife he'd begun fantasizing about.

Amber probably wasn't going to be happy watching TV in his cabin, either. But he wasn't turning his sixteen-year-old sister loose in this town, no matter what she was allowed to do at home. Besides, it seemed only fair that if she compromised his social life, he should do the same for hers. It looked like after a nice dinner, they were going to go home and be miserable together.

Maggie stared at the crowd of reporters and photographers near the back door of Fortune's Folly the next morning. She'd wondered why they hadn't been at her house. Apparently it was because they were waiting for her here. Her store was now the centerpiece of their story.

With all the news vans in the parking lot, she had to park three stores down. Tucking her head, she did a fast walk toward her back door. Someone shouted her name. For a moment she flashed on the image of a huntsman spotting the fox and sounding the horn. Then the whole mass of reporters went into motion, swarming toward her.

They yelled questions before they even reached

her. "Maggie, how long have you known Cal Drummond?"

"Maggie! What do you have to say about Rafe's warning?"

Warning? Maybe she should have picked up a newspaper.

"Is it true you accused Rafe De Luca of using violence to intimidate you?"

"Maggie! Who do you think is behind the destruction of your store?"

A man planted himself right in front of her. She shouldered by with a sharp "Excuse me."

He trotted backward, microphone extended toward her face. "Come on, Maggie, what's your response to Rafe? Did you see him on the news? Have you talked to him?"

She wanted to ask what Rafe had said that had them all stirred up, but she knew saying anything would only encourage them.

The idiot with the microphone wouldn't give up. He stepped in front of her again, letting her bump right into him. His questions were louder than the rest. "Did your sister have an affair with Rafe, too?"

Maggie stopped dead.

The crowd of reporters shuffled to a halt. Questions died out as they waited to see what she would say.

How had her sister become involved? And which one? She had a bad feeling she could guess. Fury blurred the edges of her vision as her glare settled on the reporter in front of her. He waited expectantly. When she continued her hard stare, his arm wavered, then pulled back. No one moved.

She wouldn't stoop to asking them to fill her in.

Instead, she tipped her chin up. In low, emotionless words, she said, "You are in my way. Please move."

The words died away in the warm spring breeze. A couple of questions were yelled from somewhere in the crowd, but most of them simply waited silently.

One beat. Two.

The man stepped aside.

Spine rigid and head high, Maggie walked to the back door of Fortune's Folly and unlocked it. Turning, she looked at the mass of people behind her. They crowded close, but left a little more distance than they had before. She'd have to remember that they respected bitchiness.

"Perhaps you didn't know this," she began. Microphones lifted. Cameras flashed. They waited. "This parking lot is for employees only. If you don't move those vans, you'll all be ticketed and towed." Before they could respond, she slipped inside and locked the door.

Maggie closed her eyes, leaning against the door until the pounding anger ebbed and her mind stopped spinning. *Stay calm. Be rational.* She'd find out what Rafe had said. And how it involved one of her sisters. Something inflammatory, no doubt, and meant to hurt. She could handle this.

She allowed a small smile—she'd taken those reporters by surprise. It counted as a small victory.

"What's wrong, Maggie? I thought you'd be used to notoriety."

She gasped, putting a hand to her chest.

She didn't have to search for the source of the voice—he stood right in front of her, arms folded and a small sneer twisting his lips on one side. Her heart tripped right back into high gear, thundering in her ears.

She swallowed, her mouth suddenly bone-dry. "Rafe!" It was barely more than a croak, fear turning her voice scratchy and weak. "How did you get in here?"

Chapter Ten

Oh God, he wasn't alone. A man stepped out from behind one of the stacks of boxes crowding the back room. Since packing up half her merchandise, the back room had been reduced to narrow paths between stacks of cardboard boxes and wooden crates.

At least it wasn't Rafe's hired muscle. Parker Jameson, legal watchdog, brushed dust from his suit jacket as he stepped around Rafe. "Don't answer her, Mr. De Luca. I'll handle it."

"How did you get in here?" Maggie repeated, relieved that her voice didn't shake. She couldn't say the same for her insides, which were twisting with anxiety. Not sure whether to be afraid or furious, she'd gone with both. Her stomach wasn't happy with the choice.

"The door was locked. That means you broke in. I'm calling the cops."

"We walked in through the front door, Ms. Larkin. By invitation, all nice and legal."

"How . . . ?"

"The contractor you hired to replace your front window. I believe his name is Rob Beamer, of Beamer Doors and Windows. An accommodating man. The De Lucas have used him several times themselves. He understood our desire to wait inside to avoid the very scene you encountered."

Great, the De Lucas owned her contractor. She'd fire him on the spot except no one in Barringer's Pass did better work. If there were someone else, the De Lucas would undoubtedly buy his loyalty, too.

She clenched her jaw. "What do you want?"

"To deliver a message, Miss Larkin." He paused, holding her gaze with his hard, flat stare. "You will cease and desist. Now."

"Cease what?"

"Everything. Speaking to the press. Raising speculations. Asking questions. I believe you know what I'm referring to. The De Lucas have had their privacy invaded for long enough, and they will not tolerate any more." He cocked his head, looking her over as though trying to determine how bright she was. "Do you understand the meaning of slander, Miss Larkin?"

She was on safe ground here. "I haven't made one single accusation against Rafe or his family." That wasn't exactly true, since she recalled making several during the original yelling and shoving match at The Aerie. "About the accident," she clarified. "And I never lied about Rafe to the press. I can't help it if they jump to false conclusions."

He gave her a tolerant smile, the kind usually reserved for small children. "Have you ever heard of libel by innuendo?"

She hadn't. But she could figure it out—intentionally reporting something so it would be taken the wrong way, purposely defaming someone's character. She licked her lips nervously. She'd certainly done that one. But it was probably the *Entertainment Tonight* piece that had him upset, and she had a clear conscience there. Or at least, not too murky.

"I never implied that the De Lucas had anything to do with the accident that wrecked my store." She'd left that to the media. She was getting good at careful wording.

"Yes, you carefully sidestepped that, didn't you? My firm will be contacting the *Entertainment Tonight* legal department later this morning. But I am not that easily fooled, Miss Larkin, and you are not blameless—"

"Fuck this bullshit!" Rafe exploded, causing Maggie to jump. He pushed past Parker Jameson, and she automatically took a step back. Then another. He backed her against a tower of boxes, until his snarling face was inches from her own. She froze, unable to think of anything except that no one's teeth were naturally that bright.

"Listen, bitch, I'm through playing games with you. You either make me look good in the press, or I'll rip you apart. First in the press, then in private. Understand?" With his finger he traced a line across her neck, raising shivers all the way to her toes. "No hick cunt is gonna trash my reputation—"

"Rafe."

The one word, along with Jameson's hand on his arm, halted the threat before Rafe could finish it. As intimidated as Maggie had been at the outburst, she was more unsettled by the emotionless ease with which Jameson controlled him. It spoke volumes for the power the De Lucas put in his hands.

Jameson rested his gaze on her. "I believe we have delivered the intended message, Miss Larkin. I trust you understand."

She did. But she couldn't do anything about it. "I don't even talk to the press. But I can't make the tabloids and TV stations stop asking questions, and if I don't answer them, they speculate. This thing has taken on a life of its own, and your client is as much to blame as I am."

"But you *can* do something, Miss Larkin." Jameson's voice was smooth as oil. "You can speak to the press and tell them they are off-course and out of line, that the De Lucas had nothing to do with the accident at your store or the rumors that surround you and your sisters."

Her sisters—she still didn't know what Rafe had said about them. "What rumors?"

He shrugged. "Just the same old stories of your sordid life that I'm sure you've heard before. It's unfortunate that your youngest sister has to suffer for the poor judgment shown by her older siblings. Unfortunately, your past makes it easy to believe those rumors about how she financed her education." He turned to Rafe. "What was the term they used?"

Rafe's lip curled into the semblance of a smile. "Hooking."

"Ah, yes. I believe an escort service was involved. But of course it's all unfounded rumor."

Rage burned in her chest. She fisted her hands at her sides, nails biting into her palms. "Sophie isn't part of this. Whatever you've done, undo it. Fast."

"Or what, Miss Larkin? You'll sue, engaging in a protracted public debate about your sister's character?" He lifted one eyebrow. "Frustrating, isn't it? But I believe Rafe could be persuaded to say a few kind words about the girl, if you do the same for him. You'll let us know your decision, won't you?"

Jameson walked to the back door, stuck his head outside and looked around, then held it open for his client. With a final vicious glare at Maggie, Rafe followed.

Maggie sagged against a stack of boxes. She had to call Sophie. This whole fiasco with Rafe had already endangered her sister's relationship with her boyfriend, and forced her to make awkward explanations to colleagues at the university. If Rafe's new accusations hadn't reached them yet, Sophie might be able to minimize the damage.

Her hands were still shaking with anger as she dialed Sophie's number.

"Maggie!" Sophie answered the phone after one ring.

"Hi, Sophie. I wanted to warn you about some things Rafe De Luca may have implied about—"

"I heard! I'm gonna kill that son of a bitch. Who does he think he is? Do you think those reporters would come over if I called them? I have a few things I'd like to say."

"Sophie, don't do that!" Why had she ever thought Sophie was mild-mannered?

"Why the hell not? He sure doesn't hesitate to

spread lies whenever he wants to. I could make up some dandies. If he wants to imply that we had a fling, let him. I'll be glad to fill in the juicy details about what Rafe is like in bed."

"Is that what he said?"

"He said meeting you just confirmed every impression he had about the Larkin sisters after meeting me last year at a private party in Boulder."

"That doesn't sound so bad."

"The kind of party where the entertainment for the evening is provided by an escort service with an 800 number and employees named Bambi and Ginger."

"Oh, God, Sophie, I'm sorry!" A side job with an escort service definitely wouldn't play well with the dean. "I hope your boyfriend knew it was all made up."

"I wouldn't know," Sophie replied stiffly. "He moved out."

Maggie squeezed her eyes shut. "I'm so sorry, Sophie."

"Don't be. Good riddance. And if Rafe wants to play hardball with the Larkins, let him bring it. I'll be glad to give the press details of our night together. Poor Rafe, trying to compensate for his little weenie and his problem with premature ejaculation."

Damn! Apparently beneath that sweet, studious exterior, her sister was as much of a fighter as she and Zoe. Maybe more, which meant Maggie would have to work twice as hard to end this before Sophie blew the whole thing onto the cover of *People* magazine.

"Just don't do anything yet, okay? Stay home and stay out of it. Please. I'll talk to Cal and we'll decide what to do." For once she would be glad to consult with him.

"Can't stay home. Amber and I are going shopping."

"You and Amber? How—"

"Cal got Zoe's number from the hotel, and asked her if she knew someone who might want to hang with his sister for a day while he investigated Rafe." Maggie heard a laugh in the background and some talking. "Really?" Sophie said. "Hey, Maggie, are you really sleeping with Cal?"

"No! Did Amber say that?"

"She says no," Sophie reported.

When the conversation went on without her, Maggie raised her voice. "You two have fun talking about my nonexistent sex life. I have work to do." She hung up, too aware that she'd be in a far better mood if the nonexistent part hadn't been true.

Since it was true, and since Cal wasn't knocking on her door to say he'd just ditched his little sister and was dying to ravish her luscious body, work seemed to be her only option. Starting with the message light blinking on her phone. Sighing, she picked up a pen and hit the play button.

"Hello," a woman said in precise, businesslike tones. "This is Sandra, calling for Mr. Damon Martin. Mr. Martin would like—"

Maggie hit stop. Did she say Damon Martin? As in the Academy Award–winning, to-die-for actor Damon Martin? She hit rewind.

"Hello, this is Sandra, calling for Mr. Damon Martin. Mr. Martin would like to place an order for an item shown on the Fortune's Folly website.

He is aware of the recent damage to your store and understands that shipment might be delayed. If possible, he would like to order item number 1708, the handwoven silk tapestry from India. Your website says you have two in stock, however Mr. Martin would like four of them. Please call me to confirm the order—"

Maggie hit stop again and fell back in her chair. Four? Holy shit! That tapestry retailed at $28,000! Unless her webmistress had made an error . . . Frantically, she turned on her computer and called up the Fortune's Folly website, double-checking item number 1708. She wasn't crazy. One of the biggest stars in Hollywood had just placed a $112,000 order with her store.

She stared in wonder at the phone for several seconds, then fumbled for her pen and wrote down the phone number Sandra recited. Then stared at the paper. Then giggled. Obviously, she couldn't call Sandra back until she could talk without sounding like someone was tickling her with a handful of feathers.

Grinning, she hit play again. "Hey, hi there," a man's voice said. The lazy drawl sounded vaguely familiar. "Say, I want to buy one of those fossilized dinosaur footprints you have on your website. But I'd really like one from a bigger dinosaur if you have it. And carnivorous, that would be cool. Give me a call. Ask for Mick."

Maggie blinked as recognition clicked in her brain. Mick Perry, lead singer of the rock band Changeling.

Nervous laughter bubbled from her throat. Her idea had worked! Far better than she imagined, too. A lot of powerful people must be dying to show just how much they disliked the De Lucas, and Fortune's Folly had become the vehicle for their revenge. She looked at the blinking light on the phone—six more messages.

Laughing out loud, she picked up her pen and hit play.

Cal pulled onto the highway fast enough to send the back of the truck skidding, spraying gravel, but it didn't even begin to relieve his frustration.

His investigation into Tara Kolinowski's disappearance had hit a dead end. Maybe if he had as much money and power as the De Lucas, he could buy his way past it, but he didn't. And they'd gotten there first.

Both of Tara's friends had been bought off. He didn't know if they'd seen Tara leave with Rafe on that last night of their ski trip, and he'd never find out. They wouldn't talk about it.

He wasn't even sure they had anything to hide. Each had talked freely about the details of the trip, right down to that last night, with one exception. Both claimed to know nothing about Rafe De Luca. Cal found it odd that employees at the hotel would remember that Tara had been with him the night before, but her roommates knew nothing about it. What young woman intent on meeting celebrities wouldn't brag about that?

They'd even given him the same line Tara's father had used, that asking about a celebrity would just distract people from the real investigation into Tara's disappearance. Either they thought exactly like Tara's parents, or the De Lucas had planted that line in everyone's head in addition to spreading a little financial aid around. At least Tara's old school friend had had the grace to blush when he'd asked if the Land Rover outside was hers. A high-end SUV like that had to run $80,000, at least. There was no way her job in customer service for the gas company paid that well.

He'd gone all the way to Denver again to talk to one friend, then sidetracked into the foothills to find the other. A lot of driving for nothing. It was past six o'clock when he finally pulled into the Lost Canyon Lodge—home sweet home. A quick dinner sounded good. Crashing on the bed sounded even better. He rounded a huge boulder and a stand of aspen, feeling almost fond of his rustic cabin in the woods.

He rocked the truck to an abrupt stop. He had company.

A black Explorer sat out front. On the porch, Maggie sat in one of the plastic chairs, feet up on the porch rail, reading a newspaper. He wasn't used to seeing her in jeans, and took an appreciative look at the long line of her legs. Not bad at all, even though he liked them better bare.

She looked up at the sound of his truck, grinned, and dropped the paper. Half his weariness fell away just looking at her bright face.

He had barely slammed the truck door shut when she bounded down the steps and threw herself into his arms. "It worked, Cal! I had the absolute best day!" She pushed back enough to look at him. "I hope you don't mind that I waited here. I just had to tell you about it!"

He didn't mind at all. Her infectious smile had wiped away the scowl he'd worn for the last three hours. "Tell me about what? No, wait." He ran his hand under her hair and drew her in for one long, deep kiss. The last of his tension eased away, her happiness melting it as she wrapped her arms around his neck. She smelled like flowers. He inhaled deeply, soaking in her scent along with the pine-scented air. He could get used to this place. "Okay, tell me."

Her smile was as bright as her sunlit hair. "Our plan worked, Cal! People have been calling the store since last night and placing orders online. I've done more business in one day than I usually do in a month! No, two months!"

She was nearly bouncing on her toes with excitement, making him laugh. "I'm glad to hear so many people hate the De Lucas. But it was your idea, not ours." Not ready to let go of her, he put an arm over her shoulders as he started toward the cabin.

She slipped her arm around his waist, cuddling close. "My idea, your brilliant plan for implementing it. I guess Rick gets some credit, too. He did a great job getting the media on the story."

He held the door, then followed her inside. "Why don't we leave Rick out of it for now?" He turned the lock. "I like it better when you focus on me."

Understanding flashed in her eyes. "I'm tempted to remind you that I don't like bossy men, but you don't seem so bossy lately. In fact"—she stroked a finger thoughtfully down the stubble on his cheek—"you seem pretty cooperative."

"Told you I'm all about teamwork."

"You did. I've been sitting on your porch for the past hour, thinking about that very thing."

Her sultry look said all he needed to know. His

heart probably sped up, but it was hard to tell, since every part of him had gone on high alert the second she fell into his arms. "You were sitting out there an hour? I'm flattered."

She slipped both arms around his waist. "I had some thinking to do."

"That's nice." He kissed her and forced her backward a few steps, moving with her.

"Don't you want to know what I was thinking about?"

Probably the same thing he'd been thinking about the past couple of days. The thing that had taken over his mind and wouldn't let go. But she seemed to want to talk about it, so he nibbled her ear and said, "What were you thinking about?"

"About how well we work together."

"We do." He kept her moving back, past the kitchen counter and onto the rug behind it.

"And how not exploring that chemistry might be pretty stupid."

"You're not stupid." Three more steps. He brushed kisses along her jaw.

"Mmm." She rolled her head, allowing him to drop more kisses on her collarbone. "No, I'm not. And that means . . ."

Her voice trailed off as his hands slid under her shirt and up to her breasts. He could feel her nipples poking hard against the smooth material of her bra. "What does it mean?" he asked, watching her eyes. She looked a little dazed.

"Uh . . . I don't know." She blinked slowly. "I forgot what I was going to say."

"I'll stick around while you think about it." One

more step. The back of her legs hit the foot of his bed.

She closed her eyes for a moment as his thumbs moved in lazy circles. When she opened them, her sleepy gaze focused on his as her hands went beneath his shirt. "I think I'm done thinking."

"About time," he murmured. He pulled her top off, then helped her remove his own. He supposed her bra was pretty, with all that black lace, but he didn't take time to admire it. Reaching around to unhook it, he slipped it off her arms and out of his way. Then paused to admire the view.

"Freckles." He smiled at the light scattering of color that faded out halfway down her breasts.

"Redhead."

"I like them." He cupped each breast and rubbed his thumbs over the tightly puckered nipples. She sucked in a breath and closed her eyes. "I like that, too," he said, watching her reaction before ducking his head to pull one firm nub into his mouth.

"Oh, God . . ."

He was in complete agreement.

Cal could have happily spent the next hour acquainting himself with the taste and feel of her breasts, but each delighted moan from Maggie created more pressure in his groin, until he didn't think it was possible to get any harder. The urgency to do something about it only increased when she found his erection and began stroking him through his jeans. When she unfastened them and reached inside, he groaned and pushed into her hand. Her fingers caressed as they stroked. If she kept doing that, he'd never last long enough.

He bent her backward as he held her, taking them

both down to the bed. With a last lingering kiss on her breast, he pushed up and slid her jeans off. He smiled at the scrap of black lace, wondering exactly what shade of red he'd find behind that thin little triangle. Loving the anticipation, he ran his fingers under the thin bands that crossed her hips, then down the silky front triangle where it disappeared between her legs. As his finger touched moistness, Maggie breathed a soft, "Oh," and drew a quivering breath.

That was all he could take. He pulled the black lace panties off her legs.

Blond with a hint of red. He cupped the softness, thrilling at the way she rose against his hand, seeking more.

Lifting her arms, she pulled at his shoulders. "Come here, she pleaded. "I want to feel you against me." Lifting her foot to the bed for leverage, she started to scoot toward the pillows, making room for him.

He caught her other knee, holding her in place. "Not yet, sweetheart. I think I want you right here for now." Pushing her knees apart gently, he knelt between them.

Maggie was melting from the inside out. Certainly her bones were gone, because she was as limp as a rag. All she could do was clutch the bedspread and ride the waves of pleasure Cal drove through her body. His big hands held on to her hips and caressed her legs, while his tongue . . . Oh, God, what hadn't he touched with that tongue? She quivered when he tasted her, then gasped as he licked into her most sensitive spots, arching helplessly against his mouth. She couldn't stop herself, and didn't want to. She whimpered, then panted, then nearly screamed as every muscle below her waist spasmed in ecstasy. When she finally opened her eyes, Cal was leaning over her, gray eyes dark with desire.

Was there a proper etiquette for thanking a man for the best oral sex ever? Following her instincts, she grabbed his neck and pulled him down for a passionate kiss. When their lips parted she found her voice, even though it was rough and low. "Tell me you have a condom."

He smiled. "I have several."

She lifted an eyebrow, which clearly said, "Why the hell don't you have one on already?"

He was ahead of her, slipping out of his jeans and ripping open the packet in record time. Impatience made her squirm, while watching him sheathe himself ignited a new fire between her legs. She hooked her legs around his hips, pulling him close, wanting to feel him inside her. *Needing* to feel him.

His gaze burned, too, watching her as he reached between them. His finger found her wetness. She made a small sound a pleasure in her throat. His eyes closed halfway, steady on her own, as he inserted another finger.

She bit her lip. "Cal," she breathed.

Then his fingers were gone and he slipped inside her, deep and full.

She moaned. She wanted to move, hard and fast. But he held himself there, eyes closed. "Jesus," he breathed, then gave a half chuckle. "You feel too good. Give me a second."

Her heart gave a little skip. Damn it! It seemed

like he touched every part of her, including emotions she didn't know she had. She was tempted to ask if it had been a long time for him, too, but she didn't want to know if it hadn't, so she lay still. When he moved slowly a few seconds later, she found herself right back on that desperate edge. This time he didn't hold back. Delicious pressure built with each thrust, until she thought she'd go out of her mind with desire. Seconds later she gave herself over to the waves rippling through her, aware that he reached the same pinnacle immediately after her. She arched against him, helpless, then collapsed, too tired to move another muscle. He gave a satisfied groan and settled on top of her, breathing heavily.

She stroked the cool sweat on his back and ran her hand down to his tight butt. When he got up she was definitely going to take an appreciative look at that. It had looked mighty good in jeans, high and firm, and she wasn't going to miss an opportunity to admire it naked.

Finally she turned her head, brushing his where it lay cradled on her shoulder. "You going to let me get up?"

"No." He raised his head to look at her. "I'm trying to figure out a way to keep you right where you are." He kissed her slowly, lingering at the end to take a gentle nip at her lower lip. "I forgot to tell you—Amber's with your sister."

"I know."

"Then don't leave."

She hadn't been about to. Especially not after seeing the heat in his gaze that promised more of the same. "I'm not going anywhere."

He smiled. "Good." He whispered it as he kissed her ear, sending shivers all the way down her arms. Then he pushed himself up, separating them. Cool air touched her hot body. She wanted him back already. They probably had a few hours before Amber and Sophie returned, and she intended to spend every minute of that time in his bed. From the look in his eyes, Cal agreed with that plan.

She watched him walk to the bathroom, following the ripple of muscles in his tight ass, and sighed happily. No interruptions for the next two or three hours. She owed Sophie for this one.

Maggie's phone woke her. She lifted her head from Cal's arm, spotting the phone on the chipped table beside the bed. She couldn't reach it, not with Cal's leg pinning her down, and she didn't feel like trying to move him. Being wrapped in his arms felt too good. She propped herself up, weighing the options. After two more rings, it went to voice mail. Problem solved.

"You didn't answer it."

She looked down to meet his amused gaze. "I don't want to get up."

He ran his fingers through her hair, watching lazily as the strands sifted through them to her shoulder. "Me, either. What time is it?"

She looked at the watch she hadn't bothered to take off, and widened her eyes. "Damn, it's almost ten."

He pulled her down and rolled on top of her, his naked body fitting nicely against hers. The hard line against her thigh was especially nice. He moved his hips against hers, stirring all sorts of tempting ideas.

On the table, her phone chirped, announcing a message.

He didn't say anything, waiting for her decision. She hesitated, then closed her eyes, surrendering to her responsible side. "Can you reach it?"

He did, rolling off her so she could sit up. Gathering the sheet around her, she accessed her messages while Cal lay back, hands behind his head, waiting. She was about to give in to the temptation to run her hand over his broad chest when Sophie's voice hit her ear at top volume, speaking over blaring music: "Hey, Maggie, I just wanted you to know that Amber and I are hanging out at The Aerie. We're having a great time, so don't jump out of bed or anything. See you later!"

Maggie lowered the phone. "Sophie and Amber are at The Aerie."

Cal's eyebrows drew together in a suspicious look. "Amber's sixteen."

She didn't like it either, but there was no point in getting him more upset. "It's in the hotel. And I don't think Sophie would let her order a drink."

Cal sat up. "It's not the alcohol I'm worried about. The Aerie draws a pretty sophisticated crowd."

Including the *Trust Fund Brats*. He didn't have to say it. He also didn't have to remind her that Amber was rather uninhibited, or that she and Sophie both had a chip on their shoulders about Rafe De Luca, and an aggressive attitude about payback.

"I have to shower before we go."

A spark of interest lit his eyes. "It'll be twice as fast if we shower together."

• • •

Stepping into the cool mountain night was disorient-
ing, like stepping from a dream into reality. The last
few hours in Cal's tiny cabin had been an erotic inter-
lude, suspended in time. Reality was the pine-scented
night, the other cars on the highway, and the laughter
and music that drifted from The Aerie lounge before
they even opened the doors.

Maggie paused at the entrance to The Aerie. She'd
come here countless times, but had never seen it quite
so crowded and noisy. The deep bass beat of dance
music thumped behind the wall of raised voices and
laughter in The Aerie's back room. "Do you think
they're having a wrap party for the show?" she asked.

"No idea." He dipped his head close to her ear,
but still had to speak loudly. "Did you try Sophie's
phone?"

"Went to voice mail. I'm sure she never heard it
ring."

He kept his hand on her back as they skirted the
crowd at the bar, scanning faces there before looking
at the tables and booths to their left. If Sophie and
Amber were in some dark corner, this could take quite
a while.

They were halfway through the room when Cal
suddenly exclaimed, "Shit!" He tugged her into the
mass of people around the bar, pushing through a gap
until Maggie stood wedged between two occupied
stools. Putting his mouth near her ear, he said, "Look
at the very end of the bar."

She let her gaze follow the curving bar to its end.
She spotted Cal's sister easily. With her back turned toward them, Amber's blue-streaked hair stood out, even
in the dim light around the bar. She nodded for Cal's

benefit as she peered past Amber to see the person she was talking to, expecting it to be Sophie. Amber laughed, ducking her head slightly and giving Maggie a clear view of the person next to her.

Maggie froze. Bare inches from Amber, Rafe De Luca flashed a broad smile, aiming it at both Amber and a taller blond girl standing next to her. Maggie didn't have to hear them to recognize what was happening. The girls were flirting with Rafe, and not in a subtle way.

As she watched, Amber said something to the other girl, touching her arm as if she knew her, then repeated it to Rafe. He answered and gestured with his hand, taking in both girls. Whatever he said made Amber smile and lean close to reply. When Rafe's arm went around her shoulder, she didn't resist.

Cal swore furiously. Maggie caught his hand before he could move, tugging him closer. "I don't think it's a good idea for us to get her. Someone might recognize us, and I don't want to create another scene with Amber in the middle. If Rafe's here, so are the paparazzi."

Cal's glare never left his sister, but he nodded curtly at Maggie's words. She watched his jaw tense as he thought it over. Seconds later, he raised a hand and motioned to one of the bartenders. The young man nodded, finished an order, then came over to them. "Evening. What can I get you?" he asked loudly.

Cal tucked a folded bill in his hand. "See that girl down there with the blue hair? I want you to card her."

The young man took a long look at Amber, then glanced down at the bill, turning it until the twenty showed. He hesitated. "She hasn't ordered anything," he said.

"Your sign says you have to be twenty-one to be in here," Cal pointed out.

"She's with Rafe De Luca."

"She's sixteen."

"Shit." The bartender nodded and pocketed the bill. They watched him make his way to the end of the bar and exchange a few words with Rafe, looking apologetic and nodding at Amber. Amber stiffened and appeared to do her best not to look annoyed when the bartender nodded toward the door. Rafe smiled at her and shrugged, as if to say it was too bad she got caught.

Cal tugged on Maggie's hand and she followed him back through the crowd to intercept Amber. When she saw them, she stuck her hands on her hips. "It was you!"

"Damn right," Cal growled. "And you're getting out of here right now." Not waiting for an answer, he ushered her toward the door. "Where's Sophie?"

Amber simply glared in return, but they didn't need her reply. Sophie appeared at Maggie's elbow. "What's going on?"

Her expression was altogether too innocent. "You're leaving," Maggie informed her curtly. She led the way to the door, then turned back to make sure they were behind her. As she did, her gaze caught on Rafe as he turned their way. He paused, lifting one side of his mouth in a smile that was more like a snarl. Then his gaze shifted and he watched Amber stalk past her, securely tucked next to Cal. Maggie knew he'd recognize her even from the back—that blue streak stood out.

Rafe's smile disappeared, replaced by a cold stare. His gaze shifted back to Maggie as he made the obvious connection. The blonde latched onto his arm, saying something, but he ignored her, pinning Maggie with a look that promised retribution.

She shivered and turned away quickly, following Cal into the relative quiet of the hallway that connected to the lobby.

Cal had released Amber and was already laying into her. "You don't go after killers when you have no idea what you're doing! Do you have a death wish, or are you just crazy?"

Amber narrowed her eyes. "I knew exactly what I was doing. And I wasn't alone."

"What, you thought that little blond piranha would save you? She doesn't give a damn about you. She was on the make and probably glad you're gone."

Amber gave him a look that said exactly how stupid she thought he was. "I don't even know her, we just met. But Sophie was watching me. If you hadn't butted in, I could have gotten Rafe to break at least a couple laws with no trouble at all. I don't know about you, but I want to put his ass in jail where it belongs!"

"So do I! But not because I catch him killing another young woman, even if she was foolish enough to practically dare him to do it!"

Amber curled her lip in disgust. "You know, for a cop, you're pretty dense. Sophie wouldn't have let him touch me."

Sophie didn't seem to have any more desire to get involved in the family dispute than Maggie did. She stood off to the side, but offered a weak smile at the mention of her backup role. Cal speared her with a glance that wiped the smile off her face before returning to his main target.

He barely had a chance to utter the first profanity when Rick Grady burst out of The Aerie and into the center of their small gathering. "Cal! I thought that was you. Hey, Maggie." He cast a frankly curious stare at Sophie and Amber. "What are you all doing here?"

"Where have *you* been?" Cal countered, apparently no more pleased with Rick than he had been with Amber.

"Watching Rafe, like we agreed." He looked from Amber to Cal. "What's going on?"

"What's going on is a sixteen-year-old girl trying to lure Rafe into committing God knows what crimes so she can have him arrested."

"I'll be seventeen in two weeks," Amber muttered.

Rick directed his answer at Cal. "I know. I was watching her and that girl next to her."

Cal paused, squinting at Rick. "And you didn't stop it?"

"Hell, no. That's what I've been waiting for him to do. I was ready to follow them if he took one of them out of there."

"See?" Amber said. "I was perfectly safe!"

Cal pinned Rick with a cold stare. "She's my sister. She's not involved in this."

"Okay," Rick said. "Sorry, man."

Amber rolled her eyes and muttered something about control freaks.

Cal looked at Maggie. "I'm taking Amber back to the lodge."

She nodded. "I'll catch a ride with Sophie."

"Come on." Cal urged Amber forward with a hand on her arm. Fortunately she didn't do more than huff her annoyance and throw a quick "Thanks for today" at Sophie before following his command. Rick shifted uncomfortably, then muttered a quick excuse about needing to watch Rafe and sidled back into the bar, leaving Maggie and Sophie alone in the hall.

Sophie broke the awkward silence with a soft snort of derision. "Geez, Maggie, I can see why you aren't sleeping with him. He might be a hunk, but he's also an ass. What a controlling jerk."

Maggie turned on her. "Were you part of that plan? Because you were supposed to keep yourself away from Rafe, and keep Amber safe, neither of which you did."

"Excuse me, I was supposed to keep her occupied. And she's fine. Besides, I kind of liked her idea about tempting Rafe into doing something."

"Well, I don't. Don't do it again. I'm trying my best to keep this whole mess from touching you, and you're jumping right into the middle of it."

She looked as disgusted as Amber had. "Now you're telling me how to live my life? Cal must be rubbing off on you."

Maggie bit her lip and tried not to picture Cal rubbing on her. "I don't want to argue with you, Sophie. Stay away from Rafe, and keep Amber away from him, too."

Sophie held her hands up. "Fine. But that girl's got one goal in life—to make Rafe pay for her sister's death. She's going to find a way to do it, and you can't watch her every minute."

Maggie knew Sophie was right. What's more, she couldn't blame Amber for wanting revenge. But she also couldn't stand by and let her do it. After the look Rafe had given them, she had no doubt Amber was now in as much danger as she and Cal were.

They needed to get Amber out of his reach. And just possibly, Maggie knew how to do it.

It really didn't matter that Amber wouldn't like it.

Chapter Eleven

Maggie laid it out neatly in a phone call to Cal the next morning. "You need a safe place to stash Amber where she can't hit on older guys or turn vigilante and go after Rafe."

"Right. Also for that other important reason."

Privacy. She felt her whole body grow warm. "Yes, well. I know of a place that will work."

"You know she'll sneak off and do what she wants as soon as no one's looking."

"She won't be able to do that."

"You got her a cell at the county jail?"

Maggie gave a short laugh. "She might think so, but I promise she'll have plenty of room to roam, things to do, and people who treat her well. In fact, they'd love to have her."

"I'm sold. What is this wondrous place?"

"The People's Free Earth Commune. We'd better take your truck, the road gets pretty rough."

• • •

Amber held a tight grip on the handle above the passenger door as the truck jolted over another rock. "Are you sure people live up here?"

"*I* used to live up here." Maggie braced herself against Cal's leg for the fourth time to keep from bumping against Amber on her other side, and wondered from his smug look if he was hitting all the rough spots on purpose. "There are probably ten or twelve people living permanently at the commune. Most of them have been there since it started almost forty years ago."

"They're crazy," Amber decided. "There's nothing up here but trees and rocks."

"But look at the view!" Cal exclaimed. "It's fantastic."

Amber snorted her disgust. "You live in *Ok-la-ho-ma*," she reminded him. "Probably anything looks better." Squinting at a rocky bluff, she asked, "Are those ugly dogs?"

"Goats. They belong to the commune." Maggie nodded at the curve ahead. "The house is right around that bend."

They all watched as a large log-and-stone house came into view. Several smaller buildings and a fenced corral lay behind it.

Cal gave a low whistle. "Nicer than I expected."

"The commune's done pretty well over the years." As three dogs ran toward them, barking, she reached across and leaned on the horn, giving one long blast of noise that echoed off the distant peaks. "They're probably working, but they'll be here in a minute. Let's wait outside."

He stepped out and took her hand to help her out,

looking around as he did. "I'm surprised they have a phone all the way out here."

"Cell phones. There are towers all over the mountains. They're hippies, not Amish farmers. They like technology."

They were petting the dogs when a woman rounded the corner of the house at a fast trot. She grinned when she spotted them, and sped up, long hair flying behind her.

Amber took in the calf-length flowered dress, denim vest, and sandals. "Whoa. Retro."

Maggie braced herself, but was still staggered by the encompassing hug that nearly lifted her off her feet, along with the enthusiastic greeting, "Baby!"

"Hi, Mom."

She stood still while her mother framed her face between callused palms, beamed at her daughter, and kissed her cheek. "You look wonderful, Maggie! Introduce me to your friends."

"Mom, this is Cal Drummond. Cal, my mother, Kate Larkin."

Cal already had a huge smile on his face as he stuck out his hand. "Nice to meet—" He broke off with a startled look as Kate wrapped him in a warm hug, then set him back with an admiring gaze.

"How lovely to meet you, Cal. I hope you'll make yourself right at home." Kate's sparkling gaze shifted to Amber. "And this must be the young woman we've been looking forward to having as a guest. Welcome, sweetie!" Amber stiffened slightly, allowing Kate's hug but shooting a suspicious look at Maggie.

Maggie had never seen the girl at a loss for words before, and tried to imagine what she must think of

Kate. Her mother was still a pretty woman at fifty-five despite a few lines beside her eyes and silver streaks in her faded red hair. Kate's joyous welcome had been genuine, but it wasn't enough to crack Amber's sullen reserve.

Frankly, Maggie couldn't blame her. Getting passed from an indifferent mother to a dutiful but unenthusiastic half brother would have made her cynical, too. The girl hadn't objected to moving out of Cal's tiny cabin and the extra cot that was her bed, but she hadn't shown much enthusiasm for visiting the People's Free Earth Commune, either.

"We're so excited to have you here!" Kate told her.

Amber was still taking in Kate's hippie clothes with a wide-eyed stare. Her eyes settled on the pendant Kate wore on a leather thong around her neck, an intricately wrought peace sign with small doves perched on the silver bars. "Hey, cool necklace."

"Would you like to have it?" Before Amber could close her startled mouth, Kate slipped it off and settled it over her head. "Pete makes them. He's quite a good silversmith."

"Uh, I didn't mean . . ." Amber fingered the delicate peace sign, obviously taken with it.

"Maybe you can watch him make one. We have a lot going on here, and Maggie said you might be able to stay for a while. You'll have time to try everything."

Amber shot a resentful look their way. "Yeah, well, I guess they don't want me to be in their way."

"Oh, no, they just wanted to give you something fun to do. I'm sure you weren't in anyone's way."

Amber shrugged. "Maybe they just didn't tell you everything. Cal and Maggie are sleeping together, you know. They'll probably be screwing like bunnies now that I'm gone."

Beside her, Cal swore under his breath. Amber darted a satisfied look at each of them, confident she'd taken her revenge for getting dumped in the remote reaches of the Rockies.

"Oh! Are they?" Kate clapped her hands together and turned a bright look on Cal and Maggie. "How wonderful for them!" She smiled benevolently at Amber's suddenly blank face. "And so mature of you to understand their need for privacy in the early stages of a sexual relationship. Come on, let's find you a room before I show you around."

Kate slipped her arm around Amber's shoulder and led her away. Amber threw a confused look back at them, then stumbled on a stone and started paying attention to where she was going.

Maggie tucked her arm through Cal's. "Want to see where I grew up?"

"Hell, yeah."

Cal stared at everything, fascinated. Beyond the grandeur of the land, the commune was a glimpse into Maggie's past. Despite his best intentions, she had become important to him, and he found himself intensely curious about her unorthodox beginnings.

They followed Kate and Amber to the house, where he submitted to exuberant welcomes from two women introduced as Marcy and Feather. It was like being mobbed by two overly enthusiastic grandmothers. Hippie grandmothers—he couldn't think of any other word to describe the patched jeans, loose, lacy tops, and granny glasses.

"Feather's the official housekeeper," Maggie told him. "That includes plumbing repairs and basic carpentry, when needed."

Cal looked around the great room and the connecting kitchen, then back at Feather and her long gray braids. She looked a good decade older than Kate. "That's a lot of work."

Feather beamed. "It's what I like best. We all do what we're best at."

"Marcy keeps the books for the commune, and takes care of shipments."

"Shipments?"

"Pottery, jewelry, whatever orders we're filling," Marcy told him.

"The commune supports itself by selling crafts," Maggie explained. "Very good crafts. Their pottery and jewelry get shipped to stores all over the country. I carry some at Fortune's Folly."

He looked up as Amber came downstairs with Kate. His sister didn't look happy. When the three women started questioning Maggie about recent events with Rafe, she tugged on his sleeve and pulled him aside.

Standing on tiptoe, Amber hissed in his ear. "Cal, they don't have Internet service here. Not even TV!"

"My God, you might die."

She slapped his arm. "This is serious! You're stranding me here. You'd think they'd at least have a horse to ride, but no, all they have is chickens and goats." She leaned closer. "And you'll never guess what they do with the goats."

He thought he could, but he enjoyed her horrified expression, so he tried to look alarmed. "What?"

"They drink their milk!" From the revulsion on her

face, she might have said "blood" instead of "milk"—
it was priceless. "They only eat *natural* food, like it's
unnatural to eat fast food or something. And they all
have *jobs*. No TV, no computers—what am I supposed
to do all the frickin' time, milk their goats and roll
their joints?"

He didn't know for sure about the joints, but with
the amount of work they did every day, he figured no
one had that kind of downtime. And if drugs were
an issue, Maggie wouldn't have brought her here.
"Maybe you could help them with something," he
suggested. "You didn't mind helping Maggie with her
store."

"Maggie had cool stuff. And customers I could
have talked to." Her voice dropped to a whisper as
she peered around him at Kate, Feather, and Marcy.
"There's no regular people here. Just *them*."

You'd think he was dumping her at the Bates Motel.
"Maggie lived here full-time until she was eight, and
every summer after that, and she seems perfectly normal
to me." He didn't bother adding that her grandmother
had hauled her back to civilization, along with her sisters.
"She said there were other kids, too, and I'm pretty sure
they survived. I think you'll find something to do." At
her mutinous stare, he said, "Look, give it a week. If you
still hate it, I'll take you back to my crummy little cabin,
where you can be bored with trees instead of goats."

"Three days."

"Five."

"Four."

"Five."

She ground her teeth. "We stop for a bucket of KFC
on the way back."

"Deal."

She might have pushed it further, but Kate appeared at her other side. "Amber, honey, let me show you around our work buildings. The others are dying to meet you."

Amber trudged off beside Kate as he and Maggie followed at a distance, going outside and crossing toward a small barn. "Is she pissed off?" Maggie asked.

"She'll get over it. This is a great place."

"I guess so." She stuck her hands in her pockets, pausing to scan the various buildings set among towering pines and huge outcroppings of pink granite. The trees blocked his view of the snow-covered peak of Two Bears, but the cool wind reminded him it was there. It whipped over snowfields before curling down to the dense forests and sun-drenched meadows of the commune. Maggie turned her face toward the wind, letting it toss her hair into a fiery mane. Cal watched, mesmerized. This was how he'd always think of her, he realized. Not standing up to Rafe, or working happily in her store. Not even naked and hot beneath him. He'd see her here, touched by the wild freedom of the mountain. It was part of her.

"It's a different world," she said, pulling him back to earth. "Especially for a kid. Creeks to wade in, fields to run through. I had about a dozen parents watching over me. It wasn't all play—they taught me to be industrious from the time I could walk, to accomplish something with my life." She smiled at him. "You'd like the commune's philosophy, they're heavily into teamwork."

He gave her a sidelong glance. "Not the same kind, I think."

"You have a dirty mind, Cal Drummond. I like that about you."

"I plan to take advantage of that weakness very soon."

She laughed and took his hand. They checked out the barn and chicken coop, then a small stone building where a man and woman were firing pottery in a kiln, and another one where they found a man named Pete making jewelry.

Pete looked up when they came in. Cal had a fast impression of a gray ponytail, bushy beard, and faded Grateful Dead T-shirt. Two seconds later Pete jumped to his feet with an excited whoop and wrapped Maggie in a bear hug. She disappeared in his arms, dwarfed by Pete's large body, her head nearly buried beneath the shaggy beard.

When Amber got the same treatment, Cal stood his ground warily. Thankfully, Pete merely shook his hand and gave him a hearty slap on the shoulder.

With a satisfied chuckle, Pete gestured at the leather thong around Amber's neck. "I see Kate's already pushing our products."

Amber clasped the silver circle. "Did you really make this?"

"Sure." Pete shrugged. "Make 'em all the time. Peace signs are making a comeback. That's one of the fancier ones, with the little doves on it."

"I love it," Amber admitted.

He nodded. "That's cool. Hey, why don't you watch us work, maybe try your hand at making something?"

Amber looked stunned. "Can I?"

"Yeah, why not?"

"But I . . . I'm not an artist."

A smile split the untamed hairs of his beard. "How do you know? Can't know if you're any good at a thing if you don't try it." While Amber struggled to absorb her sudden apprenticeship, Pete said, "If you don't like pendants, maybe you'll like some of Kate's stuff. She's into rings."

Amber blinked at Kate. "You are?"

Kate nodded happily. "Pete taught me. I love to find the perfect setting for a gemstone. It's such a satisfying art."

"You've seen her work," Maggie told her. "Remember the onyx ring at my shop?"

Amber's mouth dropped open. "You made that?"

"Did you like that one? So did I!" Kate gushed. "Oh, we're going to have so much fun together! Let me show you the raw gemstones I'm working with now."

While Kate led a speechless Amber across the room, Maggie tugged Cal back outside. "We've lost them both. Pete and Mom will keep her busy looking at their stones and tools and molds and God knows what else until Marcy calls them for supper." She stood at the foot of the stone steps and took a deep breath of the pine-scented air, letting it out with a relaxed sigh. She probably didn't even realize she made that little sigh of contentment, but he'd seen it every time they stepped out of a building. Coming back here relieved the stress that had built up over the past week down in Barringer's Pass.

"Fine, let's lose them. Show me something else." He'd say it even if he weren't fascinated with the place, just to keep her here.

"You've seen it all, unless you want to track down some goats."

"Sounds good."

"You want to meet the goats?"

"I want to see the property. Hike around."

She gave him a speculative look, followed by a sly smile. "I know just the place. But we'll need a flashlight."

The mountain sky was blindingly bright, so he didn't know why they needed a flashlight, but he didn't ask questions. "I have one in my truck."

It was a long hike that left the cluster of buildings behind them as they wound up a steep slope. Fewer trees clung to the rocky ground up here. Even the goats weren't around, with less to forage on. He followed Maggie, content to keep his eyes on her nicely curved ass as she climbed ahead of him. It wasn't until she paused at a flat area that he noticed the panoramic vista behind them.

"Damn, that's beautiful." The mountain sloped down to a thick forest on their left, where the commune nestled behind the trees, and sparsely wooded grassland directly below them. Beyond that, he glimpsed the highway that cut through Barringer's Pass. The majestic beauty ended at their far right, where an ugly tumble of stones and gravel cut a wide swath down the mountainside. It stood out like a scar, not recent but not as weathered as the granite ledges and deep forests.

"What's that from, a landslide?"

"It's tailings. Debris from mining, when they separated the ore from the surrounding stone." She pointed, moving her finger upward. "Follow it back up the mountain. See where it starts?"

He looked up, but instead of the expected black entrance to a mine tunnel, all he saw was scrub growth. "I don't see a mine."

"It's there. You'll see."

It only took another five minutes to reach the ledge that was the source of the tailings. Cal saw nothing but gravel-covered ground with small firs and bushes against the mountainside. Maggie pushed her way through them without hesitation, so he followed.

Branches stabbed his back, but he barely noticed. Against the side of the mountain, old timbers framed a low entrance, with newer boards nailed across it. Maggie pulled at the second and third boards up, pivoting the higher one up, and the other down, revealing a small dark hole. Cool, dank air seeped from its depths.

Excitement tingled in Cal's veins like jolts of electric current. The mysterious unknown! The boy in him wanted to plunge into the dark, but the adult made him hesitate. "Are we trespassing?"

"Always the cop, huh? The commune owns the land. Pete talked everyone into buying it nearly twenty years ago, when he had some idea about digging out the traces of silver that were too small for a mining company to go after. He shored up the tunnels, but never did much more than that. The mine was played out. It's safe to explore, though. I've been inside a few times." She flashed a smile. "Just don't tell anyone we were here. I don't want them to ruin my secret cave with safety lectures and padlocks."

"Your secret's safe with me." He unhooked the Maglite from the belt loop on his jeans, and clicked it on. The strong beam illuminated dirt walls and rusted twin tracks for ore carts, before it was swallowed up by pitch-black depths. He looked up from his crouched position, grinned, and held out a hand to help Maggie through the small opening. Keeping her hand firmly in his, he took short steps away from the small circle of light at the entrance, into the blackness. Walking upright was out—his head scraped the ceiling. He developed a shuffling gait, head tucked down and arm extended, as he aimed the flashlight ahead. With each step he shone the light around at the walls, then the ground before them, ensuring they met no surprises.

No surprises turned out to be a bit boring. No bats, no shiny streaks of silver ore along the tunnel walls, and no hint of the miners who carved out the tunnel over a hundred years before. Cal realized that the little boy inside him had been hoping to find a skeleton with a pouch of silver ore still clutched in its bony grasp.

He chuckled at the image, and heard the sound bounce eerily off the walls.

"What's funny?" she whispered.

"My imagination. Did you ever see *The Goonies*?"

She laughed softly. "I've been here before. Believe me, if there were treasure, I would have taken it."

"What is here? Not that this isn't cool, but does it go anywhere?"

"Just to dead ends. But there is something kind of neat. See right up there, where the tunnel branches? Take the one on the left."

He did, then wondered at the wisdom of it when he had to crouch even lower. But after twenty or thirty feet the tunnel suddenly widened and became higher. Within three more steps they were standing in a small round room with plenty of clearance overhead. He shone the light around, fascinated by the scrapes and gouges made by pickaxes long ago.

Maggie stood close, her shoulder touching his. "Point the light higher," she said, her voice almost a whisper.

He did. The beam hit about six feet over their heads, lighting up the wall with tiny sparkles like diamonds blazing against the dull black stone. He moved the light, leaving a trail of sparks across one side of the cavern.

"Is it silver?" he asked, awed.

"Maybe some, but Pete said it's mostly quartz and mica. Not valuable, but as pretty as any silver that ever came out of here." She gave a little sigh. "I always think of this place as the star cavern."

He let the light play around the walls and ceiling, finding the glittery crystals far more concentrated on one side of the cavern. At ground level on the far side, the light touched on strips of wood. He steadied the beam. Several boards lay side by side on the floor of the tunnel.

"It's a hole," Maggie said before he could ask. "Pete boarded it over. The shaft is pretty deep and there's water at the bottom."

There was nothing else to see in the little room, so he mounded loose gravel on the floor and propped the flashlight in it to point high on the wall, setting the tiny crystals ablaze like stars above them. Outside the narrow beam, the room remained smothered in darkness. Maggie was little more than a warm shadow beside him. Reaching for her, he slipped his arms around her waist, pulling her back against his chest. She leaned against him as they admired the display above.

"Does this mine have a name?" He spoke quietly, the deep blackness and hollow echoes inspiring a cathedral-like hush.

"You mean like the Fortune's Folly mine?" She shook her head, her hair rubbing softly against his chest. "I never heard one. It just had a number, something like 'mine fourteen twenty-seven.' That's all most of them have. Terribly unromantic."

It seemed an odd thing to say, since mine 1427 was giving him all sorts of romantic thoughts. With his eyesight effectively gone, other senses strained to compensate, overwhelming his brain with scent and sound and touch. He was acutely aware of the clammy coolness of the air around them and the pleasant, contrasting warmth of Maggie's body where it touched his. The light fragrance of her hair drifted over him. The softness of her skin was a seductive lure for his fingers, tempting him to touch every part of her. He was drunk with the feel and the scent of her.

He wanted more.

He slid his hands up, beneath her T-shirt and the loose denim shirt she'd thrown over it. Her skin felt hot, so he knew his hands must be cool, but she didn't flinch away. With a soft sigh, she laid her head back against his shoulder, arching toward his hands. Without seeing, he knew her eyes were closed, knew she delighted in the feel of his hands on her body as much as he did.

He didn't try to remove her shirt—the mine was too cool for that—but didn't hesitate when he found the front closure on her bra. She arched even more, giving herself to him, and he filled his hands with her, stroking gently until she breathed a long "Ohhh" into the darkness.

It set him on fire. Blazing with need, he turned her in his arms, finding her mouth with an urgency that pulled at something deep inside him. He hoped like hell his roughness hadn't ruined the mood.

Maggie's lips parted eagerly under his. She met his passion with her own, her hands running over his hair, fingers digging into his shoulders. He didn't need to see her face in the dark to know her desire had soared as fast and high as his own. He could feel heat from the flush in her skin, feel her heart pounding hard against his own. And he knew the need in her body as she stood on her toes, pressing her hips against his.

He wanted her right now, right here. He dropped his hands to her waist, fumbling with her jeans. Her frantic hands were faster, unbuttoning and unzipping, then shoving his jeans and shorts over his hips. Cold air moved over his skin but couldn't touch the heat that drove him.

Her hands found him and he groaned. Her fingers were cool against the heat of his erection. Soft against his hardness. Firm as they stroked and slid around to cup him. He pushed into her hand then swore under his breath at the raging need and felt for her zipper.

It slid past his hands as she fell to her knees. He barely had time to brace himself before the warmth of her mouth enveloped him. "Jesus, Maggie," he groaned, then shut up as she drove every thought from his mind, bombarding him with a hundred sensations at once, an explosion of feeling that rocked him to the core. He closed his eyes, which made no difference in the pitch dark of the mine, and stroked her hair, holding on until he couldn't take any more.

"Maggie, stop."

She did, cold air hitting him where her mouth had kept him hot. He couldn't see her, but felt her head tilt upward. Her whisper was low and throaty. "Do you have a condom?"

Her question was a jolt of reality, crashing his plans. "Oh, hell. No. Shit, I'm sorry . . ."

She didn't listen. Her mouth covered him again, her hands moving, too, her purpose clear. He couldn't have stopped her if he wanted to. Helpless, he let the need grow until it ripped through him, pulsing against her.

"Christ," he breathed seconds later, as she rose to her feet. "I didn't expect . . ." The cold air reminded him to pull his jeans up and fasten them. He moved quickly, in a hurry to reach for her, and found her arm in the dark. He didn't say anything, just walked backward slowly, pulling her with him as he felt behind his back. He didn't know if she guessed, but she followed. Three feet. Four. The wall of the cavern met his hand, rough stone curving inward as it rose. He drew her close, then turned and set her back gently against the wall.

He heard her suck in her breath as he knelt in front of her and lowered her jeans. Then there was only heavy breathing as he loved her with both his hands and his mouth. Her fingers gripped his hair as she tilted her hips toward him, holding on as he took her to the same heights she'd taken him. When she gasped and pushed against him he slowed down, pulling a long disappointed groan from her that made him smile. He did it once more, enjoying her frustration, then took her over with out stopping, fast and hard, feeling her release in the spasm of muscles as they clamped around his fingers. Her hands fell limply from his head and her knees bent as she sagged against the wall, letting the solid rock hold her up.

He slid her jeans up and fastened them, then rose to his feet. They hadn't said a word, but something had passed between them in the dark. Not the crackling electricity of the first time they'd made love, but something deep and powerful all the same. He didn't know how to put it into words, so he simply pulled her into his arms and held her. She wrapped her arms around him and nestled her head on his shoulder. They stood for a long time like that, beneath the faint glitter of stone stars, and he realized that maybe she didn't need the words right now. Or maybe she didn't know them, either. For now, this deep contentment was enough.

Maggie had never been so grateful for the dark. If it had been light, Cal might have seen the moisture that leaked from the corner of her eye, confusing her like crazy, not to mention scaring the shit out her.

You weren't supposed to get all mushy just because some guy gave you good sex. Okay, great sex, with a lot of tenderness thrown in.

It was the hug that had done it. She knew plenty of guys who would have said, *Thanks, that was great!* A few might even have high-fived her. But Cal had knocked down her defenses, then tapped right into the soft center that she tried to pretend she didn't have. And she'd practically melted in his arms. At least he couldn't see her, and by the time they got out of here she'd have herself back together. They'd be the same two people they were when they walked in here. None of this scary emotional shit that she had no experience with.

Feeling more settled, she pulled back. He did, too, although he still stood close, and his hands stayed on her arms. She already missed the warmth and the scent of him.

One of them should say something to break whatever this thing was that vibrated between them and caused weird little tingles in her chest. She opened her mouth, but before she could speak a soft rustling sound came from her right. Then another.

He must have heard it, too. "Are there animals in here?" he whispered.

"Maybe bats," she said doubtfully. "But not this far in."

They stood perfectly still, listening. Seconds later they heard it, this time a low murmur, like a far-off voice. It came from deeper in the tunnel, somewhere to their right.

His hand slid down to clasp hers. Keeping her close, he shuffled back to the flashlight and picked it up, shining it toward the far end of the cavern. They saw nothing but the boarded-up hole before the light was swallowed by the dark tunnel beyond.

Cal walked slowly forward. Maggie wasn't sure she wanted to run into someone in the mine, but she wasn't alone and curiosity was overcoming fear. She crept silently beside him, holding tight to his hand.

They reached the boards over the hole, an area only five or six feet in diameter. Cal started around it, then stopped at another sound. The voice was closer. Not distinct enough to tell what the man said, but enough to know he wasn't far away.

It came from the hole.

They knelt on the gritty floor as Cal shone the light over the boards. Most were close together, but a large gap showed where two boards had rotted away and fallen into the hole. The rest shone with moisture. Maggie realized the air felt damp, too, and looked around as Cal's flashlight explored the walls. Small rivulets of water left wet paths on the wall and snaked their way to the hole. The miners had probably only enlarged a hole or fissure that was already there, following the course of the water.

The flashlight played over the boards again and the dark gap that revealed the rough walls of the shaft below. With sudden alarm she grabbed his hand, pushing the flashlight away from the boards.

He aimed the light at her chest, not blinding her but allowing him to see her. She probably looked as shadowed and eerie as he did. "What are you doing?" he whispered.

"They might see it," she said, pointing at the hole. She wasn't even sure why she was being secretive. Why she didn't yell hello and ask how the tunnel was down there. Exploring an old mine didn't make the other people suspicious, any more than it did her and Cal.

But Cal must have felt the same caution, because he nodded and kept the light pointed up. As they stared into the hole, she noticed a faint glow lighting the bottom, creating a shiny black reflection that moved across the water. It wasn't the narrow beam of a flashlight, and she assumed someone down there had a lantern.

More murmuring reached them, still indistinct but never varying in tone. "It sounds more like one person talking to himself," she said.

"I think you're right." They listened for another minute before Cal whispered, "I don't hear splashing sounds. I thought you said there was water at the bottom of the hole."

"There is. Maybe it's a small pool, and he's near it."

"How'd he get there?"

"I don't know. Mines sometimes have more than one level, and more than one entrance. He must have come in through a different tunnel."

They listened quietly a while longer. She heard a watery sound that could have been from someone dipping into the water. Then one or two quick words and nothing more. He was gone. After a few minutes of silence, Cal helped her to her feet. "Come on. Whoever he is, if he's hiking on this mountain, I'd rather run into him outside than in here."

But there was no sign of anyone as they hiked back to the commune. Maggie led Cal straight to the tiny jewelry studio so they could ask Pete about a possible second mine entrance. She forgot all about it as soon as they opened the door.

Amber was looking at herself in the small mirror Kate held up. "Try it on the other side," Kate said, and Amber switched something to her other hand, holding it beside her lower lip as she studied her reflection. Maggie recognized one of the small silver pieces of jewelry the commune made for piercings and nearly choked.

"Mom, what are you doing?"

Kate looked up. "Oh, hi, sweetie. Amber's considering a new piercing, so we're trying to see how it might look."

"What!" Cal took a step forward, and Maggie grabbed his hand, squeezing hard. He stopped, teeth grinding as he reevaluated. "Why do you want another piercing?" he asked. She thought he sounded quite reasonable.

Amber apparently didn't. She gave him a hard stare. "Because I like them."

Cal looked at the silver ring Amber was holding up to her mouth and folded his arms. "I don't."

Kate gave him a bright smile. "Then we won't offer you one. We all get to decide what to do with our own bodies, don't we?"

Amber smiled at Kate.

Maggie grabbed Cal and left.

Chapter Twelve

He grumbled about the lip ring halfway back to town. "She hasn't done anything yet," Maggie reminded him. "Maybe she just wants to show some independence, to let you know you can't take over her life."

Actually, she didn't think there was any maybe about it. She'd felt the same way when her grandmother had tried to put sensible restrictions on her behavior—restrictions she wouldn't have had at the commune. She'd rebelled. The only difference was, she didn't do it by getting her lip pierced. She'd had sex with boys.

"It could be a lot worse," she told him.

He caught the significance in her look, and shut his mouth. "I guess," he admitted. He was quiet for some time after that. When he finally spoke, his voice had lost all its anger. "I don't know what I'm doing, Maggie. I don't know how to be a big brother to a sixteen-year-old girl. I want to tell her all the things she's doing wrong, even when I know she doesn't want to hear them. I don't know if I can do this family thing."

"Sure you can. Everyone feels that way about teenagers."

"Yeah, I see a lot of those teenagers as a cop. I don't like them."

"And most of them turn into decent people. Amber will, too."

His mouth pulled into a tight line. "At least I only have to keep her for two weeks. Maybe she won't have too many new holes in her by the time I send her home."

They were just entering Barringer's Pass when Maggie gave in to impulse. "Pull in here," she said as they approached Del Tanner's.

"A bar?" He turned into the parking lot. "You want a drink?"

"Not only a bar. They also make the best burgers and sandwiches you've ever had. My treat, to celebrate all my big orders today."

"I am hungry," he admitted.

"Me, too. I worked up an appetite on that hike."

His mouth twitched with a half smile and she knew he was thinking of one specific way they'd worked up an appetite. A million butterflies battered themselves against her stomach. Between the sexy smiles and the tender hugs, he kept her more off balance than she'd ever felt with a man.

She covered it up with a grand entrance, raising her voice to yell hello to Del when she spotted him across the room.

The middle-aged man looked up and grinned. "Hey Maggie! Have a seat, I'll be right with you."

"No rush." Grabbing one of the small laminated menus, she led Cal to the bar. It was early for supper and most of the stools were open. Leaning sideways to see the menu as Cal read, she began to point out her favorites.

"Did you find the burgers? The Silver Miner's Deluxe is my fave . . . what the hell?" She stared at the menu, which no longer offered the Silver Miner's Deluxe. It had the Rafe De Luca Special.

"Del!"

Across the room, Del lifted a hand, letting her know he'd be right there.

"I take it you weren't always a sandwich?" Cal asked.

"Me?" She grabbed the menu and looked where he pointed. *The Maggie Larkin Hot Plate.* Her eyes narrowed at the line beneath it: *Caution: This is one hot dish!*

She barely saw Del arrive through the red haze in her eyes.

"Maggie! Long time no see!"

She spun the menu around to face him, and pointed. "What's this?"

Del's laugh wasn't even a little self-conscious. "You like our new selection? Pretty clever, if I do say so myself."

"A hot dish?" she growled.

"Sizzling!" He took a good look at Cal. "Hey, you must be the mystery man!"

"Cal Drummond." He appeared to be fighting back amusement as he stuck out his hand.

"You oughta try the Mystery Man Burger with my special mystery sauce. A real kick-ass burger, like it says."

"God damn it, Del."

He gave her shoulder a friendly swipe. "Hey, it's good business, kiddo. Just like they do in New York City. I went there once and had a sandwich named for Michael Douglas. Figured you deserve your own sandwich, too, now you're famous."

"But I don't want to be famous."

"Can't fight public opinion, Maggie. The people say you're famous, you're famous."

She looked at Cal. He leaned close. "I believe it's meant to be a compliment," he murmured.

"'Course it's a compliment!" Del said. "What do you say I fix you two a couple burgers on the house? You've more than earned it, the way my business has picked up."

She sighed. "Fine. Just not the Rafe burger."

"Ten minutes," he promised happily. "Hey, Cassie, get these two something to drink, would ya?"

He left to see about the burgers and Maggie turned a helpless look on Cal. "I'm not sure if I should be horrified or embarrassed."

"Like you told me, things could be worse."

"How?"

He turned the menu around. "You could be this one."

She looked. *The Bodyguard Club Sandwich. A huge pile of meat that packs a real punch!*

"Now, that I like."

He stopped at a drugstore on the way to her house. When he came back out, he opened the box as soon as he got in the truck. "I haven't carried a condom in my wallet in years, but I'm putting one in it right now."

"Do you have room for two?"

He gave her a heated look. "I'll toss out the money."

She smiled all the way home. The man was definitely getting an invitation to spend the night, and she was sure he wouldn't refuse. Let the media hordes see his truck parked in her driveway overnight. Everyone already considered Cal her boyfriend, so it wouldn't be a news flash.

Once they were inside, he asked for a tour of the house, starting with the bedroom. It turned out to be a short tour.

He didn't rush. He undressed her, leisurely exploring each part of her he exposed. She never knew that a kiss on her wrist or behind her knee could feel so erotic, or that she could want a man so much that just the feel of his naked body against hers could bring her to the brink of orgasm. He stretched out on top of her, pinning her hands to the bed as he kissed her mouth and nibbled at her neck. Between them, his erection teased her, making her strain upward, nearly begging him to relieve the aching lust he built inside her. But he took his time, driving her to the edge of madness before he finally eased into her in one long, slow slide. She exploded before he could even move, crying out as her body convulsed around his.

When she could breathe normally again, she laughed. "I'm sorry, I couldn't wait."

"It's okay." He moved slowly, watching her.

"I . . . Oh. Mmm." Her spent body was recovering rapidly, and turned out to be not so spent after all. "Cal?"

"What?"

"Don't stop doing that."

"Wasn't planning to."

Neither was she, not until his breathing became as ragged as hers had and his eyes as feverish with need. When they finally did, she took him with her into a body-clenching, soul-rocking release.

They lay entangled for some time afterward. She hadn't intended to fall asleep, but when she opened her eyes again the bedside clock read 2:36 a.m. and her arm was numb. She rolled over. The bedroom was dark but light poured in from the hallway and the living room beyond, where they'd left the lamps on. She should probably turn them off. She could also get a snack while she was up. As she debated the idea, Cal mumbled in his sleep and looped his arm around her, spooning her against his warm body. She sighed contentedly and changed her mind about getting up.

Waking up with Cal felt normal, which was saying a lot—even when she'd had a regular sex life she'd never allowed men to sleep over. She didn't like to encourage their territorial instincts. But rolling over to Cal's kisses felt as natural as if she'd done it for years, although she was certain she'd never had a morning shower as invigorating as the one she took with him.

He even seemed to belong in her kitchen. Their movements felt choreographed as she selected cereal boxes, milk, and juice, turning to find he'd set out bowls, spoons, and glasses. She smiled to herself and sat down to eat.

Cal dug into his cereal as he asked, "What do you have planned for today?"

"I have to be at the store. I have brickmasons coming this morning, and the carpenter in the afternoon. How about you?"

"I thought I'd try to get some time with that police sergeant we talked to—what's his name?"

"Sergeant Todd?"

"Right. He seemed open to considering Rafe as a suspect, and I'd like to go over Tara's and Rachel's case files with him, if he'll let me. Might find something that was missed if we go at it from a new perspective."

She nodded. "Want to meet for dinner?"

"Sounds good."

Damn, even their conversations sounded like they'd done this forever. She couldn't understand it—men didn't mesh well with her life. Everything just felt so darn middle-class, middle-American *normal*.

He took a sip of juice. "Let's go back to Del Tanner's. I want to try the Maggie Larkin Hot Plate."

She rolled her eyes. Maybe not everything.

She prepared to feel less comfortable about being with him that evening, in case her mind was floundering in a sex-induced haze. Instead, she found herself suggesting they stop by his cabin to pick up a few changes of clothes.

His lopsided smile made her heart do little flips. "I was hoping you'd say that. But you can still ask me to leave if you feel like I'm crowding you."

She was pretty sure that wasn't going to happen.

She gritted her teeth as they approached her house, preparing for another dash past the media, except the reporters weren't there. Maggie looked up and down her street and in her neighbors' driveways as they turned in. No vans with satellite dishes on their roofs. No reporters.

"Where did everyone go?" she asked.

"No idea. Must be swarming after Rafe."

"Good. He can keep them." Part of her wondered what Rafe might be doing or saying to attract every available news team, but she wasn't going to let it ruin her night.

An odd tingle started deep in her chest as she watched Cal carry his small duffel into her house. She decided it was a good tingle. And after making room for his things in her dresser and bathroom, and making love with him in her bed, she decided *normal* might be a good thing.

They made popcorn and turned on the TV. Maggie leaned against Cal's shoulder, lazy and happy, thinking about how good the right kind of *tired* could feel. She barely stirred when Cal's phone rang.

He took the call, listened, then hung up seconds later. He turned to her with a perplexed look. "Rick says something's going down at the Alpine Sky and we'd better get up there right away. He said a couple cop cars are parked out front and they've been questioning employees."

Maggie scrunched her brow in confusion, but before she could respond, her own phone rang from the coffee table. She looked at the readout then held Cal's gaze as she picked up the call. "Hi, Zoe."

Her sister's voice was a harsh whisper in her ear. "Maggie, I think something terrible has happened."

She wouldn't have thought she had any adrenaline left, but at the panic in Zoe's voice, a tiny jolt of fear shot through her. "What is it?"

"A girl is missing. Someone who was partying here the night before last. Maggie, Rafe was here then, too. He was with her."

All the way there, Maggie kept thinking about how easily it could have been Amber. If they hadn't pulled her out when they did, if they hadn't made sure she was tucked away where Rafe couldn't get to her, they might be experiencing a whole different level of terror right now.

She turned up the truck's heater, though she was shivering from more than the frigid night air. "Maybe we're jumping to conclusions," she said, wanting to believe it. "Rafe isn't stupid. He knows you're looking into Tara's and Rachel's disappearances. He wouldn't dare kill another girl now, would he?"

"Stupid has nothing to do with it, Maggie. If he killed another girl, it was an impulsive act, a result of losing his temper. It depends on whether someone made him angry enough to lose control."

Her heart sank. "We did."

It came out small and weak, but he turned sharply, and she repeated it. "We made him that angry. He saw us when we left the bar with Amber. He looked right at me, and realized Amber was with us. I think he would have killed me on the spot if he could have."

He shook his head. "That would be premeditated. That's not his style. I meant if the girl made him angry." In the low light from the dashboard, she saw him clench his jaw. "Unless he's changed his pattern."

She shot an alarmed look at him. "Could he?"

"If he develops a taste for murder." He squeezed her hand, kept it. "He wouldn't be the first."

The Alpine Sky was ablaze with lights. Not the late-night glow of discreetly placed lamps, but the harsh glare of floodlights. They'd found the missing media convoy.

Five news vans lined the curving entrance, ceding prime curb space only to the two police cruisers near the door. Two more vans with satellite dishes sprouting from their roofs sat in the parking lot, along with three SUVs covered with the call letters and slogans of their various network, cable, and radio stations.

Maggie felt a combination of relief that they'd forgotten her, and pity for whoever would be the next victim of the media spotlight. "It doesn't take them long to move on, does it?"

Cal gave the media swarm a mistrustful glance. "Don't be so sure they have."

He parked several rows away, allowing them to stick to the shadows and skirt the news vehicles as they walked up to the main doors. Maggie didn't consider asking Zoe to let them in the side door by the kitchen. The flurry of activity around the front entrance drew her, stirring a mixture of curiosity and dread.

News crews clustered on the sidewalk just beyond the front doors, taping under the bright glare of spotlights. She paused just short of the entrance, captured by the excited voice of a reporter summarizing the situation for viewers. After spending the past week dodging this same media circus, she felt vaguely guilty to be on the other side of the camera, feeling the prickle of excitement it aroused. Especially when the cause of the excitement was a missing girl.

Or maybe it wasn't. Maggie stopped abruptly as she saw the reason for all the media attention. A few steps past the reporter, Rafe De Luca stood patiently as a hair stylist fussed with his hair and someone else dabbed makeup on his forehead. They both melted away as the cameras and reporter turned toward Rafe.

Maggie and Cal watched from a safe distance as Rafe slipped into his smooth public persona, the ultimate wolf in sheep's clothing.

The reporter explained Rafe's presence at the resort before getting to the point of the interview. "And you actually spoke to Emily shortly before she disappeared, didn't you?" she asked, thrusting the microphone under Rafe's nose.

Rafe nodded solemnly. "That's right, Vicky. As you said, the young lady was at The Aerie where our cast and crew had met for drinks. She and her friend introduced themselves to me, and we talked for a few minutes. She seemed like a very nice girl. I hope this is all a false alarm and the police find her soon."

The reporter leaned closer, oozing concern. "We all feel the same, but the police seem quite concerned. I understand you were able to give them some information about Emily?"

"I merely confirmed that Emily was there. So did a few other members of the crew. I'm afraid none of us saw her leave."

Maggie shivered at the familiar story. Somehow Rafe was always around when the missing women had slipped out, unnoticed.

Vicky pulled her microphone back for a quick question. "Are you aware that the police are looking into the possibility that Emily's disappearance might be connected to the disappearance of two other women from this area?"

Rafe looked stunned. "Are you kidding? This has happened before?" To Maggie it looked like overacting, but she imagined the viewers would eat up the drama.

"That's what a source within the police department tells us," Vicky assured him.

"Well, no offense, but I hope your source is wrong, Vicky. I would hate to think something like that could happen here. People around here call this God's country." Rafe's brow wrinkled as he pondered the painful reality that violence might have touched his heavenly hideaway. Shaking his head sadly, he went on, "This has always been such a safe town. My family has a home here, you know. It's appalling to think someone might be preying on innocent young women here in B-Pass."

Using the local shorthand for Barringer's Pass was a nice, homey touch, Maggie had to admit, even if he had protested a bit too much for comfort. Or maybe she was the only one uncomfortable with Rafe talking about the possibility of a serial killer in the area. Vicky was certainly sucked in by his deep concern for the women of Barringer's Pass.

"I'm sure everyone agrees with that sentiment, Rafe. Can you tell us anything else about Emily, anything she might have said that would indicate what she planned to do the rest of the evening, or who she was with?"

He shook his head sadly. "I'm afraid not. We only talked for a couple minutes. But hopefully her girlfriend will be able to help the police figure out where she went."

Two girls, at least one of whom had talked with Rafe at The Aerie—Maggie felt a chill slide across her shoulders. Had Amber come that close to becoming Rafe's next victim?

"Our information is that the girlfriend has disappeared and might also be missing, and that the police are trying to learn her identity. I imagine if you gave them a description, it would be very helpful."

Rafe hesitated as if this might be classified information. "Actually, I gave them her name. I'm not at liberty to tell you why, but I have reason to believe she's staying in this area."

Vicky nearly vibrated with excitement at this scoop. "You gave them her name? Rafe, you seem to have been an enormous help to the police in this investigation!"

"I don't know about that," he said, his humility lacking only some aw-shucks toe scuffing. "Anyone would have done the same. I just hope it helps them find Emily."

"I know America agrees with you, Rafe."

Rafe looked over his shoulder as if someone had called his name, turning back with the mildly preoccupied expression of a person whose time was in great demand. "I'm sorry, I have to go now."

"We understand, Rafe. Thank you so much for talking with us!" As Rafe turned away, she addressed the camera. "That was Rafe De Luca, one of—or perhaps I should say *the* star of *Trust Fund Brats,* talking with us about his possibly pivotal role in the search for the missing Emily Renee Banks."

Cal tugged on Maggie's hand, jerking her out of her stunned trance. "We have to find your sister. I need to know for sure."

She knew what he meant—he needed to see a photo of Emily Banks, needed to know if she was the blonde who'd been standing beside Amber at The Aerie, flirting with Rafe. He needed to know if Rafe had targeted Emily simply because he realized he'd missed his chance to truly hurt them by taking Amber.

She trotted to keep up as Cal strode past the lobby fountain and set a straight course toward the offices behind the reception desk, skirting clusters of guests who talked while keeping an eye on the activity outside.

Maggie felt an ache in her heart in anticipation of what she feared he would learn. He wouldn't take it well. He already felt responsible for not being there when Julie needed help. If another girl had died simply because of a connection to Cal, it would devastate him. She wanted to reassure him that Emily's disappearance was not his fault—not *their* fault—but didn't know how. In a horrifying way, it might be.

"Maggie! Cal!"

They turned to see Zoe waving at them from the concierge desk, where she appeared to be giving hasty instructions to a young man. They changed course and met her as she came around the desk.

Maggie barely had time to take in her sister's harried look before Cal demanded, "Do you have a picture of her? The missing girl?"

Zoe nodded. "The police gave out this picture from

her driver's license," she said, reaching over the concierge desk to grab a sheet of paper. "It's not a great photo. They're trying to get something better from her family."

Cal snatched the paper. Maggie moved closer so she could see, too, studying the girl's long blond hair and heart-shaped face for something familiar. They'd seen her only from the side, so she had to imagine the face in profile, picture the way the girl's small nose would turn up at the end and her crooked eyetooth would stand out in an otherwise perfect smile.

Maggie felt suddenly light-headed. Emily Banks was unmistakably the girl who'd been with Amber.

"Son of a bitch," Cal growled between clenched teeth.

Zoe stared, taking the paper from his unresisting fingers. "What's wrong?"

"Amber was with that girl at The Aerie the night before last," Maggie told her, fighting to keep her voice from trembling. "They were both flirting with Rafe. He was furious when he saw Amber leave with us. He might have even figured out she's Cal's sister—his lawyers are thorough."

Zoe looked from Cal's stiff expression back to Maggie. "You think he might have taken Emily just because he missed his chance to get Amber?"

"And because a girl's life means nothing to that depraved bastard." Cal looked at Maggie. "I didn't want to believe it, but he might have progressed to intentional killing."

Zoe's worried gaze fastened on him. "I thought you said he killed on impulse."

"He does. It's not that different. Even for serial

killers, murder is an impulse they can't control. They have to do it, and it's often related to sexual gratification. We know that's true with Rafe—it probably happens during sex. Maybe the first death was an accident, I don't know. But if it enhanced the sexual experience for him, he'd re-create it. And once he kills deliberately and likes it, he'd begin choosing his victims."

Maggie flashed back to the attack on her porch, when the man had simulated cutting her throat. The motion had been intimate, like a caress. He liked the idea, *wanted* to do it. She shivered.

Zoe didn't look convinced. "But he knows you suspect him of murder, and he knows killing another girl will attract police attention. He seems too smart and controlled to do that."

Cal shook his head. "Part of the thrill for serial killers is in fooling the police." He looked distant, almost as if he were talking to himself. Convincing himself. "They're arrogant. Huge egos, even though they might have few real talents outside of killing."

"Rafe's ego does tend to get in the way," Maggie said dryly. "His lawyer tries to keep it in check."

He nodded, then turned to her. "You've seen him lose his temper, Maggie, so tell me—are his lawyer's warnings enough to keep him under control when Jameson isn't around?"

Recalling her recent meeting with Rafe in the back room of Fortune's Folly was enough to give her chills. "The last time I saw Rafe he backed me against some crates. I think if Parker Jameson hadn't been there, he would have gotten physical. There was this wildness in his eyes, like pure hatred. . . ." She swallowed. "No.

If Jameson weren't around, I don't think Rafe would stop himself."

"So maybe he's crossed a line and taken it to another level of killing."

"He also pulled Amber into it," she reminded him. "Deliberately."

New concern wrinkled Zoe's brow. "What did Rafe say about Amber? Where is she?"

"Rafe just gave an interview outside," Maggie told her. "He said he knows the name of the girl who'd been with Emily at The Aerie. The police will want to question her."

"That little prick," Zoe said. "Is she someplace safe?"

Cal's face darkened. "Yeah, but Rafe might try to find out where she is, have one of his goons follow the police when they go to question her."

"She's with Mom," Maggie supplied.

"You took her . . ." Zoe glanced furtively around and lowered her voice. "She's at the commune?" Maggie nodded and watched Zoe's surprise turn thoughtful. "That might be good." She thought some more. "That might be brilliant. It's nearly impossible for someone to sneak into that compound, what with the dogs and so many people being around."

"As long as Amber doesn't find a way to leave."

"How could she?"

Maggie didn't know, but as much as she wanted to agree with Zoe, she wouldn't underestimate Amber—if anyone could find a way out, she would.

Zoe's gaze snagged on a man across the lobby and she straightened, smoothing back her hair. "That's my boss. Gotta go. I got him out of bed and he's not going to be happy about that, but I think he'd rather know about this now than tomorrow morning." She hurried off.

"What now?" Maggie looked at Cal. "Back to my place?"

For the first time since they'd arrived, his expression softened into a smile. "That sounds nice." He stroked a hand down her cheek, sending shivers skittering down her back. "But I think we should call Rick before we leave. I want to hear how this media blitzkrieg started." Interest sparked in his eyes. "Then back to your place."

That couldn't happen soon enough.

They met Rick at a secluded seating area near the darkened entrance to the Alpine Sky's exclusive spa. The dim lighting almost felt romantic, which Maggie thought just proved that she needed more time alone with Cal.

Rick did his best to ruin the mood, recapping the evening with his usual level of excitement when talking about Rafe De Luca. "Filming wrapped early today and Rafe was here since late afternoon. So were most of the cast and crew. I was hanging near the rest of the reporters who tail Rafe—blending in, you know? And I started noticing that some were getting messages on their phones, then cutting out. So I followed to see what was up. That's when I saw the police cars out front."

"What time was that?" Cal asked.

"About six? Maybe seven. I didn't see the cops for a while because they were back in the manager's office. They kept calling employees back to talk with them, then we'd grab 'em on their way out and ask what was going on. We finally figured out that some girl was missing and this was the last place she'd been seen."

Cal raised an eyebrow at Maggie. "I think maybe Sergeant Todd was paying attention when I told him about those other girls. They're already looking at the possibility of a pattern."

"The paparazzi would leave Rafe for a missing girl?"

"When he was the last one who saw her? You bet. Pretty soon the news stations started rolling in here, and before you know it the cops are questioning the *Trust Fund Brats* people, including Rafe. I did, too. All the reporters—they talked to anyone who'd been here the night before. And you saw the rest, I guess, because I saw you both outside when Rafe was doing his Good Samaritan bit for the cameras. I stuck with him, but he grabbed one of the girls from the show and went up to his room. I'm thinking he won't be down again tonight."

"But what about two nights ago?" Maggie asked. "You were here. Didn't you see him leave with Emily Banks?"

Even in the subdued lighting, she saw a blush creep up his neck. "I was distracted for a few minutes, and when I looked for him, he was gone. I don't know if she was, too, because I wasn't watching her." He gave Cal a sheepish look. "I'm really sorry. I know that was exactly the moment I've been waiting for, and I totally blew it."

Cal didn't look nearly as upset as Rick. "What distracted you?"

"An argument. Some girl started screaming that this guy tore her top. Someone sure did, because her boob was practically hanging completely out. It was, you know . . ." He shot Maggie an embarrassed grin. "Big. The guy was denying the whole thing. Got pretty noisy and aggressive about it, too. And the girl was so pissed she was gesturing all over and just barely hanging on to her ripped top, and, well, it kinda drew everyone's attention."

Cal nodded. "Who was the guy?"

"How should I know?"

"One of Rafe's bodyguards?"

Rick paused, brow furrowed. "I don't know. Yeah, maybe."

"How about the girl?"

"I heard she worked with the show's catering company." Realization finally hit. "You think that was a setup? A distraction so Rafe could slip out with some girl?"

"Yeah, I do."

"Damn. That was a good one."

It *was* good, which Maggie found very disturbing. Rafe was always a step ahead of them, experienced both at drawing media attention as he had tonight, and avoiding it when he slipped off with a girl. The scary part was that a notorious womanizer shouldn't need to slip away unnoticed . . . unless, as Cal suggested, he was killing no longer on impulse but with deliberate forethought. She didn't feel better having that theory confirmed.

Rick shook his head, looking disgusted with himself. "Christ, I hate falling for the De Lucas' tricks. I swear I'm going to get that bastard." He stood. "But I'm done for tonight. I'll catch up with you both tomorrow."

They watched him walk away. Maggie turned to Cal hopefully. "Home?"

He smiled. As he opened his mouth to answer, his phone rang. He pulled it out of his pocket and read the caller ID. When he looked up his smile had been replaced with a look of resignation. "The Barringer's Pass police. I think they have questions for me that won't wait until morning."

She sighed. "We're going to be up all night, aren't we?"

Chapter Thirteen

Cal called the Barringer's Pass police and told them where to find his sister. He saw Maggie make a brief call at the same time, and when he hung up, he asked, "Who'd you call?"

"My mom. Feather doesn't like to be around if the police stop by. I think there's an old warrant . . ." She slapped her hand over her mouth. "Woops. You didn't hear that."

Cal grinned. "It's probably expired by now."

"Maybe. But she'll feel better if we give her time to disappear before they get there." She stood. "Come on, let's get going."

He got slowly to his feet. "Um, Maggie, I know you want to go home . . . "

She laughed softly. "We're going to the commune. You need to be there when they question Amber."

He pulled her close and kissed her forehead. "Thanks."

•   •   •

A police car was already there when they pulled up, and thankfully, no media vans were with it. Sergeant Kyle Todd sat in the living room, his big body looking out of place on a delicate bentwood rocker. Cal wasn't surprised to see him; the man had good cop instincts. He had a new ally in his investigation of Rafe De Luca.

The hugs they got were more restrained this time, the faces concerned. Todd had obviously told them about the search for Emily Banks. Cal looked around the room, recognizing the eleven people he'd met on his first visit. Even in the middle of the night, the commune had gathered in support of their guest—everyone except Feather. He smiled.

Cal stood by silently as Amber answered Sergeant Todd's questions. Yes, she'd met Emily at The Aerie. They'd talked in the bathroom, then gone out to the bar. Yes, they'd both talked to Rafe. No, they hadn't talked about going anyplace with him—she'd left before that ever came up. Cal got a dirty look. And no, Emily had not mentioned where she intended to go later, or with whom.

He didn't care that Amber was still resentful about him getting her kicked out of The Aerie. His only concern was with how she would handle Emily's disappearance and the realization that she might have come close to being the next victim. He wanted to assure her that she was safe at the commune, and that the police wouldn't let the press know where she was.

He didn't have to worry. She set him straight about that as soon as Todd left.

"I'm not an idiot, you know." She sat on the living room couch after everyone else had gone, giving him a look that was both composed and condescending. "And I'm not a child. You don't have to warn me about strangers offering candy."

"No, you're not a child. Neither was Emily—she was twenty-one."

"Yeah. I hate to tell you, but Emily was a real noob."

"A what?"

"You know, a newbie? Naive? She probably could have used that stranger-danger info."

"Amber . . ."

"I know how to take care of myself, Cal. I was doing it for almost seventeen years before I got dumped on you, and I'll do it again when I go back to L.A."

He didn't try to tell her that Julie had felt the same way, because he hadn't really known Julie. Maybe she hadn't been as hardened by life as Amber seemed to be. And it was true that once she went back to L.A., she'd be on her own. He studied her determined expression. "So how are you doing here? You haven't expired from boredom yet."

She shrugged, looking suddenly more vague. "They keep me too busy to get bored."

"Milk any goats yet?"

She narrowed her eyes. "I don't do goats."

She hadn't pierced her lip yet, either, and he decided not to mention it. "Make any jewelry?"

She hesitated. "Not yet. I'm still learning the techniques." He saw a second of self-consciousness before annoyance flashed in her eyes. "This isn't summer camp, you know. They don't just thread beads on a string. Jewelry's an art."

He bit back a smile. "So I guess you'll be okay for another three days."

"I can manage."

"Okay." He stood. "I'll just take Maggie home, then. It's late, and we're keeping you all up."

Amber stood, too, jamming her hands in the pockets of her jeans. "Nah, they stay up late here. Header plays a mean guitar, and Ron and Marcy play, too. They do these old rock songs. That's what we were doing before you got here. It's kinda, I don't know, fun."

"Header?"

"That's Paul. Header's his nickname."

"Oh."

Before he could look too pleased with the changes in Amber and ruin the whole thing, he went off to find Maggie. He was already looking forward to coming back in three days.

The beauty of being on leave was that he could set his own hours. And if he wanted to spend an extra hour in bed with a woman who could set him on fire with just one heavy-lidded glance, he would. When that woman also had a flexible schedule because half her store had been destroyed by a truck, they could make it two hours. It was a pretty good way to start a day.

Life seemed almost normal now that they could walk out of Maggie's house without encountering the media hordes who'd abandoned them in favor of the parking lot at the resort. Maybe it was a journalistic tenet—celebrity plus abduction trumped celebrity and bad girl.

While Maggie drove into town undisturbed, Cal met Sergeant Kyle Todd at the police station.

Todd had cleared it with his chief, calling Cal an outside consultant. Cal didn't care what they called him. All that mattered was that he now had access to information he couldn't get on his own, information that came only as a result of police questioning. Like which employees at the De Luca estate might have seen Rafe the night Emily Banks disappeared, and whether he was accompanied by a blond girl.

Cal met Todd at his desk, pulling up an extra chair. Todd was already going through the case file. "What did you find out?" Cal asked eagerly.

Todd tossed a sheaf of papers down in disgust. "Nada. No one saw Rafe that night."

He didn't want to believe it. Rafe had to have taken Emily someplace where he wouldn't be seen by paparazzi, reporters, or fans. A remote road or vacant building was risky when he might be recognized coming or going. The estate was the only safe place. "His family could be covering for him."

"Maybe. Harrison—that's the cop who questioned the employees—said there were two live-in housekeepers. They have more when the De Lucas are in town, but the parents are in Switzerland now. So it's just these two women and one of the beefy De Luca guards living in the house. Two other guards stick with Rafe these days, but they stayed at the Alpine Sky that night. Verified by the hotel."

"Shit," Cal muttered. "So we've got nothing?"

"Not quite." Todd pulled out a typed report. "The three De Luca employees never saw Rafe that night, but someone saw his car. A kid, eighteen, lives with his parents just down the road from the De Lucas' place, last house before their private drive. He and his girlfriend saw Rafe's car go by about one thirty in the morning." Todd raised an amused eyebrow. "Parents weren't home. The kids say they were watching TV."

"Great. So while two teenagers are screwing their brains out on the living room sofa, they happen to see Rafe's car? On a dark mountain road with no lights?"

"Actually, they were in the kid's upstairs bedroom. Harrison says he's got a fifty-two-inch flatscreen on the wall. More important, he's got a big balcony that overlooks the front of the property and the road. The only vehicles passing their house are the ones going to the De Luca estate. The kid says he had the French doors open and heard the car coming before he saw it."

"Open doors sounds a bit fishy. It's still hitting the freezing mark here at night."

Todd shrugged, smiling. "Gotta air the place out when you're smoking weed in your bedroom."

"Ah. Good point."

"Anyway, he hears this engine roar, says he recognizes it as Rafe's car, and pulls his girlfriend out on the balcony to see it go by. Says there was enough moonlight to recognize it."

Damn, just when he'd thought it sounded promising. "Hell, that could be anyone. He couldn't even be sure it was Rafe's car."

"Ever see Rafe's ride?"

"He's always in a limo, with a driver."

"That's what the studio provides. But sometimes he goes off in his own car. He drives a bright yellow Lamborghini. V-10, 530 horsepower."

Cal smiled as he got it. "Loud?"

"Nothing like it. And fast. Asshole's gonna kill himself on these roads someday."

From the mild tone, Cal gathered that no one in the Barringer's Pass PD would much care. "Does anyone else drive it?"

"Not as far as we know."

"So we've got Rafe driving to the family estate about one thirty a.m., maybe looking for a little private time with Emily Banks. Could he get into the house without the guard or the maids knowing?"

"That's what Harrison wondered. 'Course, if we assume the neighbor kid recognized the car when he was most likely stoned and more than a little preoccupied with the girlfriend, we have to assume the household staff would also hear the car pull up."

"Right." He frowned, thinking. "Where else could he go? Are there any other buildings, maybe a guesthouse?"

"No, but there's a pole barn where they store their snowplow. Not the most romantic location, but if your idea about him advancing to deliberate kills is right, it wouldn't matter. Not being seen would be his priority."

"And he wouldn't drive by the house to get there?"

In answer, Todd got to his feet. "Let me show you."

Cal followed him to a small conference room that was nearly filled by a long table and ten chairs. They walked around the table to a large map tacked to the far wall. It looked like a satellite image with the town of Barringer's Pass at its center. Slightly above the town to the north and west, large swaths of bare ground marked ski slopes. In the winter they would stand out like wide, white roads. In the summer view, they were broad gashes in the forested slopes.

"Here's the De Luca property." Todd drew a small circle with his finger on Two Bears Mountain. The area sat on a fold in the mountain where rocky promontories jutted out, no doubt providing spectacular views of the ski resorts on both Two Bears and neighboring Tappit's Peak, and the town in the valley between them. "This thin line is the private drive to the house. The barn is off to the left, here." His finger pointed to a dark square just off the drive before the house.

Cal examined the property, trying to envision Rafe driving there at night with a very willing Emily Banks. She probably wouldn't protest even if he drove to the pole barn instead of the house. She'd been coming on to Rafe hot and heavy.

He hadn't wanted to believe that Rafe would move from impulse killing to deliberate murder, but every piece of evidence pointed toward it. Motive, opportunity, means—Rafe had them all. He had to operate on the assumption that he'd done it. He didn't know how far Rafe would take it, if he'd kill her outright or have sex with her first. Either way, the barn was private, a definite possibility.

"You search it yet?"

"Getting the warrant as we speak."

Cal nodded, envisioning his scenario. Rafe would have to dispose of Emily's body. He squinted at the featureless mountainside, wondering if the one-dimensional image hid ravines where someone could dump a body, and where animals would soon scavenge it to an unrecognizable pile of bones. He pointed to a small black shadow on an otherwise bare spot of ground. "What's that, another building?"

Todd shook his head. "It's just an old mine entrance. They're all over the place. Used to be silver mines in this area until they all played out about eighty years go. Mostly, they're boarded up. A few are open for tourists."

A mine could hide a body, especially if it was on private land. "Has anyone been inside it?"

"On what grounds? The De Lucas aren't about to let cops go tramping all over their land, looking for bodies. Maybe if we find something in the barn."

He was already looking for other dark spots that might indicate a mine. Unfortunately, the angle of the satellite image made the property to the north look foreshortened, and he couldn't see details on the wooded slope. He tapped the spot. "Who owns this land?"

Todd peered at the map. "Let's see . . ." He mumbled road names as his finger traced the route to the land on the other side of the promontory. After a few seconds, he snorted out a laugh. "That's the commune where your sister is staying. Kind of a neat place if you're there in the daylight. You ever see it?"

"What I've seen is their old silver mine. It's right in those trees on the other side of the De Luca land. Maggie and I explored their mine. There's another entrance to it that we never saw. It just might be on De Luca land." Sergeant Todd gave him a quick look. Cal said thoughtfully, "I think I might explore that mine again, maybe see if I can find the other entrance."

Todd looked thoughtful. "If you came out a different way, you wouldn't even know whose land you were on."

"Right. I'd have to look around a bit, see if I could find my way back to the commune."

"That's right. When do you think you might do that?"

He did a mental inventory. "Tomorrow, soonest. I need to get supplies first—ropes, lights, and maybe even pitons and a hammer. There's a shaft I have to go down, with water at the bottom. A small inflatable raft, too, since I don't know how deep it is."

"Expensive."

And his credit card had already taken a beating. But he had money he hadn't touched, money that felt tainted somehow, since it came from Diane's life insurance policies. He hadn't been able to bring himself to profit from her death by buying a new house, but it had felt okay to live off part of it while he took a leave from work to look for his sister's killer. And it felt okay to use more of it to spy on Rafe De Luca.

"I can manage," he told Todd. "Think I can find those supplies around here?"

"Hell yeah, no problem. B-Pass gets lot of climbers in the summer. But I don't want you poking around De Luca land without letting me know first. Someone has to cover your ass."

"It's not De Luca land," he reminded Todd. "We don't know whose land is on the other end of that mine." He smiled at Todd's narrowed eyes and gave him a friendly slap on the arm. "I'll let you know before I go. First I have to get Maggie to arrange for us to visit the commune."

Maggie stood under a mounted moose head in the hunting section of High Country Outfitters, talking into her phone. "I'm doing great," she assured Zoe. "I don't need a shopping trip to cheer me up, but thanks for asking."

She watched Cal as she talked. He was across the aisle selecting climbing and caving equipment. He seemed to know what he was doing.

"How about dinner?" Zoe persisted. "I can make that chicken teriyaki dish you like so much."

"No, thanks, really."

"Come on, we should do *something*. You want to catch a movie?"

"Not tonight." She had other things in mind that were far more fun than a movie. Unless Cal was interested in watching something a little racy . . .

"What's going on?" Zoe sounded suspicious. "Are you and Cal stalking Rafe tonight?"

"No. Cal's working with the police, and I'm not doing anything." That she wanted to talk about. She watched Cal try on some gloves and wondered how he'd look in a bathtub full of bubbles, and if he'd sit still for it. Probably, if she was in it with him.

Zoe was silent for a few seconds. "Why don't you sound tired and depressed?"

Maggie thought she must have lost the thread of the conversation. "Why should I sound tired and depressed?"

"Didn't you just spend the whole day in your demolished store talking with contractors and claims adjusters?"

"And suppliers. I have a lot of orders coming in still."

"So why do you sound as relaxed as if you're on a beach in Jamaica?"

"Do I?"

"Yes, you do."

"I guess it's because I have everything under control."

"Uh-huh." Zoe had gone from suspicious to decisive. "Or maybe it's because you've been working out all your tensions in the bedroom."

Maggie wasn't sure if she should deny it, and she couldn't even pretend to be outraged. "Why does everyone think we're sleeping together?"

"Because you are."

"Yeah, but they thought so before we actually were."

Zoe didn't respond for several seconds, and the silence cracked with tension. "I thought you were trying to be more selective about who you went to bed with."

"I am." It came out sounding defensive, but she didn't like the thought of Cal being lumped in with her past mistakes.

"Do you even know much about Cal?"

"I know his half sister, and I know how he rejected his irresponsible mother."

"I mean romantically? Does he have a girlfriend back in Oklahoma? A fiancée? A wife?"

Maggie wanted to say, "Of course not," but she didn't really know. A wife? He didn't wear a ring, but he wouldn't be the first man to take it off when he left the house.

Her silence was enough for Zoe. "Maybe you should find out," her sister said quietly.

She had to come up with some defense. "He would have told me. He's a good guy, Zoe." She glanced at the good guy in question, who held up a pair of boots much too small for him as he waved her over.

"I hope so, sweetie, I really do."

"I have to go, Zoe. Talk to you later." She pocketed the phone and smiled at Cal as she walked over to him, loving the way she could see both affection and desire in his eyes when he looked at her. There wasn't a wife back home, she was sure of it. Not even a girl-friend. Cal was better than that.

Right. And she had a history of flawless decisions about men.

She would find the right time, and ask.

They didn't leave for the commune until nearly noon the next day. Maggie liked waking up with Cal too much to rush out of bed. It should have been the per-fect time to ask him some personal questions, but it had turned into a giggling, crazy tangle of arms and legs and constantly changing positions that left her ex-hausted and happy. Too happy to let doubts about his marital status and general availability intrude.

The drive to the commune almost had a feel of ad-venture, with all the caving supplies loaded in the back of the truck and a warm breeze sucking away the last crusty patches of snow. The truck wound up fifteen hundred feet of switchback roads with high granite cliffs pressing in on one side and sheer drop-offs on the other. Dense growths of spruce clung to the steep sides, filling the air with the scent of pine. Cal rolled down the windows and gaped like a tourist.

They parked amid the commune's usual pack of barking dogs. After taking a few minutes to pass out pats and ear scratches, Cal dropped the tailgate and hauled out their large backpacks. Maggie tied her jacket around her waist before strapping her pack on.

She'd need the jacket in the mine, but it was too hot to wear it now.

Her mother found them just as they were ready to start their hike to the mine.

"Cal! How lovely to see you again!" She hugged them as well as she could with the supplies on their backs, then turned a stern look on her daughter. "Maggie May, were you going to go off without saying hello?"

"I didn't want to disturb your work. I'll stop by when we get back from the mine. I'm sure Pete will want to know where that other tunnel goes."

"Good. If you see Amber, would you tell her Marcy picked up the supplies we were waiting for and we can do her piercing now?"

Maggie gave a cautious nod, expecting Cal to make another attempt to veto the piercing, thereby incurring a lecture on free expression and a young woman's right to decide what to do with her own body. But Cal's thoughts had taken another direction.

"Amber's not here?"

"Oh, she should be back any minute now. She went for a hike."

"A hike? Amber?"

"Um-hmm." Kate nodded and repositioned a purple flower in her hair as she talked. "We were talking about the mine and how you thought it might connect to our neighbor's land, and she said she wanted to see it." Realization dawned, and she touched Cal's arm. "Oh! You're worried about her going inside the mine? No, no, don't worry. Pete warned her about not going in there alone, and she promised she wouldn't."

"And you believed her?" Cal obviously didn't.

"She promised," Kate stressed. "Amber wouldn't lie to us."

Cal raised a skeptical eyebrow. "She wouldn't mind bending the truth till it screamed."

Maggie grabbed a coiled nylon rope and shoved it at Cal, pushing him toward the path up the mountain. "We'll give her the message, Mom." She gave Cal another push, but he was already moving.

Kate waved. "I'm sure you'll run into her soon."

Maggie skipped to catch up with Cal. "Maybe Amber's starting to like the mountains," she said. "She might be looking for spring flowers. Communing with nature."

"Do you believe that?"

"I'd like to, but . . . no."

"She's up to something, and I'm afraid it has to do with sneaking onto De Luca land."

"To do what?"

He set his mouth in a grim line. "I'm afraid to guess."

They made the hike quickly. There was no sign of Amber along the trail, but the boards covering the mine entrance didn't appear to have been moved.

"You think she'd close it up behind her?" Maggie asked doubtfully as Cal pulled boards aside.

"I don't know. If she didn't want anyone to find out where she'd gone, then yes, she probably would."

"But she's smart enough to know it would be dangerous to go inside alone."

"That didn't stop you."

She didn't have an answer to that. Even after she'd moved to her grandmother's house, she'd spent every summer at the commune. They were all her family. But communal living could be overwhelming, and sometimes she'd needed to get away, to go off on her own.

She guessed Amber was like that, too. She probably would have gone in the mine alone.

Their mission to follow the new shaft suddenly had a more serious overtone. Wordlessly, they slipped out of the backpacks, put on jackets, gloves, and headlamps, then repositioned the packs. Pulling out two Maglites, they ducked under the boards and turned on the flashlights. Twin beams cut through the black maw of the mine, adding to the slightly weaker lights atop their heads. All of them faded quickly as the inky blackness swallowed them. Maggie aimed her light briefly at the floor, but the hard-packed dirt and rock held no footprints.

Cal didn't hesitate. He started down the tunnel.

They walked with surer steps this time, reaching the star cavern quickly. This time they didn't shine their lights at the ceiling, but headed straight for the other side. Maggie couldn't suppress a quick rush of heat remembering what had happened the first time they were here, but the feeling disappeared quickly. Uncertainty about Amber made any thought of romance impossible.

Ahead of her, Cal found the boarded-over hole. Maggie shrugged out of her pack as she approached and shone her light on the boards, half afraid of what she'd see.

They looked undisturbed. No rope dangled into the gap on the far side where Amber might have managed to slide through. "I don't think she's been here," she said with relief.

Cal was already pulling a hand pump out of his

backpack, but he paused to look at Maggie in the shadowy gloom. "Unless she fell through the gap. Or her rope came untied and dropped in after her."

Maybe it came with being a cop—he always thought of the worst possible scenarios. She shuffled closer to the gap and aimed her light straight down. Dark walls became slightly wider as they fell away into a deeper darkness. At the bottom water glistened faintly, black and smooth. There was no sign of Amber or a rope—which meant nothing, she reminded herself. If they'd fallen through they would have been swallowed by the water.

Rubber slid against the mine floor with a soft rustling sound. Ten feet away Cal opened the inflatable kayak. If its air pump worked as advertised, it wouldn't take long to inflate the narrow craft. She'd better get busy.

She found the weighted measuring line in her backpack and squatted near the hole, letting the line play out. She allowed it to fall quickly at first, then more slowly, listening for the sound of a splash. A possible soft sound was drowned by the rhythmic click and hiss of the air pump.

"Cal." Her voice was hollow in the empty mine shaft, but it carried well. He was only a shadow in the perimeter of the Maglite's beam so she couldn't tell if he looked at her, but he stopped pumping. "Stop for a second," she said, pulling the line back and letting it fall again. This time she heard the splash clearly. She shone her flashlight directly on the part of the line she held, leaning close to see the numbers. "Twenty-seven feet," she said.

"Good." He resumed pumping.

She recoiled the line and put it away, pulling out the rolled rope ladder. They'd selected the longest one in the store, thirty-three feet. It would work.

A few minutes of searching with her flashlight revealed what she wanted on the low ceiling—anchored iron rings used for raising and lowering men and supplies to the tunnel below. She played her light around. The rings looked rusty, but the ceiling was dry. "You were right," she called out. "Four rings. Huge ones."

Cal came over, dragging the kayak behind him. "We'll use them all. One could come loose, and I don't want to take any unnecessary risks."

What they were doing was risky enough.

Cal wove a rope through every ring and tested its strength. Nothing moved but a few flakes of rust that drifted into the hole. He attached the ladder and turned to her. "I'd feel better if you stayed up here."

They'd already covered this. "I know you would," she told him gently. "But that's not going to happen."

He made a resigned sound and didn't argue. She wasn't about to stay behind in a dark mine tunnel, staring into a black pit, wondering if Cal was okay. Or even knowing he was but not being able to see what was happening. She was going with him.

With a rope on one end of the kayak, it lowered easily through the hole, landing softly on the still water below. With the other end of the rope tied near the Maglite on his belt, Cal let the ladder unroll over the edge of the hole. It hung centered from the ropes, and easy to reach. He grabbed it and started to step onto one of the thin rungs.

"Wait!"

He stopped. "What?"

She gave him a quick kiss.

"For luck?" he asked, a smile obvious in his voice.

"I guess so. It just seemed necessary."

"It's always necessary," he said. He kissed her back, longer this time, then stepped over the edge.

The ropes above groaned as they stretched. They held, as did the anchor bolts. He descended slowly, then took his time stepping into the kayak as she provided what little light she could from above. He sat down as he steadied the bottom of the ladder and shone his light up its length. "Ready."

Maggie took a deep breath. Don't look down, she told herself. She grabbed the rope ladder and stepped gingerly onto the metal rung. The whole thing wobbled, tilting her slightly backward. Her stomach wobbled and tilted with it. For several seconds she clung to the ladder, waiting for her heart to stop racing. When both her pulse and her stomach felt steady, she took a careful step down. Then another. She tilted backward a bit more. The lower she got, the more her feet tried to angle toward the wall, dipping her back toward the water. She knew it had to have been worse for Cal, with no one to hold the other end of the ladder.

Each step felt shakier than the last, but there was no way she'd turn back. Going with Cal, no matter how uncertain the footing, was preferable to staying behind alone.

Barely more than a minute later, she felt his hand take her ankle in a secure hold. She finished the descent with Cal guiding her to the flat surface of the kayak. It moved beneath her feet but felt more secure than hanging in the cold, damp air of the shaft. Her flashlight pointed down, pooling on the red rubber bottom of the kayak and reflecting enough to show her the seat behind her. She settled in, feeling safe and snug in the fourteen inches of interior space between the tubular sides.

"You okay?" His voice was low, almost a whisper, but still echoed softly off the walls.

"Fine." She spoke just as softly, as if someone might hear them in this damp, smelly cavern. The smell wasn't overpowering, but was unpleasant enough to keep her breaths shallow. "What's that odor?"

"The water, I guess. Minerals. I wouldn't want to drink it."

Cal's flashlight began roaming the walls, and she grabbed hers to do the same. The walls were closer than she'd imagined, making the pool no more than thirty feet in diameter at the spot below their dangling ladder, and tapering gradually as it spread away from them. Shining the light directly at the water, she saw nothing but black water and the tiny ripples created by the slight rocking of the kayak.

"How deep do you think it is?" she whispered.

"No idea. Do you still have that measuring line?"

"Crap. No."

He pulled the small collapsible paddle free of the duct tape on the floor. She shone her light toward him as he extended the short handle and stuck it over the side. The water swallowed its eighteen inches without a sound. "Could be nineteen inches, could be twenty feet," he said.

If it were nineteen inches, Amber wouldn't have survived a fall into it, and her body would be submerged mere inches below the surface. If it were significantly deeper, she might have been able to swim to the edge.

She didn't say it, knowing Cal would have already concluded the same thing.

He must have felt the same urgency to find out that she did. He dipped the paddle in again, taking one long, shallow stroke that set them drifting to the right, toward the narrow end of the pool. Switching sides, he took another slow stroke. The kayak turned a bit to the left and drifted faster.

Maggie kept her light pointed ahead. About fifty feet away, the glistening surface dulled abruptly where water touched dirt. Beyond it, the cavern narrowed sharply into another black tunnel with more rusted cart rails disappearing into its depths. It was what they'd expected. If their guess was right, De Luca land was on the other end of that tunnel.

Water splashed softly with each stroke of the paddle, the only sound as they crossed the black pool. As they drew closer, Maggie's light fell on what appeared to be scuff marks on the rock at the water's edge. "Look!" she said. "Are those recent?"

"I can't tell." Cal's voice was tight with tension.

She kept the light pointed at the ground as they drew closer. Ten feet away, the kayak suddenly veered to the right between paddle strokes. Maggie looked back at Cal. "What happened?"

His Maglite lay at his feet and his face looked ghostly in the reflected light. "I think we hit something." He took a backward stroke, stopping them.

Maggie hadn't even thought about submerged rocks, and worried suddenly about gouging a hole in the kayak. She had no desire to test the depth of the water by sinking into it. But whatever they'd hit hadn't scraped or punctured the kayak. It had moved them gently to the side. She waved the light slowly over the water.

At first she saw nothing. Then the light caught something white bobbing just under the surface. Cal moved them closer. Whatever it was, it was small, slightly bigger than her hand. They inched even closer, and she suddenly saw why. It *was* a hand, bloated but recognizable. It floated back up, fingers hanging limply in a delicate gesture. Whoever it was attached to lay submerged in the black water below.

Chapter Fourteen

Maggie recoiled, sucking in a sharp breath and nearly dropping the light.

"Christ," Cal swore softly. He dipped the paddle and set them drifting gently forward, bringing him even with the hand. She heard him let out a long, shaky breath.

"It's not Amber."

She wanted to believe him, but he might be in denial. "How do you know?" Her voice sounded as shaky as his, and the chills that shook her had nothing to do with the cold in the mine.

"This body's been in the water too long. A couple days, maybe. Besides, there are no rings. Amber has silver rings on nearly every finger."

Maggie breathed a bit easier, but her heart still pounded. It was someone. "Emily Banks?" she whispered, her voice barely audible even to herself.

Cal nodded. "Maybe." He paused, then soberly amended it to "Probably."

With a sick feeling she recalled the sounds they'd heard two days before, someone talking to himself while creating a small splash in the water. Dumping a body? Checking to see if the dark pool would make a good grave? Shivers ripped through her, making the flashlight beam shake visibly in her trembling hand.

"She didn't wander in here by herself and drown." As obvious as it seemed, she had to hear him confirm it.

"No." He stared at the hand for several seconds, muttering a few more swear words. "Let's get out of here."

The pool had steep sides like the deep end of a swimming pool. They climbed out carefully, then pulled the kayak out and left it.

A day ago Maggie would have hesitated to enter a strange, dark tunnel, not knowing where it would lead. But having seen what lay in the dark water behind her, she didn't hesitate to plunge into the unknown.

They followed the rusted rails, headlamps and flashlights bobbing, neither of them talking. Cal reached for her hand, and the contact warmed more than her fingers. The tunnel was too narrow for her to walk beside him, but he never let go of her as he led the way between the rails.

They almost bumped into the exit. Faint light seeped around the edges of a sheet of plywood that was wedged against the hole. Cal ran his light over the wood from inches away. "New," he said. Proof that at least one person knew about the mine tunnel, and had been there recently.

Shoving the wood aside, they pushed through the branches of a large spruce and stepped into the sunlight. Maggie turned around. The tree only partially shielded the opening, but this side of the plywood had been painted dark gray, allowing it to blend into the shadows. No one would find the tunnel entrance unless they knew where to look.

Cal took out his phone. "No bars."

"Walk out a ways, and off to one side. There are towers all over. The people up here have money and they get cranky if they can't text their bff."

They acquired a signal within minutes, and Cal began thumbing his phone. "Gotta love these things," he said, holding it out so Maggie could see. "That's our latitude and longitude. Call the police on your phone and read it off for them. Tell them we'll wait here."

"We don't even know where we are. It could take hours."

"I have a feeling it won't. If this is De Luca land, they'll just drive through the main gates and head in this direction."

She pulled out her phone, but didn't dial yet. "Cal, what about Amber? Where do you think she is?"

"I don't have any idea. Right now I'm just glad she wasn't in there." He ran a hand through his hair, throwing a look at the mine entrance. "And sorry for whoever is."

It was hardly more than an hour before Kyle Todd found them sitting on the ground, sharing a granola bar.

Cal helped Maggie to her feet and glanced behind Todd. "Just you?"

"Three more, a few minutes back. They had to rustle up a lot of big lights, like you said."

"And the rope, and a tarp . . ."

"Yeah, got it all." He frowned suspiciously at the smooth rock face behind them. "I don't see a mine tunnel."

"Right behind that tree." Cal pointed, then nodded in the direction Todd had come. "What'll we find if we go down that way?"

He gave a short laugh. "One very nervous De Luca security guard. Probably more by now. He was making phone calls when I left him. But I need you both to stay here until we get your statement."

Maggie nodded. "Just give us a lift back to the commune when you're done here. I'm not going back the way I came."

It took forever. Maggie had fallen asleep with her head on Cal's thigh when voices woke her. She blinked at the long shadows that stretched where sunlight had been before, and sat up. Her jacket slid from her shoulders—Cal must have covered her as the temperature dropped. Looking around she saw two police officers start down the mountainside with a large blue tarp slung between them, sagging with the weight of the body from the mine. Kyle Todd followed, then made a detour toward them. They scrambled to their feet, brushing off dirt and pine needles.

She searched his grim expression. "Was it Emily Banks?"

"Yeah." He ran a hand through his hair and gave a heavy sigh. "That's not all. They found some bones while they were probing the bottom. Part of a leg. There's at least one more body in there."

She looked at Cal, knowing they had the same

thought: Rachel Anders or Tara Kolinowski. Or both.

"It's gonna be awhile before we're done up here. We're going to have to pump it out—it's about four feet deep, eight near that shaft you came down. Won't take too long once we get the equipment up here. But it'll be awhile before we get an ID on the bones, and we may never determine cause of death."

Cal clenched his jaw. "Cause of death was Rafe De Luca."

Todd met his eyes with a hard look. "Help me prove it, and I'll owe you big-time."

Cal didn't need incentive. The way he saw it, he'd just pointed a big flashing arrow at Rafe De Luca as a person of interest in the death of Emily Banks, which he hoped would be the beginning of the end for Rafe. The media hordes would have a field day. Rafe would probably be furious. Maybe scared. Cal hoped he was terrified. First, because he was sure Julie had been, and he wanted Rafe to feel as much of that terror as possible. Second, because terrified people often made mistakes.

When Rafe made his mistake, Cal would be there to catch him.

Amber was undoubtedly planning the same thing. The best way to find her—maybe the only way—was to keep Rafe in his sights.

Cal had another incentive to catch Rafe that had taken on more importance than he ever would have thought: Maggie would be free. Free of the "bar bimbo" tag, and free of the paparazzi for good. Rick could spin it for her with the press one last time—she would be the one who got away. They could have one last interview to get her version of events, then disappear from her life forever.

And then . . . what? He could feel better about walking away because her life would be back to normal—or as normal as it was before Rafe De Luca came along and fucked it up. He could leave with a clear conscience.

Except he didn't want to leave. He'd been shoving that realization aside for days now, and he needed to face it. Once Amber went back to Los Angeles he'd be free, too. He hadn't changed his mind about staying away from impulsive women with a reckless disregard for common sense, but he was no longer sure that description fit Maggie. He'd led her through a dangerous descent in the abandoned mine today, and an unnerving discovery. Her reaction had been far from reckless, following every safety precaution and never showing a hint of panic. The perfect partner, calm and sensible.

But Maggie in bed . . . Jesus. Who said reckless impulses didn't have a positive side? That impulsive episode in the star cavern had blown his mind, along with other things. He might have been too quick to judge Maggie Larkin.

He'd have to give it some serious thought. He wondered how big a jerk he was that he could think about sex while his sister was still missing. It wasn't like he trusted Amber to do something sensible. He tensed up just thinking about it.

"Kyle," he called out as they started down the mountain. "My sister's missing. I don't think she's been abducted," he added at the cop's alarmed look. He was going to operate on that assumption for another few hours. "But if you see her I wouldn't mind if you threw her in a cell until I can get there."

They followed the body procession downhill to Kyle Todd's police cruiser. He opened the back door and stood aside like a chauffeur. "Not much room up front with all the electronics we carry," he said in apology.

Cal doubted Maggie was too tired to care that she might look like a suspect in the back of the car. They braced themselves as Todd bumped along a faint track that might have been made by the narrow chassis of an off-road vehicle. The track turned into a dirt drive as they rounded a large outbuilding and came in sight of the big house. Cal's gaze wasn't drawn to the magnificent stone and wood house as much as to the three police cruisers parked in front. One was from B-Pass, the other two were state cops. "You brought the state guys in?"

"We're not big enough to handle this," Todd said. "And I'm not taking any chance that the investigation won't hold up in court when I finally nail this bastard."

Cal couldn't see any activity outside the house. "Are they talking to Rafe?"

"He's not here. He's supposedly at the Alpine Sky. His lawyer claims he's been there for the past several days." Todd's dry tone said he didn't believe it. "I hear the senior De Luca is hustling home from Europe, and he's pretty pissed off about the whole mess." Todd smiled with satisfaction.

"They're going to claim anyone could have snuck onto their land to dump those bodies."

Todd gave a derisive snort.

"Start looking for a money trail from De Luca to

Emily's family. Also the Anders and Kolinowski families. I'm pretty sure he hushed them up once before, and he'll probably try to do it again."

Todd gave a brief nod. "Thanks."

They hit pavement and accelerated through the main gate. Cal put his arm around Maggie—possibly the only couple ever to cuddle in the back of Kyle Todd's police cruiser. She settled against his side as Todd glanced at them in the mirror. "You two cozy enough back there? Need some music?"

"Got any smooth jazz?" he asked.

Todd chuckled. "Will the police radio do?"

It was dusk when he dropped them at the People's Free Earth Commune. They tossed their backpacks in the bed of the pickup and trudged up to the house.

"We look awful," Maggie said.

He glanced down at his clothes, then hers. Their shirts were clean, but the knees and seat of their pants were covered with dirt. He shrugged. "I guess I wouldn't mind washing my hands." And showering with Maggie when they got home. The thought put a little spring back in his lagging steps.

The door opened as they reached the porch. Kate and Feather tried to fill the doorway at the same time, with several heads visible behind them.

"Where is she? Did you find her?" Kate stood on tiptoe, looking past them.

Something cold gripped Cal's gut, and he realized he'd been holding on to one last desperate hope. "Amber didn't come back here?"

Kate met his worried look with one of her own and shook her head.

"We haven't seen Amber since she left on her hike," Feather told them.

Kate stepped out and grabbed Maggie by the arm, ushering her inside, and Cal after her. Everyone backed up to make room but didn't go far. The whole commune seemed to be gathered near the front door.

"Six of us hiked the property," Kate told them. "She's not here."

His fear came out as anger. "God damn it! That kid is so irresponsible! I do everything I can to keep her safe, and she goes running right back into danger. You'd think she'd appreciate the efforts everyone has gone to for her, but no, she just takes off. I can't figure out what in the hell she's thinking."

Wordlessly, Maggie took his hand. He didn't pull away, but it didn't do much to turn down the heat of his anger.

"Cal, she's grieving."

Kate's reasonable voice cut through the red haze in his mind. He frowned, concentrating on her quiet tone. "Amber's been deeply wounded by her sister's death, and she needs to feel she's doing something to avenge it. She's no different than you are, you know. She feels she should have somehow saved Julie, and she's suffering terribly from guilt because she didn't, the same as you."

"I'm not . . . She's . . ." He squeezed his eyes shut while he gathered his thoughts. "Amber has no reason to feel guilty. She couldn't have stopped Julie from seeing Rafe."

"Neither could you, but it hasn't kept you from suffering guilt, or from trying to find her killer to make up for not saving her life."

He stared at Maggie's mother. "She never said anything to me. How do you know that?"

She held her arms out in a large shrug, bracelets jangling. "It's obvious. Amber talks about Julie all the time. She misses her."

Behind Kate, several heads nodded.

Apparently Amber didn't think he was interested in listening, which made him feel like a shit all over again. Julie's death was the one thing they had in common, and he'd never once talked with her about it, thinking that his search for evidence would speak for itself. He should have known a teenage girl would need to talk.

Kate gave him a soothing pat, her nurturing instincts firmly in place. "She's not trying to be irresponsible, Cal—just the opposite. She needs to do something to help. Anything. Just like you."

He let it sink in, knowing she was right. Amber had wanted to help him investigate, and he hadn't let her do even the smallest thing, thinking it was more important to hide her away. If someone had tried to deter his efforts like that, he'd have done the same thing—he'd break away and go off on his own to find Julie's killer. It was exactly what he'd done when he took a leave from work. Why hadn't he seen that Amber needed the same thing? He was making a huge mess of this big-brother role.

He could chastise himself later; right now he needed to find Amber, make sure she didn't step into a situation that might have just reached critical mass. Finding those bodies on De Luca land could send Rafe over the edge. What that might make him do was too alarming to think about.

"Do you have any idea how she could have left? It's too far to walk, and there was no indication that she went through the mine. Is there a vehicle she could take?"

Several heads shook, and Marcy said, "There's only one and it's still here. I have the keys."

"Then how could she have left when she's alone here with no one to drive her anyplace?"

Feather spoke up hesitantly. "Amber did have a visitor this morning, but I know she didn't leave with him."

His skin prickled ominously. "A visitor? Who?"

"A man. I don't remember his name, but Amber knew him. She said he was a friend of yours."

Only one person in Barringer's Pass might qualify in Amber's eyes. "How old?"

Feather shrugged. "Forty?"

Rick. It had to be. "What did he want?" he asked, trying hard not to snap it out. They weren't responsible for Amber. He was.

"To say hi?" Feather gave a helpless shrug. "I didn't hear anything, but Amber said he just dropped by to see how she was." Cal must have looked as agitated as he felt, because she hastened to add, "I watched from the porch while she talked to him out by his car. Didn't take no more than ten minutes, then he waved at me and drove off."

And waited down the road until Amber could get away and meet him. A dismayed glance from Maggie told him she'd realized it, too. It hadn't been so hard for Amber to sneak away from her guardians after all. These people simply didn't have a devious bone in their bodies.

Cal's thoughts spun in a dizzy whirlpool. Had he told Rick where Amber was staying? He didn't think so. Rick could have followed the cops, though. Or followed Cal and Maggie. They both went to the commune last night, and all Cal had been watching for was the media vans. When none turned into the commune behind them, he thought they hadn't been followed.

Damn it, what did Rick want with Amber? He'd done a fairly good job of sticking to Rafe like a burr, but Cal could tell he'd been frustrated with the lack of action. Nothing was happening, and the one time it probably did, when Emily disappeared, Rick had lost track of Rafe.

Maggie squeezed his hand as she turned worried eyes on him. "Cal, remember how Rick wanted to set something up with Rafe, using me as bait? That's almost what he was waiting for when Emily and Amber were at The Aerie. If he decided to try again with Amber, I don't think she'd object."

Neither did he. Worse, they'd had hours to come up with a plan.

He scanned the group of concerned faces watching him. "We'll find her, don't worry. I know where to look." He grabbed Maggie's hand as he turned.

"Wait a minute." She clenched his fingers tightly as she turned to Kate, ensuring he wouldn't leave. "Mom, do you have a skirt I could borrow? I can't go anywhere looking like this." She glanced at him, seeing how well he'd taken it. She must have read his impatience. "Just give it to me, I'll change in the truck."

She trotted back to the truck with him, unbuttoning her long-sleeved shirt on the way. She was down to her white T-shirt by the time she closed the door and slipped out of her cargo pants. He wasn't so worried that he didn't sneak a look at her legs, all the way up to her skimpy underpants; he'd have to be dead before he passed on that opportunity.

She tossed the cargo pants and shirt into the backseat and shook out the skirt Kate had thrust at her. It was long and made of something lacy, the typical feminine style her mother favored. She arched her hips to slide it up, then looked at him. "Where to, the Alpine Sky?"

He forgot about Maggie's legs and skimpy underwear as irritation with Amber and fear for her life slammed back to the forefront. "Right. That's where Rafe always hangs out, and I'm betting he's there now. If he isn't, there will at least be someone from the show to ask. And if they don't know," he added grimly, "I'm calling Kyle Todd. I'm not waiting for Amber to turn up dead."

Maggie figured Cal had reached his limit. If he was ever going to ditch his analytical, rational approach and do something wildly impulsive, this would be the time. She wouldn't blame him. But she might have to stop him from tearing into Rafe for laying his hands on Amber. This time she could be the rational one and keep him from winding up as tabloid headlines, or worse.

She watched his jaw clench and grind as he drove, knowing he was thinking things over, waiting to see what direction his anger would take.

If it were her, she'd be figuring out whether to go after Rafe first, or Rick. Definitely Rafe. Move in fast, slam him against the wall, and punch his lights out.

Then grab Rick from the corner where he would be cowering and give him the same treatment. Very Clint Eastwood, and very satisfying.

Unfortunately, that's what she had to keep him from doing, otherwise Cal would end up in jail and Amber would be the newest tabloid sensation.

If he said something, she could gauge how angry he was. She knew his mind must be working furiously, but he didn't say anything. The tension was killing her. She finally went for the direct approach. "What are you thinking?"

He took his time answering. "I think your mom's pretty smart."

That was unexpected. She answered cautiously, "She is."

"I wish Amber had met her sooner. Or had someone like Kate in her life to be a good influence."

She sighed. "It doesn't always work that way, Cal. I'm the shining example of how a teenage girl can go wrong despite being surrounded by good examples."

"Are you saying nothing could have changed that?"

She thought about the resentment she'd felt toward her mother for choosing a lifestyle that left her kids open to ridicule. The resentment toward her grandmother for taking her away from her mother during the long school year. Hurting them had been part of her reason for sleeping around. Living up to what everyone else assumed was true was the other.

"Nothing would have changed it," she admitted. "Because there are other influences out there. Things you can't control. Being a good parent—or big brother—won't necessarily stop Amber from doing something stupid in response to them. You can't change her basic personality."

"Meaning she'll always be prone to stupid, reckless behavior. Great."

She blinked at his look of weary resignation. Had he even realized what he'd said? "Is that how you think I am?" she asked quietly. "Still prone to stupid, reckless behavior?"

"No, I . . ." He faltered, then stopped, pressing his mouth into a thin line. "A couple things you did weren't very smart, Maggie."

She suddenly felt as tense as he looked. "Maybe."

His lip twitched up. "Maybe?"

"I shouldn't have talked to the press that first day."

"That's all?"

Irritation sharpened her voice. "You want me to say that punching Rafe in the nose was a bad idea? Well, I won't. It might have been impulsive, but he deserved it. I'd do it again."

He gave her a long look before returning his eyes to the road. "It was reckless. You could have gotten yourself or someone else killed when that bodyguard pulled a gun."

She couldn't have known the idiot had a gun—which she didn't say, because that was his whole point. But there was something disturbing behind the worry in his eyes. "You have a big problem with that, don't you? Reckless behavior—you mentioned it before."

He was quiet for several seconds. "Yeah, I do."

"Because of that other police officer. Diane."

His hands tightened on the wheel. "She made a stupid choice and paid with her life. I don't want to see the same thing happen to you."

It was so obvious she couldn't believe she hadn't seen it before. "You were in a relationship with her, weren't you?" But it was more than that, and she didn't want to admit to the flare of jealousy she felt when the realization hit her. "You loved her."

She wished he'd look at her, soften the blow with his understanding gaze, but he just stared into the twilight ahead. "She was my wife."

Chapter
Fifteen

It shouldn't have meant anything to her. Big deal, he had a past; everyone did. But it stabbed like a knife. He'd loved someone enough to commit the rest of his life to her. It was enough to make her jealous of a dead woman.

But that was what stunned Maggie the most. She was jealous because she loved him.

Her head buzzed with confusion. When had that happened? She wasn't sure, but she knew it was true. And it didn't feel good. It hurt. Cal was the wrong man to fall in love with, and he'd just explained why—he didn't like reckless, impulsive behavior. If that included falling in love, he was right about her. She couldn't have been more reckless when she fell for a methodical, controlled man.

She became aware of the hum of the tires on asphalt. Silence hung between them, heavy and awkward. Just to break it, she repeated, "Your wife," careful to keep her tone mildly curious.

He glanced at her. "Technically."

"Um . . . I think marriage is like pregnancy—either you are or you aren't."

"We were separated. We were going to file for divorce."

"Oh. I'm sorry." It made sense, in a depressing way. He couldn't live with Diane's reckless choices.

"It had been obvious for some time that it wasn't working out between us."

"Cal, you don't owe me an explanation."

"I want you to know."

He kept checking for her reaction, and she was determined not to show one. It wouldn't have been good. How was she supposed to react to the news that he couldn't stand being married to someone like her?

"Diane and I met at the police academy, but she hired on with the city, and I went with the state cops. She loved the excitement of working the streets. It took me awhile to realize why—she was an adrenaline junkie. If a case involved high risk, she was there. Drug deals, hostage situations . . . hell, she probably married me because it was some kind of rush. The academy and her department both disapproved of two new cops getting married, and she loved to buck the system."

"But you loved her."

"I loved the person I thought she was. Maybe I was just trying to rebuild a family. Don't laugh, but I had this image from TV of what families were supposed to be."

She wouldn't laugh; it was too sad to think about how much he must have missed, living with foster families and not having one of his own. Her family might have been different from most, but they were always there for her. She couldn't imagine life without them.

"My real family didn't come close to that ideal, and I thought maybe if I started fresh I could get it right. You know, the house in the suburbs, coaching Little League, camping trips on weekends . . ." He gave her a sheepish smile. "Corny, huh?"

She thought it was achingly sweet but was suddenly choked up, so she just shook her head.

"It turned out Diane liked that I didn't have an established family life. Her job was her life. She lived for risk, for the thrill of overcoming danger. The last straw was when she pushed hard to get an undercover role in a big drug investigation. I was worried that she'd crossed a line, that she needed counseling. I even went behind her back and talked to her superiors about it. They didn't agree."

"They gave her the assignment anyway?"

He nodded. "And when she found out I'd tried to have her pulled, she left me. We called it a trial separation, but we both knew our marriage was over. She was killed three months later in a drug raid. Technically, I was still her husband."

"That's awful," she said softly.

"It was two years ago."

"But you're still touchy about people putting themselves in risky situations. I can understand why."

"Touchy?" He gave a cynical laugh. "I guess I am. But I know Amber isn't like Diane. She makes me crazy, but she's only sixteen and she's been through something really rough. I get that. The bigger question is, how am I going to handle this family thing with her?"

She thought he'd been doing fine so far, despite all the frustration. "What's so hard about being her brother?"

"Everything. What do I know about being part of a normal family? My marriage was dysfunctional. My childhood was dysfunctional. Amber's hasn't been any better, seeing that we have a mother who doesn't know the meaning of parenting. Basically, I'm Amber's whole family." His desperate gaze found hers. "Maggie, I don't know what the hell I'm doing. If that kid has nothing more than me to rely on, she's in big trouble."

That's what had him so withdrawn and worried? She shook her head, smiling. "You'll figure it out. You both will."

"I don't know. Your mom understands her so much better than I do. It makes me realize how little I know about being part of a family."

"There's no rule book, Cal. I know that's a big disappointment to you, but I think you're supposed to just make it up as you go."

"I was hoping there was a way to do it that wouldn't make her hate me. She likes your mom. Hell, I think she likes everyone at the commune more than she likes me."

"Because you're the one telling her what to do."

His eyebrows came down hard. "Someone has to. She's an idiot."

"Spoken like a big brother. I could have used one of those when I was her age."

He looked doubtful. "I don't think Amber agrees. She'd leave if she had anyplace else to go. And I have to tell you, it would be nice not to have to save her ass every couple days."

She drew her eyebrows together, suddenly worried. "You won't let her leave, will you?"

Cal set his jaw. "I'm all she has. I'm not walking away."

The Aerie looked deserted. Cal scanned the few people sipping drinks at the bar and the mostly empty booths. A twinge of dread curled inside him. If he'd guessed wrong about Rafe being here, then he had no idea where to find him.

"Where is everyone?" Maggie asked. "I've never seen it this dead."

It might be dead, but it wasn't quiet—music pounded from the lounge area in the back room. As they stood there, a loud cheer went up, rising over the fast beat. They exchanged puzzled looks. In unspoken agreement they cut past the row of booths to check it out.

Cal rounded the wall and came to a sudden halt, staring. The front of the lounge was empty but the back half had been turned into an impromptu dance floor. Tables had been pushed aside to create a space big enough for several couples. A crowd stood around the dancers, watching. It was the dancers who had stopped him in his tracks.

Men and women were fused together, moving as one to the rapid, pounding rhythm. Bodies moved in sinuous harmony, bending and leaning in ways that were blatantly sexual. As he watched, a woman turned in her partner's arms then bent double, moving her hips while her partner melded his pelvis with her backside, rocking against her in a rhythm no one could mistake. The move elicited another cheer from the crowd, mixed with shouted encouragement and a few wolf whistles.

"Wow, dirty dancing," Maggie said beside him. "Some of them look like professional dancers, too."

"It's the *Trust Fund Brats*," he muttered. "Rafe must be in there somewhere." His eyes searched the dance floor. Rafe would be a dancer, not a watcher; the man craved attention too much to sit on the sidelines.

A couple moved aside in a sinuous flow of bodies. Cal spotted them and stiffened. Rafe and Amber were plastered together, thigh to thigh, hip to hip, chest to chest. Rafe's chest was bare, his shirt obviously discarded to better show off his toned body. At least Amber was clothed, if barely. Her short, tight top looked like the sort of thing women jogged in, leaving a lot of bare skin below it. He figured with her low-slung jeans there was nearly a foot of tanned skin swaying beneath Rafe's greedy fingers. Her hands slid up his arms and over his shoulders in a dance of their own. Neither smiled. Rafe's eyes held hers with an intense gaze that promised all sorts of dark pleasures. Amber's mouth opened slightly as the tip of her tongue licked a slow path over her upper lip. Someone in the crowd yelled out, "Yeow! You got yourself a hot one, Rafe!"

Cal froze as the room swayed beneath his feet. Where the hell had a sixteen-year-old learned to dance like that?

As he watched, Rafe said something to Amber. In response, she raised one leg and hooked it around his thigh. Rafe held it, rubbing his pelvis against hers in a long, slow stroke that he repeated as she laid back on his other arm. He held her as they mimicked having sex; there was no other word for it. The crowd roared its approval.

Cal's brain was on fire. Rafe De Luca was a dead man.

His mind raced with the charges he'd slap on Rafe. Lewd behavior in public. Indecent behavior with a minor. Sexual assault. He'd even take the jail time he'd probably get for knocking his teeth out. It would be worth it. He started forward, his furious gaze steady on Rafe and Amber.

Maggie's hand shot out, grabbing his arm. "Don't!"

He shook her off, but she grabbed him again, this time with both hands. He turned and growled between clenched teeth, "Let go, Maggie. I have to do this."

"No!" She jerked hard on his arm to get his full attention. "Just wait, damn it."

His head was about to explode with pressure, but he focused an impatient stare on her. "Why?"

"Look at that crowd. Who do you see?"

He turned, running a quick gaze around the circle. "Crew members. The regular group of fans." He paused, recognizing one of the tabloid reporters that had hounded Maggie. Then another. And next to him, a cable TV reporter. "Press. God damn it."

"If you barge in there you'll create another incident like the one we started. The reporters will rip into Amber just like they did to me. Worse, probably, once they find out she's a lot younger than she looks."

He automatically glanced at Amber as she danced with Rafe's hands all over her ultrafeminine curves. "What's the age of consent in Colorado?"

"I'm pretty sure it's seventeen."

"Good." The criminal charges regarding minors

would stick. It didn't mean he wouldn't punch Rafe's lights out, just that he didn't have to kill him.

He watched the dancers as his frustration rose. What did she think she was doing, anyway? Was Rick watching from the crowd, filming them? That hardly seemed like a plan for revenge.

At the back of the crowd he heard one of the reporters yell to another, "Who's the chick with Rafe? She a local groupie, or is she somebody?"

The other man shrugged. "Nobody."

Cold panic grabbed Cal's gut. How long would it take them to find out?

The music changed, the melody fading behind a hard, driving beat. Amber turned in Rafe's arms, putting her back to his chest. Rafe's hands immediately covered her breasts as his pelvis ground against her ass in time to the beat.

The press might not know who Amber was, but Rafe did. Cal imagined he was enjoying this even more, knowing she was his sister.

Rage ripped through him. Fuck waiting. He'd have to create a distraction, something that would clear everyone out of there. A fire alarm would work. It would probably mean fines or charges later, but what the hell? He was already going to spend time in jail for hitting Rafe, so what was one more misdemeanor? "Do you see a fire alarm?" he asked Maggie.

She jerked as if her thoughts had been elsewhere. "What? No, don't do that, you'll get arrested, and Amber will be part of a police report. I have a better idea."

"What is it?"

"Never mind, just trust me."

"Maggie, I need to clear this place out, now."

"I know." She took both his hands in hers and gave him a pleading look. "Just give me a few minutes, okay? For Amber's sake. Don't do anything."

She turned on her heel and rushed back around the wall, toward the bar. Cal shot a glare at the dancers. Whatever Maggie was planning, it better happen fast.

Fear blossomed in Maggie's chest at the thought of what she was about to do. She shoved it down, refusing to think of consequences. Nothing mattered as much as saving Amber from the publicity that was inches away from crashing on top of her.

She raced blindly around the dividing wall, nearly colliding with a young woman. She recognized her as one of Rafe's fellow *Trust Fund Brats*, Lara Somebody, a spoiled heiress with too much money and not enough common sense.

Maggie grinned at Lara. This was perfect.

"Hey, what's going on back there?" Lara nodded toward the room where Rafe and Amber were setting the dance floor on fire. "Is it a good party?"

"It's Rafe De Luca hogging the attention again. But if you're up for some action and you don't mind getting your picture on the front page of every tabloid, you might want to come with me."

Lara might have known laughably little about middle-class life, but she knew the value of publicity. Without a blink, she took Maggie's hand. "Let's go."

She rushed around the corner, Lara in tow, and slapped the bar. "Bartender!"

A young man at the other end turned with a start.

Maggie knew everyone else in the room would be looking at her, too. And at Lara.

"Bring me two margaritas and a pair of scissors." She put one foot on the rung of a bar stool and began unlacing the hiking boots she'd worn for exploring the mine. "If you don't have scissors, I'll take a sharp knife."

She didn't bother to look at the dozen or so people scattered around the room as she kicked off both shoes and socks. If her announcement hadn't gotten their attention, her next move would.

"Follow my lead," she told Lara, who was already slipping out of fashionable, spiky heels. She hadn't even asked why. Damn, you had to hand it to the *über*-wealthy—they knew how to leap at opportunity.

Gathering the long skirt, she stepped onto a barstool, and from there onto the bar. Two middle-aged men sitting nearby lifted their beers off her new runway, watching with interest. Hands on hips, she surveyed the room. "Let's get this party started, people!"

Lara got a boost from a couple of helpful men, landing beside her. "Fucking brilliant," she told Maggie.

A couple women stared in shock as two others raised their glasses in a toast to her. The men looked like they might be up for some entertainment, but several cast skeptical glances at her ankle-length skirt.

"Is that the best you can do?" one called.

She grinned back. "You're right. These aren't exactly party clothes."

"Uh, miss?"

She looked down at the bartender. He held two frosty margaritas, a large pair of scissors dangling next to one. "Scissors first," she said, stooping to snatch them from his hand. "And a drink for my friend."

He held a margarita aloft, and Lara snatched it, drinking deeply.

"You're not supposed to be on the bar."

She ignored him. Lifting the hem of the skirt, she eyed the seam for guidance and began cutting a straight line up the side.

"Now, that's a party," her critic agreed, deserting his table for the bar. Several others followed.

When the scissors reached her upper thigh, she cut across, then down again. Tossing the strip of fabric to the floor, she pointed her toes and angled her leg toward the men in front of her. "What do you think?"

A six-inch-wide gap ran from hip to hem, revealing the full length of her leg nearly up to her panties.

Several men called out approval as her former critic slapped the bar with a happy shout of, "More!"

Others turned it into a chant, slapping and yelling for "More!" She cut more, swishing this way and that so they could admire her handiwork, adding a few bump-and-grind hip thrusts. Cheers and whistles rose over the thrumming music in the other room. Yes! She needed more of that. She'd do whatever it took to get it.

Lara took the scissors, not pausing as she ripped a slit up her skirt.

The bartender still held her margarita, a worried crease on his forehead. "Hey, it's a party," she called out. "Drink up!" She grabbed her margarita and took a healthy sip before setting it on the bar.

"Two beers over here," someone ordered, finding a place at the bar. Someone else called for a refill. She turned a smile on the bartender, who shrugged and turned to fill the orders.

She quickly cut another strip up the side of the skirt, to the accompaniment of rhythmic clapping. Dancing around her margarita, she swayed down the bar, making use of the heavy beat pounding through the walls behind her. Her audience was getting into the spirit of the dance, clapping and yelling out requests, mostly to "Take it off!"

She'd known it would turn into a strip show the second she stepped on the bar. The consequences didn't matter; saving Amber from a paparazzi feeding frenzy was worth it. She gave her T-shirt one last look of regret before raising the scissors.

Cal hung back in the shadows, furious with Amber and unable to take his eyes off her. As if watching could stop Rafe's hand from roaming down to squeeze her ass in a firm grip as he did now. Cal clenched his fists and swore.

A cheer rose up from the front room, briefly rising over the music and noise in the lounge. He couldn't imagine what Maggie was doing to arouse them. A few people broke off from the back of the crowd, wandering toward the bar. Most still didn't seem to hear the whistles and shouts from the other room, or didn't care.

Whatever she was doing, it wasn't enough. He scanned the walls for a fire alarm.

Maggie had her T-shirt cut off just below her bra and her skirt shoved low enough to reveal her belly button. What remained looked more like a fringed belt than a skirt. Her small crowd was getting louder and larger. But not large enough. The people she needed were still in the other room.

Next to her, Lara was getting into the mood. Stripped to a cami and eight inches of skirt, she thrust out her chest and wiggled for the boys.

Maggie grabbed her. "Turn your back to me." When she did, Maggie plastered herself against Lara, shoulder to shoulder and butt to butt. Sensuously, she began moving against her.

Lara was obviously no slouch when it came to sex and seduction. She immediately began swaying in time with Maggie, reaching back to put her hands over Maggie's hips, keeping them in perfect rhythm and keeping the audience hooting and cheering. Maggie thanked fate for uninhibited, happily tarnished rich girls.

Still swaying, she scanned the back of the room. Three familiar faces—finally, the right people had noticed. She didn't have to wonder if the recognition was mutual.

"Hey, it's Maggie and Lara!" The shout came from a man at the back of the room, a reporter she recognized from one of the cable TV stations. Excitement rippled through her audience eliciting several more yells of recognition.

"Maggie! I thought you gave up your wild life."

So had she, yet here she was throwing gasoline on the flames.

She refused to think about the consequences. She had no choice. If the media vultures realized they were watching Cal's sixteen-year-old sister throwing herself at Rafe in the next room, they'd trash her life in a way she'd never live down. Maggie had already been sacrificed on that public altar. This way there were no new victims.

A new voice called out from the back, "Our old Maggie's back! Hey Maggie, where's Zoe?"

Pain stabbed her, but before she could respond, Lara shouted, "We're all you need, guys!" To prove it, she spun around and fused her pelvis to Maggie's rocking backside.

Holy shit. Maggie nearly staggered, and Lara's hands came up to steady her.

Landing over each breast.

Someone held up her margarita. Maggie tossed back a healthy gulp to loud cheers, feeling the burn as it went down while trying to ignore the warm fingers covering her breasts. She'd needed a distraction, and she got it. No turning back. "Woohoo!" she yelled, holding her drink aloft. "Let's hear it for tequila!"

"Tequila!" the group at her feet chorused.

It was wonderfully raucous. She glanced to see if the bartender was getting upset, but he was busy pouring drinks. "Is that the best you can do?" she admonished her fans, while trying to ignore Lara's hand as it roamed down to her hips. Raising her margarita higher, she yelled, "Tequila!"

"Tequila!" the room roared. The sound rolled over her in a deafening wave, while from the side a camera flashed. Then another. She tried not to think about it.

"Patrón!" Lara shouted, going for top-shelf. Maggie laughed. You can take the girl out of the penthouse, but you can't take the penthouse out of the girl.

"Patrón!" they cried, stomping and whistling. A

few independent thinkers called out their own preferred beverages, getting enthusiastic support.

She kept up her sinuous movements, letting Lara
guide them. Who'd have guessed the girl had hidden
leadership ability? Her hands caressed Maggie's hips,
skimmed her breasts, and threaded through her hair.
The room went wild.

And on the fringes, a couple paparazzi drifted back
toward the lounge. To call their friends or because they
were bored? She couldn't take the chance.

There was only one way to hold them. Her stomach
rebelled at giving up the last bit of respect she'd fought
for. But it was either that, or let a sixteen-year-old girl
suffer an even more widespread public humiliation.

It was no contest.

It had taken Cal several minutes to locate an alarm on
the back wall, and another one to pry off the cover.
Rafe was getting bolder by the minute. Cal's breaths
came hard and fast as he pulled the alarm.

Nothing happened.

What the fuck? He flipped the switch several times
with no result. Shit! As soon as this was over, he'd make
sure the Alpine Sky got slapped with a heavy fine.

Still fuming, he turned back to Amber. It was bad
enough when Rafe's hands were on her waist, pulling her against him. The little pervert had to be hard
as a rock by now. But now his hands slid up to cup
the sides of her breasts. Only a thin layer of material
kept him from crossing the line from bold to lewd.
Even Amber looked more cautious than before as Rafe
slowed their dance, making his moves seem all the
more intimate.

Amber gave a sudden jerk and pulled back. It was enough to let Cal see what had startled her—Rafe's thumbs had crept beneath her top to stroke the underside of her breasts.

That was it. Paparazzi or not, the creep was going down.

He started forward, barely aware of a sudden increase in the whoops and whistles from the bar. Someone yelled, "Do it, Maggie!" and others took up the call of "Do it! Do it!"

Whatever *it* was, it worked. The last of the crowd around the dancers made a mass exodus for the bar. Cal paused impatiently as the dancers followed—all except Rafe and Amber, who stood locked in a kiss.

No one was in his way. Cal surged forward and went in low, hitting Rafe in a leg tackle. The bastard didn't even have time to yell as Cal hit hard, knocking him sideways to the floor. Amber staggered back with a small sound of surprise. He didn't bother to look at her. Rising up to his knees, he flipped Rafe onto his back.

Rafe blinked groggily. "What the fuck?"

Cal hauled his fist back and punched him in the face. His knuckles collided with Rafe's jaw, hurting like hell but making a satisfying smack. Rafe's eyes rolled, then closed as his head sagged.

Damn it! The wimp had a glass jaw. How could he beat a man when he was unconscious? He slapped Rafe's slack cheek, hard. "Wake up. I'm not done with you."

"Cal! Get off him, you stupid idiot!"

Amber clutched his shirt. Since Rafe wasn't responding, he let her pull him to his feet. She stood with her hands fisted on her hips, glaring and all but breathing fire. "What the hell are you doing? Stop being my freakin' watchdog!" She emphasized the last word with a sock to his biceps. "You're a goddamn control freak! You ruined everything!" One tear slipped down her cheek and she swiped it aside angrily.

Her language wasn't helping his disposition. "You're out of here." Wrapping a hand around her arm, he turned her toward the bar.

She grabbed a pair of red shoes from a table, slipping them on, then doing her best to stalk ahead of him as she tottered on four-inch heels. "Fine! Everything's gone to hell, so what difference does it make?"

At least she was walking on her own; he'd been afraid he'd have to drag her out, which wouldn't look good as they passed by all the reporters and photographers in the next room. Rick should be with them, but he hadn't noticed him in the crowd. "Where the hell is Rick?" he grumbled. "He's supposed to be watching you."

"He's waiting for me upstairs in our room, what do you think?"

Alarm jolted through him as he stared at the back of Amber's head. In five quick strides he caught up and blocked her path. "Hold on!" The hand he laid on her shoulder earned him another pissed-off glare, but he didn't care. "Did you say *your room,* as in both of you together?"

She planted her feet in a furious stance. "Of course. What did you think we were doing? We checked in just like regular guests."

"Son of a bitch." This was how she handled grief? Grabbing Amber's hand, he pulled her into the bar.

"Wait!"

He ignored her protests, cutting through the empty aisle along the booths. Everyone was across the room, cheering and pounding their fists on the bar. He thanked God for the efficient job Maggie had done in distracting them. No one so much as turned around to see him drag Amber out of there. Everyone's eyes were on the bar.

He looked.

It took a couple of seconds to realize that the woman in the tattered skirt-thing was Maggie, partly because he couldn't see her face and her distinctive red hair. They were hidden by the scrap of T-shirt she was lifting over her head. With a victorious tug she whipped it aloft and faced the madly cheering crowd in nothing but a barely-there skirt and a lacy black bra.

Her mouth opened in shock as she met his eyes.

Chapter Sixteen

Maggie couldn't move. Knowing this moment would happen and living through it were two different things. She couldn't even wipe the humiliating smile off her face. All she could do was stare as her life crashed around her like shattered crystal.

The man she might possibly love aimed his startled glance at her bra, then down to the tattered remnants of her skirt. He blinked. That's all she had time to note as he tugged Amber through The Aerie's front entrance and hurried toward the lobby. He didn't look back.

Sensation slowly returned to her frozen body. At her feet, men whooped and whistled and shouted her name. At the other end of the bar, two women who had been dancing in the lounge climbed up to join Lara. Jumping into the spirit of things, they threw off their snug crop tops. They weren't wearing bras.

The roar from the crowd brought Maggie back to her senses. Her impromptu party was out of control and she no longer needed to be here. In fact, if she didn't want to add an arrest to her new reputation, she'd better move fast. In one lithe move she jumped down behind the bar. The bartender grinned at her over his shoulder as he drew a beer. "Nice show. Hey, are you leaving? Don't forget your tips."

He nodded at a shelf below the bar. A pile of crumpled dollar bills lay next to a bowl of sliced limes. "I pulled them off the bar so they wouldn't fall on the floor."

A new low—men were now paying her to strip in bars. Grandma would *not* be proud when she heard about it. And she would hear. With the number of cameras that had been flashing, everyone would hear about it.

"Keep it," she said. Tugging her T-shirt over her head, she turned to go but was brought up short by a hard stare from twenty feet away.

Zoe.

Her sister stood at the entrance to the bar, hands on hips. The fitted navy blazer and name tag meant she was on duty. The furious look on her face meant Maggie wasn't leaving the premises anytime soon.

Maggie tugged her T-shirt in place and did her best to look dignified as she opened the side panel and walked over to Zoe.

"I can explain."

Zoe keyed the microphone on her lapel and spoke in a clipped voice. "Send extra security." She looked Maggie up and down, then settled her tight gaze on Maggie's eyes. She stepped aside and gestured down the hall. "In my office."

Maggie nodded meekly and held up a finger. "Just let me get my boots. They're new."

• • •

Cal couldn't process what he'd seen. Maggie stripping on a bar? Was that what she'd resorted to in order to provide a distraction for Amber's escape? Since he'd first met her she'd been doing everything she could to defend her reputation and convince people that the old Maggie was gone for good. Now it seemed she was back, her reputation so thoroughly trashed she'd never live it down. It wasn't the Maggie he thought he knew.

He couldn't process it now. Right now he had to deal with a forty-year-old who'd possibly tried to sneak off for a quickie with Cal's sixteen-year-old sister. As soon as he beat Rick to a pulp he could find out if they still had nunneries. It was the only solution he could come up with for a girl who just didn't get it.

"What are you so upset about?" Amber asked in that snotty tone that teenagers do to perfection. She tottered after him, apparently having a difficult time keeping up in her high heels.

"How about the fact that you keep daring Rafe De Luca to kill you, like it's some kind of game? I find that just a little upsetting, not to mention a whole lot stupid!"

She made him crazy; he couldn't deal with Amber and Rick at the same time. As they crossed the lobby he spotted a security guard hurrying toward them. He stepped into his path, forcing the man to stop. With one hand he reached into his pocket for his ID, while with the other he thrust Amber at the man. "Here. Watch her until I get back."

He talked over her protest. Flipping open his ID, he flashed the shiny badge. "This girl is a possible escaped felon. Don't let her get away."

"Uh, yes, sir," the man stammered. "What are you . . . I mean, where are you going?"

"I have to arrest her partner upstairs. I won't be long."

"You can't do that!" Amber yelled, then turned her pleas on the guard who had a firm hold on her arm. "I'm not a felon. He's lying. Let me go!"

"You got a badge?" the guard asked.

Amber wrinkled her nose indignantly. "No."

"He does."

Cal jogged across the lobby. One problem down, one to go.

He used the badge again at the registration desk, flashing it long enough for the young woman to notice the silver shield but not long enough to read it. "State police," he said, which wasn't technically a misrepresentation. "What's the room number for a Rick Grady?"

She consulted her computer. "Four thirty-seven." When he turned and hesitated, she added, "West elevators, to your right."

"Thanks." He sprinted for the elevators.

Maggie walked fast to keep up with Zoe's angry stride. She hadn't said a word as they walked toward the lobby and the administrative offices, but whatever her sister was holding back was going to make a big explosion once she closed her office door.

The fountain splashing in the center of the lobby atrium created a soothing white noise, but it wasn't enough to drown out the angry voice of a young woman whose tirade was slipping into the profane.

Maggie gave the argument a curious glance,

privately commiserating with whoever else was having a bad day. With a start she recognized Amber. Clutching Zoe's arm, she said, "It's Amber."

Zoe took one glance, changed course, and marched up to the guard. "What's this about, Marvin?"

"Some cop told me to hold this girl until he got back. He went after her partner upstairs."

"He's being a jerk," Amber declared. "Do something!"

Zoe said decisively, "I'll take her. When the officer gets back, tell him she's in my office."

Amber tugged, but he didn't release her. "Miss Larkin, that might not be a wise idea. The cop said she might be an escaped felon."

Maggie choked back a laugh. Zoe kept a straight face as she said, "I know the girl and the situation. It's okay." She looked at Amber with a glare that dared her to try anything. "Come with us. And don't try to run—I know every cop in this town."

Amber nodded meekly as the guard's hand fell away. She sidled close to Maggie. "I didn't think she was such a bitch," she said in a low voice.

"Not usually. This is a special occasion."

Cal ground his teeth impatiently as the elevator stopped at the second floor and an elderly couple got off. He should have taken the stairs. It would be just as fast and he might work off some of the nervous energy that had his muscles jumping.

When the doors opened on the fourth floor he burst out, pausing only long enough to read the signs. Room 437 was down the hall to the left. He jogged, scanning numbers until he pulled up at Rick's room. Rick and

Amber's room, he reminded himself. As if he needed any more motivation for what he was about to do.

He knocked. Faint shuffling sounds came from inside, followed by silence as someone looked through the peep hole. The door opened.

Rick had a surprised look on his face. "Cal! I wasn't expecting you."

"I'll bet." Cal punched him in the face.

Zoe had sent someone to the spa to fetch a robe, so at least Maggie didn't feel half naked. That didn't mean she felt comfortable. Zoe's expression was hard as stone as she listened to their explanation.

Amber had gone first, explaining how Rick had waited for her down the road from the commune, then driven her to the Alpine Sky, where they'd cooked up a plan to trap Rafe into revealing his true character. They reasoned that if Amber looked like a guest and took Rafe back to her own room, Rick could be hiding there, ready to record incriminating evidence or stop Rafe if he got violent.

"And you thought that was going to work?" Zoe asked.

Amber huffed her disgust. "Traitor. You liked the idea a few days ago."

"This is different."

"It's stupid," Maggie said flatly. "You can't push Rafe to the edge of violence to catch him in the act. It's not like he kills every girl who makes him mad, and all you have to do is push the right buttons."

Zoe rocked back in her chair. "Sounds more like a plan to get Amber raped and get Rick beaten beyond recognition."

"Which is why we had to stop her."

Zoe turned her attention to Maggie. "And how does stripping on The Aerie bar accomplish that?"

Maggie was impressed with Zoe's restraint, knowing she'd rather have her hands around Maggie's neck right now than folded on her lap as she waited patiently for an explanation. The resort cultivated a reputation for being sophisticated and upscale. Bar strippers and topless dancers were not going to go over well with Zoe's boss.

"Stripping?" Amber shot a startled look at Maggie.

Thank goodness—she must have been so angry with Cal that she hadn't looked at the bar when they passed through the room.

Maggie turned to Zoe. "That lounge was full of paparazzi and they were starting to ask who Rafe's dance partner was. If we hadn't pulled her out of there, she would have been their next sensational headline. But we had to get rid of the reporters before we could rip Amber away from Rafe, and it's not easy to compete with hot, sexy dancing, so . . ." She shrugged and let it hang there.

"You *stripped*?" Amber asked.

"Not all the way," she corrected.

"Far enough," Zoe said. But the anger was gone and she looked at Maggie with sympathy. "You sacrificed your reputation to save hers."

"I took one for the team. It's no big deal. I don't have as much to lose."

Amber frowned, trying to figure it out. Zoe didn't say anything, but Maggie saw the pain on her face and knew she understood the lie. In ten minutes on that bar she'd thrown away everything she'd spent the last ten years fighting for. Maggie Larkin was once again the wild girl of Barringer's Pass. Her personal reputation was trashed. She didn't know how it would affect Fortune's Folly, but it couldn't be good.

"And what happened to Rafe?"

Maggie sent Amber a questioning glance. Amber shook her head. "Beats me."

Zoe started to look worried. "Was he angry? Yelling threats?"

"He was unconscious," Amber told her. "Cal knocked him out."

"Really?" Maggie couldn't help a smile.

"Oh, shit," Zoe mumbled and snatched up her desk phone. Seconds later, she said, "It's Zoe. Do you have Rafe De Luca there?" Maggie saw the corner of her eye twitch. "Right now?" She listened for several seconds, then mumbled "Thanks" and hung up. She cleared her throat before meeting Maggie's eyes. "Security says Rafe is in their office, waiting for his personal physician and his lawyer. He thinks he has a concussion and a broken jaw, and is threatening to sue both the resort and the man who assaulted him."

"The big baby," Amber scoffed.

"Don't worry, he won't do it."

Zoe didn't look convinced. "The De Lucas aren't afraid to throw lawyers at their problems to make them go away." She studied Maggie's serene expression. "What do you know that I don't?"

"It's what Rafe doesn't know. Amber is only sixteen. I doubt he wants the world to know he was dirty-dancing with a high school girl when her older brother punched his lights out."

Zoe looked thoughtful. "You may be right."

"I am. In fact, I'll go set him straight right now." Shutting down both Rafe and his watchdog, Attorney Parker Jameson, had great appeal. She stood, pointing at Amber, who looked ready to follow. "You stay here."

"No way! I had to let him touch me, Maggie. If Rafe is going to be humiliated because of me, I should at least get to watch."

"I sympathize with your position, Amber. I really do. But if Rafe is at security, you can bet a dozen reporters are there, too. We can't let them see you again, and risk them discovering your age and your connection to Cal. I'm already tomorrow's big story, so it doesn't matter if they see me talking to Rafe."

Amber flopped hard against the back of her chair. "Great, lock me up again. What am I supposed to do here?"

"Cal should be back any minute. If I were you, I'd practice acting contrite."

Cal ripped the cellophane wrapper off a glass and filled it with water. He carried it back to where Rick lay on the floor, arms out and mouth open. Why did these tough-talking morons always crumple like a used tissue when you hit them?

He kicked Rick's foot. "Hey, Grady, wake up. We have more to discuss."

Rick uttered a low moan but didn't move.

Cal threw the water in his face.

Rick sputtered and coughed and finally propped himself on his elbows. Squinting, he looked around. "What happened?" His gaze found Cal and recognition sparked. "What the fuck did you do that for?"

"For using my sixteen-year-old sister for your own selfish purposes. Get up so I can hit you again."

Rick's face screwed up in disbelief. "It's not like I was sleeping with Amber!" He sat up and probed his jaw gingerly. "She was supposed to . . . Ow! Christ, that hurts."

"She was supposed to what?" Cal folded his arms, sure the explanation wouldn't make him happy, but interested in making him say it anyway.

"To entice Rafe back to the room so we could catch him in a compromising position. Ruin his image." Rick worked his jaw back and forth, then seemed to think better of it and left it alone.

"So you were going to let *Rafe* fuck my sister. Get up."

"No! She wasn't going to sleep with him." He narrowed his eyes at Cal. "Or with me."

"I told you trying to catch Rafe attacking a woman was a stupid idea the first time you proposed it. You agreed to try it my way."

"Yeah, well, your investigation wasn't getting anywhere. I had to do something."

"I found the bodies."

His mouth opened and he blinked several times. "You found bodies?"

"At least two, in an old mine on De Luca land. One was Emily Banks. The police are investigating."

"Wow." Rick's stare was unfocused as he thought. "That's great. I could sell your firsthand account for . . ." He looked up. "You'll give me an exclusive, right?"

His distaste for Rick was mounting by the second.

"I'll cut you in. You'll see, we can both make money

off this." Rick scrambled to his feet with newfound energy, but kept a wary distance from Cal. "When can I interview you?"

"The first thing we do is take Amber back to the commune, and you can explain to everyone there how you won't be taking her away again."

"Yeah, whatever." He folded a tripod and tossed it into a small duffel bag, along with a video camera. "Let's go. The sooner I get this story, the better. Man, I'm gonna nail Rafe's ass this time." He paused at the door and motioned to Cal. "Come on, we gotta get back before someone else gets the jump on me."

"That would be tragic." Cal thought the sarcasm was obvious, but he wasn't sure Rick got it.

They wouldn't let Maggie see Rafe.

"He's being examined by his doctor," the security guard said. He swiveled his chair, putting his back to the bank of monitor screens. She noticed various views of the lobby, the spa, and the parking lot glowing brightly under halogen lamps. She couldn't tell if one of the other screens showed the bar in The Aerie, and sincerely hoped it didn't.

"Does he really have a broken jaw?"

"Doubt it. He'll probably need a few new caps on his teeth, though."

The little office held one other chair and a desk, but it was unoccupied. "Is another guard with him?"

"Nope."

"What if he leaves?"

"I hope he does. We got no reason to hold him, and if he leaves, the pack of paparazzi will go with him. Makes my night a whole lot easier."

Damn. She'd been all psyched about crushing Rafe's hopes for a giant lawsuit. But telling Parker Jameson might be just as good. Propositioning a minor—that should crack Jameson's cool exterior. If the press got wind of it, it wouldn't matter if the minor in question had looked willing. It was the kind of publicity Jameson was paid to cover up.

"Do you know where his lawyer is?"

"Haven't seen him." The guard cocked his head, looking her over. "Aren't you Zoe Larkin's sister?"

She nodded.

He leaned back and laced his fingers over his belly. "Heard you put on a pretty good show tonight."

The little room suddenly felt claustrophobic. "Someone must have exaggerated."

"Hey, I ain't criticizin'. Fact, I wish I'd been there to see it." His eyes took another tour of her body, lingering on her breasts. "You planning on doin' an encore?"

Never, but that didn't matter. The newspapers would make sure no one forgot. Photos of her in her bra and fringe skirt would be everywhere, even on the Internet. God, she'd never live this down.

And Cal . . . Heat bloomed on her cheeks. She knew from the shocked look on his face that he'd never forget, either.

"Thanks for the information," she mumbled, and made a quick exit.

The enormity of what she'd done was starting to sink in. She'd known there were possible repercussions, but hadn't thought about them at the time. She did what had to be done. She'd dealt with a reputation tarnished by rumors before. But this was more than rumors, and it was far more than local. By tomorrow, Wild Maggie Larkin would be national news.

And Cal Drummond would never want to see her again.

Loud laughter made her look toward the lobby. A group of reporters had gathered by the fountain, probably waiting for Rafe to emerge from the administrative offices. She didn't want to face them. She didn't feel like being shut up in Zoe's office, either, answering Amber's questions. Her only other option was the alarmed exit at the end of the hall, with darkness and cool night air beyond. It sounded perfect.

Opening Zoe's office door a crack, she motioned for her sister to step into the hall. "Can you override that alarm for me? I need to get my cargo pants from Cal's truck, and the lobby's full of reporters. I can't go that way."

Zoe led the way down the hall. She keyed the override, then held the door open. "Call me when you're ready to come back in." Maggie nodded and slipped outside. The door clicked shut behind her.

The night wasn't dark here, or quiet. Even though there was no moon, the mountainside above her glowed with light. Floodlights bathed each ski run in white as snow guns spit long arcs of snow over the slopes, the white fountains adding a layer of powder to fight off the spring melt. By morning, huge snowcats would have the runs packed and groomed for the last skiers of the season. It might be after 2:00 a.m., but the slopes were busy.

At least the people out here weren't reporters. She ran to Cal's truck and was relieved to find he hadn't locked it. Her pants might be dirty, but they were a lot warmer than bare legs. She traded the robe for her jacket while she was there.

Going back inside wasn't appealing. She wandered toward the equipment barn, staying close to the pine trees that shielded it from the view of guests. Away from buildings, among the fragrant branches of the pines, she at least had the illusion of solitude. Even the diesel exhaust from the snow groomer idling in front of the barn drifted in another direction. The air among the trees was fresh, filled with the spring smells of damp earth and new growth—just what she needed. Maggie closed her eyes and inhaled deeply.

The faint trace of cigarette smoke touched her nostrils. Someone else was out here, not too far away.

Cal skirted the reporters as he scanned the lobby. No Amber, no security guard. The man had looked too earnest and impressed with Cal's badge to have let her go; they had to be close by. His best bet was the security office. If the guard wasn't there, someone would know where to find him.

"Looks like something's going on," said Rick, taking in the mass of reporters and photographers by the fountain. Cal had nearly forgotten about him in his eagerness to wring Amber's neck.

Maggie's bartop striptease would explain the paparazzi. So would Rafe's bruised face. Since the reporters were keeping an eye on the door that led to the administrative offices, he figured one or both of them were in there.

He hadn't told Rick what had happened in The Aerie. He didn't intend to, either—Rick had chosen sides when he tried to use Amber. Encouraging him to mingle with his own kind could be a good way to get rid of him. "I'll check with Zoe. Why don't you stay here, find out what's going on?"

"Right." Rick sauntered over to a group of reporters. He didn't even realize he'd been dumped.

Cal nodded to the desk clerk and slipped through the doorway to the administrative offices. He'd check with security first, and hope they had Amber. Then he could find Maggie. Of the two, Amber was the slipperier, the one who'd run if he turned his back. Maggie would just . . . actually, he wasn't sure *what* to expect from Maggie, after that striptease on the bar. But he would start with Amber.

He paused with his hand on the door to the security office. Sergeant Kyle Todd walked toward him from the direction of Zoe's office.

A cold spot formed inside Cal, an icy lump of fatalism. He could think of two reasons for Todd to be here—one, to arrest him for smashing Rafe in the face, or two, to arrest Maggie for public indecency. Like any good criminal, he acted innocent. "Hey, Kyle. What's up?"

"I got word that Rafe De Luca was here. We've been trying to find him for questioning ever since you led us to those bodies."

He wouldn't mind having a word with Rafe himself, especially if he was in there with Amber. "Mind if I watch?"

Todd only gave it a second's thought. "I guess you've got a stake in this, too."

He had no idea how much. Cal followed him through the door.

A man turned from the bank of monitors he was

watching. At a desk on the other side of the tiny office, Rafe sat holding an ice bag to the side of his face.

"I'm looking for a girl named Amber," Cal told the security guard at the monitors. "I left her with another—"

"Assistant manager's office," the guy cut him off. "Down the hall."

If Zoe had her, Amber was safe. Rafe didn't look interested, anyway. He glanced at Sergeant Todd and sank into a scowl. "Don't waste your time. I don't talk to cops without my lawyer present."

Todd arched an eyebrow. "You get a lot of practice being questioned?"

Rafe's narrowed glance took in Cal. "If you've already talked to him, I'm not giving my side without my lawyer."

Todd turned a questioning look on Cal. "His side?"

Cal gave a half smile in return. "I'm the one who gave him the lump on his jaw."

Todd turned back to Rafe. "You have a lump?"

Rafe glared and lowered the ice bag. Cal stepped forward to see. Purple bloomed along Rafe's finely chiseled jaw, with red stretching over the cheekbone. Cal smiled; the golf ball–size swelling was coming in nicely.

Todd smiled. "This should be good."

"Arrest him!"

"Well now, I might get to that later," Todd said, as unconcerned as if Rafe had requested a can of soda. "But that's not what I'm here for."

Rafe sat straighter. "Why the hell not? I want to press charges against that asshole. I don't care if he *is* a cop, he didn't have the right to hit me. You really slipped in shit this time, cowboy. You ever seen the press go after a cop for police brutality? I got witnesses."

"And I have pictures—of you with your hands all over a sixteen-year-old girl."

Rafe clamped his mouth shut.

Todd said, "I came to ask you about Emily Banks."

Rafe returned the ice bag to his face. "I already talked to the cops about that. I don't know where she went that night."

"We found her body."

Rafe met Todd's eyes briefly, unconcerned. Pretty damn composed for a killer. "Yeah? So what? Everyone figured she was dead. Now you have proof. Go do your forensic stuff, find out who did it, and leave me alone."

"That's such a touching testimonial for a girl you spent most of an evening with."

"I'm all sniffly," Cal agreed.

"Fuck you." Rafe moved the ice bag for an unimpeded glare. "You're out of your jurisdiction, cowboy."

"I'm not," Todd said, his voice suddenly several degrees colder. "And I'm the one talking to you."

Rafe gave him a sullen stare. "Like I said, I'm waiting for my lawyer."

"Fine. Here's something to think about while you wait. I got a dead girl who was last seen with you, and whose body was found on your parents' property. Their gated, guarded property that you have access to. I want to know how she got there."

Cal knew he wasn't fishing for an answer, not after Rafe had mentioned his lawyer. He just wanted to see Rafe's uncensored reaction to the news. So did Cal.

Denial wouldn't have surprised him. The furious, self-righteous arrogance of a criminal who knows he can use the law to protect himself.

What he hadn't expected was shock. Rafe's face went slack and drained of color. He lowered the ice bag. "Her *body* was at my parents' house?"

"Are you speaking to me voluntarily, without your lawyer?" Todd glanced at the security guard by the monitors to make sure he had a witness. No problem—the guy hadn't looked at his screens since they walked in.

"Yeah, yeah, no lawyer," Rafe said, waving his hand impatiently. "Tell me where you found her body."

Cal noted the mix of puzzlement and concern in Rafe's eyes, and frowned. He hadn't thought the asshole was a good enough actor to fake it so convincingly.

"In a pool of water inside an abandoned mine."

"A mine? What mine?" Rafe's forehead showed deep creases, then cleared as he shook his head. "There's no mine on that property. You'd better check a map." His confidence returned rapidly. "And get yourself a whole damn law firm while you're at it, because you just implied some very damaging shit that's going to end your career."

"It's on De Luca land," Todd told him, unruffled. "No question."

They exchanged stares for several seconds, while doubt grew on Rafe's face. "Where?"

"The sharp rise east of the house. There's at least one more body in there, too."

"*What?* You mean there was another missing girl? I

thought it was just those other two, a long time ago."
Panic crept into his voice. "Besides, I only did her in
my car, I never . . ." He stopped, wild eyes narrowing
to slits. "I'm not talking to you anymore. I'm talking
to my lawyer."

"Fine. I'll see you both at the police station." Todd
turned abruptly and walked out. Cal followed, his
mind buzzing with confusion.

Todd stopped in the empty hallway. "I didn't say
the second body was a girl. And I didn't say how long
the body had been there."

"I know." Rafe had jumped to conclusions. The
wrong conclusions.

"I saw him in that movie where he played a racecar
driver," Todd said. "The kid can't act worth a damn."

"I know."

"I don't think he knew about that mine."

Cal nodded slowly. "I don't either." It was infuriat-
ing. Just when all the puzzle pieces seemed to be coming together, this scattered them all over the board.
"But I'm certain he was with Emily and those other
two girls before they disappeared. Maybe someone else
disposed of the bodies for him."

"Or maybe someone else killed them."

He didn't want to admit it, but it looked possible.
Rafe was a sneaky, lying creep who used and abused
women—he was sure of that much. But it was possible
someone else around him was just as sick and abusive.
Someone who might look down on the women who
threw themselves at Rafe and went home with him for
one-night stands.

The pieces were starting to move back into place.
Maybe someone was charged with taking the girls

home when Rafe was done with them. His personal security guards would be an obvious choice. Plus, they were all beefy enough to be pumped up on steroids, which would give them an aggressive attitude. They might easily overreact, like the one who'd gone after Maggie.

Maggie—he had to tell her about this. He pulled out his phone and called her. He hadn't been aware of his tension until she answered and he let out a quiet sigh of relief. "Where are you?"

"Outside, near the equipment barn. I needed some air."

"Stay there. I'll pick up Amber and meet you."

Maggie pocketed the phone, walking aimlessly. She wasn't up for this, but she had to face Cal's outrage sooner or later. They hadn't discussed what constituted a reckless impulse, but she was pretty sure stripping on a bar in front of a whistling, stomping crowd of men would qualify. The longer she put off their breakup, the more it would hurt.

Pine needles rustled behind her. "I believe we need to talk."

Maggie gasped and spun around. Parker Jameson stood three feet away, dressed in his usual three-piece suit even in the middle of the night. Maybe he slept in it.

She didn't have to ask what they needed to talk about. It would be the same thing they always talked about—Rafe. His image needs and her stubborn demands. Only this time, she and Cal had the upper hand, and she was going to get her way.

She hadn't noticed the cigarette he was holding until

he raised it for a long pull, exhaling a cloud of smoke. "I didn't know you smoked."

"Only when I'm having a bad day." He smiled faintly. "This has been a *very* bad day."

Not as bad as hers, but at least it was some consolation that she'd helped put the De Lucas and their lawyer in a tight spot. "You heard about the mine?"

"I did." He gave her a considering look that was not nearly as unfriendly as she'd expected. "And what a coincidence that it should be you and your friend who discovered the bodies there."

He seemed strangely calm in spite of his bad day, but that might be normal for a soulless minion of Satan. "There's nothing coincidental about it. Cal knew Rafe is a murderer, he just had to prove it."

"Yes, Mr. Drummond has been persistent in going after my client."

His placid expression was starting to bug her. Why wasn't he more worried? "Because he's guilty."

Jameson gave her a condescending smile. "Because Mr. Drummond wanted to make him *appear* guilty. Of course, that's to be expected from serial killers, trying to make the evidence point to someone else."

Her mouth dropped open. "Are you talking about Cal? You've got to be kidding! If that's your idea of a defense, I can tell you no one's going to believe it."

"Naturally, you'd defend him. You've let your emotions delude you."

It was true a lot of emotion surrounded her feelings for Cal. Love, especially. But that wasn't delusion, it was a deep, heartwarming truth, one that looked like it was about to become a heart-wrenching loss. "I'm not the one who's deluded."

Jameson shook his head sadly. "Consider it from an objective point of view. Cal Drummond is estranged from his mother, openly criticizing her lifestyle. When his sister seems to be emulating that lifestyle, wantonly chasing after celebrities, Cal confronts her. In a rage, he kills her."

"What!"

"Perhaps he didn't mean to, but I suspect he did. Because she wasn't the first."

She snorted a laugh. "What's in that cigarette?"

"He killed at least twice before," Jameson mused, ignoring her question. "Right here in Barringer's Pass. He chose women known to be easy, women who were looking for a man who would show them a good time, maybe solve all their problems. Rather like his mother's relationship with men, wouldn't you say? That seems to be the thing that sets him off. Do you see the pattern?"

The way he twisted things around made her dizzy. "Cal never met those girls. But Rafe did—he's the one with a pattern of dead girlfriends."

"Ah, yes. Rafe. For some reason Mr. Drummond decided to make my client look guilty. Perhaps he was envious of Rafe's well-known success with women? Whatever the case, he invented this idea that Rafe was involved in their disappearance, and planted it with the family and friends of the two women he had killed, all the while pretending to conduct a murder investigation—which he is unauthorized to do, by the way. Of course, it would be difficult to convince those families that they had been manipulated by the De Lucas, when the De Lucas were the ones who set up a reward for finding their daughters' killer. They also established charitable funds in the girls' names as a memorial to them. The families were quite touched."

She stared, speechless. The De Lucas had been more thorough than they'd guessed. No wonder Cal got no help from the families of the missing girls.

"Convincing argument, isn't it?" He took a satisfied pull on his cigarette.

"No."

"More so than your case against Rafe. But then, you haven't heard the most convincing part." He paused, making sure he had her attention. "While my client was sitting in the Alpine Sky's security office tonight, nursing his wounds and talking with the police, Mr. Drummond flew into a rage over the lewd behavior exhibited just an hour earlier by his own girlfriend, who apparently chose to dance on top of a bar, nearly nude, in front of a gawking crowd. Rather alarming to any man, especially one as judgmental as Cal Drummond. And as vengeful."

She didn't know whether to be outraged or to laugh in his face. "Are you implying Cal's going to kill me?"

"Sadly, yes."

"Don't get your hopes up. Cal's not a killer. Rafe is the one who snaps and loses control. I know you're paid to keep his image clean, but you can't change who he is. And Cal isn't the least bit like that, no matter what you think."

"Of course he isn't." He gave her a tolerant smile. "You misunderstand. It's the scenario we'll use in court. Psychiatrists will confirm that Mr. Drummond's unfortunate childhood permanently damaged his opinion of women. I believe his history of reporting his mother to social services, in addition to his mother's own actions, will go far to support our claim."

It wouldn't work. It couldn't. Could it? "You'd go that far to protect a killer?"

"As you said, it's my job. But to be fair, Rafe didn't kill those girls. He simply choked them into unconsciousness. He has a bit of a temper, but you can't blame him, really."

Oh, she really could, but she didn't think Parker Jameson was open to arguments.

"A woman who would allow herself to be used like that has to know that different men have different preferences. To offer sex, then pretend she only meant a certain kind of sex . . . well, you can't blame a man for taking what he wants in those circumstances, even if he has to do it forcibly. Unfortunately, the De Lucas can't have stories like that getting around. My job is to keep Rafe's image clean; the girls had to be silenced."

She tried to swallow, but her mouth felt like it was full of sand. "Who . . . ?" There was no good answer, but one was better than the other. "You mean you had Rafe's bodyguards . . . ?"

"No." He flicked the cigarette butt to the ground.

That's what she was afraid of. "It was you."

Jameson smiled. "I knew you were smart."

Chapter Seventeen

He was lightning fast. He grabbed her arm and spun her around, then kicked her behind the knee. Her leg buckled and she dropped to her knees before she knew what had happened. He knelt behind her, straddling her lower legs as he slipped one arm around her neck and pulled her against him. From the corner of her eye she saw his other hand move and heard a soft click. A blade flashed.

"Remember this?" His voice feathered the hair next to her ear, soft and seductive, and she flashed back to the attack on her front porch. Him! Only this time with a real knife instead of a gloved finger. "I'm beginning to like having you in this position," he murmured. "Too bad it has to end."

He bent her back, exposing her neck. Her mind raced as fast as her heart. *Do something!* She tried to grab him, grab anything, but her scrabbling fingers couldn't reach the dirt. Her left hand flailed uselessly at air, while her right hand hit the long bough of a pine tree. It was all she had. Grasping the thin limb, she directed it toward his face and stabbed.

It was a sloppy aim—needles poked through her hair and pricked her cheek. But enough of the long, sharp needles must have found his face, because he screamed and reflexively reached for his eyes. The knife slid harmlessly to the ground.

Maggie scrambled to her feet.

"Bitch!" Jameson staggered to his feet, too.

She ran.

"You can let go, I'm not a child." Amber trotted to keep up with Cal's long strides, her hand firmly caught in his.

"All the more reason to hold on to you," he grumbled. If Cal had ever thought of her as a child, he didn't after that dirty-dancing demonstration. She'd terrified him. How had their mother ever thought she could turn Amber loose without supervision? That was no way to raise a kid.

"Explain it again," she demanded. "Are you *sure* Rafe didn't kill Julie?"

"No, I'm not sure, but it's a strong possibility."

She humphed her dissatisfaction as she kept up her walking-jogging pace. "Then who did?"

It was the same question that churned in his gut. "I don't know."

He slowed as they reached the shelter of the trees. He didn't see Maggie, so he raised his voice and called her name. No one answered.

"Where is she?" Amber asked.

"She said she was here, just a few minutes ago. She couldn't have gone far." It was also possible she couldn't hear him over the deep rumble of the diesel engine he heard beyond the trees. He pushed through the breakwall of pines until he saw the source, a large snowcat idling in front of the open doors of the equipment barn. He could see better on this side of the tree line, too, thanks to the luminous glow of the barn lights and the snowcat's running lights. It was enough to see that Maggie wasn't standing along the line of trees. And barely enough to see the faint white spot on the ground near his feet.

He bent to pick it up. A cigarette butt. A warm one. "Damn, I need a flashlight."

"Hang on." He watched as Amber dug through her purse and came up with a set of keys with various charms and doodads hanging from it. One was a miniature flashlight. She flicked it on. "It's not much."

"It's enough. Thanks." He gave her an appreciative smile before squatting to shine the light on the ground.

"What are you looking for?"

"This." As she squatted beside him he used his other hand to indicate the faint footprints of a smooth-soled shoe.

"Those are big feet," Amber said doubtfully.

"Maggie was wearing hiking boots. But you're right, those aren't hers." He shone the light a short distance away. "These are."

The deep indentation from the tread on the hard rubber soles showed up clearly. They both examined the ground as he looked for more of the squiggly treads. A clod of dirt and pine needles showed where she had pivoted sharply. The print next to it was deeper, from a foot stamping down forcefully. He shone the little light back and forth impatiently, look-ing for another print. He couldn't find one, and the cheap little light was already fading.

"Here," Amber said.

He directed the weak beam at the spot she indi-cated. It was too far away for a regular footstep. He'd either missed one, or . . . He found the next step even farther away, and the next. "She started running."

"So did the other person." Amber pointed out the impression almost on top of Maggie's print. She looked at him, worry showing in her shadowed eyes. "Something made them run away."

"Or she ran, and he chased her." Fear already quiv-ered in his voice, and he saw it reflected in Amber's eyes as he stood, looking in the direction Maggie had run. The equipment barn.

"Stay here!" he ordered, and took off. He doubted she'd obey—when did she ever?—but he didn't have time to argue about it. Not while Maggie was in danger.

Maggie hesitated a fraction of a second, caught by the first spark of passion she'd ever seen in Parker Jameson's eyes. The change was dramatic. His serene stare dissolved, replaced by the flare of something that looked unnervingly like lust. It compounded the effect of the knife.

He'd hesitated, too, almost as if he wanted her to run, and she understood that catching her would be part of his satisfaction. Killing her would be the rest.

She ran. Instinct drove her toward what seemed the most likely source of help, the large metal pole barn.

The snowcat was still idling out front; there had to be a driver nearby.

The ground around the barn had been torn up by the caterpillar treads of the snowcats, and she slipped once, catching herself with one hand before stumbling on, her desperate mind consumed with the thought that she would not be one of those women, the ones who would have made it to safety if not for the fact that they tripped and fell, screaming their last scream as the scene faded to black. She would not be a helpless victim.

The snowcat's caterpillar treads were huge with wide, staggered blades. When she got close she realized they were only waist high, low compared to the height of the trucklike cab perched on top of them, towering over her head. The 'cats normally trundled the slopes with plows in front and drags behind, their humped shapes making them look like semis that had lost their trailers, then mated with a tank. Humongous semis, with five passenger cabs and tinted windows, fitted with winches and hydraulic arms and bristling with spotlights and rearview mirrors.

She couldn't see a thing through the tinted windows, and would have had to climb up on the treads to reach the cab. She didn't have time. Waving her arms and yelling, "Help me!" she rounded the front of the snowcat so the driver could see her. Surely anyone inside would open the door to see what was wrong.

The door didn't open. The cab was empty. Parker Jameson was no more than ten steps behind her. Without pausing, she ran toward the gaping cavern of the barn.

The barn was huge, dark, and nearly empty with all the snowcats out grooming the slopes. Her ragged breaths echoed off the high metal roof as she squinted into the deep gray interior, then veered left across the concrete floor toward darker blobs that might offer cover. She was winded, and Jameson was gaining on her. If she could just find something to use as a weapon . . .

Jameson's footsteps were loud behind her as she cut between a snowmobile and an all-terrain vehicle. The barn wall loomed ahead, wooden beams crossing corrugated metal. Bare beams, and bare metal; no shelves or pegboards or storage closets. Not even a spare board she could swing as a weapon. This friggin' resort must have something smaller than an all-terrain vehicle. Where the hell were the snow shovels?

No time to search. A few yards behind her, smooth leather shoes slid on cement—Jameson had rounded the snowmobile. With a spurt of adrenaline, Maggie took off.

Two more ATVs. Then suddenly what looked like a table with something above it. She skidded to a stop. Her heart leapt with hope. Tools! A workbench backed by a pegboard wall. Directly in front of her, wrenches hung in a neat row of decreasing size.

Grabbing the largest one, she turned and threw it. A few yards away, Jameson shouted and the wrench clattered to the concrete floor. Her throw had been wide and low, but she must have nicked his leg.

It was better than nothing. Yanking frantically at the wrenches, she pulled off several more and began throwing. Wildly at first, laying down a barrage of tools, then trying for more accuracy. Jameson swore and crouched low, shielding his head as wrenches rained around him. Her aim got better, but the wrenches got smaller. And smaller. Braving the last few, he stood and charged toward her.

Panic grabbed her. Running would only delay the inevitable—in a footrace, he'd win. She needed a bigger weapon, not these wimpy tools they probably used on the snowmobiles and ATVs. They had snowcats; they *must* have bigger tools.

But she was out of time—he was on her. She reached for the longest piece of metal she saw, lifted it off its hook, and swung it toward Jameson.

She wasn't fast enough. He was already there, slicing at her arm with his knife. She felt the sting on her forearm and faltered in mid-swing, her weapon missing him entirely. She backed away, two hands on the piece of metal, wielding it like a bat as she watched him cautiously. Jameson eyed it, and she glanced at what she held.

A lug wrench. It was about a foot and a half long, with an angled end. Solid and dangerous—no wonder a wary look had crossed his face.

He held the knife at the ready, but it was his eyes that unnerved her, making her heart pound against her ribs. Despite the deep shadows, she noted the barely veiled excitement. Cutting her had been a thrill; killing her would be exhilarating.

She pressed her lips together and tightened her grip on the wrench. Something wet ran down her arm, and she knew it was blood. The cut must be deep, but she couldn't feel it. Her left hand felt weak, but her right one made up for it. She raised it like a batter ready for the pitch, and kept her eyes on the knife.

He feinted toward her, and she skipped backward. She wouldn't fall for that trick. If she swung he'd rush her before she could swing again. She had to make each one count.

She didn't have to wait long. He lunged, arm outstretched to stab. She swung the wrench. It whipped through air, barely missing him. He stabbed again, and she had to jump away as she swung, clipping the knife without knocking it loose. Before she could recover, he sliced at her hand. A line welled with dark blood.

Jameson smiled. "Shall I keep score? That's two for me." He moved the knife down, then up, watching with amusement as her eyes tracked it. "This is even better than when they're helpless. It prolongs the pleasure. Your death will be memorable, Maggie Larkin."

She didn't answer. It was what he wanted.

"They usually plead for their lives. Plead for me, Maggie. Beg me to spare your life. If you're convincing, I will."

"Liar."

He grinned in response, then jabbed toward her thigh. She swung, connecting with a dull crack. The knife fell, clattering on the cement floor.

"Fucking whore!" Jameson's mouth pulled into a snarl as he grabbed his elbow. She swung again, and he ducked, coming up with the knife in his other hand. He jabbed, and she barely evaded the blade.

She gripped the wrench with two hands, waiting for his next move. He was still dangerous, but probably not as good with his left hand as his right. The odds had evened up.

She did her best to look calm while her heart thundered so hard she heard each beat in her ears. She tried to tune out the distracting pounding, louder even than her panting, until the sound resolved into running footsteps and a dark form charged toward them.

"Maggie!" The sound echoed in hollow vibrations from the walls and roof. Cal!

Jameson whipped around. In that moment, she swung her wrench.

The connection was fast, ricocheting off his forearm with another crack. The dangling, injured arm jerked back at an unnatural angle.

Jameson yelled, a roar of pain and fury, as he clutched the useless arm to his body. His eyes flashed, outraged, wild. He crouched, ready to tear into her despite the lug wrench, when his head jerked toward Cal's racing footsteps.

Close. He rounded the two ATVs without slowing, charging toward them.

With a snarled curse, Jameson turned and ran into the darkness.

And vanished.

Maggie stared at the spot where he'd disappeared. Cal stopped abruptly, and she knew he was confused, too. She listened for footsteps over his rapid breaths. Nothing.

"Where'd he go?" Cal searched the darkness, braced to spring into action. She heard his worry, and knew he was afraid Jameson was hiding nearby.

She shook her head. "He ran toward that big grease spot, then disappeared."

Cal walked cautiously toward the dark spot on the floor.

"Cal?" Amber's voice carried across the barn, trembling with fear. "Where are you?" She didn't seem to be entering. Seconds later, fluorescent lights flickered high above them.

Blinding light filled the front of the barn. More lights flickered to life, row by row, until the entire barn blazed with it.

Maggie blinked and squinted at Cal. He stood by the oil-blackened area where Jameson had disappeared. Except it wasn't oil.

She approached slowly, peering into the hole in the floor. Cal grabbed her arm to keep her away from the edge, then just held on to her even though she wasn't going anywhere. She didn't have to. She could see the hoist, the huge hydraulic cylinder standing like a pillar in the center of the rectangular pit. Next to its base Jameson lay still on the cement floor.

"Is he dead?"

"I'm pretty sure. Looks like he hit his head on the hoist."

She didn't need to see it. Amber apparently did. She trotted across the open center of the barn, stopping at the other side of the hole. She peered down, unflinching. "Is he the one who killed them?" she asked. "The one who killed Julie?"

"Yes." They said it at the same time, and Cal gave her a questioning look. "He told me. He said Rafe choked them when he . . ." She didn't want to say while he raped them, even though Amber probably knew, judging by the angry look on her face. "They might have been unconscious." Let Amber believe that. "They knew what Rafe had done and they would talk. Jameson couldn't let anyone find out. So he killed them. Rafe must have known."

Cal sighed and ran a hand through his hair. "I'm not so sure about that. He doesn't expect to see women again after he's done with them. Maybe he'd started to wonder these past few days, after the police questioned him about so many women disappearing after he was with them. But I don't think he knew."

"He's still a slimy little prick," Amber said. No one disagreed. She looked back into the hole at Jameson's body. "I'm glad he's dead." A moment later, her gaze settled on Maggie's arm. "You're bleeding."

Cal was instantly alarmed. "Where? Did he hurt you?" He grabbed her shoulders, looking her up and down. It didn't take him long to see the blood dripping from her arm. Worry changed to outright horror. Gently, he took her hand, lifting her arm.

His fingers brushed the cut by her thumb and she finally felt it, sucking in a sudden breath at the pain. Cal let go immediately, and she held her arm up for him to see. "It's not too bad. I didn't even feel it until now."

A scowl darkened his face as he glanced at the cut on her hand, then examined the deeper one that curved from the top of her arm to the underside just below the elbow. His mouth tightened in a grim line. "Maggie, this is deep. You need stitches." His gaze darted over her before he began unbuttoning his own shirt. "Why didn't you say something?" he demanded, directing his scowl at her.

"I forgot." Although, now that he'd pointed it out, she became aware of a dull throbbing in her arm. It wouldn't be long before her shock wore off and the pain hit her full force. She watched him wrap his shirt around her arm, and winced at the tight knot he made with the sleeves. Blood was already seeping through the shirt.

"Come on, we're getting you to the hospital. Amber, will you get my truck and drive it up here so Maggie doesn't have to walk so far?" He pulled keys from his pocket and tossed them to her. "Put it in four-wheel drive, the ground's soft."

Amber took off at a jog. Cal wrapped his arm around Maggie as they walked across the barn. It felt good, and not only because she was cold. Shock was beginning to set in, the aftermath of operating on pure adrenaline.

"Cal, we can't just leave with a dead body back there. This is a crime scene."

"I'll call it in. But they'll have to question us at the ER. We're not waiting for EMTs to get here when you're bleeding like that and there's a twenty-four-hour clinic a couple miles away."

She gave in meekly. Truthfully, she would be glad to find a warm place to sit down, curl into a ball, and stare at the walls. A psycho had just tried to kill her. Probably would have succeeded, too. She didn't want to think about what he would have put her through before finishing the job.

And it felt awfully good to be wrapped in Cal's protective embrace. She sank into silence, content to be with him as he called the police, as he drove to the clinic, while they hustled her back to a room. Cal was given a scrub shirt to wear while the nurse sliced through the one he'd wrapped around her arm.

He touched her uninjured arm. "Will you be okay if I leave you? The police will be right behind us and they're going to want to question Amber. She's a minor, so I want to be with her and make sure no one digs for information they don't need to know. That whole dancing thing with Rafe has nothing to do with Jameson trying to kill you."

"Sure, go ahead."

He smiled and squeezed her hand. "I'll find you when we're done."

He didn't come back while they put twenty-six stitches in her arm, but she hadn't expected him to. She gave a statement to the officer who came, then sat in the lobby to wait. Two hours later, she was still waiting when Zoe called.

"Maggie! I haven't had a chance to call until now. Are you okay? They told me you got cut, and someone said it was pretty bad, and someone else said it was nothing, and I don't know what's going on!"

"I'm okay, just got a few stitches in my arm."

"Did that De Luca lawyer really try to kill you?"

She didn't want to increase Zoe's anxiety, but didn't know how to play down attempted murder. "Yeah, he did. But I'm fine, really."

"Oh, my God, how can you be fine? You must have been terrified!"

More than she had ever been in her life. "I'm okay now, honest. Zoe, could you do me a favor? Could you give me a ride home?"

"I'll be right there."

She ended the call and dialed Cal, but got shunted to voice mail. He hadn't called back by the time Zoe's car pulled up to the emergency entrance.

He did after she got home; a quick message to say they were still talking to Amber and he'd see her later. He sounded tired and dejected. She wasn't sure if it had to do with her, and didn't want to ask. She felt pretty dejected herself. With the crisis over, her R-rated dance on the bar loomed larger than ever.

Chapter Eighteen

Cal looked at the clock on the dashboard. Nearly five-thirty in the morning. Not the usual time to bring someone home.

"Do they get up early at the commune?"

For a few seconds Amber's face was blank while she processed the question. She'd answered a lot of questions in the last couple hours. They both had. Blinking sleep away, she said, "Some do. Flynn and Amy. Marcy."

Good enough. He started the truck and left the Alpine Sky for the second time that night. Away from the news vans and police cars, Two Bears Mountain was quiet, still cloaked in predawn darkness. Cal opened his window a few inches despite the cool temperature, just enough to feel part of the peace and solitude of the mountain. He breathed deeply as the wilderness worked its magic, dissolving his tension. The only sound was the soft rumble of the engine, the only light the glow from the dash.

"I don't want to go home."

Amber's soft words startled him. He'd thought she was asleep, but the pain in her eyes told him her mind had been far from peaceful. Apparently she wasn't as attached to the members of the commune as they were to her. "I can take you back to my cabin if you don't want to stay at the commune."

"No, I don't mean the commune. I mean *home*. Los Angeles. I don't want to go back there."

"You don't have to leave yet if—"

"Ever." Her troubled gaze stabbed at his heart. "I don't ever want to go back there."

"Your mother . . ." He left it hanging, not sure where to go with the thought.

"She won't miss me. You know she won't."

She was right. And he couldn't blame her. It wasn't that Sherrie June Drummond Ellis Howard Whatever was mean or abusive to her children. She just didn't care. He knew what it was like to live in a home without love. It sucked. He'd be glad not to send Amber back to that.

But she was too young to be on her own—she hadn't even finished high school yet. She needed a home.

The idea had been in the back of his mind for several days, and needed no deliberation. "You can live with me." It wouldn't be the "normal" family life he'd envisioned, but they'd manage.

"You mean in *Oklahoma*?"

You'd have thought he'd said Lower Slobovia. "Oklahoma City, to be exact. It's a great place, and it has anything you'd want—theaters, museums, parks." The horrified look hadn't gone away. "Malls."

"I want to stay *here*. At the commune."

He frowned. "I thought you hated being there."

Her gaze shifted away, evading his. "It's not so bad. The people are nice, and Kate and Pete are pretty cool."

He suspected he knew why she said that. "Yeah, they encouraged you to pierce your lip. Real cool."

She glared. "For your information, Kate talked me out of the lip ring. And I already got a new piercing. Here." She turned her head, holding the long brown and blue strands away from her ear. A shiny silver cuff shone at the top of her ear, with a delicate chain connecting it to a black stone midway down. Different maybe, but not weird.

"Oh." He almost hated losing that bargaining chip. "So you want to stay and learn to make jewelry?"

"No, I'm not interested in making it. But did you know there are people who travel all over the world, finding things to sell in stores over here? Maggie buys stuff from people who do that. That's what I want to do, after I learn about jewelry and maybe some other stuff. Kate and Pete are teaching me a lot."

"And what about school? Kate and Pete won't let you drop out." At least, he hoped they wouldn't. "If you did, they wouldn't take you in. You have to finish high school at least, and you can't do that living in a remote commune in the mountains. Even Maggie and her sisters had to move to town with their grandma during the school year."

She didn't look discouraged. "Then I'll do that, too. I'll find someone to stay with in B-Pass," she said, adopting the local abbreviation like a native. "Maybe I could even stay with Maggie. Or her grandmother. It's just for the school year."

She'd already shoved him out of the picture. He should be relieved. He didn't need a stubborn, impulsive teenager messing up his plans. But someone had to take responsibility for the kid, and if it wasn't going to be her mother, then it would damn well be him. He refused to examine the idea that he'd grown fond of her, might even love her in a brotherly way. She wouldn't care, and that wasn't the point. A kid needed a home, and he wasn't going to let his little sister be passed around from family to family because she didn't have one.

"We're family," he told her firmly. "And you're a minor. It's Oklahoma City or Los Angeles, take your pick. Next summer if you want to come back here, I'll bring you."

She clamped her jaws together and folded her arms. "I knew you wouldn't understand. You're such a control freak. *Don't do anything reckless*," she mimicked in a deliberately taunting voice. "*Don't talk to strangers*. You think you get to tell everyone how to run their lives. Plus, you're boring." She made it sound like a disease. She slouched down in her seat and turned away, staring out the side window.

Cal ground his teeth. The name-calling might be immature, but it still hit a sore spot. He wasn't boring. Hell, he was a lot of fun. She'd only known him while he was hunting down their sister's killer. After she'd known him a few more months, she'd see how wrong she was. And he didn't try to tell everyone how to live their lives, either. He just wanted to keep Maggie safe from reckless impulses.

Not that it had worked. That last one in the bar had been a doozy.

He sank into a grumpy silence. He'd done the right thing. Amber would have a home, and someone who cared about her. Someday she'd appreciate what he'd done, how he'd given her stability. She might even decide to go to college. They'd both finally have a normal life.

And Maggie . . . He flinched at how he'd messed up her life. She'd nearly lost her store and had probably destroyed her reputation, two things she cared fiercely about. And it could have been worse—helping him investigate Rafe had nearly gotten her killed.

She'd be better off without him.

He waited several hours before calling the West Coast, but it still sounded like he'd gotten his mother out of bed. The gravel-voiced "'Lo?" sounded sleepy, but could also be part hangover.

"It's Cal," he told her.

"Cal? Hang on." He heard rustling sounds, murmured voices, and finally the click of a door closing. "What are you calling for?"

Nice to hear from you, too, he thought. "It's about Amber."

"What about her? Didn't she show up?"

Fine time to ask. But that attitude just made it all the more likely that she'd agree to let him take her. "She's here, but now I'm leaving Colorado. I'd like to take her with me to Oklahoma if it's all right with you."

"What for?"

"To live with me for a while. She could go to

school there and we could get to know each other."

"Live with you?" Her voice rose in disbelief. "I need her back here."

Caught off-guard, he just blinked for a few seconds. He hadn't expected to run up against maternal instinct, and wondered if Julie's death had somehow awoken it. "You want her back?"

"Damn right. Bud and me need her to watch his dogs while we go on a cruise."

The glimmer of hope faded to black. "Tell Bud he can put them in a kennel."

"They *are* in a kennel. Bud raises greyhounds for racing. He's got fifty or sixty of 'em. But his kennel manager just up and quit. We figure if Amber takes over the kennel job for the summer, it'll save us a pretty penny."

It didn't sound like any of those pennies would be going to Amber, either. "Does Amber know about this?"

"Not yet, but it don't matter because she likes dogs, and she don't have a job. This'll be good experience."

For what, indentured servitude? "I forgot to mention, Amber broke her arm. The cast has to stay on for at least six weeks, and she can't do much. Can hardly even wiggle her fingers."

He waited through a long pause. "Well, shit. Now what am I supposed to do?"

"Hire someone to run the kennel, I guess. But it'll be best if you stick around until she gets that cast off, because she'll need help with stuff. Getting dressed, cutting her meat, stuff like that."

"Fuck that. I ain't givin' up my Mediterranean

cruise. If she can't take care of herself, then she can just stay with you."

"Okay. I just wanted to make sure you didn't mind . . ." He didn't finish the sentence, because the line had gone dead.

No way in hell would he let Amber go back to Los Angeles. Ever.

Maggie refused to answer the incessant knocks on the back door of Fortune's Folly. She had no desire to hear the shouted questions from the reporters camped in the parking lot.

Zoe found her anyway. Maggie looked up from taping a box as her sister came through from the shop area.

"Where are the flooring guys?" Zoe gestured at the front of the store. "Your carpenter let me in. He's the only one out there."

"There was some snafu with the wood. They tell me they have to reorder and it'll take another week." Maggie gave her a cynical smile. "Just one more thing that's gone wrong with my life lately."

Zoe settled on the stool at the end of the worktable, fiddling with a spool of packing tape as she watched Maggie finish the box. She nodded toward the bulky bandage circling Maggie's arm above and below her elbow. "How's your arm feel?"

"Hurts a little. Everything works, though." She wiggled her fingers in demonstration. It didn't even pull on the five stitches at the base of her thumb.

"That's good." Zoe twirled the spool absently. "I saw the De Lucas on TV this morning. They were already distancing themselves, expressing shock that such a deranged man was allowed to handle their son's legal affairs. They're making noises about seeking damages against his firm."

Maggie looked up. "They're suing their own law firm?"

"Deflecting attention from Rafe. They say the firm was negligent for entrusting their son's legal affairs to a man who was obviously insane. He put others in jeopardy, too—that would be you. The De Luca family is outraged on your behalf."

"I feel warm all over."

Zoe set the tape aside. "So. Did he call?"

Maggie nodded, not wanting to talk about it but knowing she couldn't avoid it. "Yeah. He said he was taking Amber back to the commune."

"And?"

"And nothing. It was nearly dawn and we were both tired. I told him I was just getting into bed. He said I needed a good night's sleep so he'd just go back to the lodge."

Zoe thought it over. "Considerate."

"Don't bother trying to find the bright side, Zoe. He wanted to be there so he could check out first thing this morning."

"Check out?" Alarm made her voice ratchet up to near-squeaky. "What's that mean—he's leaving already?"

Maggie shrugged without meeting her eyes. "Can you blame him?"

"Yes! And I can't believe he'd leave without saying good-bye."

"He asked where I'd be, then said he'd stop by here. I haven't seen him yet."

Maggie dumped a bag of Styrofoam peanuts into the box and refused to meet Zoe's eyes. She knew her sister was watching her closely, weighing whether to offer supportive platitudes or unleash a string of expletives denouncing men in general and Cal Drummond in particular. Maggie wasn't sure which would make her feel better.

"It's still early," Zoe finally said.

Maggie looked pointedly at the clock. Past two—not what she would call early.

"He wouldn't just leave, Mags."

"After what I did? He might. He's looking for normal, Zoe. The kind of woman who makes rational decisions based on careful thought. That's not me. It never was. In case there was any doubt, I resolved it with my little demonstration at the bar last night. I'm not only reckless, I'm back to being a bar bimbo. Not exactly what a man like Cal wants. Not even close."

She could see Zoe struggling to find an argument and failing. Her sister watched as she spread out packaging paper, then lifted a small slab of fossilized trilobites onto the center and began wrapping.

The door from the shop opened. Maggie looked up sharply, then relaxed as Sophie came in.

"You didn't give me the secret password, Maggie. I actually had to show that carpenter guy my ID before he'd believe I was your sister and let me in."

Maggie smiled with relief that he was taking her orders seriously. "You might have been a reporter." Her gaze went to the folded newspaper in Sophie's hand. "Which one is that? I've already seen 'Bar Bimbo Strikes Again.'"

Reluctantly, Sophie laid it on the table between Maggie and Zoe. "The B-Pass *Echo*. I wanted to see how the local press handled it."

Maggie stared at the front-page picture of herself in a bra and skimpy, fringed skirt, waving her T-shirt over her head. In consideration of family values, the paper had slapped a black bar across her chest, covering her bra, so it was hard to tell if she wore anything at all. The headline read, "Wild Party at Alpine Sky Ends in Death." The caption beneath the picture proclaimed, "Local businesswoman Maggie Larkin is said to have initiated the rowdy celebration." Maggie made a face and shoved the paper away. This was worse than when she was a teenager; at least then they couldn't tie her to a murder investigation.

Sophie took a critical look at the picture. "It's not so bad, Maggie. Really. I've worn less at the beach."

"I wasn't at the beach."

She waved the objection away. "So what? It's not like you were topless, like a couple of those dancers."

Maggie gave her a pointed stare. "But they don't live in B-Pass, and they aren't on the front page of the paper." She sighed softly. "Look, you don't have to try to make me feel better. I knew what I was doing, and I knew what the result would be. I appreciate your support, but I wish you two would just stay away and let them focus on me. Let it be wild Maggie Larkin, not the wild Larkin sisters. Maybe this doesn't have to ruin your lives, too."

"Sorry, can't do that," Zoe said.

Sophie straightened, narrowing her eyes. "Seriously? You think we should throw you to the wolves and watch while they tear you apart? What kind of sisters do you think we are?"

Maggie raised an eyebrow.

"That would be like saying we're ashamed of you! Well, we're not. We're proud of you." She stuck her hands on her hips. "If you think we're going to let them slander you without saying a thing in your defense, you're wrong. If they take on one of the Larkin sisters, they take on all of us. Don't think just because—"

"Down, girl." Zoe tugged on Sophie's arm to silence her, smiling at Maggie. "I guess she feels she missed out the first time around."

"You sheltered me," Sophie muttered. "But I'm not a little kid anymore."

"You're one of the Larkin sisters. I get it." Maggie smiled at her youngest sister. "Welcome to the scandal."

The shop door opened again. She had to stop tensing every time that happened.

She almost didn't recognize Sergent Todd in jeans and a knit shirt. He glanced around, smiled in recognition. "Hi, Zoe."

"Hi, Kyle." She raised a questioning eyebrow at Maggie.

Maggie lifted a shoulder at Zoe, and gave him a friendly "Hi."

"Maggie, I'm not here as a member of the B-Pass PD."

She smiled, glancing at the jeans. "I see that. Want something to drink? There's soda in the mini-fridge."

"No, thanks. I just wanted to make sure you were aware of something."

His gaze flicked to the copy of the *Echo* on the table, so it had to be something other than the usual accusations and rumors. She found herself tensing again.

"I read the statement you gave last night, so I know how everything went down between you and Jameson. And I saw the De Lucas on TV this morning, spinning their relationship with him to make Rafe look like a victim. Deflecting attention from the fact that he was the one who had violent sex with the girls that Jameson later killed."

"I heard."

"It pisses me off that no one's out there standing up for you, even though you were the one who stopped a murderer and helped us find his previous victims."

It felt good to hear someone say it, but she gestured ruefully at the newspaper. "I'm afraid I eclipsed that particular scoop."

He scowled at the *Echo*. "It doesn't have to be that way. It shouldn't. Do you have a lawyer?"

"I have a lawyer I try not to use. Hurts the bank account too much. And thanks for your support, really, but I'm not a celebrity and my last name's not De Luca. I can't afford to sue every tabloid that misrepresents me, and I can't hire a team of lawyers to make sure my side of the story gets a fair hearing."

"But you can." His mouth curved into a sly smile. "What do you want to bet Jameson's firm is huddling around conference tables right now, trying to figure out what to do if it occurs to you that a senior lawyer in their firm repeatedly threatened you, attempted to coerce you into keeping silent, and, oh yeah, tried to kill you? They're liable, Maggie, in a very big way."

She raised her eyebrows. "You think I should sue them?"

"If that's what you want. You certainly have a case, and you'd get more than enough money to sue those tabloids and get them to retract their lies."

"But it's not all lies." She lifted the newspaper. "This isn't a lie, it's just not the complete story. They print what they want, the parts that appall and titillate."

She slapped the paper down, then looked at it thoughtfully. "It's called libel by innuendo." She looked up, ideas falling into place. "Maybe they'd pay attention if a powerful law firm threatened them with that."

"Bet they would."

She smiled at Kyle. "Perhaps Jameson's firm would be willing to do that if it would keep me from going after them."

"There you go," Kyle said. "Get your side of the story out there, Maggie. It will go a long way toward countering those bar bimbo headlines." He straightened and pulled keys out of his pocket. "That's all I wanted to say, just to let you know you don't have to take all this bullshit they're saying about you."

"Thank you." She grinned. "Really."

"Okay if I slip out the back door?"

"As long as you don't let any reporters sneak in."

He nodded at Zoe and Sophie. "Ladies."

The door closed behind him. They all looked at each other, then broke into grins. "It could work, couldn't it?" she asked her sisters.

"Absolutely! I love it," Sophie exclaimed.

Zoe nodded. "Call Jameson's firm. Today."

"I will." She was still smiling when the shop door opened. She looked up, expecting to see Sam coming to tell her he was a carpenter, not a bouncer, and he was tired of checking IDs. But it wasn't Sam.

Her smile faded. She bit her lip and felt her heart take off at a gallop.

He was tall and tanned from the high-altitude sunlight, and his long, sexy stride nearly made her knees buckle. Cal's eyes found hers and stayed there, ignoring Zoe and Sophie.

"I had to show my badge before your carpenter would let me in here."

"Sorry. Paparazzi problems." She didn't trust herself to say more, afraid he might hear something in her voice she didn't want him to hear. No matter how much she dreaded this meeting, and how much she knew it would hurt, she couldn't make her body stop reacting with pleasure when Cal walked into a room. It wasn't fair. She didn't want to love him, didn't want her heart to race every time she saw him. It was going to make their breakup talk even harder.

He stopped within three feet of her. "I checked out of the lodge."

She nodded.

"All my stuff's packed in the truck."

She didn't think that needed a response, so she just ran her dry tongue over her drier lips and waited.

"I'm leaving for Oklahoma today."

"I heard." She thought it was audible, but there wasn't much breath behind it, so maybe it wasn't. She cleared her throat. "So I guess you came to say good-bye." Maybe fast and neat was the best way, but that didn't make it hurt less.

"We need to talk."

Off to the side, she saw Sophie and Zoe watching alertly. She stared at them until their fascinated gazes finally turned toward her, no doubt waiting for her reply. She stared harder.

Zoe snapped out of it first. "Oh. Yeah. Come on, Sophie. We gotta go . . . do that thing." She plucked Sophie's sleeve. With a significant look at Maggie, she made the universal thumb-and-pinkie sign for a phone call and mouthed, "Call me later."

The door closed behind them.

Maggie shifted her gaze back to Cal, wishing she weren't so darned *aware* of him. His presence filled the room until she could barely breathe. Hoping she sounded more composed than she felt, she said, "So talk." The quicker they got this done, the better.

"I've decided to keep Amber with me instead of sending her back to L.A."

It wasn't exactly what she'd expected to hear, but she could guess where this was going. With a sister already prone to headstrong, reckless behavior, the last thing Cal needed was someone else in his life who would only set a bad example. It looked like Amber got the guy. She couldn't even resent her for it, because his little sister had a prior claim and deserved to have her brother in her life. "That's nice," she said around the lump in her throat.

"I worked it all out this morning. I'll buy a house in a good neighborhood and see that she has what I didn't have—a place to put down roots, to call home. A yard, neighbors, backyard barbecues . . . hell, I might even get a dog. Amber can finish high school, and if she wants to go to college, she can do that, too."

Something warmed deep inside her as she recognized the reality he was trying to create. "You'll have that normal family life you always wanted." She smiled, trying not to think about how she didn't figure into that picture, because it was probably best this way. She didn't belong in a TV-land fantasy family. "I'm happy for you, Cal, I really am. For both of you."

He nodded thoughtfully. "It sounds perfect, doesn't it? It's everything I didn't have growing up, the American dream."

She nodded too, wishing he wouldn't rub it in.

"That's why I was surprised when I realized that just thinking about it makes me miserable."

She started. "What?"

"Amber, too. She was pissed as hell at the idea."

She shook her head. "I don't get it."

He shrugged. "It's a nice reality for some people. It turns out I'm not one of those people. Amber either. We're fine with being an unconventional family. Besides, Amber wants to stay at the commune and learn more about jewelry from your mom and Pete."

She must be hearing him wrong. "Amber wants to join the People's Free Earth Commune and become a hippie?"

"No, she wants to be an international buyer for retail outlets. At least, that's what she thinks now."

"She does?" She could see Amber doing that.

"Maybe that will change, but that's the option she wants to explore. Not high school volleyball or glee club or cheerleading. So today I went up to the commune and talked to them about it. Your family's great, you know. They were excited about having her stay there for the summer. She'll have to live with me during the school year, but they said she could come back again next summer, too."

"So she'll finish high school in Oklahoma."

"That's the other part. Maggie, I live in Oklahoma because that's where I found a job. I like it there. But then I came here and found something I like even more. No, something I love."

She hated herself for it, but for one second she ignored the reasons she was all wrong for him, and dared to hope.

"The mountains." Excitement flashed in his eyes. "They're breathtaking. The clean air, the spectacular scenery—but I don't have to tell you, do I?"

She shook her head, swallowing hard against the disappointment she had no right to feel.

"So the perfect answer is to move to Barringer's Pass. Amber can live with me during the school year and still visit the commune on weekends."

Oh, God, he'd be right here. She'd always be reminded of what she'd almost had before she recklessly threw it away.

"By the way, Amber might be hitting you up for a part-time job at Fortune's Folly, but I'll bet she'd work for free if you let her. She's fascinated with the different kinds of jewelry you carry."

"I'd love to hire her," Maggie said, but couldn't pretend she hadn't focused on the other part of what he'd said. He was jumping into this so fast it made her head spin. "How can you move here when you don't even know if you can find a job?"

"Because I do know. I called Kyle Todd at home

and talked with him about job openings for cops around here."

Maggie felt light-headed. "You've been busy today."

"That's why I'm running late. Kyle said there's a guy on the force who will be retiring next year. I've made some good connections with the people there, and Kyle said he'd put in a strong recommendation for me. It looks good."

"Next year." That gave her time to get over him before she had to risk running into him around town. Not enough, but it was a start.

"But I thought maybe I'd give notice now so I can get moved in as soon as I find a place. I've got enough money to get by until a job opens up."

She tried to absorb it. There were so many changes, all happening so quickly. It wasn't like Cal. In fact . . . She gave him a disbelieving look. "Isn't this all a bit impulsive?"

"You think?" He hooked his thumbs in his pockets and actually looked proud of himself. "I'm trying it out. I did figure out the financial side and logistics, but I didn't hesitate. Does that still count as impulsive?"

"For you, it's damn near reckless."

"Then this will really blow your mind." Before she realized what he was doing, he pulled her against him, wrapping her in a strong embrace. "Move in with me, Maggie."

Her brain stumbled. "What?"

"Move in with me. Damn, I'm getting fond of these reckless choices. Come live with me. I know I have a part-time teenage roommate, but she's pretty cool once you get past the blue hair and the piercings."

She felt torn in two, half of her hopelessly giddy,

and the other half wondering if he'd lost his mind. She went with the most likely one. "Have you seen the papers this morning? Weren't you the least bit curious when you had to wade hip deep through paparazzi to get in here?"

He assumed an air of peaceful contemplation as he slid his hands beneath her hair, letting the strands fall between his fingers. Maybe he was on tranquilizers. "I saw them," he told her calmly.

"Then you know I'm a pariah again. The town slut."

He smiled. "You're a fraud."

"Excuse me?"

"That's not you. Besides, do you think I care what they say?"

"I think you care that I'm impulsive and reckless. I'd like to pretend you don't, and that last night never happened, but unfortunately there are pictures. By now the whole world has seen them. I really wish I were the woman you want me to be, Cal." Especially when he ran his hands beneath her hair like he was doing now, making her sigh with longing. "But I can't pretend to be something I'm not. Obviously, you've blocked what you saw from your mind, maybe because of everything that happened afterward. But those pictures are real. I really was that impulsive and reckless."

She expected to see his expression fall as the disappointing truth sank in. It didn't. The crooked smirk that touched his mouth made her squirm with desire and wish really, really hard that he wasn't deluding himself. Teasing her with what she couldn't have was unfair.

He shook his head sadly. "See? You're perpetrating a fraud."

My God, maybe he really was so deep in denial that he refused to see the truth. She should break it to him gently. "You were in the other room, so you didn't see—"

"Maggie, what I saw was the most selfless act of bravery I've ever seen from anyone."

Her mouth hung open for several seconds before she could speak. "You did?"

He caressed her cheek and looked at her with a tenderness that made her heart skip several beats. "I saw someone sacrifice herself to save someone else. Your reputation in this town means more to you than anything. I know what they used to say about you, Maggie, and I know how much it hurt. You spent years trying to repair that damage, and it was finally working. Then in ten minutes' time you threw it all away so Amber wouldn't have to face the same ridicule."

"You know that?" she said weakly.

"I know that," he affirmed softly. "And I know it wasn't an impulsive decision. I think you knew exactly what the consequences would be, and you did it anyway. It was amazing and brave, and I'm sorry I didn't get a chance to thank you for it last night, but I got a bit distracted by watching a serial killer try to carve you up with a hunting knife."

Understandable. "I forgive you."

He smiled and tucked a lock of hair behind her ear, and she nearly melted at his touch. Her heart would be happy never to move out of the moment, but her brain insisted on making sense of her spinning thoughts. "So I'm a fraud, and you're the reckless one for deciding to quit your job and move to Colorado?"

"Actually, I'm a fraud, too." He lowered his voice as if letting her in on a secret. "Moving here isn't reckless, it's simple self-preservation. If I left here I'd die. I love you too much to live without you, Maggie."

The words were soft and gentle, and slammed into her heart with enough power to collapse her lungs.

"What?" She'd heard perfectly. She wanted to hear it again.

"I love you." He framed her face and kissed her gently. "Move in with me, Maggie. What do you say?"

She checked to see if she could breathe first. "Okay."

He smiled.

She had to say it, but took her time, smoothing her hands over his chest as she savored the warm, fuzzy feeling. "I love you, too."

"Good. Then, I'll give you the summer to think about marrying me, because by fall we'll have an impressionable young girl in the house and I wouldn't want to shock her delicate sensibilities by living in sin."

She ignored her tripping heart and bit her lip to keep from grinning. "Bad argument. Not even looking at the cracked head of a dead serial killer shocked Amber."

"Good point. How about the fact that making an honest woman of you would help repair your tarnished reputation?"

Probably not so tarnished after she got through

with Jameson's law firm. "Maybe," she allowed, because jumping up and down and shouting yes would have been too embarrassing.

"Maybe" seemed to be good enough, because he took her mouth in a long, delicious kiss that knocked her thoughts back into a happy muddle. It took a long time to remember the one incongruent fact. Reluctantly breaking away, she said, "You said you were leaving for Oklahoma today."

"I am. I have to quit my job and pack up my stuff. Wanna come?"

She almost gave an automatic "no," then stopped. She didn't have to worry about the store—it wasn't open. She could stand around watching contractors for a couple more weeks, or she could ask Sophie to cover for her and spend every day with Cal. And every night.

"Sure."

That was good for another long kiss. Cal finally pulled away, directing a startled look toward the worktable. "That's not George, is it?"

She glanced at the slab of fossilized trilobites she'd been wrapping when he walked in. "No, it's a smaller piece."

"Good, because I'm rather fond of old George. I was thinking of buying him."

She was surprised he even remembered what she called the giant trilobite. "Cal, did you see the price tag on that thing?"

"I have plenty of money."

She laughed. "You don't hear that every day."

"Plus, you could give him to me at cost. Sort of a family discount."

She could tell he was really going to push the family

idea. Surprisingly, she was all right with it. "I could do that. Why are you so fond of George?"

"Because he's brilliant, a trilobite ahead of his time. He found the secret to love five hundred million years ago." He laid his forehead against her, holding her close. "When you find the right woman, you stick with her. Forever."

Turn the page
for a sneak peek
at the next sexy adventure
by

Starr Ambrose

Coming Soon from Pocket Books

Z oe Larkin stepped inside the Rusty Wire Saloon
and felt her sling-back pump stick to the floor.
She looked down. Her right foot rested squarely in a
half-dried puddle of beer.

Leaving was tempting. Unfortunately, it wasn't an
option. It was either brave the sticky beer puddles at
ten in the morning or the raucous crowd that created
them at night. Wrinkling her nose, she stepped around
the beer and surveyed the saloon.

Directly across a vast open area of floor, a long
bar looked as it probably had a hundred years ago
when the place was new. As she watched, a bartender
sloshed soapy water onto the top and attacked the surface with a brush. At least they kept something clean.

The spacious dance floor would be crowded at
night, but only three customers were in the place
now. At one end of the bar, a man sat hunched over a
glass, getting an early start on his drinking. A woman
in jeans and a T-shirt sat beside him, talking quietly.
Across the room, a man sat at a table. Or rather,

reclined. He slouched in one chair with boots propped on another, hands folded on his stomach, and cowboy hat over his face. She hoped he was left over from last night and not sleeping off an early buzz.

She crossed to the bar, trying to ignore that every other step nearly glued her right foot to the floor. The young man with the scrub brush looked up.

"We're not open."

Zoe readjusted the purse strap on her shoulder as she flashed a professional smile. "I know. I'm Zoe Larkin from The Alpine Sky. I'd like to speak to the owner, please."

The young man took his time looking over her business suit as if he'd never seen one before. "He don't like to be disturbed this time of day. What can I do for you?"

"I'm afraid I can only speak to the owner."

"Oh. Um, I see . . ." The young man's gaze flicked to the drunk by the tables, uncertainty obvious in the nervous twitches that pulled his mouth into various puckered shapes as he stammered and stalled.

A chair scraped as the man kicked his footrest out of the way and eased into a sitting position. With the hat centered on his head, she could see the firm lines of his face beneath at least a day's stubble. It was the rugged sort of face that quickened female hearts and imaginations, and could make a woman lust after cowboys—if she didn't know she was better off with the suit-and-tie type. He would have looked even better if it weren't for a put-upon frown that said forcing his body into an erect posture was more work than he'd intended to do all day.

Leaning his forearms on the table, he turned a

tired gaze on her. "I'm the owner, lady. What do you want?"

She approached slowly, taking in the wrinkled shirt that went with the faded jeans and worn boots she'd glimpsed earlier. Instead of making him look shabby, they added to the magnetic pull that tickled the nape of her neck and made her wonder what kind of hard living got them that way. His eyes were clear and steady beneath the shadow of his hat, not the blood-shot gaze she'd expected.

He might not be drunk, but if he could sit there and nap while his saloon needed cleaning, he was a lazy slob. She'd spent some time hanging out with people like him, and recognized the type. Party all night, sleep all day, and never do a bit of work you don't have to do. She'd narrowly escaped getting sucked into that mire herself, and would prefer to stay far away from it. People in Barringer's Pass had long memories.

Luckily, this would be a brief association. "Are you Jason Garrett?"

"It's just Jase."

She stuck out her hand. "Hello, Mr. Garrett. I'm Zoe—"

"Yeah, yeah, Zoe Larkin, assistant manager from the Alpine Sky. I heard." He waved her hand away. "You wanted the owner, you got him. What do you need?"

She took a deep breath, forcing herself not to glare. It didn't matter if he was rude, only that he accept her offer. She was fairly certain that hearing it would wipe that irritated look right off his face.

"I'm here to make you an offer on behalf of Ruth Ann Flemming, the owner of the Alpine Sky."

She paused a couple seconds for dramatic effect. "Mrs. Flemming would like to buy the Rusty Wire saloon."

Behind her, a glass thunked onto the bar. The rhythmic sound of the scrub brush stopped. Jase Garrett didn't move, not even the flicker of an eyelid. His gaze was steady on hers for several long seconds, while she tried not to fidget. "Is that so," he finally said.

Since he hadn't made it a question, she didn't answer. She wished he'd ask one though, because his thoughtful stare made her nervous.

"What does the exalted Alpine Sky want with my saloon?"

"We would like to expand our business."

His gaze took a slow trip up and down her suit. "A honky-tonk doesn't seem like your style."

"Thank you, it isn't. But the Alpine Sky doesn't actually want your saloon, Mr. Garrett. We want your land. As you know, our resort is a popular winter destination for skiers. We would like to offer summer activities, too, which means building a golf course. For that we need a semi-flat piece of land, like the one your saloon sits on."

The stillness at the bar behind her was palpable, as if all three people were holding their breath. Jase's shadowed eyes gave nothing away. "You want to tear down the Rusty Wire?"

"I imagine if the building is in good condition, it might be used for something else." She gave the room a quick glance, deciding not tell him the chances of that were next to zero. "The town's records show that the lot size, including parking, is two acres. You also own the fifty behind it. Those acres adjoin the Alpine

Sky, and they would be ideal for an eighteen-hole course."

"That land is untouched wilderness."

She raised an eyebrow. "Mr. Garrett, the Rocky Mountains are full of untouched wilderness. You can buy as much as you want. The only thing special about *your* piece of wilderness is that it adjoins our resort."

"And it's flat."

"Yes, relatively."

His expressionless gaze held hers for a long time. A barstool squeaked behind her, but she didn't turn.

"The Rusty Wire's not for sale."

She smiled. "You haven't heard our offer yet, Mr. Garrett. It's more than generous."

"Doesn't matter."

"Two point five million."

Zoe heard the woman suck in her breath. She tried not to look smug as she waited for Jase Garrett's eyes to widen and his mouth to drop open in shock. It didn't happen. Nothing happened.

"No, thanks." He all but yawned.

No thanks, that was it? Irritation prickled just under her skin, making it hard to keep up an appearance of calm. "Mr. Garrett, perhaps you should take some time to explore the price of real estate around Barringer's Pass. Two and a half million is an incredibly high price for fifty-two acres of mostly undeveloped land."

Finally, his expression changed. His eyebrows drew together and a muscle clenched along his jaw, a decisive expression that warned her she'd roused a determined man behind the lazy exterior. "I said no, Miss Larkin. That's my answer. Go make your pitch to whoever owns land on the other side of the Alpine Sky."

It was more wordy than his other responses, but just as negative. It also revealed their weakest bargaining point. She pressed her mouth together, reluctant to admit what she had to say. "The other side is Federal land. It's too steep, and even if it weren't, the government isn't open to an offer."

"Neither am I."

She closed her eyes and sighed, making a big deal out of her reluctance to give in. Let him think he'd made a crafty bargain. She dropped her voice. "I'm not authorized to offer more money, Mr. Garrett, but just between the two of us, if you gave me a counter-offer of three million, I might be able to convince Mrs. Flemming to pay it."

He actually scowled. "Miss Larkin, I appreciate your dedication to your job, but I've given my answer. Now run along." Tugging his footrest chair closer, he propped his feet up, slouched down, and dropped the hat back over his eyes.

She stared. A show of resistance wouldn't have surprised her, but she hadn't been prepared for a flat rejection. Who turned down three million dollars for a crappy saloon and a few acres of trees? She was missing something here, and she wasn't leaving until she figured out what it was.

Jase waited for the click of heels across the dance floor, interested enough to take a peek at the resort lady's legs to see if they matched the shapely body he'd detected under that stuffy business suit. For one of the infamous Larkin girls, she wasn't what he expected. But then, rumors were often wrong.

He didn't hear retreating footsteps. He poked a cautious finger at his hat brim and lifted it an inch. She was still standing there, her pretty lips pulled into a tight line and her irritated gaze boring into him. A no-nonsense look, right down to the twisty bun-thing she did with what would have otherwise been a beautiful fall of red-blond hair. The kind of hair that shone like it was shot through with fire, waking a man's fantasies about the hot woman that came with it.

But it wasn't his fantasies keeping her here. Clenching his teeth over a curse, he pushed the hat up a couple inches. "Miss Larkin, I can't help but notice you're still here."

"Nothing gets past you, does it, Mr. Garrett?"

"What else do you want?"

"I want an explanation. I offered you far more than this old place and that undeveloped land is worth. In fact, my guess is that the Rusty Wire is aptly named, and that rust isn't even the worst of your problems in a building this old." She looked around the saloon, taking in the century-old bar along with the new light fixtures and new windows. "You've probably had to dump a ton of cash into plumbing and electrical updates, just to mention the obvious. I think it's safe to assume it takes most of your profits to keep this place up to code."

That was accurate enough to raise her a notch in his estimation; she wasn't just some corporate lackey delivering a message. Assistant manager, she'd said. She probably knew a lot about running an establishment that served the public. Not that it would help her argument any. "What's your point?"

"My point is that I just offered you the equivalent of a winning lottery ticket, and you turned it down without a thought."

"I thought about it. Maybe I just think faster than you."

She ignored the jab. "Why would you turn down a small fortune, when keeping the Rusty Wire open will eventually *cost* you a small fortune?"

He flashed a cocky smile so she wouldn't know how little he knew about his own saloon's finances.

"Keeping the Rusty Wire open *doesn't* cost me a small fortune, Miss Larkin. If you work up the hill, I'm sure you've seen how busy this place is on a Friday or Saturday night. We turn a nice profit. But thanks for your concern."

Her frown said she wasn't buying it, and he didn't want to argue the details, since he didn't know them. He kicked the chair aside again and got to his feet, walking around the table to place a guiding hand on her elbow. Impulsively, he leaned close, as if to confide a secret, enjoying her light scent as much as the shiver that ran over her skin when his breath touched her ear. "Not that it's any of your business, Miss Larkin, but you might say I already won the lottery. I don't need your three million."

She stared as he guided her out the double doors. Let her figure that one out. "You can't buy me, Miss Larkin. You run back up to that fancy palace on the hill and tell that to the lady who sent you here. Have a nice day now, you hear?" Before she could argue that with him, he turned and walked back inside, locking the door behind him.

The smile that had lurked in his mind spread across

his face. He hadn't intended to pull her so close, to lean in and inhale her fragrance, but damn, he'd had to know if she felt and smelled as good as she looked. He grinned to himself; she did.

The rest of her visit wasn't even worth considering. He'd never sell the Rusty Wire. The Alpine Sky might be determined to buy, but they didn't know what they were up against.

Thankfully, Zoe Larkin hadn't seemed like the type who was easily discouraged. His smile grew bigger. He hoped the pretty little tycoon-in-training came back to try again.

Zoe fumed as she drove the half mile up the mountain to the Alpine Sky Village. She was a professional, presenting a major business deal. Or trying to. He might as well have patted her on the head and told her to run along. He *had* told her to run along, the patronizing jerk.

Jase Garrett obviously didn't know her—she wasn't a quitter. She was going to do some homework on him, and hope like hell he was too lazy to do any on her. Next time she went to the Rusty Wire, she'd know everything there was to know about both Jase and his saloon, including what might tempt him to sell.

If she was lucky, she could do it before she had to report back to her boss.

She realized how unlikely that was as soon as she crossed the marble floor of the lobby. David was behind the admissions desk. Their new clerk appeared to be hanging on his every instruction, already captivated by her boss's handsome face and air of authority. It didn't matter that David was twenty years older than the desk clerk, with hair gone prematurely silver-gray. It never did. They always fell for his sophisticated look and charm, and the cool way he passed all the problems on to Zoe, as if they were no more than minor blips on his radar screen. If James Bond had gone into hotel management and been merely passably good at his job, he would have been David Brand.

Zoe seemed to be the only one who found him condescending and arrogant. His feelings for her weren't any warmer.

They both knew she'd be a better manager than David. Buck Flemming, the original owner of the Alpine Sky, preferred keeping women where he insisted they belonged—beneath men—so David had skated by while she did all the work. Then Buck had died. Ruth Ann took a couple minutes to play the grieving widow before freeing up her social calendar by making her son, Matt, the new general manager. Zoe hadn't met him, but David had. He didn't give her the details of the meeting, but his irritation made it obvious—finally, someone else had not been charmed by David Brand.

Matt had given her the golf course deal without even meeting her. She and David both knew her success might result in a shake-up in management.

Gloves off, game on. David wanted nothing more than for her to fail. Hearing him gloat had zero appeal, so she tried to sneak past the front desk. He looked up and caught her eye with a cool smile. "Excuse me, Victoria," he told the starry-eyed clerk. "I need to talk to Zoe, but I'm confident you can handle things on your own. You're doing beautifully." She beamed, but he didn't see it as he intercepted Zoe at the back hallway.

"I'm just here to pick up my laptop," she told him.

His smile almost looked sincere. "Let's take a minute to chat in my office, shall we?"

She tried not to roll her eyes. Let's chat meant, *Let me find something to criticize about the way you handled things so I can enjoy how bad you'll look when Mrs. Flemming hears about it.* It killed her that she was about to make his day.

He closed his office door and sat behind the desk before giving her an expectant look. "I heard your car was at the Rusty Wire."

Crap, he had snitches. "I stopped by to meet the owner."

"Oh, let's not be coy. We both know why you were there. So how good are you at high level negotiations? Did he go for two point five?"

She felt her whole body tighten, and told herself he'd find out soon, anyway, being her supervisor. "No."

"That's too bad." He clicked his tongue in mock disappointment. "It would have looked good if you could have brought this deal in at two-five. But I suppose Ruth Ann and Matt won't be *too* disappointed with three."

She clenched her teeth and made herself say it. "He didn't go for three, either."

"Really?" He savored it, a smile playing at the side of his mouth as he tried to look concerned. "How disappointing for you. How much does he want?"

"He says he won't sell at any price." David nearly lit up, and she rushed to squash his hopes. "I haven't given up. I'll get to him, I just haven't found his weak spot yet."

David's smile was serene. "Maybe he doesn't have

one. It would be awful to disappoint the Flemmings, though. I heard Ruth Ann put Matt in charge of the whole expansion project, and I've heard how she is about her baby boy. He's not the person you want to piss off." He looked positively thrilled that she might.

"He won't be disappointed."

He punched the air like a cheerleader. "That's the spirit."

She looked around, wondering if there was anything she could accidentally bash his teeth in with. Her gaze fell on a large box in the corner. Beneath packing labels and tape, the box bore the distinctive double-E logo of Everton Equipment.

She frowned. As far as she knew, Everton didn't make ski equipment. But they did make an exclusive line of clothing and equipment for golf. She gave David a puzzled look. "Are we already ordering for a golf line? They don't even know if the project is a go."

"More pressure on you, huh?" He enjoyed it for a moment before nodding at the box. "Those are sample shirts direct from the factory. Naturally, if the Alpine Sky builds the golf course, we'll only carry the best brand in our pro shop. I imagine Everton heard rumors and decided to do some early lobbying for their brand."

Really early; she was surprised they even knew about it. That meant Ruth Ann and Matt must be operating on the assumption that buying the Rusty Wire was a done deal. Zoe had to convince Jase Garrett to sell fast.

David went to the box and lifted the flaps. "Here, take one." He pulled out a polo shirt and tossed it at her. "Wear it to the Rusty Wire, maybe it'll help." For some reason that made him grin.

She'd had enough of David's encouragement. Clutching the shirt, she stood. "I'm not giving up, you know. I'll find a way to convince him to sell."

He smirked. "Good luck."

She wasn't stupid enough to count on luck.

Fantasy.
Temptation.
Adventure.

Visit PocketAfterDark.com,
an all-new website just for Urban
Fantasy and Romance Readers!

• Exclusive access to the hottest
urban fantasy and romance titles!

• Read and share reviews on
the latest books!

• Live chats with your favorite
romance authors!

• Vote in online polls!

 www.PocketAfterDark.com